D0251875

DOROTHY MUST DIE

STORIES

WITHDRAWN

Novels
Dorothy Must Die
The Wicked Will Rise

Digital Novellas
No Place Like Oz
The Witch Must Burn
The Wizard Returns

Novella Collections
Dorothy Must Die Stories

Y
PBK
Paige

NO PLACE LIKE OZ
THE WITCH MUST BURN
THE WIZARD RETURNS

DOROTHY MUST DIE

STORIES

DANIELLE PAIGE

HARPER
An Imprint of HarperCollinsPublishers

Beverly Hills Public Library
WITHDRAWN
Beverly Hills, California

Dorothy Must Die Stories

No Place Like Oz © 2013 by Full Fathom Five, LLC

The Witch Must Burn © 2014 by Full Fathom Five, LLC

The Wizard Returns © 2015 by Full Fathom Five, LLC

All rights reserved. Printed in the United States of America.

No part of this book may be used or reproduced in any manner

whatsoever without written permission except in the case of

brief quotations embodied in critical articles and reviews.

For information address HarperCollins Children's Books,

a division of HarperCollins Publishers, 195 Broadway,

New York, NY 10007. www.epicreads.com

ISBN 978-0-06-228079-4

Typography by Ray Shappell

Hand lettering by Erin Fitzsimmons

15 16 17 18 19   PC/RRDH   10 9 8 7 6 5 4 3

❖

First Edition

CONTENTS

NO PLACE LIKE

Thanks to Angela and Darren Croucher for all their help

ONE

They say you can't go home again. I'm not entirely sure *who* said that, but it's something they say. I know it because my aunt Em has it embroidered on a throw pillow in the sitting room.

You can't go home again. Well, even if they put it on a pillow, whoever said it was wrong. I'm proof alone that it's not true.

Because, you see, I left home. And I came back. Lickety-split, knock your heels together, and there you are. Oh, it wasn't quite so simple, of course, but look at me now: I'm still here, same as before, and it's just as if I was never gone in the first place.

So every time I see that little pillow on Aunt Em's good sofa, with its pretty pink piping around the edges and colorful bouquets of daisies and wildflowers stitched alongside those cheerful words (but *are* they even cheerful? I sometimes wonder), I'm halfway tempted to laugh. When I consider everything that's happened! A certain sort of person might say that it's ironic.

Not that I'm that sort of person. This is Kansas, and we

Kansans don't put much truck in anything as foolish as *irony*.

Things we do put truck in:

Hard work.

Practicality.

Gumption.

Crop yields and healthy livestock and mild winters. Things you can touch and feel and see with your own two eyes. Things that do you at least two licks of good.

Because this is the prairie, and the prairie is no place for day-dreaming. All that matters out here is what gets you through the winter. A Kansas winter will grind a dreamer right up and feed it to the pigs.

As my uncle Henry always says: *You can't trade a boatload of wishes for a bucket of slop.* (Maybe I should embroider that on a pillow for Aunt Em, too. I wonder if it would make her laugh.)

I don't know about wishes, but a bucket of slop was exactly what I had in my hand on the afternoon of my sixteenth birthday, a day in September with a chill already in the air, as I made my way across the field, away from the shed and the farmhouse toward the pigpen.

It was feeding time, and the pigs knew it. Even from fifty feet away, I could already hear them—Jeannie and Ezekiel and Bertha—squealing and snorting in anticipation of their next meal.

"Well, really!" I said to myself. "Who in the world could get so excited about a bit of slop!?"

As I said it, my old friend Miss Millicent poked her little red face out from a gap of wire in the chicken coop and squawked in greeting. "And hello to you, too, Miss Millicent," I said cheerily. "Don't you worry. You'll be getting your own food soon enough."

But Miss Millicent was looking for companionship, not food, and she squeezed herself out of her coop and began to follow on my heels as I kept on my way. I had been ignoring her lately, and the old red hen was starting to be cross about it, a feeling she expressed today by squawking loudly and shadowing my every step, fluttering her wings and fussing underfoot.

She meant well enough, surely, but when I felt her hard beak nipping at my ankle, I finally snapped at her. "Miss Millie! You get out of here. I have chores to do! We'll have a nice, long heart-to-heart later, I promise."

The chicken clucked reproachfully and darted ahead, stopping in her tracks just in the spot where I was about to set my foot down. It was like she wanted me to know that I couldn't get away from her that easily—that I was going to pay her some mind whether I liked it or not.

Sometimes that chicken could be impossible. And without even really meaning to, I kicked at her. "Shoo!"

Miss Millie jumped aside just before my foot connected, and I felt myself lose my balance as I missed her, stumbling backward with a yelp and landing on my rear end in the grass.

I looked down at myself in horror and saw my dress covered in pig slop. My knee was scraped, I had dirt all over my hands, and my slop bucket was upturned at my side.

"Millie!" I screeched. "See what you've done? You've ruined

everything!" I swatted at her again, this time even more angrily than when I'd kicked her, but she just stepped nimbly aside and stood there, looking at me like she just didn't know what to do with me anymore.

"Oh dear," I said, sighing. "I didn't mean to yell at you. Come here, you silly hen."

Millie bobbled her head up and down like she was considering the proposition before she hopped right into my lap, where she burrowed in and clucked softly as I ruffled her feathers. This was all she had wanted in the first place. To be my friend.

It used to be that it was all I wanted, too. It used to be that Miss Millicent and even Jeannie the pig were some of my favorite people in the world. Back then, I didn't care a bit that a pig and a chicken hardly qualified as people at all.

They were there for me when I was sad, or when something was funny, or when I just needed company, and that was what mattered. Even though Millie couldn't talk, it always felt like she understood everything I said. Sometimes it even almost seemed like she *was* talking to me, giving me her sensible, no-nonsense advice in a raspy cackle. "Don't you worry, dearie," she'd say. "There's no problem in this whole world that can't be fixed with a little spit and elbow grease."

But lately, things hadn't been quite the same between me and my chicken. Lately, I had found myself becoming more impatient with her infuriating cackling, with the way she was always pecking and worrying after me.

"I'm sorry, Miss Millicent," I said. "I know I haven't been

myself lately. I promise I'll be back to normal soon."

She fluffed her wings and puffed her chest out, and I looked around: at the dusty, gray-green fields merging on the horizon with the almost-matching gray-blue sky, and all of it stretching out so far into nothing that it seemed like it would be possible to travel and travel and travel—just set off in a straight line heading east or west, north or south, it didn't matter—and never get anywhere at all.

"Sometimes I wonder if this is what the rest of life's going to be like," I said. "Gray fields and gray skies and buckets of slop. The world's a big place, Miss Millicent—just look at that sky. So why does it feel so small from where we're sitting? I'll tell you one thing. If I ever get the chance to go somewhere else again, I'm going to stay there."

I felt a bit ashamed of myself. I knew how I sounded.

"Get yourself together and stop moping, Little Miss Fancy," I responded to myself, now in my raspy, stern, Miss Millicent voice, imagining that the words were coming out of her mouth instead of my own. "A prairie girl doesn't worry her pretty little head about places she'll never go and things she'll never see. A prairie girl worries about the here and now."

This is what a place like this does to you. It makes you put words in the beaks of chickens.

I sighed and shrugged anyway. Miss Millie didn't know there was anything else out there. She just knew her coop, her feed, and *me*.

These days, I envied her for that. Because I was a girl, not a chicken, and I knew what was out there.

Past the prairie, where I sat with my old chicken in my lap, there were oceans and more oceans. Beyond those were deserts and pyramids and jungles and mountains and glittering palaces. I had heard about all those places and all those things from newsreels and newspapers.

And even if I was the only one who knew it, I'd seen with my own eyes that there were more directions to move in than just north and south and east and west, places more incredible than Paris and Los Angeles, more exotic than Kathmandu and Shanghai, even. There were whole worlds out there that weren't on any map, and things that you would never believe.

I didn't need to believe. I *knew*. I just sometimes wished I didn't.

I thought of Jeannie and Ezekiel and Bertha, all of them in their pen beside themselves in excitement for the same slop they'd had yesterday and would have again tomorrow. The slop I'd have to refill into the bucket and haul back out to them.

"It must be nice not to know any better," I said to Miss Millicent.

In the end, a chicken is a good thing to hold in your lap for a few minutes. It's a good thing to pretend to talk to when there's no one else around. But in the end, if you want the honest-to-goodness truth, it's possible that a chicken doesn't make the greatest friend.

Setting Miss Millicent aside, I dusted myself off and headed back toward the farmhouse to clean myself up, change my dress, and get myself ready for my big party. Bertha and Jeannie and

Ezekiel would have to wait until tomorrow for their slop.

It wasn't like me to let them go hungry. At least, it wasn't like the *old* me.

But the old me was getting older by the second. It had been two years since the tornado. Two years since I'd gone away. Since I had met Glinda the Good Witch, and the Lion, the Tin Woodman, and the Scarecrow. Since I had traveled the Road of Yellow Brick and defeated the Wicked Witch of the West. In Oz, I had been a hero. I could have stayed. But I hadn't. Aunt Em and Uncle Henry were in Kansas. Home was in Kansas. It had been my decision and mine alone.

Well, I had made my choice, and like any good Kansas girl, I would live with it. I would pick up my chin, put on a smile, and be on my way.

The animals could just go hungry for now. It was my birthday, after all.

TWO

"Happy Swoot Sixtoon," the cake said, the letters spelled out in smudged icing. I beamed up at my aunt Em with my brightest smile.

"It's beautiful," I said. I'd already changed into my party dress—which wasn't that much different from the dress I'd just gotten all dirty in the field—and had cleaned myself up as best as I could, scrubbing the dirt from my hands and the blood from my knee until you could hardly tell I'd fallen.

Uncle Henry hovered off to the side, looking as proud and hopeful as if he'd baked it himself. He'd certainly helped, gathering the ingredients from around the farm: coaxing the eggs from Miss Millicent (who never seemed in the mood to lay any), milking the cow, and making sure Aunt Em had everything she needed.

"Sometimes I wonder if I didn't marry a master chef!" Henry said, putting his arm around her waist.

Even Toto was excited. He was hopping around on the floor yipping at us eagerly.

"You really like it?" Aunt Em asked, a note of doubt in her voice. "I know the writing isn't perfect, but penmanship has never been my strong suit."

"It's wonderful!" I exclaimed, pushing down the tiny feeling of disappointment that was bubbling in my chest. A little white lie never hurt anyone, and I didn't doubt the cake would be delicious. Aunt Em's food might not usually come out looking fancy, but it always *tastes* better than anything else.

Oh, I know that it's how a cake *tastes* that matters. I know there's no point in concerning yourself with what it looks like on the outside when you'll be eating it in just a few minutes.

But as it sat lopsided on the table with its brown icing and the words "Happy Sweet Sixteen" written out so the *e*'s looked more like blobby *o*'s, I found myself wishing for something more.

I just couldn't let Aunt Em know that. I couldn't let her have even the smallest hint that anything was wrong. So I wrapped her up in a hug to let her know that it didn't matter: that even if the cake wasn't perfect, it was good enough for me. But then something else occurred to me.

"Are you sure it's big enough?" I asked. "A lot of people are coming." I had invited everyone from school, not that that was so many people, and everyone from all the neighboring farms, plus the store owners at every shop I'd been to on my last trip into town. I'd invited my best friend, Mitzi Blair, and even awful Suzanna Hellman and *her* best friend, Marian Stiles, not to mention a reporter from the *Carrier* who had taken a special interest in my life since the tornado. Plus, Suzanna would be dragging her horrible little sister, Jill, along.

Aunt Em glanced down nervously. "There was going to be another layer, dear, but we were running low on eggs . . . ," she said, trailing off, her weathered face suddenly rosy with embarrassment.

Uncle Henry came quickly to the rescue. "I just won't have a second helping," he said, rubbing his belly, which is not small. "It wouldn't hurt me to skip a first helping, come to think of it."

My aunt swatted his arm and chuckled, her worry momentarily gone. All those years of hard Kansas life had taken their toll on her, but when she was around my uncle, her eyes still lit up; when he made a joke, she still laughed a laugh that sounded like it belonged to a girl my age. "You'd eat the whole thing if I let you!" He swiped a bit of frosting with his finger and grinned.

Seeing them together like that, happy and playful and still as much in love as they'd ever been, I felt a swell of affection for them, followed immediately by sadness. I knew that, once upon a time, they had been as young as I was. Aunt Em had wanted to travel the world; Uncle Henry had wanted to set off to California and strike gold. They just hadn't had the chance to do any of those things.

Instead, they had stayed here, and when I asked them about those days now, they waved away my questions like they were ashamed to admit that they'd ever had dreams at all. To them, our farm was all there was.

Will I be like them, someday? I wondered. Happy with crooked cakes and gray skies and cleaning out the pig trough?

"I'm going to go hang the lanterns outside," Henry said, walking to the door and reaching for his toolbox. "People expect this place to look nice. After all, they helped build it."

"Only after you got it started," Aunt Em reminded him.

After the tornado had swept our house away—with me in it—everyone had figured I was dead. Aunt Em and Uncle Henry had been heartbroken. They'd even started planning my memorial service.

Imagine that! My funeral! Well, sometimes I did imagine it. I imagined my teachers from school all standing up one by one to say what a wonderful student I was, that there was something *truly* special about me.

I imagined Aunt Em all in black, weeping silently into her handkerchief and Uncle Henry the very picture of stoic grief, only a single tear rolling down his stony face as he helped lower my coffin into an open grave. Yes, I know that without a body there could be no coffin, but this was a fantasy. And it was at that moment in my fantasy that Aunt Em would bolt up, wailing, and would race forward to fling herself in after my corpse, stopped only at the last minute by Tom Furnish and Benjamin Slocombe, two handsome farmhands from the Shiffletts' farm. Tom and Benjamin would be crying, too, because of course, they both harbored a secret admiration for me.

Well, if one's going to daydream, one might just as well make it a good one, don't you suppose?

Of course, I know it's vain, and petty, and downright spoiled of me to do such a thing as daydream about my own funeral. I know it's downright wicked to take even the slightest pleasure in imagining the misery of others, especially my poor aunt and uncle, who have so little happiness in their lives as it is.

I try not to be vain and petty and spoiled. I *certainly* try not to be wicked (after my experiences with Wickedness). But we all have our bad points, don't we? I might as well admit that those happen to be mine, and I can only hope to make up for them with the good ones.

There was no funeral anyway, so no harm was done. Just the opposite, in fact! When I showed up again a few days after the cyclone—without so much as a scratch on me, sitting by the chicken coop, which had somehow remained undisturbed through everything—people had assumed that my survival was some kind of miracle.

They were wrong. Miracles are not the same as magic.

But whether you want to call it a miracle or something else, every paper from Wichita to Topeka put me on the front page. They threw a parade for me that year, and a few months later I was asked to be the head judge at the annual blueberry pie contest at the Kansas State Fair. Best of all, because I came back from my adventures *minus* one house, everyone in town pitched in to build us a new one.

That was how we got this new house, to replace the old one that was still back in you-know-where. It was quite a spectacle to behold: it was bigger than any other for miles around, with a second story and a separate bedroom just for me, and even an indoor commode and a jaunty coat of blue paint, though that was just as gray as everything else in Kansas soon enough.

Henry and Em didn't seem particularly happy about any of it. They were humbled, naturally, that our neighbors had done all this for us, especially seeing as how they had all suffered their losses in the cyclone, some of them bigger than ours. Of course we were grateful.

But when the neighbors had done their work and gone home, my aunt and uncle had examined all the unfamiliar extravagances and had concluded that the old house had suited them just fine.

"An indoor commode!" Aunt Em exclaimed. "It just doesn't seem decent!"

How silly they were being. Grumbling about the gift that had been so kindly given to us.

On the other hand, I had to admit that even *I* felt that the new house left a few things to be desired. Nothing could compare to what I had seen while I had been gone. How do you go back to a two-bedroom farmhouse in Kansas when you've been in a palace made of emeralds?

Once you've seen castles and Munchkins and roads of yellow brick, once you've faced down monsters and witches and come face-to-face with true magic, well then, no matter how much you might have missed it while you were gone, the prairie can seem somewhat dull and—truly—downright dreary.

All I wanted to do upon my return was tell my aunt and uncle everything about what I'd seen. The whole time I'd been in Oz,

I'd imagined Aunt Em's amazed face when I told her about the fields of giant poppies that put you right to sleep, and I'd thought about how Uncle Henry would sputter and spit his coffee back into his cup when he heard about the town where all the people were made of china.

They hadn't given me quite the reaction I'd been hoping for. In fact, they'd hardly reacted at all. Instead, they'd just exchanged a worried glance and told me that it must have been some fanciful dream I'd had when I hit my head during the cyclone. They warned me not to repeat the story, and to get some rest. They said nobody liked a tale-teller.

Never mind that a bump on the head didn't explain where the house was now, or why no one had ever found it. And it didn't explain how I'd gotten home. When I told them about the magical Silver Shoes that had carried me back across the Deadly Desert, they seemed even less convinced than ever. After all, the shoes had slipped from my feet somewhere along the way.

I can see why some people might have thought I was crazy, or a liar, or had made the whole thing up. Around here, they don't believe in anything they can't see with their own two eyes.

Aunt Em and I brought the cake into the living room and set it on the table by the modest spread of food she'd already laid out. As I looked at the room, all spruced up and decorated with a careful, loving hand, I reminded myself of how much they were doing.

The birthday party had been my aunt and uncle's idea—I'd overheard them talking just a few weeks ago about how blue they thought I'd seemed lately, and how a big birthday party might be just the thing to cheer me up.

I'd asked them not to do it, of course. I knew we didn't really have the money to spare.

Even so, I must admit that I was secretly pleased when they insisted on doing it anyway. As my "wild ride"—as so many people called it—had begun to recede further into memory, I was growing eager for something to break the monotony of the farm and school and then the farm again.

"Dorothy, what is your scrapbook doing out?" Aunt Em asked, noticing the book with all my newspaper clippings sitting on the table next to the buffet. "Your guests will be here any moment."

I quickly picked the book up and moved it aside so that it didn't fall victim to any smudges of icing or stray crumbs. "Oh," I said. "I thought someone might like to look through it at the party. A lot of people who are coming were quoted in the articles about me, after all. It might be fun for them to see their names in print."

Aunt Em didn't appear to think that was a very good idea, but she didn't try to dissuade me. She just shook her head and started humming one of her old songs again as she scurried around, busying herself with last-minute tasks.

I sat down and began to flip through the pages of my scrapbook myself. Toto hopped up into my lap and read along with me. At least I had him. *He* knew it was all real. He'd been there, too. I wondered if he missed it the same way I did.

THE GIRL WHO RODE THE CYCLONE.

That headline, from the *Star*, was my favorite. I liked the way it made me seem powerful, as if I'd been in control rather than just some little kid swept up by forces of nature.

In Oz, I hadn't been just some little kid either. I'd been a hero. I had killed two witches and freed their subjects from tyranny; I'd exposed the humbug Wizard and restored order to the kingdom by helping my friend the Scarecrow, the smartest creature I've ever met, claim the throne.

If only *those* things were in my scrapbook!

Here, I knew that I would never, ever make as much of myself as I did in my short time in Oz. It just wasn't possible. Here, it wasn't even considered proper to think about such things.

And yet I had wanted to come back here. All those brave things I'd done: I wasn't trying to be a hero. I was just trying to get home.

It would have been too cruel to leave Uncle Henry and Aunt Em all alone here, thinking that I was dead. It wasn't all to spare *their* grief either. I would have missed them terribly if I had stayed. All the magic in the world—all the palaces and beautiful gowns and fields full of magical flowers—all the friends I'd found—could never have replaced the people who had taken me and raised me as their own after my parents had died. I would never have been able to be happy with them here and me there.

But sometimes I still wondered. Could there have been another way? Was this really home at all?

"Oh, Toto," I said, closing the cover of the scrapbook harder than I intended to and tossing it aside onto the couch, where it landed just next to Aunt Em's embroidered throw pillow. Maybe the words on that pillow were more right than I knew. Maybe you *couldn't* go home again.

Either way, it would have been a nice consolation if I'd gotten to keep those shoes.

THREE

"Here," Mitzi Blair said, thrusting a small gift into my arms as soon as I opened the front door and found her standing on the stoop. "Happy birthday. Is Suzanna here yet?"

I eyed Mitzi uncertainly and she gave me the same look right back, but with a hint of a question, like *Well?*

I don't know what had come over me. Mitzi was my best friend and here I was treating her like a stranger at my birthday party. Luckily, I caught myself in my momentary rudeness, smiled brightly, and ushered her inside.

"Thank you!" I exclaimed, placing her present on the little table that Aunt Em had set aside for that purpose. "Suzanna and Jill are by the—"

I didn't get a chance to finish my sentence. "My mom says happy birthday, too," Mitzi said over her shoulder, already making a beeline for the corner, where snobby Suzanna Hellman was slumped against the wall, looking straight out of a magazine ad in her brand-new dress with a fashionable wide collar and a bright pink sash while her sister, Jill, helped herself to Aunt Em's signature potato puff balls from the snack table.

"Thank goodness you're here," Suzanna said, her face cheering in relief when she saw Mitzi approaching. "I was beginning to wonder if Jill and I would be the only people under a hundred. Not counting Dorothy, of course."

I giggled at the barb—probably more enthusiastically than I should have—and tried to pretend that it wasn't at my expense.

It would have been easier to let it roll right off me if Suzanna didn't seem so *right*. The sparse crowd milling around the living room was almost entirely made up of Uncle Henry's friends from neighboring farms, and none of whom were a day under forty, if that. I had been hoping for a few of the handsome farmhands, at least, but I guess they'd all been left behind to keep an eye on the livestock.

"So, Dorothy," Suzanna said, turning her gimlet-eyed gaze in my direction. "Been in any good parades lately?"

This time, there was no sense in pretending she wasn't poking fun at me. Suzanna couldn't bear to see anyone else getting more attention than her, and was always acting like the one little parade they'd thrown for me after I'd survived the tornado made me some sort of spotlight-hogging monster. It had been years ago, but she would never let me forget it.

Frankly, I hadn't wanted snobby, mean-spirited Suzanna Hellman at my party in the first place, but Mitzi had insisted

that there was no point in throwing a party if you weren't going
to invite the richest girl at school—the *only* rich girl at school,
actually—and so I'd relented.

Now I looked over at my friend, expecting to see her indig-
nant, but she just averted her eyes to the floor, her face flushing.
If I hadn't known better, I almost would have thought she was
stifling a laugh.

Fine. I might as well admit it. When I say that Mitzi Blair is
my best friend, what I mean to say is that she *used* to be my best
friend. For most of my life, the two of us had been inseparable,
but that had all changed after I'd ridden the cyclone.

Mitzi was the only one—other than my aunt and uncle—
who I'd told the truth about my adventures in Oz after I'd come
back. It hadn't gone well. Instead of marveling at everything I'd
been through, Mitzi had called me a liar and a show-off.

We'd made up a few weeks later, but that didn't mean things
had gone back to normal. These days she was spending more
and more time hanging around with awful Suzanna Hellman,
not to mention with Marian Stiles and Marjory Mumford. As for
me—I was spending more and more time by myself.

Oh, I didn't care. This was my birthday, and Aunt Em had
put so much effort into it, not to mention money that we couldn't
well afford, with the farm doing the way it was. If she and Uncle
Henry were kind enough to throw me a party then I was going
to enjoy it whether Suzanna Hellman wanted me to or not.

If only there were a few more people to talk to.

Of course, Uncle Henry had already warned me that not

everyone I'd invited would be able to make it. It was harvesting season, after all, the busiest time for anyone on a farm, and anyway, most of my classmates lived too far away to easily make the trip all the way out here. Still, I had been hoping that a *few* more girls my own age would be able to make it.

So, even though I'm not exactly their biggest fan, I breathed a sigh of relief when Marian Stiles and Marjory Mumford walked through the door. I was happily greeting them when Mitzi tapped my shoulder. Suzanna's little sister was at her side, hopping impatiently from one foot to another.

"Excuse me, Dorothy?" Jill asked innocently. "When do you suppose the cake will be?"

"After the presents, I think," I replied. "It's one of Aunt Em's best."

"Well, when are presents, then? Mother said we had to stay till the cake."

Suzanna snorted back a laugh and *shhh*-ed her.

I sighed. The truth is, I had been planning on waiting for the reporter from the *Carrier* to arrive before opening the presents. He'd told me that my Sweet Sixteen would make the perfect story for the Sunday edition. People were still interested in my doings, even if they weren't throwing me any more parades.

But the reporter was nowhere to be seen and people were starting to seem bored. Maybe one gift wouldn't hurt. It would make it feel more like a party. Plus—I had a feeling I knew exactly what my gift from Aunt Em would be. "I guess I could do a little preview," I said.

"Aunt Em," I said, wandering over to where she was sitting alone on the couch. (Aunt Em has never had Uncle Henry's gift for chatter.) "I think I should open *your* present. So everyone can see it."

"Of course, dear—if you say so. But . . . don't you think you should open some of the others first, though?"

"I'll get to them," I said. "I just can't *wait* for yours."

"Okay, dear. I'll ask Henry to bring it down." My aunt set her tea down and went to fetch Henry.

I'd been dropping hints for weeks that I wanted a new dress more than anything, and from the way my aunt's eyebrows had shot up into an arch every time I mentioned it, I had a feeling I'd be getting my wish. I didn't know how she was going to manage it—they'd already spent more money than they could really afford on the party itself—but if anyone could pull it off, it was Aunt Em.

Suzanna Hellman wouldn't be so smug once she saw me descending the stairs in a dress that was sure to put hers to shame. The more I thought about it, the more it seemed like just the thing to turn the party around.

A few minutes later, Toto was wagging his tail excitedly and racing around the room as Uncle Henry came out of the kitchen carrying a large, floppy package wrapped in tissue paper. There was no box and the paper was crinkled and creased in all the wrong places, but I didn't mind.

It's what's on the *inside* that counts. And it certainly looked like what was on the inside was exactly what I thought it was.

Henry placed the present with the rest of the gifts, and every-one began to gather around. I picked it up and held it to my chest, and as I did, my eyes met Aunt Em's. She looked away with an expression that almost seemed worried.

"*Well?*" Suzanna urged me. "Are you going to open it or not?"

I peeled away the wrapping as Suzanna leaned in close, eager to get a good look. I heard her stifle a snort as heavy twill fabric came into view. My heart stopped.

The rest of the paper crumpled to the floor and the dress swung loose.

It was long and brownish green. Not sparkling green, or for-est green or even blue green like the ocean. It certainly wasn't Emerald City green. No. It was green like . . . well, it was green like Aunt Em's old dress.

That's because it *was* Aunt Em's old dress. She'd tailored it to my size, fixed it up to make it look new by cinching the waist, giving it a fuller skirt, and adding poufy ruffles to the shoulders.

There was no getting around it. The dress was hideous.

The whole room knew it. Even Mr. Shifflett from the next farm over had a look of shocked horror on his face, and I'd never seen him wear anything fancier than a pair of clean coveralls.

My cheeks burned in embarrassment. The only sound in the room was coming from Suzanna, who was fighting to conceal outright laughter.

Toto snarled loudly at her, ever faithful, but that only made her suppressed giggles louder.

The worst, though, was the look on Aunt Em's face—a crushed mixture of hopefulness and humiliation that broke my heart.

She had tried—there was no question about that. Just like she'd tried with the cake. But I could see what she had done: the color of the dress was faded and the edges of the fabric were worn. The red embroidery on the sleeves looked out of place, and I knew it was there to hide the tear from when she'd caught it on the chicken coop.

Suzanna gave up all attempts to cover her snickering once the dress was fully unfurled. "Oh, how nice," she said. "It'll be sure to keep you warm when you're working out in the fields. And you won't need to worry about getting it dirty!" At that, her sister burst out laughing and buried her face in her hands.

If I'd had a bucket of dirty water to throw in Suzanna's face, I would have. If I had, I'm curious whether Suzanna, like many a witch before her, would have melted right before the eyes of me and all my guests. I for one would not have been astonished. It wouldn't have been anything I hadn't seen before.

But I was empty-handed, and I knew the only way to stave off the angry, hot tears that were prickling at the corners of my eyes was to maintain my dignity. "My, what a dress!" I exclaimed jubilantly to no one in particular, least of all Suzanna.

"You *have* to try it on," she singsonged mockingly. "Go ahead. Show it off."

At that, Marian Stiles began to giggle into her hands, too, and then Marjory Mumford. When Mitzi began laughing along with them—like the Benedict Arnold that she was—I realized the sad, final truth: I had no friends.

None of these people belonged at my birthday party. The people who belonged here were the ones who really cared about me: the Scarecrow and the Tin Woodman and the Lion and Glinda and all the other people I'd met in Oz. *They* were my true friends.

"Well," Suzanna prodded me again. "When's the fashion show?"

I had had more than enough. I was Dorothy Gale. I was the *Girl Who Rode the Cyclone*. Not to mention the girl who went to Oz, and defeated two *real* witches on my own pluck alone. She was nothing compared to them.

And now I was angry. It was one thing to be cruel to me. I could take it. But I didn't understand why anyone would want to hurt my aunt.

"I don't think you know who you're talking to," I said to Suzanna with every ounce of imperiousness I could muster. Which happened to be quite a lot.

Suzanna just hooted, and Marian looked as if she was about to burst.

"Oh, I know," Suzanna managed to reply through her giggles. "You're the Fairy Princess Dorothy. I wonder, though: why aren't your fairy friends here? Is it because you made them all up? It's too bad—a straw man and a big tiger at your birthday would probably fetch you another newspaper article for your precious scrapbook, now wouldn't they?"

I turned on Mitzi, whose face, redder than Glinda's ruby castle, betrayed her guilt. She had told them.

That was enough. Without another look at anyone, I whirled on my heels.

"Never mind. I'll go try it on right now."

It was the last thing in the world that I wanted to do. But what other choice did I have? Give in to them? Let them get the best of me? I wouldn't give them the satisfaction.

When I reached the stairs, though, each step seemed more hopeless and daunting than the last as I made my way to my bedroom, the awful gown draped heavily over my arm and Toto following right behind me.

In my room, I stood in front of the mirror and held the dress up to my chest.

It was a perfectly respectable dress. It really was. I could see how Aunt Em would have been pleased at her ingenious scheme to refurbish it, could see her happily sewing and cutting, congratulating herself for her thriftiness and creativity and pioneer spirit.

That was when all my anger and resolve fell away, leaving only a sense of sad, empty hopelessness.

Because of course it didn't matter at all. Even the finest dress money could buy—a dress befitting Her Majesty Suzanna Hellman herself!—wouldn't have been the dress I'd been dreaming of.

The dress I'd been dreaming of would have been magical. It

would have come from Oz.

"I know you're disappointed," Aunt Em's soft voice said from the doorway. "I'm sorry those girls were mean to you. I *surely* don't know what's come over Mitzi Blair. But we did tell you not to share your tales. . . ."

I looked up at her.

This was the moral of the story, to her? This was *my* fault, for telling my friend the truth about what had happened to me?

"They're not *tales*," I snapped. "And I'm not disappointed. I just . . ."

I trailed off. I didn't know how to end the sentence without hurting her feelings more.

"You know that things have been tough," Aunt Em said. "We just have to get through this rough patch. I promise, there will be a new dress someday soon. A dress and a bigger cake, and—"

"How?" I asked before I could stop myself. "How will we get any of those things? What's going to be different about tomorrow or the next day? Every day is the same!"

Aunt Em's face fell even further than it already had, further than even seemed possible.

"Our luck will turn," she said. "Maybe next year will be a good crop, and we'll be able to go into town and buy you whatever dress you want."

It all came rushing out. "It's not about a dress or a cake, Aunt Em. It's about this whole place. Nothing ever changes around here, and everyone likes it just the way it is. But I'm sixteen now, and I can't imagine spending the rest of my life here. Doing the same thing every single day, never wanting more."

I was starting to cry now. "I just wish you could see what it's like," I said. "Then you'd understand, and Uncle Henry would, too. There's magic out there in the world, Aunt Em. There're things so wonderful that you could spend your whole life trying to think them up and you'd never come close."

The tears in Aunt Em's eyes evaporated in an instant. Her gaze went steely. It's a trick my aunt has. She's not as much of a pushover as she first appears. I had to get it from somewhere, didn't I?

"Dorothy Gale," she said. "You are indeed sixteen now, and it's time you put your tall tales aside. There is no such thing as magic."

There was just no arguing with her like this. "I'm not feeling well," I said, turning away from her. "Could you give my apologies to my guests? I need to lie down."

She just shook her head in frustration as she closed the door behind her.

I didn't need to say anything to Toto as I pulled him up into my arms and collapsed into bed. He understood. His big, wet eyes said as much. They said he missed it as much as I did.

As angry as I was—at Mitzi and Marian and Suzanna and even at Aunt Em and Uncle Henry—I knew that Aunt Em was right about one thing.

It didn't matter that it had been real. I was never going back there.

Kansas may not have felt like home anymore, but it was where

I lived, and it was where I was going to live. I knew I had to put everything else in the past where it belonged.

I knew all those things, and yet there was a part of me that couldn't let go.

"There's no place like Oz," I mumbled, pulling Toto even closer to my chest. I barely knew I was saying it. I might have already been asleep.

FOUR

When I woke up, the sky outside my window was black. I didn't know how long I'd slept for or what time it was, and Toto was licking my face.

"Oh, Toto," I said sleepily. "I was having the nicest dream—let me go back to sleep."

My dog wasn't listening. He was spinning in circles on the old quilt that Aunt Em had made for me right after I'd come to live with her and Uncle Henry after my parents died, when I was just a baby.

He was trying to get my attention.

"What is it?" I sat up sluggishly and dropped my legs to the floor as Toto jumped down in excitement and scampered under the bed. When he came back out a few seconds later, he was huffing and puffing and dragging something in his mouth. It was a box.

It was wrapped in glittering, red paper that looked thick and expensive, with every corner perfectly creased. The package was tied with a bright green bow. "What in the world?" I gasped.

I took the box from him and carefully ripped through the paper to the box beneath. It was pink, the color of a perfect sunset.

Where had it come from? Was Uncle Henry trying to cheer me up? Had he snuck in here and hidden the box under my bed while I'd been asleep?

No. I knew instinctively that this was something else. The shade of pink looked so familiar. But there was no way . . . was there?

Or maybe there was.

I pulled the lid off and found myself looking at a pair of shoes. That was when I was certain.

Because they weren't just any shoes. They were the most beautiful shoes I'd ever seen. They were red to match the wrapping paper and had sharp, pointy heels—the highest I'd ever seen, high enough that they would scandalize all of Kansas if I ever tried wearing them out of my bedroom.

They were lacquered and shinier than the glossiest patent leather, glowing with a warm radiance that seemed to come from within. No—not from within. It seemed to come from somewhere else. From another world.

I knew in my heart that that was *exactly* where it came from.

I reached down and ran my fingers over the heels. The shoes were smooth and strangely warm to the touch. These were the heels of a young woman who had never set foot inside a chicken coop. These were shoes fit for a princess. A *fairy* princess, if it would make Mitzi Blair happy to hear me say it.

I could barely breathe as I pulled them out of the box and set them on the floor, slipping off my worn, brown flats.

I heard a knocking at my door, but it sounded like it was coming from very far away.

I sat there, paralyzed, afraid that if I reached out to touch them again they would disappear, like food you try to eat in a dream. All I could do was stare at them in awe.

The spell was only broken when Toto barked one more time and dove into the box, emerging a few seconds later with a pink slip of paper in his mouth. He dropped it in my lap. It was a note written in fastidious cursive handwriting, the ink red and sparkly.

Dear Dorothy,

Happy birthday! I hope you like these.
I thought about silver to match the ones you lost,
but in the end I decided that red was more your
color. I think you know what to do with them.

G

P.S. If anyone happens to ask, let's keep this
just between us girls.

When another knock came at the door, louder this time, I ignored it again.

Trembling, I lifted my feet and, one after the other, slid them into the red heels. They fit perfectly. The warmth I'd felt when I'd touched them before now coursed through my body, rising up through my toes, into my legs, and beyond. A smile spread across my face. I felt like my heart was expanding by the second.

The knocking on the door got louder. "Dorothy? Everyone's gone now." It was Uncle Henry's voice, anxious and urgent. "Can you open up the door, please?"

I rose to my feet. "Come in," I said, my voice strong and commanding, reverberating through the room. The sound of it surprised even me.

Uncle Henry opened the door and stepped into the room with Aunt Em right behind him. At first, he opened his arms to give me a hug, but then he gasped when he saw my feet. A split second later, Aunt Em gasped, too.

Aunt Em's hand flew to her bosom. "Oh my word," she said.

"Where . . . ," Uncle Henry trailed off.

Toto yapped and sprang into the air. Without even thinking about it, I scooped him into my arms and drew him to my chest.

"You were wrong, Aunt Em," I said softly. "You both were. It *is* real."

I knew what I had to do. I knew how I could get back. And I knew I *wanted* to go back. Before either of them could reply, I knocked the heels together. Once. Twice.

Three times.

The shoes constricted around my feet like they wanted to be part of me. A red glow began to snake through the room like smoke. The shoes took three steps forward. Aunt Em and Uncle Henry both grabbed my arms, trying to stop me, but I wouldn't let them. I *couldn't* let them.

"Dorothy!" Uncle Henry yelled. "What in the world . . . ?"

"There's no place like *Oz*," I whispered. The room exploded in a crimson flash.

FIVE

Everything around me blurred and folded in on itself, twisting into a hazy whirlpool of brilliant light and color. Aunt Em was screaming. Toto was barking madly, squirming in my arms. Somewhere, I heard Uncle Henry's voice. "Dorothy!" he bellowed.

I couldn't see any of them. All I saw was red and blue and green and purple and yellow as I plunged headlong into a liquid rainbow with no idea which way was up and which was down.

And then the colors stopped swirling and a new world constructed itself below me as I fell. I was just opening my mouth to scream when I hit the ground with a crash. Toto went flying out of my grip.

When I sat up a moment later, in the middle of a field, my head was still spinning but everything else was finally still again. I rubbed my eyes, trying to piece it all together.

Toto, though, had recovered himself more quickly, and was

already bounding through the grass toward me. He jumped right up, barking wildly, and licked my face in excitement.

The grass underneath us was bluish green. The sky above was even bluer. Not gray. Not white. Not whitish gray. But blue. The sun was warm on my face, and a light breeze ruffled the tall grass around me.

It wasn't a dream or a fantasy. I knew it as well as I'd ever known anything. I could feel magic in every blade of grass.

A few feet away a grove of trees bore strange and luscious-looking fruit that cycled steadily through a rainbow of colors. Farther off was a gurgling brook that I could have sworn was singing to me, saying, "Welcome home." On the banks of the stream, enormous flowers swayed in the wind, their giant blue blossoms—some as big as beach balls—opening and closing hypnotically, as if they were breathing.

Their scent wafted toward me on the breeze. I took a deep breath. It smelled like the ocean and fresh-baked blueberry pie and like the aftershave Uncle Henry wore for special occasions. It smelled like all those things at once, in a good way.

As if all that wasn't enough to tell me I was back in Munchkin Country, the only *real* proof I needed was staring right at me. Not ten paces from the stream, a little old farmhouse was situated crookedly in a patch of dirt.

Just where I had left it.

The wood was rotting, the roof was beginning to cave in, and huge tangles of twisting vines crawled out from every crevice. The windows were broken, the porch was near collapse, and the whole place appeared to be well on its way to sinking into the ground.

It had only been two years since I'd landed here, but the house looked like it had been sitting here for a century.

Still, there was no mistaking it. And I wasn't the only one who recognized it.

I heard a high-pitched gasp, and I turned around to see Aunt Em sprawled out in a bank of wildflowers, her eyes wide in astonishment, one hand covering her mouth and the other pointing at the crumbling shack.

"Henry! Look!"

At her side, Uncle Henry rubbed his forehead as he sat up creakily. "Now see here, Dorothy," he said irritably. Then he saw it, too.

"Well I'll be," he muttered. He squeezed his eyes shut and opened them again, like he was expecting to get a different picture this time. When nothing had changed, he jerked his head back and let out a wheezing noise that was a little like a burp. "Oh my," he said. "I knew I shouldn't have had that drink at your party. . . . I never did have a taste for the strong stuff."

I laughed. "Don't you see?" I exclaimed. "We're here! We're *all* here."

After the disastrous start my birthday had gotten off to, I was now sure I'd never been so happy in my life. I was back in Oz and this time my family had come with me. Now that Aunt Em and Uncle Henry were here, we could finally all be happy together. We would never need to go home, because home had come *with* me.

Aunt Em stood up, carefully dusting off her gray smocked dress.

She looked unsteady, and began to fan herself with her hand. For a second I worried that she was about to faint, but Uncle Henry stood, too, and put an arm around her waist. "There, there, Emily," he said. "Take a minute. Breathe." He gave me a strange look. "What have you gotten us into?" he asked. His gaze dropped to my feet accusingly. "And where on earth did you get those preposterous shoes?"

Aunt Em didn't seem to care about the how or the why of any of this, though. Once she managed to catch her breath, she pulled herself from his grip, suddenly back in perfect form, and marched straight for the old house.

"Just *look*," she marveled. "Henry, can you even believe it?"

Henry hurried after, her but he wasn't as easy on his feet as she was, and he stumbled a few times as he tried to catch up.

"No, I can't believe it," he said, wheezing breathlessly.

Aunt Em pressed her palm to the weathered shingles in awe. "Remember when you painted the window frames?"

"Yes, dear," he replied. "But I don't think you're in your right mind at the moment. We have more important things to worry about. Like where we are and how we got here."

She brushed him off with a wave of her hand.

I furrowed my brow and raced over to join them. "Excuse me," I said. "I know it's a wonderful house and everything. But haven't you noticed that we're not exactly in Kansas anymore?"

Henry jerked his face toward me sharply. "I did indeed notice, young lady. And we're going to have a talk about that in a bit. But as you can see, your aunt isn't well. Let's just let her get her bearings."

"I *do* have my bearings," Aunt Em said. "Look! I'd forgotten all about this door knocker! The one you bought in Topeka just after you came home from the Great War!"

Henry's face spread into an involuntary grin at the mention of the knocker. "Yes," he replied softly. "I sure do remember that."

It was just like Aunt Em and Uncle Henry to be so wrapped up in fond feelings toward our old house that they didn't even notice where we were. You had to give it to them—my aunt and uncle had *heart*.

Still, I wanted them to understand the gravity of the situation. I wanted them to be as happy as I was.

"Look over here," I said, trying to shift their attention to a bush that had sprung up next to what used to be the kitchen window. "This shrub is growing little puffballs with eyes instead of fruit."

One of the puffballs sneezed right in my face. I jumped back in surprise, but my aunt and uncle went on ignoring me. Uncle Henry rubbed Aunt Em's back as she examined the molding around the door frame, remarking admiringly on the craftsmanship.

Then, before I could say anything else, something happened that not even they could ignore. On the little ramshackle porch, the air began to shimmer with energy. It was pink and glittery, like a little pink fish was swimming through the air, twisting and looping in little spirals, growing brighter and stronger and pinker by the second until Aunt Em was moved to shield her eyes.

Henry clenched his fists at his sides as if preparing for a fight. I wasn't worried. I'd already seen such strange things in this land that I just watched in excited curiosity as the energy crackled and glittered and grew until, slowly, it began to resolve itself into something resembling a form. Into something resembling a person.

Her face appeared first, pushing its way through the light as though emerging from a pool of water. Next came her golden crown, then finally the rest of her. She was standing right there on the porch, regal and glowing, just as beautiful as I remembered her. Her face was porcelain-white, punctuated with piercing blue eyes and a perfectly red, perfectly tiny little mouth. She was sheathed in a slinky pink evening gown that looked almost liquid and hugged her body scandalously.

"My oh my," Henry said under his breath.

I knew exactly who it was. And I can't say I was very surprised to see her. "Glinda!" I exclaimed joyfully, running to hug her.

I stopped in my tracks when I saw that she wasn't responding. She wasn't even looking at me. It was like she hadn't heard me at all.

Then I noticed that her image was flickering and translucent. I could even see the faint impression of Henry's prized door knocker shining through her image from somewhere behind her rib cage. She was fading in and out, getting clearer but then more indistinct, like she wasn't entirely here yet.

"Dorothy," she said, still not turning her face to meet mine. "Help me." Her voice was a hoarse, urgent whisper.

"What's wrong?" I asked, moving instinctively toward her. "What do you need from me? How do I help?"

Now I was standing right in front of her, but her eyes remained unfocused. She still didn't hear me. "Help," she repeated. "Help." Her image came fully into focus for a last, brief moment. I lunged forward and reached for her, trying to grab her hand.

"Glinda!" I screamed.

But before I reached her, there was a bright flash of pink light, and with that, she was gone.

SIX

"Well," Aunt Em said shakily, as if it had just dawned on her that something funny was going on. "That was unusual. Was that woman some kind of actress?"

"Of course not," I said. I do try not to lose my patience with them, but sometimes it's an effort. "She's a *sorceress*. I've told you all about Glinda, remember?"

She and Henry both stared back at me with a look of blank confusion.

"A . . . sorceress?" Aunt Em seemed hesitant. "I suppose it did *seem* magical. . . ."

"It seems magical because we're in *Oz*. You may have noticed the sneezing flower and the fruit that changes colors?"

My aunt and uncle exchanged a look. "Now see here, young lady," Henry said. "I don't care if this is Oz or Shangri-la or Timbuktu. You can't just go spiriting people away like that with not so much as a how-do-you-do. It's the busiest time of year and

I have work to do tomorrow. I need to get a good night's sleep if I'm going to be up before dawn to milk the cows."

Aunt Em was nodding along with him as he spoke. "I'm not quite sure what's going on here," she said slowly. "But it's all very strange and, well, I would feel a lot better if I could sleep in my own bed tonight. Wouldn't you, dear? It's been a long day for you."

I'm the first one to admit that Oz is a lot to wrap your head around all at once, especially for two people who had always been perfectly content to spend their lives on the farm. At the same time, I had told them about this place so many times. You would think that would have given them at least a bit of a head start.

I tried again, this time speaking slowly and simply and trying to keep the creeping frustration out of my voice. "We have been transported to Oz," I said. "My friend Glinda the Sorceress must have brought me here. She's in trouble. I need to help her."

Toto barked one sharp *yip* of approval.

Neither of them looked very convinced, but before they could protest any more, Toto and I were already on the move, charging across the clearing, away from the house and the stream, in the direction of the Munchkin village I knew to be close by. I guess Aunt Em and Uncle Henry didn't want to be left alone in this strange place that might as well be Timbuktu because they began to follow.

I had imagined my triumphant return to Oz a thousand times. Probably more. This had not been exactly how I'd pictured it. I thought that I'd cleared up every last bit of trouble last time I was here. This time, I'd assumed my family and I would get to enjoy all the luxuries a magical kingdom had to offer without me having to go to the trouble of battling evil and saving the land.

I should have known better than that. Of course the very reason I'd been brought back would be because they needed my help. I'd saved Oz before. If Glinda was in trouble, that meant Oz needed rescuing. Again.

I have to say—it was nice to feel special, but I would have preferred to be able to just relax and see the sights with my family. You know, like a vacation.

But it occurred to me that maybe a quest is the price of admission into a magical kingdom, and if that was the case I wasn't going to complain. I just hoped I could get it over with quickly. And the only way to do *that* was to keep moving.

It didn't take long for us to spot the Munchkin town in the distance, and as we got closer, I remembered that it was hardly a village at all—it was just a circle of squat, domed houses ringed around a cobblestone plaza with a statue in the center of it.

A statue. I didn't remember that part. And when I stepped onto the cobblestone plaza I suddenly understood why.

Towering over the square, looking every bit the hero, was a girl in a familiar checked gingham dress, her hair pulled into two long braids. She had her hands on her hips and was staring triumphantly into the distance. The statue had been cast in marble and was entirely colorless except for one important feature: the shoes on its feet were silver, and they were sparkling in the afternoon sun.

This was Oz, where the unexpected wasn't unexpected at all. A hippopotamus in a tutu, a fat man walking on his hands, a pack of wild polar bears dancing the cha-cha—you could have put almost anything in the center of that square and I wouldn't have been surprised.

The statue, though, surprised me.

It was me. They had built a statue of *me*. I would have loved to see the look on Mitzi Blair's face if only she were here. I would have loved to see the look on my *own* face for that matter.

"Is that . . . ," Aunt Em asked.

"It can't be," Uncle Henry said. "Can it?"

I stepped over to the base and gazed up at myself, awestruck.

"'HERE STANDS DOROTHY GALE,'" I read aloud from the placard at the base, my voice wavering a little as I spoke the words. "'SHE WHO ARRIVED ON THE WIND, SLAYED THE WICKED, AND FREED THE MUNCHKINS.'" I turned around to face my aunt and uncle.

They just stared at me, dumbfounded. A wave of triumph washed over me.

"Can't you see now? Everything I told you was true. It's written right here. Written in *stone*."

Uncle Henry was rubbing his head. "Maybe *I'm* the one who's not in his right mind," he muttered to himself. "I did take quite a tumble."

Aunt Em, though, was still staring at the statue. Her face rippling with emotions. It was all sinking in for her. She turned to me.

"I never—well, I suppose I just didn't want to believe it," Aunt Em said, her voice still unsteady but decisive now, too. "I *still* don't want to believe it. It's all too strange, you understand. Your uncle and I—we're not like you. We've always been ordinary people. Something like *magic* . . ." She paused, marveling at the very word. "Magic! Well, that doesn't come easily to people like us. But this is all too real. It doesn't matter whether I want to believe it. I can *feel* it."

Uncle Henry was still rubbing his head, but he was listening. And Uncle Henry never, ever doubts my aunt when she sets her mind to something. He swiveled his head toward her, then to the statue, and finally back over to me.

"In all the generations of Gales, there's never been a liar," he mused, trying the idea out.

"Or a crazy person," I pointed out.

"Never had one of those either," he agreed.

Now Aunt Em was getting excited. "Oh, Dorothy," she said. "I'm so sorry we didn't believe you. I've always known you were something special, ever since the day you came to live with us. And now!" She gestured at the statue. "To think you did something so brave and important that they put up a monument to you! I just wish your poor father and mother were here to see it. They'd be so proud of you."

With that, she wrapped her thin, strong arms around me and

hugged me tight. I hugged her back, too overwhelmed to say anything at all.

"I'm so proud of you," she said.

"Yes, we're very proud," Uncle Henry said gruffly. "Of course," he added, "that doesn't mean we don't need to get home. . . ."

For a tiny woman, Aunt Em has a strong grip, and I was trying to peel myself out of her embrace when I began to hear excited chatter and whispering coming from all around us. "Hello?" I called. "Munchkins?"

They began to reveal themselves, a few at a time, their little faces slowly popping out of bushes and shadows and doorways and everywhere else you could imagine, like frogs after a rainstorm. Soon, we were surrounded by at least two dozen of the little people, none of whom were more than three feet high and *all* of whom were wearing little blue breeches and gold-embroidered bolero jackets, and funny pointy hats with bells around the brim.

"Declare yourself!" a voice shouted out from the crowd.

"It's me!" I replied, not sure who I was supposed to be addressing. "I've returned. I'm so happy to be back—I've missed you all so much."

A Munchkin man stepped forward, looking up at me quizzically. He glanced at my outstretched hand, but made no move to return my shake. "Excuse me, young lady," he said. "I am Cos, the alderman of this Munchkin village. And who are you?"

I cocked my head in surprise, and looked around.

"Well it's me of course. Dorothy Gale." I gestured up at the statue. "See?"

Cos looked up, back and forth between the figure and me, comparing the resemblance.

For a second there was silence. Next, a murmur spread through the crowd. Then, as one, they began to roar, "Dorothy!"

Cos took off his hat, twisting the brim in his hand like he was embarrassed to have forgotten me. There still seemed to be some uncertainty in his eyes, though, as he examined me intently. "Dorothy? The Witchslayer? Is it really you?"

Witchslayer? I liked that. "It's me," I said happily.

"It's been a very long time," Cos said slowly. "We never thought we'd see you again."

"I've been trying and trying to get back," I said, kneeling so that we were face-to-face. "It's not so easy, you know. A good, strong wind only comes around once every so often."

I rose back up to my feet and looked around at the growing throng surrounding us, all of them gazing up at me in awed admiration.

I wanted to stay and talk, to hear about everything that had happened in Oz since I'd been gone. But there wasn't time for that. There were more pressing things to worry about now. Like finding Glinda.

I wasn't sure how much I should say about what I'd seen back at the old farmhouse. It was possible that no one knew, yet, that anything was wrong with Glinda. If that was the case, it was probably a wiser idea not to let the cat out of the bag in front of an entire village of Munchkins, who, truthfully, are known for being an anxious and high-strung people.

Instead, I decided it was better just to try to get as much information as I could before I decided what to do next. "How has everything been lately?" I asked.

"What do you mean?" Cos seemed befuddled by my question, and the Munchkins began to chatter amongst themselves.

"I mean, how has Oz been, since I've been gone? There haven't been any more witches causing trouble, or anything like that, have there?"

"Oh no, Miss Dorothy," Cos replied, bobbing his red, cheerful face up and down. "We Munchkins have never been happier, since you slayed the witches all those many moons ago. The crops grow, the sun shines, and there is good magic everywhere. Praise Ozma!"

Hmm. So whatever had happened to Glinda, the Munchkins *didn't* seem to know about it.

But what was Ozma?

"Miss Dorothy, would you and your family like to stay for a feast?" A murmur of approval rippled through the crowd at Cos's invitation. "We would like to celebrate your visit."

It sounded tempting. A big Munchkin feast—all in celebration of *me!*—would certainly be a good way to make up for the disaster that had been my Sweet Sixteen. And Munchkins are known to be magicians in the kitchen—literally. But . . .

"I'm sorry," I said, kneeling down again. "But it's very

important that I see the king right away."

"Now, Dorothy . . . ," Uncle Henry interjected.

"The king?" Cos asked. "What king?"

"Why, the King of Oz, of course," I said in surprise.

When I first came to Oz, before the humbug Wizard had packed up his balloon to head back to America, he had chosen to appoint my friend the Scarecrow as the new king, and the people of Oz had immediately embraced him as their ruler. My friend the Tin Woodman had been made the governor of Winkie Country, and the Lion the King of Beasts. When I'd gone back to Kansas, I'd done it knowing that I was leaving Oz in good hands.

But now it seemed that the Munchkins didn't know who I was talking about.

"We don't have a king," Cos said. The rest of them all nodded their agreement.

"But I was there when they put the crown on his head," I said.

They all began to mutter confusedly amongst themselves. "Oz has only one true monarch," Cos said. "Princess Ozma. The rightful and just ruler of our land."

"Princess *what*?" I had never heard of any *princess* before.

They all began talking over each other, trying to explain how great this Ozma person was. "Princess Ozma is beautiful and kind! Princess Ozma is our one true ruler! Long live Ozma!"

"What about the Scarecrow?" I asked.

Cos's face brightened. "Oh," he said. "The *Scarecrow*. I'd forgotten all about him. Well, I suppose he *was* king. But that was for a very short time indeed, and it was ages ago."

"It was only two years ago!"

"Two years?" Cos frowned. "No . . . it seems to me that it was much longer than that. Perhaps your calendar in the outside world is different from ours." He fixed me with a serious look. "Dorothy, much time has passed since the days of the witches."

Uncle Henry cleared his throat. "Dorothy," he said. "This is all very interesting, but we need to be getting home. Mr. Munchkin, can you advise us on the best way back to Kansas?"

Cos looked at my uncle and blinked. "Where's that?"

I didn't have time to worry about Uncle Henry's grumbling. Between Glinda's plea for help and the news that the Scarecrow was no longer the king, it was becoming more and more clear that Oz had changed since I'd been gone. And I had an uneasy feeling that it wasn't for the better.

If I was going to put it right, I had to find my old friend.

"Never mind Kansas, Cos. It's very important that we see the Scarecrow right away. Does he still live in the Emerald City?"

"Oh no," Cos said. "He lives quite near here, as a matter of fact, in a mansion made of corncobs just off the Road of Yellow Brick. It's less than a day's walk." He pointed into the distance. "You'll find the road that way. Just be wary—the trees are restless today."

"The trees?" I heard Aunt Em whisper to Uncle Henry.

"Thank you, Munchkins," I announced. "Next time I see you, I hope I'll be able to feast with you." Then, confident in my path but nervous about what other surprises Oz had in store for me, I gave my most dignified good-bye wave.

As the people of Munchkin Country began to cheer my name, I knew that no matter what Oz had in store for me this time, one thing was clear:

I was home.

SEVEN

"Couldn't we have at least stayed for the banquet?" Aunt Em asked as we made our way from the Munchkin village, toward where Cos had told us the Road of Yellow Brick began. "I'm getting a touch hungry."

"I'm not sure I'd want to see the food those strange little folks serve," Uncle Henry said, raising his eyebrow skeptically. "Back in the war, they forced us to eat monkey brains and lizard tongues for breakfast, you know, and I didn't care for that one bit."

Uncle Henry was always talking about his days in the war, but sometimes it seemed hard to believe that he'd ever left Kansas at all. Some of his stories seemed much more bizarre than anything Oz could dream up.

Then again there had never been a Gale who was a liar, so who was I to doubt him?

"Henry Gale," Aunt Em admonished him. "They did no such

thing. Anyway, I'm sure the food here is just fine."

"They could serve me Lobster Newburg and Baked Alaska and it would still be time to get on home," he replied.

"Oh, don't you see?" I exclaimed, trying to make him understand. "Don't you see? We're in Oz now! You don't need to worry about the cows, or the crops, or the pigs, or anything like that anymore. Life here is so much better—can't you see already how beautiful it is? In Oz, you won't need to wake up at dawn to milk the cows ever again!"

Aunt Em touched my shoulder gently, calming me down. I hadn't even realized how worked up I'd gotten. "Now, Dorothy," she said. "It *is* lovely here. And we're so proud of your statue and all we've learned about you today. But your uncle is right. We can't stay here. This is no place for us."

"Anyway, I *like* milking the cows," Uncle Henry said.

I stopped dead in my tracks, right there on the yellow bricks. For all of Henry's griping and Aunt Em's nervousness, it had never occurred to me that they would still want to go home once they got a taste of Oz. How could anyone want to go back to a dry, dusty field and a few irritable pigs when there were fantastic things around every corner here?

"Of course we're going to stay," I said. "Why in the world would we go home?"

My uncle looked downright aghast. "Because it's our *home* and that's where we all belong," Uncle Henry said. "I'm glad the people love you here, but that doesn't change who you are, missy."

"Don't lose your temper, Henry," Aunt Em cautioned him. "But I *do* have sewing circle next week, and the house is still a mess from your party, Dorothy. If we don't go home soon, I'll never have time to clean up all the dishes."

Suddenly I wanted to scream. They had to be joking. I had wished so hard to have a second chance here, never expecting it would actually happen. And now it *had* happened, and we were walking happily through Munchkin Country on a day more beautiful than Kansas had ever seen or *would* ever see. They wanted to give it all up so that Aunt Em could go do the dishes for her sewing circle?

At least I had one foolproof ace up my sleeve. I didn't even have to lie. Well, not exactly.

"I don't know *how* to get home," I said irritably, fighting back anger. "I don't even know how we got here in the first place! The only one who can send us back to Kansas is Glinda, and she needs our help. Once we find her, we can all talk it over."

As I spoke, I felt my shoes pulsing against my feet with a warm, tingling feeling, as if I'd just dipped them in a whirlpool of warm water. So maybe it was a tiny lie after all—the shoes had brought us here, and it wouldn't surprise me one bit if they could bring us home, too. But Uncle Henry and Aunt Em didn't need to know that.

Neither of them looked too thrilled with my plan, but it's not like they had a choice. So Toto and I stomped ahead and we all moved on.

The first signs that we were nearing the road were some scattered bricks here and there—they almost looked like they were growing out of the dirt. After a few more minutes of walking, there were more and more of them, and then the road sprang up in the middle of a wide, overgrown field, unfurling itself into the horizon like a golden ribbon.

Aunt Em was so surprised when she saw it that she let out a squeak and jumped back on her heels. Uncle Henry shook his head as if he couldn't believe what he was seeing.

I'd spent my share of time on this road, but even I was taken aback by how radiant it was in the afternoon sunlight, at the dazzling golden contrast against the blue-green of the grass and the cornfields and the sky, at the way it twisted and spiraled through the fields and hills, winding out into the distance like it would lead us anywhere we could possibly imagine, if only we could name the place.

Toto was already a few paces ahead of us, panting and wagging his tail in excitement. He barked three times, ready to lead the way.

"Well, I suppose it won't hurt to explore just a bit," Uncle Henry said. "Now that we're here anyway."

Aunt Em didn't say anything at all. She just stepped forward and set a foot onto the road. She looked back at us with a small, playful smile. "I guess the dishes can wait," she said. "For now at least."

The thing about the yellow road is that it's enchanted. It wants you to follow it—not for any devious reason, but just because it likes to have a purpose. It's very hard to resist a road with such infectious enthusiasm. I knew from experience.

My feet tingled against the bricks as we eased our way down the road, letting it lead us lazily through the hills and fields and valleys of Munchkin Country. With every step I took, it was like I could feel magic flowing up from the road and into my body. Surprisingly, even after as long as we'd been walking—even in heels higher than any I'd ever seen before, let alone *worn*—my feet didn't hurt. It was just the opposite actually. It felt like I was getting a very pleasant foot rub.

We strolled for hours without getting tired. Everyone seemed so happy. Uncle Henry was whistling one after another of the old songs he'd learned in the war, and Aunt Em was peppering me with questions, like, "Where was it that you met your friend the Scarecrow?" And, "I still don't understand why this Tin Man of yours wanted a *heart* so very desperately. He sounds like he was perfectly kind and loving and gentle without one, so why bother?"

She often gasped in amazement at a strange plant or animal— she was practically beside herself with glee when we came upon a resting flock of flying piglets, no bigger than sparrows, who were nibbling at some apples that had fallen into the road—but other times, like when we passed by the waterfall that fell up instead of down, she was simply caught without anything to say.

When we walked through the field of poppies that I remembered so well, I told everyone to hold their noses so we wouldn't be tempted to lie down for an endless nap. We walked right on through, admiring the ruby-red blossoms and the little puffs of pink smoke that shot into the air every so often.

We made it through without our eyelids even fluttering.

"In some ways it's so different from Kansas and in others it's just the same," Aunt Em remarked a bit later as we strolled through a flourishing field of corn that grew over our heads on either side. Clearly she was trying to put a positive spin on things. "I mean, we grow a lot of corn back home, too."

"This corn's different, Aunt Em," I said. "It comes right out of the husk already buttered, and it's like nothing you ever tasted."

"Never had a problem buttering my own corn, thank you very much," Henry sniffed. But I could tell even he was impressed. Back home, butter was for special occasions only. When I plucked an ear from a stalk and shucked it, the smell wafted up enticingly. Aunt Em took a nervous bite and her eyes widened. As soon as he saw her reaction, Uncle Henry helped himself to his own, and soon all three of us were sitting by the side of the road munching to our hearts' content.

It was so wonderful that I almost forgot anything was wrong. I almost forgot Glinda's desperate plea for help, and the fact that if Glinda was in trouble, Oz was in trouble, too. If wickedness was allowed to run rampant, the lush, magical cornfields would probably be replaced with barbed-wire orchards or bulldozed to make way for pincushion factories or something even more terrible.

I couldn't forget that. I was here with a job to do.

But for now the corn was plentiful, there was nothing wicked in sight, and all seemed right with the world.

That is, until we'd finished our lovely picnic, set off traveling again, and made our way a few more miles down the road.

That's when the screaming started.

EIGHT

Soon after we left the cornfield, the sky darkened into dusk and the picturesque fields and farmland we had been traveling through began to give way to a barren, burned-out landscape of stunted, sickly trees and shrubs, which made the constant screaming even eerier. The grass thinned out until the ground was mostly just blue-gray dirt dotted with sad and dried-out patches of weeds. Even the road itself was different here, dull and worn down, the bricks cracked or loose or missing entirely. Crows swooped overhead, their dark wings casting long shadows on the pale yellow bricks.

Up ahead, a forest loomed. It was deep and black, thick with vines. It stretched on and on endlessly in either direction.

The screaming was coming from somewhere deep in the forest, a deep guttural wail that shook me to my core.

It was a scream, but it was also something like a song, too. It was like all the pain and sorrow in the world was being dredged up from the bottom of the earth and was twisting itself into a horrible, tortured melody.

We all stopped walking. Even Toto, who was usually brave in the face of any danger, crouched in a ball at my feet, quivering with fear.

"I don't like the sound of that, Dorothy," Uncle Henry said with a grave expression.

"No," Aunt Em agreed. Her face turned pale. "I don't like it one bit."

I had to give them credit for putting it so mildly. Sometimes people you think you know well can still surprise you. They were being brave. Or, at least, they were trying.

I wasn't sure if I was capable of the same. Everything in my body was telling me to give up and run away. Back to the cornfield, to the Munchkin village, to the little old farmhouse by the riverbank in the woods. Back to Kansas, even.

But when I turned around, I saw that single path we had been following now forked out behind us in five unfamiliar directions. Some force wanted us to pick one of those paths in the hope it would lead us back to where we had come from.

I had a feeling none of them would. In my experience, when a dark force you don't understand wants you to do something that badly, it's best to do exactly the opposite.

I looked into the distance. The road plunged straight ahead like a golden knife through the heart of the forest. However horrible that screaming, the only choice was straight ahead.

"Come on," I said.

My aunt and uncle and my dog all looked at me like I had lost my mind. But when I took a step forward to show them it was possible, I saw that my shoes were burning red in the dusky, spooky, evening light, their comforting glow pulsing against the washed-out yellow bricks in time with my heartbeat, and I knew it was the right thing.

"Come on," I repeated, firmer this time. I took another step. Then Toto took one, too, still shaking, and then Aunt Em did the same. Uncle Henry grabbed her by the elbow and followed. If she was going, he was going, too. You could always count on him for that much.

So we moved slowly toward the woods, together, and as we got closer that moaning yowl shattered and reshaped itself into something else: a scratchy, violent squall so loud that my whole skull vibrated from the force of it.

Aunt Em and Uncle Henry doubled over as it hit them, both screaming and covering their ears in pain.

As unpleasant as it was, though, I wanted to hear it. The only way to understand it was to listen.

It was the sound of ravens screeching and rivers running dry, the sound of milk curdling into blood and children being torn from their mothers' arms.

It was the sound of death. The sound of evil.

I took one more step forward anyway, feeling as if I was being propelled by a force outside myself, and that was when I saw their faces.

Each tree had one, and each face was worse than the last, each formed out of thick, silvery-black bark, gnarled and distorted into tortured grimaces and angry, curled scowls and gape-mouthed expressions of terror.

That's when I understood: the sound wasn't coming from *inside* the woods. It was coming from the woods themselves. The trees were screaming.

And I recognized them. Sort of.

"They're not supposed to be here," I said under my breath. I don't think anyone heard me over the noise.

On my first trip to Oz, after the Wizard had gone home, the Scarecrow, the Lion, the Tin Woodman, and I had all made our way to Quadling Country to see Glinda the Good in the hopes that she would have the key to sending me home. Along the way, we'd had no choice but to travel through the Forest of the Fighting Trees.

That forest had been a lot like this one. The trees there had been mean and cruel, with ugly, hollowed-out faces and branches that bent and twined around you, tossing you to the ground when you tried to pass underneath them.

But they hadn't screamed like this.

Were the two forests related? And if so, how? This one hadn't been here the last time I'd walked this road. Where had it come from?

It didn't matter. Nothing mattered except getting through it. I forged ahead with Toto at my side and my aunt and uncle only a few steps behind.

The screaming became louder and louder until it hardly

seemed like sound at all anymore, and more like a hopelessness so strong I could almost feel it as an aching pain, lodged somewhere in the back of my gut.

It was so loud I wanted to tear my hair from my skull, to scratch at my face until it bled.

And then it was over. Just like that, everything went silent. Deadly silent.

I looked to Aunt Em and Uncle Henry, and they looked back at me, just as shaken and surprised as I was. None of us said anything for fear of upsetting the quiet.

Then we all looked up together, and saw the trees towering over us. We had made it to the edge of the wood.

They were tall and thin, hardly wider around than Aunt Em, and were almost entirely bare of leaves. Their cruel, twisted faces took up almost the entire lengths of their trunks, and their knotty, spindly branches spidered out into sharp claws.

Two trees, taller and older-looking than the rest, stood on either side of the brick road at the spot where it disappeared into the dark tangle of woods. Their faces were frozen into gargoyle masks of torment and despair.

I wondered how they had gotten this way. Had they been people once? Were they being punished for something they had done in another life? Or was it something else entirely?

In the time I'd been back in Kansas, I'd almost let myself forget this part of Oz: the witches and the monsters and the ugly, dangerous things. I'd let myself forget that magic is slippery and unpredictable. It likes to change things. Sometimes it changes things into something incredible and wonderful—something to take your breath away. Other times it twists it and corrupts them into something you barely recognize.

For everything that's wonderful, there's something wicked, too. That's the price you pay for magic.

It's worth it, I thought. Even here, standing at the mouth of a place that radiated the purest evil I'd ever felt, I knew it would always be worth it.

Because without magic, you're just left with Kansas.

Without warning, there was a loud creaking sound, followed by a groan, and then a crack as the large tree to the left side of the road lurched forward and began to uproot itself from the ground, scattering dirt everywhere.

It pulled itself toward us by its roots, dragging itself in our direction. My feet began to tingle.

It was coming right for me. It hissed and snapped its jaws.

The only way out was through. So I began to run.

I picked up Toto, ducked around the tree, and plunged myself into the forest, knowing from the sound of footsteps that Uncle Henry and Aunt Em were right behind me.

The road through the forest wasn't anything like the road that had taken us through Munchkin Country. The bricks were still yellow, but they were grown over with leaves and brush; they were crumbling and warped where the roots of the trees were moving in on their territory.

I didn't care. I raced down the path as fast as I could, as narrow and obstructed as it was, praying with each stride that my foot found a solid landing.

The forest was dark and overgrown. The trees grasped and clawed; they swiped at me with their sharp branches and bent their trunks to trip me.

Instead of screaming, they were now grunting and hissing and whispering taunts in my ear that I couldn't quite make out.

Behind us, I could hear that sick, scraping, creaking sound as the first tree dragged itself across the bricks in pursuit of me and my aunt and uncle and my dog. When I heard more snapping and cracking sounds, I knew that it wasn't just one anymore: his brothers and sisters were uprooting themselves to chase after us now, too.

I ran faster, still baffled by how easy it was in my five-inch heels.

The whole time, I made sure I was listening for the sound of Aunt Em and Uncle Henry close behind me. They might have been old, but at least they could still outrun a few trees.

And then Aunt Em tripped. She let out a sharp scream and went flying onto the ground in front of me, landing on her chest with a thump.

"Em!" I cried.

"I've got her!" Uncle Henry raced up from behind me. It's a good thing my aunt was so tiny and a good thing Uncle Henry was stronger than he looked, after all those years of working alone in the fields. Without even pausing in his stride, he swept Aunt Em up into his arms, threw her over his shoulder, and kept on running.

It didn't matter. It was too late. The trees had closed in on us, blocking the path forward.

They were behind us as well, their branches weaving tightly into one another, trapping us completely.

One of the trees snarled and lunged for Aunt Em. She cried out in terror as it slashed its wooden claws against her face, leaving three thin lines of blood on the ridge of her cheekbone.

I didn't look at him, but I could feel my uncle trembling next to me. I should have been scared, too, but I wasn't. Just the adrenaline, I guess. Instead, I felt myself go white-hot with rage.

How dare these trees threaten me? How dare they harm the people I cared about? I didn't even think they wanted to *hurt* us. I think they were just trying to humiliate me. Just like Suzanna and Mitzi had done at my birthday party.

Maybe that would work back in Kansas, but here in Oz, I demanded respect.

"*Stop,*" I commanded.

My shoes pulled tight on my feet, like they'd just gotten a size smaller. A shock of energy sizzled up from where my heels dug against the bricks and spread through my body. It felt strange, but I welcomed it.

It felt like another person had taken hold of me. "*I am Dorothy Gale,*" I said. The words sounded strange and foreign as they came out of my mouth, reverberating through the endless tangle of branches.

The trees were listening. "I am the Witchslayer. Allow us to pass, or suffer the fate of all the others that have stood in my way."

Just like that, the trees began to relax their branches. They shrank away, stifling their hissing like it had all been one big accident. Slowly, they crawled out of the road and back into the forest, where, one by one, they began to settle their roots back into the dirt.

We were free to go on.

I had done that somehow. All I'd had to do was ask. Were the trees just big pushovers in the end? Or was it something about *me* that had scared them?

"How——" Aunt Em said. Uncle Henry dropped her out of his arms and placed her upright again.

"What came over you, girl?" my uncle asked. "Not to say I'm not grateful, but . . . you didn't even sound like yourself."

"I don't know how I did it," I said uncertainly. I had found a power somewhere within myself, and I had used it. Or had *it* used me? It was hard to tell. I wasn't sure I wanted to know the answer.

"Next time," Aunt Em suggested, "it might be wise to bring an ax." She glanced over at me nervously. There was relief in her eyes that we'd made it through the woods alive but I thought I saw something like fear, too. Not fear of the trees either. Fear of *me*.

"There's not going to be a next time," Uncle Henry spat. "Because we are going home. I'll spread my own butter if it means I never have to go through anything like that again as long as I live."

The four of us carefully made our way through the rest of the forest not saying anything else about what had happened. The trees were still scowling and making jack-o'-lantern faces at us from the side of the road, but they didn't make a peep. We walked quickly. Toto hopped into my arms, where he stayed, keeping careful watch on our surroundings.

Soon, moonlight began to streak through the gaps in the branches, and then the path opened up. We had made it out of the woods. A silvery vista unfolded before us, the winding path of yellow bricks shimmering like water and dipping down into a huge, breathtaking valley. All along the road, little flowers lit the way, their centers glowing with flickering blue flames.

I collapsed onto the road and caught my breath, finally able to let down my guard. I put a palm against my face and drew back blood from where one of the trees had scratched me. My calves were shooting with pain from running. Or was it from something else?

And yet, I wasn't really tired. Winded, yes, but not tired. Actually, I felt more alive than ever, like I had energy seeping from every pore on my body.

I followed the road into the valley and then up the crest of the next hill, and I saw that we had finally reached our destination: there on the horizon was the Scarecrow's house, golden and radiant against the night sky, lit from within. Just like the

Munchkins had told us, the house was made entirely from enormous corncobs as tall as trees and five times as wide around, each one forming a single, towering turret. It wasn't just a house. It was a castle, really.

I pointed. "That's where we're headed. That's where my friend the Scarecrow lives."

Uncle Henry whistled. "I've heard about the Corn Palace in South Dakota, but I don't think it's anything compared to *that*."

We followed the road down the hill, into the valley. The evening was cool and the breeze felt good against my skin and everything was so pleasant that our frightful experience in the woods was almost forgotten. Almost.

What had *I done back there?* I wondered. Had the trees' bark simply been worse than their bite? Or had my shoes had something to do with it?

I was still considering the question when a certain feeling of *familiarness* came over me, and then I saw it: at the edge of the field, a wooden post was sticking up out of the ground at a lop-sided angle.

Something about seeing it there, like nothing had changed, made me almost want to cry. I knew that post. It was where I had first found the Scarecrow. Without him, I would never have made it to the Emerald City, would never have been able to defeat the Wicked Witch of the West. I would never have learned how brave I could really be.

Seeing it there, for the first time I knew that I was back. I was really, really back. He had been my friend, and I had missed him so much. Now I was going to see him again.

"What is it, Dorothy?" Aunt Em asked, seeing a small smile on my face.

"Nothing," I said. "I'm just happy."

NINE

Uncle Henry and Aunt Em were still huffing and puffing from the climb up the hill when we finally approached the entrance to the corncob mansion. It was even bigger up close than it had looked from far away, and I felt almost nervous as I reached for the corncob knocker on the door.

What if he was different? What if he didn't remember me? What if he was old and gray? (Could Scarecrows *get* old? There was still so much about Oz that I didn't know.)

There wasn't much time to wonder anything. The door opened before I could knock, and there he was, right before my eyes, just exactly the very same as I'd left him; just the same as I'd remembered him every day since Glinda had sent me home.

"Dorothy!" the Scarecrow exclaimed. I threw myself into his straw arms and he swept me up and spun me around, whooping with elation. "The Munchkins sent a bluebird to tell me you were on your way, but I was afraid to believe it!"

"You know I'd never leave you for good," I said, laughing.

I was still grinning from ear to ear when he set me back down again, but the Scarecrow's face looked more serious. "We missed you, Dorothy," he said, and his kind, smiling, drawn-on eyes—the ones I'd never forgotten—began to fill with tears. "Oz hasn't been the same without you. I didn't think you were ever coming back."

"I didn't either," I said, reaching out to touch his arm. "But I'm back because of Glinda. I know she's in trouble, and I have to rescue her. Do you know where she is?"

The Scarecrow cocked his stuffed head to the side.

"Glinda?" he asked. "What have you heard about her?"

"I saw her," I said. He looked even more surprised at that. "She was at my old house by the Munchkin village. Well—it wasn't her exactly. It was more like some kind of *vision*. Like she was trying to send me a message. She told me she needed my help."

The Scarecrow looked concerned. He was stroking his chin in thought. I knew that if anyone would know what to do, it was him—he was the wisest creature in all of Oz, and probably anywhere else, too.

"We have much to talk about," he said after a spell. "But first, introduce me to your friends."

I laughed. I'd been so excited to see him that I'd forgotten all about my aunt and uncle. They were still standing in the doorway looking like they had absolutely no idea what they'd gotten themselves into.

"They're not my *friends*, silly. They're my *family*—my aunt Em and uncle Henry." As I said their names, Uncle Henry gave a funny little half wave and Aunt Em bowed awkwardly.

The Scarecrow lit up—it's amazing how expressive a painted-on face can be. He clapped his gloved hands together and he bounded for them, practically tackling them as he wrapped his flimsy arms around their waists. "Of course! I've heard so much about both of you! How have your travels in Oz been so far?"

Aunt Em, Uncle Henry, and I all exchanged a glance.

"Oh, it was all just grand until we came to the screaming monster trees that tried to murder us," Uncle Henry said.

"Oh dear," the Scarecrow said. "The Forest of Fear? Don't tell me the Munchkins didn't warn you."

"How could we *not* pass through the forest?" I asked. "There's no way around it, at least as far as I could tell."

"Of course you have to pass through it but—the Munchkins really didn't tell you to stuff your ears with Pixie thread?"

I shook my head. "I don't even know what a Pixie thread is."

"It keeps you from hearing that infernal racket the trees love to make. If you can't *hear* them, you won't be afraid. And if you're not afraid, they won't even know you're there. Won't bother you a bit. They'll just look like exceedingly ugly trees. Which, in the end, is really all they are."

They sensed fear. Was *that* how I had managed to get rid of them? Just by showing them that I wasn't scared?

No. Aunt Em and Uncle Henry and Toto had all been frightened. Somehow, I had made the trees afraid of *me*.

The problem was that it wasn't just the trees who had been scared of me. I'd scared myself, too.

"I don't think we'll be traveling back that way anytime soon if we can avoid it," I said. "With or without Pixie thread."

The Scarecrow sighed. "A reasonable response. Those trees are such a nuisance. Bad for tourism, especially when the Munchkins can be so forgetful about reminding passers-through to protect themselves. I keep telling the princess that she should just set a match to the whole forest, but she won't hear of it. She says they're part of Oz—that destroying them would upset the whole magical balance."

"If that's balance," Aunt Em said, shuddering at the memory of the afternoon, "I'd hate to think what it looks like when the scales start to tilt."

The Scarecrow tipped his hat to her. "A very good question, Mrs. Gale," he said. "Let's hope you never find out the answer. Now, come, let's eat. You must be starving after what you've been through."

He turned to a doorway that led deeper into the castle and cupped his hands to his mouth. "Munchkins, prepare a feast for our special guests!"

As we entered a great dining room two Munchkins dressed in yellow and green—with tiny, pointy hats perched atop their bald heads—appeared out of nowhere.

We took our seats at the banquet table—even Toto had been given a place next to me—and before we knew it, our table settings flew in front of us only to land gently at our places: the napkins perfectly folded, the forks on the left, none of it even a smidgen askew.

Within seconds, our glasses were filled to the top with a delicious-looking beverage I didn't recognize, and it was only five minutes before tray after heaping tray of piping-hot food appeared on the table.

"I took the liberty of having food prepared that I thought you'd be familiar with, rather than some of Oz's more . . . *exotic* native dishes," the Scarecrow said, much to the relief of my aunt and uncle, who, despite their experience with the self-buttering corn, still seemed apprehensive at the idea of eating magical food.

"And very kind it was of you! There's enough grub here to feed my old army platoon," Uncle Henry said. He picked up a serving spoon and helped himself to a generous portion of mashed potatoes.

"It sure does look good. I think," Aunt Em said, eyeing a heaping bowl of caviar, which, even though it wasn't the least bit magical, was probably just as exotic as anything else Oz had to offer as far as she was concerned. At least Uncle Henry had gotten the chance to see a few scattered corners of the world, back in his army days. This was the first time Aunt Em had ever set foot outside of Kansas.

She was taking her maiden voyage in remarkable stride.

I'd never eaten so much in my life and I'm pretty sure Uncle Henry and Aunt Em hadn't either. Yet somehow we managed to finish each course just as another even larger one came. I guess a day of traveling will make a girl hungry.

"Aren't you going to have any food, Mr. Scarecrow?" Aunt Em asked around the time that they brought out the stuffed goose.

"Oh," the Scarecrow said, waving her question aside. "I don't eat. The Wizard may have given me an exceptional set of brains but I'm still shy a working stomach. Now, Dorothy, tell me what brought you here. I've been dying to know!"

I wasn't sure how much to tell him just yet. I'm not sure why, but I didn't want Em and Henry knowing about the shoes, though they *had* to have an inkling.

"Well," I said, smiling brightly. "I made a wish, and before you know it, we were all here!"

"Is that so," the Scarecrow said thoughtfully. I could tell he wasn't buying it.

"We landed right in the same spot as last time—my old house was still there, if you can even imagine."

"Of course it is," he replied with a smile. "That little house is considered one of Oz's most important landmarks."

Uncle Henry looked up from his Waldorf salad. "Mr. Scarecrow," he said. "Dorothy tells us you're the smartest character in all the land."

The Scarecrow nodded modestly, and Uncle Henry continued. "My wife, Emily, and I, we were hoping you'd have some idea of how the three of us might be able to get back—"

"Oh, drop it already!" I snapped. Aunt Em gasped, and I instantly clapped my hand to my mouth. I have to say that I was

shocked at myself. Never in my life had I spoken so disrespect-
fully to my uncle. Or to anyone, really.

But it had been *such* a long day, and my aunt and uncle were
being *so* troublesome. Here they were, eating the greatest meal
they'd ever dared to dream of, and all they could think of was
how to go back to our sad little farmhouse and our dusty pig-
pens.

I must *try to control my temper,* I chided myself. If I wanted
my aunt and uncle to see things my way, it wouldn't do to make
them angry.

The Scarecrow shot me a curious sidelong glance but otherwise ignored my outburst. "It's true that I've been blessed with
an excess of the finest brains known to man or beast, Munchkin,
witch, or wizard," he said, tapping his head with a stuffed glove.
"But I'm sad to say that traveling between Oz and the outside
world is no simple feat."

"I see," Henry said.

"Dorothy thinks a lady by the name of Glinda might be able
to help," Aunt Em said. "Do you have any idea of where we
might find her?"

Again, the Scarecrow gave me a meaningful look that said,
We'll discuss this later. "I do not," he said. "Glinda's whereabouts
have been unknown for quite some time now."

"For how long?" I asked, putting my fork down, suddenly
interested again in the conversation.

"Oh, it's hard to say," the Scarecrow replied. He fiddled with
a piece of straw that was poking out of his head. "You know

we're not much for time here in Oz. No one gets older here, and we celebrate the holidays whenever we're of a mood for it. But it was sometime after Ozma took the crown. Glinda let it be known that she had important magical business beyond the Deadly Desert, and that we shouldn't worry about her—that she would return when the time was right. That must have been, oh, at least ten years ago, if I venture a guess."

"Ten years!" I exclaimed. "But, how long have I been gone?"

The Scarecrow turned in his seat and fixed his eyes on me seriously. "I don't know, but I daresay there are many people here in Oz who won't remember you at all. I, myself, had almost forgotten what you looked like."

My last adventure here had lasted for what felt like almost a month, but when I'd returned home, only a few days had passed. Still, the idea that I had been gone so long that I'd been forgotten was unimaginable. All of my memories were still so fresh in my head.

I had so much to ask the Scarecrow. Why wasn't he king anymore? Who *was* this Ozma person? Did he have any suspicions about where Glinda had *really* gone? But I had the impression that he didn't want to talk about any of it in front of my aunt and uncle, and so I finished my meal in silence.

But there was so much on my mind that I hardly touched my food. Uncle Henry was a different story. I hadn't even made a dent in my Waldorf salad, and he had already scarfed down a goblet full of maraschino cherries, a small mincemeat pie, several hunks of lamb slathered with green mint jelly, and—despite the fact that I was unsure where exactly shellfish came from in Oz, where there were no oceans that I knew of—a giant portion of shrimp cocktail served in a crystal goblet brimming with crushed ice.

And then they brought out the ice cream.

"Oh dear," Aunt Em said when she saw it. "I'm afraid I can't possibly eat any more. The meal was just perfect, Mr. Scarecrow, but I'm afraid it's been *quite* a day. Would it be terribly rude of me to excuse myself?"

"Of course not," the Scarecrow said. He clapped his hands and another Munchkin, this one dressed all in yellow, appeared. "This is BonBon. He'll show you to your rooms."

"Thank you, sir," Uncle Henry said, standing along with Em. "Dorothy, don't you stay up too late. Tomorrow we'll need to be up at the crack of dawn to find Miss Glinda so that we can head on home."

BonBon bowed and led them away.

As soon as they were gone, I pulled Toto into my lap and turned my chair to face the Scarecrow.

"Now tell me what is going on here," I said. "I know there must be more to the story than you were telling me."

He sighed. "You first," he said. "I don't for a moment believe that you wished your way here. It doesn't work that way."

So I told him the story: of my terrible birthday party, of the shoes, and the note that had come with them.

"They *must* have come from Glinda," I finished. "Who else could have sent them?"

"It certainly sounds like her doing," the Scarecrow mused. "But until now, I believed that Glinda was dead—or gone for good."

"No," I said, so emphatically that it came out as something approaching a shout. "No. Someone's done something to her. She's still in Oz, and she's in trouble. That's why she brought me here. To save her."

"You may be right," he said. "We'll go to see Ozma tomorrow. She needs to be apprised of the situation."

Every time anyone said the name *Ozma*, a terrible feeling came over me. I'd never met her and I barely knew who she was, but I didn't like the sound of her. "Who *is* this Ozma?" I finally was able to ask. "And why aren't you the king anymore?"

A look of something like regret passed across the Scarecrow's face. He glanced down at his plate.

"Ozma is Oz's true monarch," he said. "She's a direct descendant of Oz's founder, the fairy Lurline. She was just a baby when the Wizard rose to power, and unable to inherit her throne. Still, the Wizard worried about the power she would eventually be able to wield. It's hard to seize control of a kingdom when you have the True Princess swanning about in her prime. So he sent her to the North—to Gillikin Country. What happened to her there is a mystery. Only a few people are privy to all the details, and I am not one of them. What I do know is that she eventually managed to grow up, and made her way back to the Emerald City to reclaim her crown. Unfortunately for me, that was just a few months after I'd been made king. I ceded the crown to her immediately, of course." He sighed and shrugged. "It was nice while it lasted."

It sounded like a bunch of hooey to me. "So this Ozma can just march in and kick you out on your rear end? That's not fair!"

"I had no choice. It is the way of Oz that Lurline's heirs should rule. The people were happy with me as their king, but I must admit that Ozma has been a good ruler, too. The kingdom has never been more peaceful, or more prosperous." He sounded cheerful, but it was obvious he was putting on a brave face.

I scowled. "I don't care," I said, outraged by the injustice. "You would have been better. You deserved that crown! What did *she* do to earn it, except show up when it was convenient for her?"

"Oh, it's not so bad," he said with a wave of his hand. "I like it here amidst my corncobs. There's plenty of time to think, here. And Ozma made me one of her top advisers—she always calls me into the palace when she needs someone with real brains."

"What about the Tin Woodman? What'd she do with him? Send him off to be sold for scrap?"

The Scarecrow chuckled. "Now, now, Dorothy. There's no need for that. The Tin Woodman is still where you last saw him. He still lives in the Wicked Witch's old castle, if you can believe it. He's spruced it up quite nicely; it's nothing like it was before."

"And the Lion?"

"Still ruling over the beasts, just as ever. He lives deep in the Forbidden Forest, in Gillikin Country." The Scarecrow sighed.

"He's become a bit of a recluse, though. The three of us haven't been in the same room since I left the castle."

It broke my heart to think about. Glinda missing; the Scarecrow deposed; my friends scattered across Oz. I had expected to come back to Oz to find it just as I'd left it. But nothing was the same.

"Now let's take a look at these shoes of yours," he said, after BonBon had served me an after-dinner root beer float.

I stood, extending my foot proudly, and the Scarecrow studied the mysterious shoes.

"Have you tried removing them?" he asked after examining them for a bit.

"Why no," I said, surprised that it hadn't even occurred to me. But as hard as I tugged at the heels, they wouldn't so much as budge.

"Just as I suspected," he mused.

"How strange," I said. "How will I bathe?"

The Scarecrow chuckled. "I'm sure you'll find a way. At any rate, they're magical, that much is evident. And they seem to have fused themselves to you. The *red* is certainly Glinda's signature. But she . . ."

"It has to have been Glinda," I said. "I've never been so certain of anything. Especially after she appeared to me and asked for help earlier today. We *have* to help her."

"We'll get to the bottom of it," he said. "Tomorrow, we will travel to the palace. Ozma will have heard of your arrival and will be expecting you. She's very interested in you, you know.

The princess is an avid student of history, and she's always been fascinated by your story."

"I'm not so sure I care to see *her*," I sniffed. "She doesn't sound very pleasant in my opinion."

The truth was that I didn't trust the sound of her. Was it just coincidence that Glinda had disappeared just after this new princess had seized the palace?

The Scarecrow brushed aside my protests. "Oh, she's nothing if not pleasant. I think you two will be great friends. She's about your age, after all."

"But . . ." I hesitated, not sure whether to voice my concerns, and then decided that if I couldn't trust the Scarecrow, my oldest friend, all was lost anyway. "What if Ozma's the one who did something to Glinda?"

I was of half a mind that the Scarecrow would dismiss the notion as ridiculous. But he didn't.

"The princess is very powerful," he said, lowering his voice. "She is very shrewd. But she is also very lonely, and in need of companionship. I urge you, go to the palace and befriend her. She will never be defeated by force, but I've always found force to be overrated anyway. If Ozma knows *anything* about Glinda's whereabouts, you will be the one who can learn about it. Become close with her. Give her no reason to doubt your intentions."

I nodded. I understood. I didn't like it, but I understood.

At that, the Scarecrow summoned BonBon, who appeared out of nowhere as if he'd squeezed himself up out of a gap in the floorboards.

"Follow me to your quarters, Miss Gale," he said, extending a gentlemanly hand.

"One more thing," the Scarecrow said as I scooped a now-dozing Toto into my arms. "For now, I think it's better that you don't tell the princess that you've seen Glinda at all."

"Okay." I nodded.

"And Dorothy: don't mention the shoes."

TEN

The next morning, the Scarecrow and I stepped out of his mansion into a bright and breezy day. Every ear of corn and every wildflower glistened and sparkled in the sun, and I took a deep breath, inhaling dewy morning air. It smelled like just-baked cookies.

When I looked closely, I saw that the air was filled with thousands of specks floating on the breeze like dandelion fuzz. The difference was that these specks were silvery and slippery, flying through the air like tiny beads of mercury from a broken thermometer.

One of them landed gently on my face. When I crossed my eyes to get a look at it, I was shocked to see a dainty little person with butterfly wings and a wild tuft of silver hair sitting right on the tip of my nose. And without so much as a hello.

"Oh, don't mind them," the Scarecrow said. "It's Pixie season. They can be quite irritating, but they're harmless."

Just as he said it, the creature sank its sharp little teeth into my nose. I was more surprised than actually hurt, but I screamed, swatting at it and spinning around in a circle trying to get it off me.

The Pixie jumped from my face and buzzed around my head, letting out a high-pitched staccato squeal. She was laughing at me.

"Er, *mostly* harmless," the Scarecrow said.

"I don't remember *those* things from last time," I said, rubbing at my injury to check for blood.

"They stayed in their hives back in those days," he explained. "They were afraid of the witches. But Ozma believes in letting them run wild, and they've been getting bolder and bolder. You should see what they do to my cornfields."

"I'm all for Pixies having their freedom," I sniffed. "I'm an American, after all. But they might be a little more grateful to the girl who *gave* it to them, don't you suppose?"

"All the magic in the world couldn't give a Pixie manners," the Scarecrow said ruefully. "If I were king, I'd do away with all of them. But Ozma is of the opinion that even Oz's lowest creatures deserve their freedom. Pixies, Screaming Trees, even Nomes, for heaven's sake—they've all flourished under the princess's rule."

They might have been rude, but I couldn't help being charmed as I watched the little things flitting through the air. "I hope they at least do pretty little spells or something," I said. "To make up for the nastiness and biting."

"They certainly do. If you catch one, they'll grant you exactly one wish," the Scarecrow said.

"Oh!" I exclaimed. "Then what are we waiting for?" I was about to go chasing after the Pixie who had bit me—it would serve her right!—but the Scarecrow caught me by the elbow.

"Don't bother," he said. "You can only wish for three things and none of them is very interesting. A dried cod, a hunk of coal, or a darning kit."

"Aunt Em might like a darning kit," I said, but I quickly dropped my chase.

That's when I saw our carriage sitting by the Road of Yellow Brick—a vehicle that would put Henry Ford's finest automobile to shame. It was a jeweled green sphere of glass etched with delicate swirling patterns, about as big as Uncle Henry's toolshed, and rather than having wheels it was hovering in the air a few feet off the ground. It was hitched to a crude wooden horse composed of a log sitting on top of four sturdy sticks. It had two knots for eyes, a notch for a mouth, and a twig for a tail.

"Hello there," the log said.

By now I knew not to be surprised by anything around here, especially not a talking log in the shape of a horse. "Well, hello there," I greeted him—if you could call a log a *him*. "I'm Dorothy Gale. Pleased to meet you."

He turned toward me and whinnied. "I'm the Saw-Horse," he said. "The fastest horse in all of Oz, of course, and the captain of Ozma's Royal Guard. I'll get you to the Emerald City in no time at all."

Just then, Toto came racing out of the house, followed by Aunt Em and Uncle Henry, who were looking around in a daze, like they hadn't really expected any of this to still be here. Toto began barking and leaping into the air, trying to catch the Pixies, who dipped and dove around him, taunting him with their squeaky giggles. I hoped he liked dried cod.

"Aunt Em!" I called. "Uncle Henry! The Scarecrow is going to take us to the Emerald City. Isn't the carriage marvelous?"

"It looks like a big Fabergé egg," Aunt Em said. "I always found them a bit gaudy myself." But I could tell from the way she was staring that she was more impressed than she cared to admit.

"The Emerald City?" Uncle Henry asked. "I thought we were going to find your friend Glinda?"

"We're going to meet with *Ozma*," I said, trying to reassure them. "She's the princess of Oz. She'll help us find Glinda. Besides, don't you want to see the magnificent Emerald City?"

The Scarecrow was extremely diplomatic about the whole thing. "You can't come all the way to Oz and miss out on the Emerald City," he said. When my aunt and uncle looked at him dubiously, he added: "The princess is a formidable magic user in her own right. If she can't send you home herself, she will no doubt be eager to help you find the Sorceress."

It took a little convincing, but eventually they gave in, and soon Uncle Henry was helping Aunt Em up into the carriage. At least we had a ride this time. I think after yesterday's ordeals, we were all more than happy to be traveling in comfort.

* * *

The inside of the carriage was lined with plush velvet cushions, and the Scarecrow and I sat on one side with my aunt and uncle on the other. A tea service floated on a tray between us.

"Tea?" the Scarecrow asked Aunt Em, handing her a little pink cup.

She looked like she wanted to say no, but Aunt Em can never resist a good cup of tea.

"Do you have Earl Grey?" she asked.

"I have whatever you'd like," he replied. He pointed at the kettle on the tray.

"How do I brew it?" she asked curiously.

"Just pour it and imagine the best cup of tea you can think of."

Aunt Em looked dubious, but she gingerly poured herself a serving, and when she took a sip, her eyes lit up. "That's Earl Grey, all right!" she said in delight. And then, curiously: "Did you cast a spell on it?"

The Scarecrow chortled. "A spell! I should think not. I'm a man of science. In fact, it's the milk of the rare Chimera. While it remains inside the kettle, it exists in infinite liquid forms—it's not until you pour it that it takes on the qualities you desire of it."

"Does it serve up scotch, too?" Uncle Henry joked.

"I don't see why not," the Scarecrow said.

Soon my uncle was contentedly tippling his favorite Glenlivet vintage and I had poured myself a cup of rich, dark hot chocolate, and then we were off. The carriage shot forward down the road like a bolt of lightning. The scenery was whipping past us in a green and gold blur, but we were perfectly comfortable inside our cozy little bubble. Every time we curved into a hairpin turn or went speeding down a hill, our vehicle would adjust itself so that we didn't even shift in our seats.

"Henry Ford could take a lesson from whoever built this," Uncle Henry marveled, gazing out the window.

Outside the carriage, forests, villages, and rivers all appeared and disappeared as quickly as they'd popped into sight while the Saw-Horse sped ahead, moving with such speed that his wooden feet didn't even make a sound against the brick road.

"He really is fast," I said to the Scarecrow.

"He is indeed. He claims to be the fastest horse in the land, and I don't doubt him. He's also Ozma's closest confidant, you know. He's been with her longer than anyone. He's the one who brought her back to the city after her exile, and he's been her most loyal servant ever since."

It almost made me sorry for this Ozma, to think that her only friend was a wooden horse that looked more like a piece of scrap lumber than an animal. Even Miss Millicent had to make a better friend than a talking log jammed together with a few twigs.

When he was certain that Aunt Em and Uncle Henry weren't paying attention, wrapped up as they were in their own conversation and in watching the scenery, the Scarecrow put his arm around me casually and leaned in close, whispering, "Be careful what you say in the Saw-Horse's presence. Rest assured that anything you tell him will find its way to the princess's ear."

I nodded slowly, not sure what to make of any of it.

After a bit, the Saw-Horse began to slow his pace, and I saw that we had come to a wide river.

"Oh dear," the Scarecrow said. "Isn't this always the way. It's the Wandering Water."

"What's that?" Aunt Em asked nervously.

"Just another of Munchkin Country's many nuisances," the Scarecrow explained with a wave of his stuffed hand.

"If it's anything like the Forest of Fear, I'm turning back now," Henry said firmly. "And Emily is coming with me."

I didn't speak up, but I had to agree that, after yesterday, we had all had more than our fill of Oz's alliterative annoyances.

"Not to worry," the Scarecrow said. "The Wandering Water isn't unpleasant—just inconvenient. It's a river with a mind of its own, you see. You can never tell where you're going to find it. In a few hours it will have moved on to somewhere else entirely. Never fear, though, the road isn't without its own personality. It will get us across with as little delay as possible."

As we galloped toward the water, I saw what the Scarecrow meant. The river was actually moving, shifting and undulating, snaking its way across the landscape, paying no attention to the fact that it cut right through the middle of the road, leaving no way to cross.

But as we approached, the Road of Yellow Brick began reconfiguring itself, too. As if it sensed us coming, golden bricks began to float into the air, one by one, constructing themselves into a curving bridge that led high up into the sky, where it took a meandering, curlicued route across the water.

The only problem was, it didn't look very stable.

"We're not going over that, are we?" Aunt Em asked, craning her neck out the window and turning a shade of pale green.

"Oh yes," the Scarecrow said. "Not to worry, though. The Saw-Horse has never lost a passenger."

Soon we were trotting upward into the clouds, the river hundreds of feet below us. The bridge of yellow bricks continued building itself as we made our way across it, fluttering in the breeze like a ribbon.

Aunt Em's eyes were squeezed shut, and her knuckles were white, her hands clasped together in her lap. Uncle Henry gripped her arm tight, not looking much braver than she did.

Back in Kansas I'd never been much for heights myself, but now that I was in Oz, I discovered that I didn't care. It was all part of the adventure. Why come to a place like this and then turn away the secret things it has to offer you?

So as we climbed higher and higher into the sky, I forced myself to keep my eyes open.

All of Oz was spread out below us like a patchwork quilt. When I squinted, I almost thought I could see the red towns of Quadling Country to the south and the yellow hills of Winkie territory to the west. The purple Gillikin mountain range stretched north as far as the eye could see. That is, until I saw the Emerald City glowing on the horizon, and I forgot everything else.

I would never forget that glittering skyline.

From high above the Wandering Water, the city appeared

first as a green glimmer against the blue sky and then popped into focus, rippling like a mirage beyond a massive glass wall that rose over the trees. The curved rooftops of the skyline blended into each other in a series of sloping, gentle waves, all surrounded by a halo of light.

In the center of it all, the pointed spires of the palace rose straight up into the air, scraping the clouds. I wondered what it would be like to stand at the top of one of those towers and look out over all of Oz. I wondered how far you could see from up there; I wondered what it would be like to know that all this magic was yours. Did Ozma appreciate what she'd been given?

I hoped she did. If I had all that, I would never let myself lose sight of how lucky I was. Not for a moment.

ELEVEN

We all breathed sighs of relief as the flying road began to make its descent back to the riverbank, and before we knew it, we were on land again. After that, it was only a matter of minutes before we were approaching the majestic emerald walls of the city.

Everyone was silent as we pulled up to the gates, which were intricately carved with twisting vines, gilded and studded with jewels. I noticed with some curiosity, though, that the gates were solid all the way through, and there was no obvious place for them to swing open, or even a mechanism for them to rise up. How were we going to get through?

The Saw-Horse answered my question by thumping his hoof, three times, loudly against the ground. As he did it, the entranceway rippled, and it began to melt away until it was just a smooth puddle on the ground, leaving an opening where it had just stood.

"What happened to the Guardian of the Gates?" I asked.

"That funny little man who used to hand out the glasses?"

"Ozma reassigned him," the Scarecrow explained. "That was just one of the Wizard's many idiosyncrasies. Now that he's gone, people are allowed to see clearly again. The city's green enough without the glasses anyway. Ozma installed quite a bit more emerald once she took over, and anyway, she doesn't believe in guarding the gates at all." He sniffed at what he obviously considered to be a preposterous flight of girlish fancy. "'It's everyone's city,' she says. 'Why would I want to keep anyone out of it?' The former guardian works as an optometrist now, and I'm told he's quite happy. Most people in Oz have perfect vision, so he leads a very relaxed lifestyle."

I looked over my shoulder as the Saw-Horse trotted us into the city, and as soon as we had cleared the opening in the wall, the gate sprang right back up and re-formed itself, closing behind us.

As we made our way through the city streets, I took in the sights. Little round houses were arranged in clusters around open plazas with burbling fountains and vibrant gardens where townspeople chattered amongst themselves. The smell of baking pies and fresh flowers filled my nose.

It was strange to be back in this city that I had so many memories of. It was both the same and different. For one thing, it really *was* green now, just like the Scarecrow said. From the funny little domed buildings whose roofs were reinforced with giant, smooth-polished emeralds the size of dinner plates to the towering skyscrapers that somehow seemed to be formed entirely of huge, seamless jewels, every surface in sight managed to incorporate the city's signature gemstone in one way or another. Even the yellow bricks of the road weren't immune to the treatment: the road hadn't ended at the gates, but instead continued on into the city, toward the palace, and each and every individual brick was inlaid with a single emerald at the center.

I think I liked them better when they were just plain yellow. Ironically, it was only now that the Guardian of the Gates was gone that I actually could have *used* some glasses—not to create the illusion of opulence but to shield my eyes from the glare.

At an open market, Munchkins and Winkies peddled produce and clothes and trinkets to laughing townspeople. There was a snake charmer, like in storybooks I'd read, and a sword swallower and a team of acrobats who flipped and twirled in the air as if they were propelled by an unseen force.

Everyone was smiling and laughing, milling around without a care in the world. A sense of liveliness permeated everything and everyone.

And yet I couldn't help feeling uneasy.

It was all too happy. Nothing was this perfect, not even Oz.

My shoes sent a now-familiar pulse of energy up my legs, and as I looked back out at the bustling city, the cheerful scene suddenly seemed sinister: the smiles of the people turned to leers and the candy-bright colors took on a garish, desperate tint.

Glinda was gone, I reminded myself, off somewhere no one seemed to know about.

Something wasn't right here.

***

Our carriage finally ground to a halt where the yellow brick opened up into a large, circular courtyard outside the palace entrance. Toto was the first out, followed by the Scarecrow. I clambered out after him, then helped Aunt Em and Uncle Henry down. The air was still and there was a lovely sound of water burbling in fountains. In the distance, I could hear singing.

The plaza was an explosion of azaleas that blossomed in a rainbow of colors: they were pink and purple and blue, but also striped and polka-dotted and paisley-patterned. A large marble fountain shot a waterfall of what looked like liquid diamonds high into the air.

Aunt Em trailed her fingers through the pool, then held them up in front of her and watched them glitter in the sun.

"I don't suppose your friend Ozma would mind if we took a few of her jewels back to Kansas, would she?" my aunt asked me with a twinkle in her eye. "They have so many of them here and just one of the big ones would pay for a year's worth of chicken feed and pig slop."

I groaned. "First of all," I snapped, "Ozma isn't my friend. I've never even met her before. Secondly, I don't want to hear another word of Kansas talk. Not while we're standing outside the royal palace in the most beautiful city in the universe."

Aunt Em crossed her arms at her chest. She clucked her tongue and shook her head. "My word, Dorothy. You've certainly lost your sense of humor lately. Of course I'm not going to steal from our hosts. And if I *was* going to, it wouldn't be to buy pig slop. I'd make myself a beautiful necklace with diamonds so big it would scandalize all of Topeka."

Only then did I realize she had been teasing me. "Sorry," I said sheepishly. "I just—"

"See here, Dorothy," she said. "I know your uncle doesn't approve of staying here just as well as I know that you don't want to ever go home if you can help it. Myself, I can see both sides of it. This *is* a lovely country—not counting those terrible trees—but our whole life is back on the farm."

"We could have a new life *here*. A better life."

"We *could*," she agreed. "But would it really be so much better? What would we do all day, with no cows to milk or fences to mend? We'd go stir-crazy before long."

I shook my head emphatically. "There's so much to do here," I said. "You've hardly seen any of it."

"Maybe," Aunt Em said with a shrug. "And maybe it wouldn't matter. At any rate, I say we're here now, and we might as well enjoy ourselves."

"I *am* enjoying myself," I said.

"It seems to me that you're awfully sour for someone who's having the time of her life," Aunt Em said.

I was trying to decide how to respond to that when the enormous doors of the palace swung open and a small, delicate figure came hurtling down the grand, emerald-studded steps. She raced toward me, her diaphanous white dress and dark, wavy hair flowing behind her, all tangled together in a whirling cloud.

"Dorothy!" she shouted. "It's really you! I've been waiting for this day forever!"

She bounded across the courtyard and threw her arms around my neck, pulling me against her in a tight embrace before stepping back and giving me a warm, searching smile.

It wasn't the greeting I'd been expecting. When I'd sought out an audience with the Wizard, in this very palace, it had been an arduous, hours-long process of being patted down by guards, standing in endless lines, and waiting in antechamber after antechamber before finally being allowed ten minutes alone with Oz's supposed ruler.

Ozma, apparently, was less formal than all that.

Her eyes were a vivid, haunting green, lined with kohl and shadowed with gold, and they had a kindness behind them that took me by surprise. Her mouth was a ruby-red exclamation point in the center of her round, pale face. She was tiny, too: the top of her head barely reached my shoulders.

She wore a tall, golden crown with the word *Oz* inscribed on it, and had two big red poppies tied into her hair, one on either side of her face, fastened with long green ribbons. She had a golden scepter tucked under her arm as casually as a normal person would carry an umbrella.

"I can't believe I'm finally meeting you," she said. "I was so excited when I heard from the Munchkins that you had come back. The famous Dorothy Gale. The Witchslayer! I suppose I owe you a thank-you for saving my kingdom."

"Anyone would have done the same," I said, waving the

praise away. I stole a quick glance over at my aunt and uncle and saw that Uncle Henry had his arm around Aunt Em and was pointing out various buildings in the distance.

"Are these your parents?" the princess asked, gesturing at them with her scepter, which I now saw was topped with the same insignia that was on her crown: a gold O the size of my palm that enclosed a smaller, stylized Z.

"Oh no," I said. "This is my aunt Em and uncle Henry. I live with them, back in—"

Her eyes lit up. "Oh yes! Kansas! It sounds like such a fantastic place. They say the roads there are made of dust! Or was it dirt?"

"Well . . . ," I said, "both?" I couldn't imagine being excited by dirt roads considering the opulence that was all around us here, but Ozma was already rushing over to Aunt Em and Uncle Henry. For their part, they seemed to be adjusting to the idea of meeting royalty. They wore the same friendly expressions that they used for greeting a neighbor's out-of-town cousin at the church breakfast.

Ozma leaned down and patted Toto on the head. He was so happy to be back that he was running in circles. "And this is little Tutu?"

He snarled at her. Toto didn't like it when people got his name wrong.

"Toto," I corrected quickly.

"Of course!" she said. "How silly of me. I guess I owe him my thanks as well." She knelt down and scruffed his fur, and while he bristled at first, soon he was happily licking her hand.

The princess turned her attention back to Aunt Em and Uncle Henry.

"We have rooms for all of you, and the finest clothes in the city," she said. "I want you to know that, for as long as you're here, you can make full use of everything in the palace. My servants are yours to command."

"That won't be necessary," Uncle Henry said hesitantly. "We're not planning on staying long."

Ozma tilted her head in concern. "Oh?"

"Uncle Henry . . . ," I started. "We only just got here."

"We need to get home," Aunt Em explained apologetically to Ozma. "You have a beautiful kingdom, but we're not the magical types. We have a farm back home, you see, and responsibilities."

Ozma waved her scepter with an air of dismissal. "Of course! I've heard such things about Kansas; I don't doubt that you're eager to get back there. But I've waited so long to meet Dorothy; surely you can stay for a *bit*."

Ozma called out: "Jellia! Show the Gales to their quarters, please. And please make sure their every need is attended to."

Before they could protest, a round, cheery-faced maid with blond hair and a green uniform emerged from the main building and led Aunt Em and Uncle Henry up the stairs inside. They glanced back at me over their shoulders as they stepped through the entrance, a look of trepidation on their faces. "Toto," I said, feeling almost guilty when I saw how out of their element they looked. "Why don't you keep them company?" With a sharp bark, he went bounding after them.

Ozma moved her attention to the Scarecrow, who hadn't said a word since we'd arrived. "I'm so pleased you came today," she said. "There's a delegation here from Gillikin Country and I could really use someone with brains in the room when it comes to dealing with them."

She looked at me with an air of wry conspiracy. "Keeping everyone in Oz happy is no small feat," she said. "Every day there's a new visitor with a new list of requests. Easily met, most of them, but you have no idea how dull it can be, sitting in those meetings."

The Scarecrow bowed. "I am at your service, Princess."

"Oh, stop that," she said, rolling her eyes. "You know bowing makes me uncomfortable."

"Of course," he said.

"The delegation is in the reception room," Ozma said. "They shouldn't give you too much trouble, but you know how the Gillikins are—always bickering amongst themselves and forgetting what they even want in the first place. It could take some time."

"Well, then it's a good thing I don't require sleep." The Scarecrow leaned in to give me a peck on the cheek, and as he did, he whispered: "Remember. Be careful. And not a word about the shoes."

As I watched him go, Ozma grabbed me by the elbow. "Come inside the castle. Let me show you what I've done."

The main hall of the palace was magnificent, but there was a surprising coziness to it, too—you could tell someone actually lived here. Ozma had lined the walls with damask wallpaper, and filled the space with plush velvet couches overflowing with throw pillows and ornate end tables and carved oak chairs upholstered in leather. From the diamond-shaped black-and-white tiles on the floor to the crystal chandeliers to the lush, exotic-looking plants sprouting from every corner of the room, it felt stately and elegant but warm and welcoming, too.

"What do you think?" Ozma asked, almost nervously, as we walked past a dramatic, sweeping staircase. It almost felt like she wanted me to be impressed.

I was a bit surprised that she seemed to care so much about my opinion—she was the princess after all, a descendant of the fairy Lurline, supposedly, and the heir to the greatest kingdom in the world. I was just an ordinary farm girl from dusty, gray Kansas. What did I know about interior decoration?

"It's very nice," I said, as if I saw beautiful, grand things all the time and this was just another one of them. "You've made it so much nicer than when the Wizard lived here."

"Yes, well, he did have a bachelor's taste, didn't he? Anyway, all this is thanks to you, Dorothy. You saved my kingdom when I was"—she paused—"you know. Indisposed. If it wasn't for you, the witches would probably be living here now." She shuddered. "Can you imagine what they would have done with the place? You have no idea how much I owe you."

I looked around at this dream palace full of treasure and beauty and luxury, and suddenly I had a pretty good notion of what she owed me, actually. Maybe I was just the teeniest bit jealous that she got to live like this, all thanks to me. There was a part of me that wondered if *I* would have been the princess if I'd stayed.

"Of course," I said, forcing a smile. "Oz was in danger. I only did what any decent person would have."

"No, Dorothy. Not everyone would have done it. *You* did it. You're more special than you know."

How could I argue with that? "Okay," I admitted modestly. "Maybe I'm a *little* special."

Ozma threw her head back and let out a lilting, musical giggle. "I think we're going to be great friends," she said, wrapping an arm around my waist and tipping her head against my shoulder. She led me through the great entrance hall to a series of French doors that looked out onto a lush, expansive garden dotted with fountains and topiary sculptures.

"So do I," I said, remembering what the Scarecrow had told me. If I was going to find Glinda, it appeared that I had to make Ozma trust me. I had to become her friend. Truthfully, it didn't seem like it would be very difficult.

"It's a beautiful day," Ozma said. "Well, it's always a beautiful day here, but still. Let's take a walk in the gardens. I've got so much to ask you. Starting with how in the world you got here!"

TWELVE

In Ozma's gardens, the hedges were tall and greener than green, and were sculpted into strange, looming figures that were three times as tall as either of us. Some of them were covered in strange little blossoms, others were grown over with vines and fragrant honeysuckle and jacaranda and flowers that I didn't recognize.

Some of the flowers had tiny little eyes like the funny little puffballs that were growing all over the old farmhouse back in Munchkin Country. They all twisted in my direction to stare at me.

If you've never had fifty plants with human eyeballs stare at you, you have no idea how disconcerting a feeling it is.

A path wound its way through the grounds, forking off into other trails that led into little grassy valleys, groves of orange trees, little sitting areas with wrought-iron benches. Back home what passed for a garden was usually a couple of tomato plants and maybe some scraggly old petunias. This was something else.

Ozma wandered down the main path idly, her scepter slung casually over her shoulder and the train of her dress trailing on the ground behind her.

"Don't keep me in suspense," she said. "So what was it? Another cyclone? I know it's not easy to get here from your world, believe me. I've looked into bringing you here myself, actually—we've had some political trouble, and since you were so good at handling it the first time—well, but that kind of magic is very complicated. There are few in Oz who can manage it."

A part of me didn't want to lie to her. I've always believed that honesty will get you farthest. And it was hard to believe that someone as seemingly sweet and guileless as the princess could possibly have had anything to do with Glinda's disappearance. But the Scarecrow was my oldest friend in this world, not to mention the smartest person I'd ever met. If he thought it was best to keep a few things secret from her, I knew that I should trust him.

"Well," I explained, remembering that it's always best to base a lie in some version of the truth. "It was my birthday, and you see, in Kansas, on your birthday, you get one wish. I wished I was back here, and next thing I knew, poof! We were all crash-landing in the middle of Munchkin Country."

Ozma looked skeptical.

"That's it?"

"I wished very hard," I clarified.

"But it's so odd," she said, touching a finger to her red lips. "I thought magic didn't exist in your world. It seems that something would have had to *bring* you here."

"It was my *sixteenth* birthday," I scrambled to elaborate. "That's kind of a big deal over there. So that's probably why it worked. Besides, I always felt like being in Oz the first time changed me somehow. Maybe I brought a little bit of magic back with me."

She *hmmm*-ed. Her tone was still unconvinced, but her eyes were open and trusting. It wasn't that she didn't believe me. She just thought there was more to the story.

I decided to change the subject. "But I want to know all about *you*," I said. "Are you really a fairy?"

The path we'd been following had ended at a wall of tall, thick hedges, no more than twenty feet wide, right smack-dab in the middle of the courtyard.

"Hold on," Ozma said, suddenly distracted. "I want to show you something."

She waved her scepter in a wide arc, and as she did it, the hedges parted, revealing a small opening. Ozma slipped right through it. After a moment's hesitation I followed, and as the opening grew shut behind us, I found myself in a hedge maze. To my left and right, narrow grassy paths were bounded by impenetrable shrubbery that rose high over our heads. In front of us was another opening, and on the other side of that more paths and another hedge wall.

Something about being in here made me nervous. The maze had looked small from the outside, but now that we were in it, I could see that it was much bigger than I had realized, the paths leading far into the distance in either direction.

The atmosphere crackled with energy. I didn't like the feeling of this place. Even though the sun was as big and bright as ever when I looked up, its light somehow wasn't reaching us in here.

I could feel magic everywhere. The leaves on the hedges nearly vibrated with it. But it was a different kind of magic than the magic that ran through the fields of Munchkin Country like a babbling brook. It was different from the dark, threatening magic in the Forest of Fear, too.

This magic was old and ancient. It was gnarled and weathered and fossilized. I don't know how I knew it. I just did. And I knew that if you stood still for too long in here it could swallow you.

For the first time, my shoes hurt.

"Which way do we go?" I asked.

"It's all the same," Ozma said. She was different in here, too. In the garden, she had been girlish and sunny. In here, though, her spine had straightened and her chin was raised. Her dark hair was suddenly wild and tangled; her delicate, girlish beauty was now fierce and fiery. She seemed older. She seemed less like a princess and more like a queen.

"All the paths lead to the same place," she said.

I wanted to ask where, exactly, that place was, but the words wouldn't come out of my mouth.

So we walked aimlessly, the bushes growing thornier and more overgrown and the leafy corridors narrower as we went. The air was still and quiet, and although the spires of the palace were just barely visible over the tops of the hedges if you craned your neck to see them, the city seemed very far away.

We took one corner and then another and another. Were we walking in a circle? My shoes burned on my feet, and I found myself wondering, again, what kind of magic exactly was pulsing through them. Were they communicating somehow with the magic in the hedge maze?

Ozma kept on walking. She had said it didn't matter which way we went, but I started to suspect, from the way she carefully considered each gap in the maze before deciding which one to turn down, that there was more to it than she was letting on.

I had so many questions to ask, but it was like the maze had cast a spell over me that kept me from speaking at all. It was a creepy feeling, but I felt oddly calm about it. It was hard not to when it was so peaceful in here. Ozma was the one who finally broke the silence.

"Oz is bordered on all four sides by the Deadly Desert," she said out of nowhere when we had rounded a corner into a twisty section of the maze where the hedges were overgrown with thick, brown vines. They were dotted with tiny blossoms, deep purple and smaller than my thumbnail, and they stretched over our heads in a canopy that hid the sky. "A desert so dry that you touch just a grain of its sand and it will suck all the life right out of you. One touch and *poof*, you're dust."

"Oh," I said, not knowing what else to say.

"But, you know, when Queen Lurline and her band of fairies first came to this place, ages ago, Oz was nothing *but* desert. It wasn't quite so deadly back then—Oz had no magic to speak of in those days—but it was still dry and hot and dusty and flat and it went on and on and on. There was no Emerald City. There wasn't even a tree. It was no place for life."

"Sounds like Kansas," I said. "Though, at least we have trees there."

The princess gave me a curious look. "I've always thought Kansas sounded very nice," she said. "Anyway, the fairies were passing through the desert on their way to somewhere else, and they had been traveling for a long time. A *very* long time. They were hungry and tired and thirsty. They had used the last of their magic."

"Where were they trying to go?" I asked.

"No one knows," Ozma said. She plucked a blossom from a vine overhead and tucked it into her hair. "Pieces of the story get lost over time, you know. All we know is that they were coming from somewhere and they were going somewhere else, and wherever it was, they had to cross Oz on foot to get there. But Oz is a big place. You probably know that better than I do. I have a carriage, after all, and you've walked so much of Oz. Can you imagine doing that without anything to drink or eat? Fairies are powerful, but even they have their limits. After a while, Lurline and her people were too exhausted to go any farther. She knew that resting really meant *dying*, but what else could she do?

"So they stopped. They just sat down and stopped, right there in the sand. Their travels had finally come to an end. Well, they thought they had, at any rate. But just when she had given up hope, Lurline put her hand down and felt a dampness in the dirt. When she scratched at it a bit, she could hardly believe her eyes—it was water, the first she'd seen in weeks. It was a cool, fresh spring. It was mostly covered over by the sand, but it only took a minute of digging for it all to come bubbling up."

"Someone put it there by magic," I said. "To help her."

"No. It was just good luck. Lurline was the magic one. And as she drank from the pool, she felt her magic coming back to her. With the little bit of energy the water from the spring gave her, she was able to conjure a pomegranate tree, and she and the rest of the fairies ate. The food made her stronger, and so Lurline summoned another tree, and then another and another until a whole orchard had sprung up."

The path began to curl into a spiral. Ozma's voice was dreamy and far away, and I wondered if she was talking to herself more than to me.

"They rested there for eight days, eating and drinking and dancing, regaining their strength after all the hardship they had been through, and on the eighth day, Lurline was so grateful and happy that she pricked her thumb with her knife and let a drop of her blood fall into the pool. I don't know why she did it, really. Just to say *thank you*, I guess. But whatever the reason, she gave Oz a piece of herself, and as soon as her blood hit the spring, the land began to change around them. Just like that. Lush, green grass grew where there had only been dirt and sand. Rivers sprang up, and they wandered wherever they wanted to wander. Hills and mountains burst out of the flatness. On the path that the fairies had walked, yellow bricks began to sprout like flowers. Lurline's blood had blessed the spring with magic, and that magic began to flow through everything."

The spiral we were walking in grew tighter and tighter as it looped in on itself toward a center. The path grew narrower and narrower until my shoulder touched Ozma's. Then it was narrower still, and I felt my nervousness mounting. I dropped behind her as she continued with her story. She didn't bother looking back at me.

"What had once been a barren desert had become a magical, untamed wilderness. It became Oz. But the queen knew that she and her band had already stopped for too long. It was time for them to keep going where they were going. And yet—it was so beautiful. She couldn't just abandon it. So she left her favorite daughter behind, a girl not much older than me, and the smallest of the group. She was small but tough. It was left to her to look after the land in Lurline's absence. To take care of it and nurture its magic the way you tend to a garden.

"That daughter stayed behind, alone, to become Oz's first true princess. That daughter was my grandmother. Or was it my great-grandmother? Or my great-great-grandmother?" Ozma shrugged, finally stepping forward through an arbor into a clearing where the sun was warm and bright again. Birds were chirping.

We had come to the center of the maze.

And as soon as the sunlight hit her green eyes, the laughing, girlish Ozma who had greeted me at the gate returned in a flash. She giggled a little to herself, putting a hand to her mouth. "Great-great-great-grandmother? Well, who knows! At any rate she was the first princess—whatever her name was. I honestly have no idea! Me, I'm the last. At least for now until the next one comes. Sometimes I wish she would hurry up." She gave a theatrical sigh.

The center of the maze was a circular area paved with flagstones. It was about fifteen feet across, with a ring of squat little trees inside the larger ring of tall hedges.

In the very center of it all was a single wooden bench that had obviously seen better days: it was silver and weathered and close to rotting. At the foot of the bench was a muddy, mossy puddle. All of it had a burned-out, sun-bleached look to it, as colorless as one of the old sepia photographs Aunt Em kept of herself as a child.

"So," Ozma said. "I suppose that's a very long way of answering your question. Yes, I'm a fairy. The truth is, it's really not as exciting as you might think. It's actually not so much different from being a regular girl."

She was so matter-of-fact about the way she said it—the same way I would say that my aunt and uncle were farmers, or that I was from Kansas. I couldn't imagine being a fairy princess and not even *caring*. And how could she think it was the same as being a regular girl?

"I know it's stupid," I asked. "But do you have wings? Fairies do usually, right?"

Ozma didn't mind. She laughed and flipped her palms up as if to say, *You caught me.* She tossed her black hair and shook it out, and as she did, two huge butterfly wings unfurled from her back and fluttered a few times.

The wings were golden and translucent, lined with veins, and so delicate that they barely looked like they were there at all. They looked like nothing more than the impressions that burn into your eyes when you look at the light for too long.

"They don't do me much good," she admitted, flapping them a bit to demonstrate. She hovered a few inches from the ground and then let herself down again. "They work, but flying makes my stomach queasy, and anyway, I have the Saw-Horse to take me wherever I want to go. I hardly use them at all."

The oddest feeling came over me. I wanted to reach out and touch those shining, beautiful wings so badly. If I had just asked, she probably would have let me, but I didn't want to ask. It wasn't like me at all, but I wanted to reach out and grab one of them and hold it in my fist. I wanted to know what it would feel like for it to be mine and not hers.

But I didn't do it. I held my hand back, and Ozma drew the golden wings in. Rather than folding them up neatly like a bug's wings, or a bird's, her body just seemed to absorb them back into itself. If she noticed my reaction, it didn't seem to bother her.

The princess walked to the bench and sat, letting her scepter clatter to the ground. She tucked her legs under her body and stretched her arms lazily to the sky. "This is my favorite place in the whole Emerald City. Maybe in all of Oz," Ozma said. "I'd spend days here, if they let me."

With an entire palace, an amazing garden filled with magical plants, and a whole Emerald City as a personal playground on top of it, I found it hard to believe that *this* drab little sitting area, with its broken bench and its muddy puddle, and its stunted, gray little trees—all surrounded by an enchanted hedge maze with obviously sinister intentions—was the best place the fairy princess could think to spend her free time.

"Really?" I carefully sat down on the bench next to her. "Why?"

She pressed a lock of her perfect hair behind her ear sheepishly. "Oh, who can say? It's quiet, for one thing. No one bothers me in here—I don't even think anyone else knows how to get in. In here, I don't have to be a princess. The strange thing is that in here I'm more alone than anywhere else, and yet it's the one place I don't feel quite so lonely."

"Oh," I said. I didn't know how else to answer that. Who wouldn't want to be the ruler of your very own magical kingdom? I could think of at least ten girls back home who would gladly claw each other's eyes out for the privilege.

"Maybe it's because of what happened here," Ozma said. "Maybe that's why I like it."

I gave her a blank stare. I didn't know what she was talking about.

"Can't you tell? This is the place where Oz began."

I looked at the ring of squat little trees, branches heavy with round, red fruit. Pomegranate.

I looked at the puddle, and saw that it wasn't a puddle at all, but a pool that bubbled up from deep within the earth. Floating in the center, so tiny that I'd missed it at first, was a brilliant green lily pad with a vibrant red flower at the center, its petals as red and glittering as rubies.

This was the spring that Lurline had found. This was where all of Oz's magic came from. I was at the source of all of it.

My shoes burned.

THIRTEEN

The peculiar sight of Aunt Em and Uncle Henry dressed in some of the finest clothes in Oz greeted me in the great drawing room of the palace. They were draped in colorful silks and satins and their collars were so high that they couldn't turn their heads.

It wasn't just their clothes that had been gussied up either—apparently someone had seen fit to style their hairdos according to the latest Oz fashions. Uncle Henry's hair had been swept up into a funny little triangle and his beard was trimmed into a sharp point. Aunt Em's hair, freshly coiffed into a gigantic updo, had been dyed a ridiculous lime shade with emerald combs holding it tightly in place.

Even poor Toto hadn't been spared. He looked like a giant black puffball, his fur blown out so that he was twice his normal size. The greatest indignity of all was that they had tied a bright green ribbon around his neck.

I couldn't help but giggle at the sight. They looked wonderful by Oz standards of course, but I wasn't used to seeing Uncle Henry out of his coveralls, or Aunt Em out of her gray muslin frock.

They all glared at me. Toto snarled.

Ozma entered the sitting room a moment after me. "My, don't you look wonderful!" she exclaimed at the sight of them. "Like real members of the court." They glared at her, too. This was as mad as I'd seen them since the time that the Shiffletts down the way had let the cows loose and they'd trampled Aunt Em's prize petunias.

I clasped my hands together, quickly changing the subject. "I have something wonderful to tell you!" I gushed, hoping to sweep them up in my excitement.

"You brought me a pair of coveralls and some old work boots?" Uncle Henry asked.

I shook my head, grinning from ear to ear. "Better! Princess Ozma has invited the Lion and the Tin Man to come visit us in the palace tomorrow."

Ozma had informed me of the plan after we'd left the maze when we were heading back to the castle. She'd sent word to the Lion and the Tin Woodman that I was back as soon as she'd heard herself, and the Saw-Horse was already on his way to fetch them. Tomorrow, they would be here. We would all be together again, just like before.

It was all more perfect than I could have imagined. It was so perfect that, for a minute, I let myself forget that Glinda was missing. There was no use fretting about it now anyway—when my friends arrived, we'd be able to put our heads together and try to figure out what had happened to her. In the meantime, I didn't see the harm in enjoying myself.

I may have shoved the thought of home conveniently from my mind for now, but Uncle Henry and Aunt Em weren't going to let me forget it.

They struggled to look at each other over the folds of their enormous clothes.

"That's a very lovely offer from Miss Ozma," Uncle Henry said carefully. "But this has gone on long enough. It's time we find your friend Glinda and head on home."

At the name *Glinda*, Ozma turned sharply toward me.

"Glinda?" she asked. For the briefest of instants, I thought I saw a fire behind her green eyes.

"Well," I said, thinking fast. "Uncle Henry and Aunt Em *do* so want to go home. And Glinda was the one who sent me home last time . . . so . . ."

"So it's high time that we go back to the farm!" Uncle Henry said, nearly shouting. Aunt Em put a calming hand on his shoulder, but it only got him more worked up. He tugged at his collar. "Enough of this royal bull-pucky!" he barked. Then, noticing that Ozma was still standing right there, he got even more flustered. "I mean, begging your pardon, your royal Ozma."

The princess shook her head kindly as if she would never think of being offended.

As usual, Aunt Em was slightly more diplomatic than Henry.

Grasping my hands, she said, "I'm just not so sure this is the right place for us, Dorothy. We're not cut out for palaces and fancy frocks like these. The only princess I ever knew before this was the Sunflower Princess at the state fair, and she's not really a real princess at all, if you think about it."

No, I thought. She most certainly was not. "I know it all seems silly to you, Dorothy," she went on. "But the farm is all your uncle and I have. What do you suppose the poor animals are eating?"

Ozma stepped in. "Time moves differently here in Oz than it does back in your world," she explained to my aunt and uncle patiently, even though it had already been explained to them. "It's more than likely your animals haven't even noticed you've been gone."

"I don't . . . ," Uncle Henry started. But he's old-fashioned enough that when a princess talks to him, he listens. And at this moment, Ozma was acting every bit a princess. I was starting to see that she could turn it on and off, just like that.

"You certainly wouldn't want Dorothy to miss seeing her old companions, would you? And I know that the Tin Woodman and the Lion have been so looking forward to meeting you, too. Please, just stay for tomorrow's dinner."

"And then?" Uncle Henry asked.

Ozma smiled kindly. "Well," she said. "I'm afraid Glinda can't help you. She's been missing for some time now, and I've already searched the kingdom high and low for her." She glanced at me. "I'm sure she's safe—nothing could possibly harm a witch as powerful as she is—but wherever she is, she's hidden herself well."

Ozma had been so funny and open and warm—nothing like what I'd imagined. I'd heeded the Scarecrow's warnings not to tell her about the shoes, or to ask directly about Glinda, but I'd started to mostly dismiss the idea that she could have done anything to her.

Now I was unsure again. I had the strongest feeling she was lying to me.

"I'm not experienced with the type of magic it would take to send you all back to Kansasland," Ozma continued. Her warm, smooth voice had just enough of a tone of authority to silence my aunt and uncle into submission, for now. "But after tomorrow, I'll begin looking into ways to send all of you back. I'm sure I can find something."

Uncle Henry and Aunt Em were nodding in resigned agreement, but I was surprised to feel my entire body shaking with anger, my fists clenched so tightly they hurt.

"No!" I shouted. The marble floors magnified the sound of my voice several times over, but I didn't care. "No, no, no!"

Aunt Em and Uncle Henry's jaws both dropped in astonishment. They'd seen me lose my temper before, of course, but never like this. Even Ozma turned and looked at me like she was seeing me for the first time.

I was surprised at myself, even. It wasn't like me to behave this way. I just didn't care.

"I'm not going back there," I said. "Not now, not tomorrow, and not *ever*. I belong here. *We* belong here. I'm not making the same mistake twice—you can go home without me if you want, but I'm not leaving."

Aunt Em's eyes welled with tears and even Uncle Henry was speechless.

Ozma took me by the hand. "It's been a long day for all of you," she said. "We'll talk about this again tomorrow. I'm sure we can work something out when our heads are cooler."

Uncle Henry and Aunt Em stared as Ozma led me out of the parlor. Toto hesitated for a second like he was unsure whose side he was supposed to be on, but by the time Ozma and I were climbing the grand staircase toward her private chambers, he was nipping at my heels.

The princess looked at me in concern. "Dorothy," she said. "What was that about?"

Although I was still surprised at how strong my reaction had been, it didn't change what I had said. "I'm not going back there," I said, summoning every bit of Kansas grit I had. "They can't make me."

"But I thought you loved Kansas," she said, furrowing her brow in confusion. "You know, your story is famous here in Oz. We tell it all the time. And in the story we tell, the important part is that you wanted to go home. You could have stayed here, but you wanted to go back to Kansas. You would have done anything to get back there. Is that story wrong?"

My face flushed in shame. "It's just . . . ," I started. "No. The story isn't wrong. I did want to go home. I missed it. But once I was there, nothing was the way I remembered it. Once you've seen a place like Oz, nowhere else is the same again. How could it be?"

"Your aunt and uncle will come around," Ozma said with quiet confidence as we reached the top of the steps and turned down a long, dim hall that was carpeted in green velvet. She clasped my hand tightly in hers. "I'm sure of it. But for now, I think I have just the thing to cheer you up."

The room was full of lights. Chandeliers sparkled from the ceiling, and little luminescent orbs drifted around the room. The space was stuffed with plush velvet pillows and chairs and brocade lounges, and, against the far wall, several floor-to-ceiling mirrors set in elaborate gilt frames. The air was fragrant with Ozma's perfume—bergamot and sandalwood and something else I couldn't place.

"Is this your bedroom?" I asked in awe, looking around the room in search of a bed. Did she sleep on a divan? Or maybe fairies didn't need to sleep at all.

Ozma giggled. "No, silly," she said. "It's my closet."

My closet back home could barely fit a coat hanger, much less all this furniture.

But if it *was* a closet, there was something strange about it. Even stranger than a bedroom with no bed. "Where are the clothes?"

Ozma smiled mischievously. Then she closed her eyes and moved her hands in the air like she was playing an invisible harp. The lights dimmed, and the air grew heavier, like we were standing in a pool of warm water. Goose bumps crept over my skin.

It was magic. Real magic.

As she moved her hands through the air, plucking unseen strings, I felt a rush of energy coursing through my body. A feeling that reminded me of the shoes. Catching a glimpse of myself in the mirror, I saw that she was working magic on *me*. On *us*.

Our hair changed first: mine began weaving itself into a complex series of braids while hers whirled itself up into an elegantly messy chignon. Next, my clothes tingled against my skin. I felt buzzy all over as my dress became shorter and more fitted, glistening with silver embroidery across the chest. Sparkling bracelets appeared on my wrists, and a glittering necklace materialized around my neck.

I stared at myself in the mirror. "It's beautiful," I said, truly shocked. I'd never believed I could look this *alive* before. I didn't think I ever could back in Kansas—the gray sky and gray plains washed out everything, eventually. "I look beautiful."

"Something funny happened when I was doing the spell, though. I tried to give you new shoes. It didn't work."

I looked down at my feet. The red heels I'd gotten for my birthday were still there. They looked more beautiful than ever with the stunning dress. I shrugged. "I guess it's because they're already perfect," I said guiltily, hoping Ozma would buy it.

She smiled. "They *are* beautiful," she said. "Where did you get them?"

"Birthday present." I twirled, admiring my reflection.

I couldn't believe it was even me. Was it really just yesterday morning that I had been hauling pig slop across the field? I felt like someone brand-new. Someone better than I had been before; someone who belonged here, not there.

Ozma was still looking at my shoes. "Who gave them to you?" she asked.

"My friend Mitzi," I said quickly.

"I see," Ozma said with a tight smile. "Well, your friend Mitzi has wonderful taste."

She knew something in my story wasn't right.

But I couldn't tell exactly what she *did* know. Could she tell that the shoes had come from Glinda? What would happen if she figured out I was lying? And, finally, why had the Scarecrow asked me to hide the truth in the first place?

I thought about telling her everything right there. She had been so nice so far, and I found it hard to believe that she was anything other than what she was presenting herself as. But my shoes were burning on my feet and their heat spread through my whole body. *No,* they seemed to be saying. So I followed the Scarecrow's advice and kept my mouth shut.

"Can you teach me?" I asked instead.

"Teach you?" Ozma asked.

"To do *this*." I gestured at my new clothes. "To do magic."

Ozma looked at me long and hard, searching me like I was a puzzle to be worked out. Finally, she shook her head. "No," she said softly. "I can't. Magic is dangerous. Even for those of us who are native to Oz, it's dangerous. For people who aren't from here, it can be too much to handle. It can do . . . strange things to you."

"Strange things like what?" I was annoyed. How did Ozma know what I could handle? How did she know anything about people from my world, when I was the first that she had ever met?

"It can twist you," Ozma said. And then, as if she was reading my thoughts, "You know, Dorothy, you're not the first visitor to come here from the outside world. The Wizard wasn't the first either. There have been others, over the years."

"Who?" I asked.

She just shook her head, like the story was too sad to tell. And then she brightened and flung herself onto one of her lounges. She threw her feet up, took off her crown, and dropped it carelessly to the floor. "It gets heavy," she explained. "It *all* gets heavy. The crown, the scepter, this big empty palace. It's so much responsibility. It's so *lonely*. I'm just happy you're here."

"I'm happy I'm here, too," I said. But I didn't like the way she had changed the subject so quickly. Who were the others who had come here before me? What had happened to them? What had happened to *Glinda*? And what was Ozma keeping from me?

"I've *tried*," Ozma said. "Really, I have. At first, I thought Jellia and I could be the greatest of friends. But she's so focused on the fact that I'm the princess, and that she's my servant. I told her to stop calling me *miss* and *Your Highness* and that I didn't even care if she brushed my hair and brought me my breakfast in the mornings. She wouldn't listen. After that I invited the

Patchwork Girl to come stay with me for a while. She's so much fun—she's stuffed, like the Scarecrow, but with cotton instead of straw, you know, which might be one reason for the lack of common sense and conversational skills. You can only keep up with someone like her for so long before it wears you down. But now that you're here, Dorothy, it's like I've finally found someone who I have something in common with. I just wish you didn't have to go home."

"I'm not going home," I said firmly.

Ozma twisted her lips in thought. "You really don't want to, do you?" she said.

"I don't want to and I'm not going to," I said. My mind was made up. I was staying here. In Oz. In the palace. No matter what.

"Well," the princess said after a bit. "We'll just have to make your aunt and uncle understand, then, won't we?" She stood up and faced me. She took my hands in hers.

I wanted to trust her. I wanted to be her friend. But as I looked back into her big, glittering eyes, she averted her gaze for just the briefest moment, and I knew that she was hiding something from me. She'd said we were friends and I believed her but something gnawed at me—and it wasn't just Glinda, or the Scarecrow's warnings.

The bedroom that Jellia escorted me to after dinner was everything I had dreamed. It was three times as big as my room back in Kansas, with a panoramic window that looked out over the shimmering Emerald City skyline.

There was a huge vanity and a jewelry box overflowing with earrings and bracelets and necklaces, any one of which I was sure would have cost more than Uncle Henry earned in a year back in Kansas. The ebony wardrobe in the corner was stuffed with any kind of gown I could imagine, not to mention more than a few that I never would have been able to dream up on my own.

This was what I had wanted. Sitting alone in the field back in Kansas, covered in pig slop, with Miss Millicent in my lap, I had made a wish without even realizing it, and the wish had come true.

It was *too* good to be true, though. As I stood in front of the open wardrobe, wondering which dress to try on first, I had an itchy feeling in the back of my head that was telling me Ozma knew me too well. Like she was giving me all this because she knew it was what I wanted, and she thought that if she kept me happy, I wouldn't question her.

She had seemed so adamant when I'd asked her to teach me magic. Adamant, and a little sad, like it was exactly what she'd been afraid of. And she'd certainly been interested in my shoes.

Of course, the shoes were magic. I'd already figured out they were more than just a key that had unlocked the door to Oz for me. The way they'd been impossible to take off my feet for the Scarecrow, the strange feelings that had come from them all along my journey: all of that had suggested they could do more than I knew. And, of course, there was the way they had seemed to help me fight off the Screaming Trees in the forest.

Maybe I was a little afraid of them.

But Glinda had sent them to me to bring me here, I was *certain* of it.

And really—it seemed ridiculous that Ozma should be so against me doing magic. This was the Land of Oz. There was magic in the earth, in the *air*.

At the same time, it seemed obvious that she had figured out there was more to the shoes than I was telling. I was fairly certain she knew at least part of the truth. If she really didn't want me doing magic, why hadn't she taken them away from me?

What if she knew she couldn't? What if she was *afraid* of them, too?

What if my shoes were the key to finding Glinda?

It all made a certain upside-down sense. Last time I'd been to Oz, I'd had the power in my Silver Shoes all along, and I hadn't even realized it. It would be incredibly stupid to make the same mistake twice.

So I sat down on the edge of my bed and tried to call for the Sorceress. I knocked my heels together. I squeezed my eyes shut and tried to conjure her kind, motherly spirit. I pictured her smiling, impossibly beautiful face.

Something was happening. I could feel the red shoes trying as hard as I was. They constricted on my feet; they burned and tingled, glowing with energy. A few times, I even felt like I was getting somewhere: I could feel the Good Witch's presence filling the room. Once, I even thought I smelled her perfume. But, no matter what I did, she didn't appear.

I could feel the magic inside myself. I could practically *see* it sparking from my fingertips as I waved them through the air trying to bring her forth. Still nothing.

Maybe it was just that I needed to start with something smaller.

I walked to the vanity, sat down, and looked at myself. I examined my face closely. I thought about what Ozma had done earlier that day—about the way she had woven her fingers through the air and changed my hair and my clothes, and I wondered if I could do the same. So I closed my eyes.

And I know it sounds strange of me. I don't even know where it came from. I know, but I imagined myself as a giant tree standing in the center of the Road of Yellow Brick, with roots that spread out from my feet and pushed deep into the core of Oz, drawing up magic like it was water. I imagined that Oz was feeding me. That was sort of what my shoes had felt like on the Road of Yellow Brick—like the roots of a tree that connected me to Oz.

I could feel it working. I could feel the power filling my body, and the more it did, the hungrier it made me. I felt more alive than I ever had before. I felt like I could do anything.

But I was going to start small. I squeezed my eyes, touched my hair, and imagined the magic working on it. I imagined it changing colors, flipping through all the different possibilities the rainbow had to offer until I landed on the most beautiful color I could: pink. The pink of a sunset. The pink of Glinda's dress.

And when I saw myself staring back from the mirror, a lock of hair tumbled across my forehead, and it was even pinker than I had hoped.

I had *done* it. I had performed real magic. If I could change the color of my hair, what else could I do?

Well, I had the whole night to find out, didn't I?

Once I started, I almost couldn't stop. Some things were beyond me—I spent close to an hour trying to make myself fly, and the closest I could manage was something along the lines of a little bunny hop that probably wasn't magic at all. I tried to make myself invisible, but all I accomplished was a distressing pallor in my complexion. And try as I might, I just couldn't bring back Glinda.

However, there was *plenty* that I could do. Oh, just little things—useless things, really—but little is relative when you're a girl from the prairie.

I transformed a crumpled-up stocking into a little mouse that Toto chased furiously around the room before reacting with utter shock when it turned right back into a sock. He turned to glare reproachfully at me when he saw that I was doubled over with laughter in bed. I gave myself a lovely manicure; I made a fountain pen float across the room. I made a pair of earrings disappear from my jewelry box and reappear underneath my pillow. I didn't *have* to knock my heels to do any of it, but I found that if something was proving difficult, it did help.

I turned the pink stripe in my hair green, then purple, and finally gold before I decided that I liked my hair just fine the way it was before, and I waved it all away with a thought.

Once I started, it seemed like there was almost no end to it. All I had to do was think of something, and if I thought hard enough, I could at least nudge it toward reality. With a little practice—and a bit more imagination—I was certain I would be able to manage much more.

I fell asleep, still in my clothes, just as the sun was coming up, filled with happiness. I was in Oz, and in just a few hours I would be reunited with my old friends the Lion and the Tin Woodman. I was in my own beautiful room in the Emerald Palace, and, for now, no one—not even Aunt Em and Uncle Henry—could make me leave.

Best of all, I had magic. It was mine, and Ozma herself couldn't take it away from me.

FOURTEEN

I hadn't even stepped all the way into the great hall the next morning when I was tackled. A ball of golden fur came flying right for me, knocking me backward onto the carpeted floor of the hallway. A big, wet tongue licked my face.

It only took me a short moment to figure out what was going on. "Lion!" I squealed, wrapping my arms around him. Or, at least as far around as they would go. "Is it really you?"

"Who else would it be?" he asked in a low rumble, drawing back onto his haunches and licking his lips, gazing down on me kindly.

The Lion looked different than I remembered—he was bigger and wilder now, his yellow-brown mane tangled and matted, his arms and legs more powerful. When I'd first met him, the Lion had been timid and frightened, startling at the slightest sound. Even after the Wizard had given him his courage, he'd seemed as if he didn't quite know *how* to be brave.

Now I could see, he'd grown into it.

"I can't believe it's really you," I said breathlessly, sitting up and blinking.

"And not just me either," the Lion replied. "Look who else is here to see you."

At the long banquet table inside the great hall, another familiar face rose to his feet, grinning from ear to ear. The Tin Woodman stood and held out a rose. "My dear," he said, presenting the flower almost shyly. "I didn't think it was possible for my heart to get any bigger, but seeing you again, it feels about to burst."

I just ran to him. I didn't bother taking the flower; I just flung myself against him, planting a kiss on his cheek. And if you didn't think tin could blush, then, well, you should have seen his face at that moment.

Aunt Em and Uncle Henry were seated at the table, looking on at the scene politely. I was embarrassed to see that they were back in their tatty old clothes and, though Em's hair was still green, she and Henry both had combed their new 'dos back into as close to their normal styles as they would go. They just wouldn't accept *any* changes.

Ozma had said we'd get them to come around, but I didn't see how we ever would.

While Toto and the Lion wrestled playfully on the marble floor, I joined everyone else at the table.

"It's so nice to see old friends reunited," Ozma said, raising a champagne glass, filled with something purple, in a toast. "Here's to Dorothy—beloved by all who meet her."

"I think a certain Wicked Witch would disagree with you there," I said, but I clinked with everyone—even Em and Henry.

The table was covered in everything you could want for breakfast—and a lot of things I'd never thought to want.

There were fantastical fruits that sang witchy, enchanting little songs when you weren't looking at them and fresh eggs with bright yellow speckles that cooked themselves however you wanted as soon as you cracked them open onto your plate. There were oddly shaped pastries and a rainbow of juices in little crystal pitchers. Some of the food seemed like a bit of a nuisance, really—like the sticky buns that wouldn't let go of the plate and the flapjacks that flipped out of your way when you tried to take one—but it was definitely the most exciting breakfast I'd seen in all my life.

I helped myself to a little bit of everything, chattering in excitement as I heaped food onto my plate.

"You have to tell me everything!" I said. "Everything that's happened since I've been gone. The Scarecrow told me a bit, but, Lion, have you really been living up in the mountains with all the beasts? And—oh!"

I let out a scream as a piece of toast that I had just dropped onto my plate burst into flames.

Everyone laughed—even Aunt Em and Uncle Henry.

"Same thing happened to me," Henry said as the flame grew. "I venture to say my scream was even higher pitched than yours. Just wait."

I waited, and when the flame burned out, a piping-hot glazed doughnut was sitting on my plate. It practically melted in my mouth as I bit into it.

"Tin Woodman," I asked, still chewing. "How is Winkie Country now that the Wicked Witch of the West is gone? Are the Winged Monkeys happy these days? I hope that you've found yourself a lady to keep you company, now that you have your new heart and all."

The Tin Woodman's metal cheeks flushed with a glow even rosier than before. "I can't say I have," he said. "But I've been very happy anyway."

"Happier now that *you're* here, Dorothy," the Scarecrow said. "We all miss you."

"We've all missed you," the Lion said, finally turning his attention to those of us at the table. He picked Toto up in his jaws and carried him by the scruff of his neck over to me, dropping my panting dog into my lap.

"And there's so much for you to see and do," the Tin Woodman said. "Oz has changed so much since you went away. With the witches killed and the Wizard gone, it's a much happier place now. You won't believe your eyes when we visit Polychrome at the Rainbow Falls. And your aunt and uncle are going to love Sky Island."

"Oh, I don't think so," Henry interrupted. I knew what was coming before the words were out. "We're not going to have time for sightseeing. We have to get back to Kansas just as soon as we're able to."

I rolled my eyes openly and took a blueberry scone from a

tray in the center of the table. As soon as it was in my hand, another one appeared on the tray to take its place.

"Don't you and Em have anything better to do than bother us with more boring Kansas talk?" I asked with every bit of fake-sweetness I could muster. "Maybe there are some slop buckets in the garden that you can haul around all day. Or a field to plow?"

Henry's jaw dropped in surprise at my sudden rudeness. I have to admit, I was surprised at myself, too, but I really didn't see why he had to keep picking at me like this when he could see perfectly well how much it upset me. Still, I didn't want to embarrass everyone with another nasty argument.

I decided to try something. I looked him square in the eye and focused on my shoes, feeling them grow warm.

Using magic to control another human being wasn't anything that had even occurred to me when I had been practicing back in my room. Of course, I knew it wasn't right, and I promised myself I wouldn't make a habit of it. But if I could use the power I had to make my aunt and uncle see that staying in Oz was the only sensible choice for us, well, wasn't that a case where we *all* got what we wanted?

With every bit of confidence that I was doing the thing that was more than justified, I invited the magic in. With just a thought, I pulled it up through my body and then directed it out at my uncle, imagining him saying the words I wanted to hear.

"I think your aunt and I are going to go take a walk," he muttered stiffly, just as if I had scripted it myself. Well, I *had*, hadn't I? "After all, there's so much to see in this beautiful land, and I want to take in every single bit of it if it takes me all year."

Aunt Em looked too surprised to question him when Henry pulled himself away from the banquet table and took her hand to get up. Without even saying good-bye, they walked mechanically out of the room.

The Scarecrow and the Lion and the Tin Woodman were all staring at their backs, confused at what had just happened. "Lovely to meet you!" the Tin Woodman called after them, but they were already gone.

Ozma was the only one not watching my aunt and uncle go. She was looking at *me*. "Dorothy—" she said.

I cut her off. "Thank *goodness*," I sighed. "Finally, we can have a real conversation without all their bothersome complaining."

Ozma nodded slowly, her brow furrowing in concern. Frustration started to boil beneath my skin. She was just as bad as they were, in her own way. But she let the issue drop, for now at least, and silently took another dainty sip of her fizzy purple drink.

I wasn't going to let her ruin my reunion with my best friends—my *only* friends, really. Actually, I wanted to jump for joy. I had just done magic. Real, live, actual *magic*! It hadn't even been that difficult. I'd just imagined what I wanted Henry to do, and he'd done it, like he was a marionette and I was standing over him pulling the strings. If that was all it took, they would *never* be able to make me go back to Kansas. And imagine what else I could do.

I knew, suddenly, that the shoes weren't just meant to get me back to Oz. They were meant to teach me things. To show me what Ozma—the spoilsport!—wouldn't.

Now the Tin Woodman was waxing on about the beauty of Sky Island with its rivers of lemonade and its cloud mountains, and how he *so* wished we could all visit it together. The Scarecrow was listening closely, interrupting from time to time with a detail the Tin Woodman had forgotten, and the Lion roamed around the room restlessly, with Toto following after him like— well, like a puppy, actually.

Through it all, Ozma was cheerful and bright-eyed, happy to be part of the conversation, but every now and then she'd glance over at me searchingly, like she was looking for something.

I kept wishing that she would just leave. I had to talk to my friends. *Alone.* The Scarecrow knew it, too. He kept suggesting things to her—things like, "Oh, it's getting late, isn't it time for you to go find Jellia and discuss your schedule for the day?" But Ozma didn't take the bait. I wondered if she was just having a good time or if there was more to it—if maybe she didn't trust us to be alone together.

It was risky to try using magic on her. Doing a little spell on my uncle was bound to be different from doing it on a fairy who already knew a thing or two about spells herself. Then again, my shoes were powerful. When she'd given me my makeover yesterday, her own magic hadn't even been able to touch them. If they were powerful, it meant that *I* was powerful, too. Maybe even more powerful than she was.

So I gave it a spin. I changed her mind. This time, I tried to be more precise about what I was doing, so she wouldn't be able to detect it and fight back.

I envisioned the magic as a tendril of ruby-red smoke, as thin and delicate as the smoke rings that Henry sometimes blew to make me laugh when he was smoking his pipe. I pulled it up from my shoes and sent it drifting invisibly across the table to burrow itself into Ozma's ear.

A distant, distracted look made its way across her face. She looked as though she was trying to remember something. "I . . . ," she said.

Go, I commanded silently. As soon as I thought the word, Ozma's expression resolved itself into one of surprised realization.

"Please excuse me," she said. "I think I left something in my chambers. Give me just a few minutes." With that, she stood up, set her napkin down, and hurried out.

He didn't say anything, but I was pretty sure I saw the Scarecrow smirk approvingly in my direction.

It wasn't right. I do realize that. People aren't little marionettes to be pulled this way and that without their say-so in the matter. On the other hand, just because it wasn't right didn't mean it wasn't fun.

As soon as Her Royal Highness was out of earshot, he turned to me.

"Did you learn anything?" he asked. "Do you know where Glinda is?"

Everyone looked at me eagerly. Apparently the Scarecrow had filled them all in on his suspicions. *Our* suspicions, now.

"We've been waiting to hear," the Lion rumbled. "We've all had our doubts about the princess from the very get-go. The way she just marched in here and acted like she owned the place. As if the Scarecrow here hadn't been ruling perfectly well in her absence."

The Tin Woodman set his fork down. "And where did she come from? How do we even know she's the real princess? Just because she says so? She'll offer up no explanation for where she'd been. I'm the governor of Winkie Country and the gentlest soul in all the land—you would think she would feel that she owed at least *me* an explanation. With my heart, I would be sure to understand."

I leaned in and whispered. "I'm almost certain the princess is keeping something from me," I confessed. "I don't know what, but . . ."

"Oh dear," the Tin Woodman said, a grave expression on his face.

"My brains almost never fail me," the Scarecrow said. "And I truly think Ozma had something to do with Glinda's disappearance. She's never showed more than the most cursory concern for the Sorceress's whereabouts. Dorothy, you're back here for a reason. You have to find our friend. But keep your wits about you. Ozma may seem sweet. But everything I know tells me she's dangerous."

"I have to agree," the Tin Woodman said. "I can feel it in the bottom of my heart."

The Lion just growled softly.

I knew they were all right. But . . .

I wasn't afraid of her. Suddenly I wasn't afraid of *anything*. There was real power in my shoes. I could feel it. Every time I used them to cast a spell, I could feel myself getting better, stronger. And I wanted more.

Why should I be afraid? She was the one who should be afraid of *me*.

FIFTEEN

We spent hours sitting around the breakfast table. Long after the plates had cleared themselves and the morning had passed into afternoon, we'd laughed and commiserated, retelling stories of our old adventures and some new stories, too.

The Lion told me all about his adventures in the Northern lands—exotic by even Oz standards—and the Tin Woodman told me all about his experiences governing the unruly Winkie folk.

I told the story of my sixteenth birthday party, and I saw that it had moved my tin friend so greatly that a tear was trickling down his metal face.

"Oh dear," he said, when he saw that I had caught him in his tenderheartedness. He dabbed at his face with a napkin. "This heart of mine is a wonderful gift, but it does make rust a significant concern."

Soon after, he and the Scarecrow decided it was time to go

tidy themselves up. The Lion ventured off to the forest just outside the city for his afternoon jog. I was still trying to decide
what *I* was going to do with what was left of my day when Jellia
Jamb, Ozma's handmaid, appeared, summoning me to meet the
princess in the garden.

The day was sunny and warm, and I found her sitting on a
wrought-iron bench next to a tinkling fountain. She was looking fondly at a tiny little Pixie who was perched on her extended
finger. They seemed to be deep in conversation.

"Oh!" Ozma exclaimed when she saw me approaching. The
Pixie went fluttering away. "The little thing was just telling me
the silliest joke. Everyone else thinks these Pixies are so irritating, but I think they're amusing. Anyway, they're part of Oz,
aren't they? And everything here has its place in the order of
things."

Is she kidding? I wondered. This Little Miss Sunshine act
would make Shirley Temple herself want to tap-dance right off
a cliff.

"Anyway," she said brightly. "I wanted to talk to you about
something."

I folded my arms and prepared myself for the haughty lecture
she was about to give me. About how I'd lied to her about the
shoes, about how she had warned me not to do magic, and how
I'd had the *nerve* to disobey her. About how reckless she thought
I was being.

Maybe she didn't know it, but even if I was in Oz, I was still
a citizen of the United States, and where I came from we didn't

put much stock in self-appointed *monarchs*—no matter whether their blood was blue or purple or sprinkled with fairy dust.

Sometimes even a princess can surprise you, though. "I think I'd like to throw you a big party," Ozma said. "What do you think about that?"

She had caught me off guard. "What kind of party?" I asked, suspicious. A party? I was *sure* she'd seen what I'd done at the breakfast table. Even if she hadn't felt me magicking *her*, she had to have noticed me casting a spell on Henry. I'd seen the expression on her face. Now she wanted to throw me a party? There had to be some sort of catch.

Ozma stood up and did a playful little pirouette across the grass, and I remembered suddenly that, fairy princess or not, she was really just a girl. A girl who was lonely—a girl who had been waiting and waiting for someone like me to keep her company. She *needed* me. Maybe she was willing to let a spell here and there slide. What's a little magic between girlfriends, right?

"Oh, a *wonderful* party," she said dreamily. "I don't suppose you're sick of your birthday already, are you?"

"Sixteen *is* a big one," I allowed hesitantly.

"Perfect!" she exclaimed. "It's been too long since I threw a ball. We so rarely have an occasion. I don't even know when my own birthday *is*—isn't that terrible? But all of Oz loves a party, and the whole city's already abuzz with your return. A celebration is in order!"

I had to admit I liked the sound of it. "The party Aunt Em threw for me was . . . well, it wasn't quite what either of us hoped," I said. "Maybe this can be a do-over. I'm sure it would make her happy, too, to get it right this time."

Ozma clapped her hands. "Of course! A do-over!" She said the word as if she had never heard it before, as if she was savoring each syllable as it rolled off her tongue. "We'll invite everyone," she said. "The Munchkins, the Winkies, even the Nomes and the Pixies and the Winged Monkeys and all of Oz's most important personalities. Polychrome will come from the Rainbow Falls; and I hope the Wogglebug can tear himself away from his classes at the university. We'll even invite General Jinjur—though I'm sure she won't make it. She's not much for dances." Ozma rolled her eyes. "I have to tell you about Jinjur and her all-girl army sometime."

I sat on the bench and studied her as she drifted into a party-planning reverie. To think I'd almost sympathized with her when she'd complained about the burdens of royalty. If this was the extent of her duties, it didn't seem so bad at all.

Still . . . a party. For *me*. What better way for me to announce my return to Oz for good?

Ozma slid back down onto the bench beside me and draped a slender arm over my shoulder. Her wrist of bangles glinted in the sunlight.

"And," she said, raising her eyebrows in conspiracy, "it will be the perfect way to show your aunt and uncle what *fun* it is here. Once they've seen a royal ball, they'll never think of going home. You won't even need to use those special shoes of yours to convince them."

The words hung in the air. So there it was. I'd almost let her trick me into buying her act.

"I don't know what you mean," I sniffed. I wasn't fooling anyone, naturally—she knew, and I knew she knew, and she knew I knew she knew—but I didn't want to give her the satisfaction of hearing me come clean.

"Oh, Dorothy," she said. "You don't need to hide it. I knew those shoes were enchanted from the moment I laid eyes on them. And I don't blame you for experimenting with them. Magic can be quite intoxicating." Her eyes darkened. "*Too* intoxicating," she said, the singsong of her voice giving way to sternness. "So let's just get them off, okay? That way you won't be tempted."

She twirled a finger and pointed it at my feet, at my beautiful, shiny shoes. A green spark sizzled from her fingertip, zigzagged through the air, and bounced right off my heel. The shoes glowed in response to the insult, but they didn't budge.

Ozma frowned, seeing that her spell hadn't worked. I was already on my feet. I spun around and faced her in a rage.

"They're *mine*," I said. "She gave them to me, and you can't do anything about it."

Ozma's mild smile didn't flicker. She was one cool cucumber when she set her mind to it, I had to give her that much. "She?" the princess asked, cocking her head to the side.

"Don't play innocent," I hissed. "Neither of us was born yesterday. You know who *she* is. Glinda. What, were you jealous of her? Did you want her out of the way so you could keep all the power for yourself?"

Ozma put a hand to her cheek like she'd just been slapped. She shook her head. "You're not in your right mind. Those shoes. The magic is already beginning to twist you. The way it did with—"

I didn't care to let her finish. I was too upset. Rightfully so, I should say! Glinda had been the one who had watched over Oz while she'd been off wherever she was, and Ozma had gone and done away with her without so much as a how-do-you-do. She had some nerve playing innocent with me now—as if it was anything other than a power grab worthy of a true tyrant. "A Scarecrow's one thing," I said, sneering openly. "You surely got him out of the palace fast enough. A Sorceress, though, that's another story, isn't it? Couldn't have her mucking things up for you, now could you?"

Ozma bit her lip and looked away like she couldn't believe what she was hearing. "Glinda didn't have Oz's best interests at heart," she murmured. "Trust me, Dorothy. I know that she was kind to you, but the Sorceress is not everything that she appears at first. I had no choice. It's my duty to keep Oz safe."

"*Naturally*," I said. "After all, *you're* the one true ruler, and everyone else can just fall in line. Why, you call yourself a fairy, but you're no better than a wicked witch. And you know my history with them."

Ozma's gaze turned steely at my threat, and I knew that she was through with arguing. She rose to her feet.

"I need the shoes. Now." Ozma reached for her scepter on the bench. "It's for your own good."

I didn't give her a chance to get to it.

It was easy-peasy this time. I barely even had to think about what I was doing. With every spell I cast, I was becoming more powerful. It was like my shoes were doing the work *for* me.

This time, I could actually *see* the magic with my own two eyes as it unspooled from my palm as a gauzy scarlet thread and curled toward her. Ozma could see it, too: her eyes widened in dismay and she took an unsteady step back. I guess she hadn't expected this.

That would teach her to underestimate me, Dorothy Gale, the Witchslayer herself. There was nothing she could do. My magic was already twisting its way into her skull like a corkscrew.

Her gaze turned to mush. The side of her mouth drooped a bit.

I felt a sick joy in my chest as I used the magical filament like a piece of dental floss, pulling back and forth with my mind, carefully scraping Ozma's memory clean of our conversation.

When I'd changed Uncle Henry's mind just a few hours ago, I'd sworn to myself that I wouldn't do it again. But then I had, just a few minutes later. And now I was *literally* changing Ozma's mind. Sprucing it up and making it presentable the way one would change the sheets on the bed.

Somewhere in the back of my mind, I had the vaguest notion that *I* was the one being wicked. But I found that I didn't care. In fact, I almost enjoyed it.

I made her forget the shoes, and our talk of Glinda, and the incident with Uncle Henry at the breakfast table. When I was done, I was just Dorothy Gale, her dear friend and confidante, a spunky, headstrong girl from Kansas to whom the people of Oz—her loyal subjects—owed a debt of gratitude. Or three. A girl with an unusually lovely pair of red high heels.

I let her keep the party idea, though. No point in throwing the baby out with the bathwater, is there?

SIXTEEN

Over the next week, Ozma put all thoughts of ruling the kingdom aside as she made plans for what she promised me would be the grandest event Oz had seen in most people's lifetimes. Every day, chefs, bakers, dressmakers, and party planners visited the palace, each one of them bursting with wild ideas and begging for the princess's favor.

I was pleased to notice that they also took a special interest in me. Every new visitor who passed through the palace stopped to shake my hand, or to give me a kiss on the cheek and to marvel at what a wonder it was to have the famous Dorothy Gale back in Oz.

I half expected Ozma to be jealous of all the attention I was getting. But she masked it well, and never failed to appear delighted when yet another one of her subjects treated me as if *I* was just as important as she——maybe even more important. One day, when a little furry Nome peddling jeweled goblets thanked me for ridding the land of the witches, I almost wanted to wink at him and whisper in his ear, "Just you wait. My work isn't done quite yet."

Except for one thing: ever since I'd flossed Ozma's brain, I was having a hard time hating her. In fact, when I set aside the unfortunate fact that she had imprisoned Glinda and tried to steal my shoes, we were getting on well.

We spent our days planning the menu and picking out decorations: bright, blooming flowers that changed colors every time you looked away; handfuls of stardust sprinkled over everything—we even coaxed the Wandering Water to form a babbling brook around the outside of the ballroom. I have to say, it put to shame the streamers and tea candles that passed for lavish back in Kansas. We spent countless hours lying on the grass in the garden, threading flowers through our hair, speculating about who was coming to the party, and daydreaming about the possibility that there might be a few suitable princes in attendance.

My spell had done the trick—she had no recollection of our fight by the fountain, or of the controversy over my magic shoes. As far as she knew, we were just *friends*.

In fact, Ozma was starting to feel like the closest I had to a best friend. It had been so long since I'd had a friend like that. Of course, the Lion and the Tin Woodman and the Scarecrow were my loyal friends and the most wonderful companions anyone could hope to have, but they were different. It wasn't like having a girlfriend my own age.

All the Scarecrow ever wanted to talk about was his

magnificent brains, which made me wonder what good was it to be the greatest mind in all the kingdom if you never actually *thought* about anything except your own intelligence.

The Tin Woodman spent most of his time in the palace's musty old library with his nose in boring old books of love poetry. When I agreed to let him read one aloud to me, I was so mortified at how romantic it was that I could barely stand to look at him afterward.

As for the Lion—well, he was usually off in the woods, hunting or whatever it is lions do in their alone time. When he did deign to set foot on the palace grounds, he could barely go ten minutes before his newfound courage got the best of him and he tried to pick a fight with the first palace servant who crossed his path.

With the three of them as my only other choices for company, who could blame me for preferring to spend my days dreaming and party planning with Oz's sweet little despot? At least she was capable of carrying on a real conversation. And she seemed to actually *want* to spend time with me. I just had to be careful not to do any magic around her.

I knew now that I could subdue her, if necessary—just wash her brain clear of any tension between us. But to be honest, I felt a little uneasy about having to do it again. Why go to the trouble?

"Can I ask you a question?" Ozma asked one afternoon, just a few days before my ball when we were in her closet trying on party outfits for the umpteenth time. I nodded absently, trying to decide between slinky silk or dramatic tulle and chiffon—I was leaning toward slinky.

I must admit, it felt like such a sweet victory to think that I'd be celebrating my sixteenth birthday again, like *this*, after the disaster of the first party.

Ozma turned and fixed me with a penetrating look. "Why do you live with your aunt and uncle?" she asked, out of nowhere. "What happened to your mother and father?"

I paused in surprise. "Oh," I said quietly. It wasn't the kind of question I was expecting.

"I'm sorry—I shouldn't have . . . it must be such a sad story. You don't have to talk about it."

I shrugged. "No," I said. "It's all right. I don't even remember them. My mother died when she gave birth to me, and my father was killed just a few months later. There was an accident with a plow. I know I should miss them, but it's hard to be sad about people you never even knew."

Ozma smiled in sympathy.

"What about you?" I asked. "You've never mentioned your parents at all, I don't think. Just Lur-whoozit."

Ozma passed her hand down the length of her body and her emerald-green dress turned to bloodred.

"Maybe add a train?" I suggested.

"Perhaps. No, they're so easy to trip over. Think of how embarrassing *that* would be."

"You can have a team of Munchkins on hand just to hold it

up," I said, and we both laughed over the absurdity of the idea.

"The truth is," Ozma said, when we had recovered. "I don't *have* parents. I never did."

"You must have at *some* point. Everyone has parents."

"Everyone except fairies," she said. "I was born from the pool in the center of the maze. Remember that little red flower, floating in the pool?"

"Yes," I said, vaguely remembering.

"That's where I came from. The next princess is somewhere in there, biding her time. When the flower is big and full and about to shed its petals, it means she's close to being born, and I'll know that it's time for me to go rejoin Lurline and my people. I'll go off to find them, and my successor will rise up out of that flower to take my place. Of course, it takes a very long time, and after she's born she'll be a baby for a bit—that's when Oz is most vulnerable. That's how the Wizard managed to do away with me the first time."

"How strange," I said. "But where did he send you? I've been wondering."

"Does it matter?" Ozma asked.

"Why wouldn't it?"

"Does it matter that you're from Kansas? You're here now. The past is gone. Especially in Oz—that's the way time works. In Oz, it's always right now."

I thought about it for a moment. It *did* matter. I didn't necessarily like to think about where I was from, and I certainly didn't want to go back there, but it had made me who I was, just as much as my trip to Oz had made me who I was.

Wherever Ozma had been had made her who she was, too. How could it not have?

And who was she, really? Was she the sweet, charming new friend I'd made—a girl who wanted nothing more than to try on dresses and plan parties—or was she the regal, majestic, fairy princess I'd seen that day in the hedge maze?

Was she the girl who would do anything to be a good ruler to a kingdom she didn't even really want, or was she so desperate for power that she had banished Glinda to some terrible, faraway place to get her out of the way, just the same way the Wizard, once upon a time, had done to Ozma herself?

It didn't occur to me that maybe she could be both. All I knew was that I had to find out the truth.

So even though I knew it was risky, I cast a spell. I knew I couldn't be too obvious this time. Ozma may have looked sweet and innocent, but she was dangerous, too. She was a fairy. If she had done something to Glinda, she might be able to do it to me, too, if I wasn't careful.

I gave her just the tiniest little nudge. I had been practicing at night, in my room alone, and I was getting better at using the magic. I didn't have to knock my shoes together anymore; I didn't even need to feel the tingling in my feet. The magic wasn't just in the shoes. It was in every bit of my body, and all I had to do was take a tiny little piece of it and send it out into the world to bring me back what I wanted.

There in Ozma's dressing room, I looked down at my

fingertip and saw a little red butterfly sitting on it, glowing and pulsing its jeweled little wings.

Tell me, I told it, without speaking the words aloud. And the butterfly took flight. It fluttered into the air and circled around Ozma's head in a scattered halo.

"Dorothy?" Ozma said. "Are you okay? You have the strangest look on your face."

The butterfly landed on her forehead. She didn't react. She didn't seem to notice it.

"What are you thinking about?" Ozma asked, looking deep into my eyes. "You look like you're a million miles away."

Tell me, I thought. *Tell me where Glinda is.*

The butterfly crawled across her brow, like it was looking for a way into her mind, and then it disappeared—just evaporated in a tiny puff of red dust. I had lost it.

Ozma didn't seem to know what had just happened, I don't think. But her mind was still her own. Her magic was more powerful than she let on.

I knew then, without a doubt, that she *was* the one who had done something to Glinda. You don't guard secrets that you don't have in the first place. And there was definitely something in her mind that she was guarding closely.

"Yes," I said. "I was thinking of my mother."

It was a lie, and it wasn't. I had been thinking of Glinda, who was as close to a mother as I'd ever had. Closer than my own mother had ever been, that's for sure. Closer than Aunt Em was, even.

Glinda had brought me here. She had helped me get home to Kansas, once upon a time, when it was all I wanted in the world. I had to find her. I had to help her. Even Ozma—as lovely a friend as she could be—wasn't going to stand in my way.

The night before the ball, I walked into my bedchambers. I knew that it was important to get a good night's sleep, but there was so much on my mind that it was impossible to quiet it.

Toto was curled in the corner, asleep, dreaming about whatever it is that dogs dream about.

Without even having to think about it, I used my magic to strip my dress off; to untie the ribbons that held my hair into plaits. I sent them drifting off to the corner of the room, where I let them drop into a messy pile. I let an ethereal nightgown slip over my head. The shoes, of course, stayed on. I never took them off. I couldn't even if I tried.

I levitated myself off the floor and floated myself to my bed, letting myself drop gently onto the cloud-soft mattress. I drifted off to sleep, not bothering to pull the sheets over my body. Instead, I wrapped myself in magic like it was a heavy down quilt.

As it enveloped me, I felt both happy and content—and emptier than ever.

Tomorrow was the party. I was in Oz, and there was a party being thrown for *me*. I had gotten exactly what I had wanted, and still it wasn't enough. I had wanted. And now I wanted *more*.

That was who I was, I realized as I drifted off to sleep. This wanting itself was a kind of magic—one that I'd had since I was just a little girl. Since even before I'd been to Oz. Even before I'd had a pair of magic shoes, silver or red. I had always wanted more.

It was what had brought the tornado to me. It was what had brought me to Oz in the first place. It was what had sent me home, too, and it was what had allowed Glinda to find me again, to reach out through the walls that separated Oz from the rest of the world and bring me back. Now that I was here—now that I had my shoes, my magic, my party—the wanting was still with me. It always would be.

I wanted more. I wanted what Ozma had. I wanted everything.

SEVENTEEN

Ozma sent Jellia Jamb for me in the morning so that we could get ready together, but I sent the plain little servant away. This was my big day, and I wanted to be alone—I wanted to take the time to think about everything that had brought me to this place, and about what the future held for me.

For *me*. Not for Aunt Em and Uncle Henry. Not for Ozma, or for Oz, or the Scarecrow or the Tin Woodman or the Lion or even poor, missing Glinda, but for me alone.

So I spent the day in my room. I magicked up a light breakfast of those wonderful Anything Eggs and some Chimera's milk, and, later, for lunch, ambrosia and Emeraldfruit.

I stood in front of the mirror, trying to decide how I should look for the party. Toto sat in the corner, just watching me, understanding, I guess, that I was in a world of my own.

I tried on every gown in my closet, but none of them felt special. I summoned Jellia and requested more, but I still knew that none of them would be good enough. The right dress would come from magic—not Ozma's magic, but the magic of the shoes. The magic that belonged to me.

An hour before the party, Jellia delivered one more dress to my door. This one was from Ozma.

The skirt was green and flowing, made from the finest chiffon, with a bodice studded with a rainbow of jewels.

My Dearest Dorothy, the note read. *My new friend. I am so happy to have you at my side.*

I set the note on my vanity and took one look at the dress Ozma had given me before I tossed it aside, into the corner where my pile of castoffs was turning into a mountain.

The dress from Ozma was beautiful, but it wasn't the dress I was supposed to wear on my sixteenth birthday, the day I announced my official return to Oz. It was what she wanted for me, not what I wanted for myself. I didn't want to be at her side while she ruled Oz. I was no one's lady-in-waiting. And suddenly I knew *exactly* what I wanted.

I no longer cared about hiding my magic from her. Why should I have to hide what belonged to me? This was Oz. Everything else was magic. Why shouldn't I be magic, too?

So I called it forth. Using it was second nature to me now. All I needed to do was *want* and it was mine.

The room was twitching with energy as I stood in front of the mirror. Atoms rewrote themselves around me. I felt the world twisting and turning at my silent command. Fabric wove itself against my body; my hair grew even longer, twisting, taking the shape I wanted from it until it fell around my face in two perfect auburn braids with curls that scraped my shoulders. I felt my skin becoming smoother and softer. My eyes brightened; my lips reddened. My cheeks flushed with the perfect rosy glow.

My dress took form.

When I was done, Toto barked in approval. I looked just how I wanted to look. I looked both like myself and like something greater.

There was a knock on my door. I opened it to find that Aunt Em and Uncle Henry were waiting for me outside. They gasped when they saw me.

"Why, Dorothy . . . ," Uncle Henry started. I saw him blush, and he squeezed his eyes shut.

"You look . . . ," Aunt Em began to say. She was at a loss for words, too. A look of scandal crested her face. She put her hand nervously to her mouth.

"I look like a princess," I said. I knew that it was what they meant. "And not just like any princess. I look like Princess Dorothy. The Witchslayer. The Girl Who Rode the Cyclone. The One *True* Princess of Oz."

They both looked away. They didn't say anything. They didn't have to. It was what they were thinking.

"Now let's go to my party," I said.

"Dorothy?" Ozma asked in surprise when I entered the ballroom, where the gala was just getting under way. "That's not the dress I sent you." Her face looked hurt and suspicious as she surveyed me.

My dress was blue gingham, just like the blue gingham I'd worn on the day I'd first landed in Oz. But it was different, too. Rather than being made from that scratchy, cheap fabric, it was made from the finest silk. The blue checks were stitched with glittering gold thread so subtle that you barely could see it until you looked closely.

It was short—shorter than anything I'd ever worn before. It was shorter than any dress I'd ever *seen* before, revealing my long, bare legs.

All of it did nothing more than draw attention to the shoes on my feet. They shone brighter than anything else in the room: brighter than Ozma's crown, or her scepter, or the tiny jewels that were braided through her dark hair.

"Your dress was lovely," I said, breezily. "But it wasn't what I envisioned. Today is *my* day."

"But where . . . ?" she asked.

Before she could finish the question, I stepped past her, into the ball, where everyone was waiting. They were waiting for *me*.

It barely looked like a ballroom at all. The sky was a brilliant galaxy of stars studded with giant, red poppies that opened and closed in time with the music, emitting a shimmering, heavenly light. The dance floor was a deep purple sunset.

Swarms of Pixies flew throughout the room, carrying trays of drinks and hors d'oeuvres.

The whole place was filled with Oz's strange and notable

personalities. Some of them I recognized from hearing Ozma talk about them: there was Polychrome, the Daughter of the Rainbow, wrapped in a diaphanous gown that looked like it was woven out of the sky itself. There was Scraps, the Patchwork Girl, cartwheeling across the floor like a whirling dervish, whooping with laughter as she went. There was a giant, dignified frog in a three-piece suit, and a man with a jack-o'-lantern in place of a head.

There were Nomes and Munchkins and Winkies and a man and woman made entirely of china, dancing carefully apart from the rest of the crowd so as not to risk breaking into pieces.

I whirled joyfully through the room, gliding from one citizen of Oz to the next, smiling and kissing each one on the cheek in greeting before spinning on to the next one. Each one of them looked up at me with love and gratitude. I meant so much to them. I had done so much for them—so much more than Ozma could ever think of doing. And they all wanted to meet *me*. I was famous. I was their hero.

When I got to the Scarecrow, he was ready for me. He took me up into his stuffed arms and spun me around and I laughed, kicking my feet up as the crowd parted to make way for us. The orchestra was playing a happy, energetic ragtime number and the trumpets blasted as the Scarecrow tossed me over his head as if I was light as a feather. He caught me, laughing, in his arms as I came back down before twirling me across the floor to where the Tin Woodman was waiting for me.

My metal friend grabbed my hand, and his metal palm felt

softer and warmer than I would have imagined was possible. He pulled me close against his chest, and the orchestra slowed up its tempo into something tender and sentimental. We waltzed across the dance floor. Everyone else had paused in their own dancing to watch us. They surrounded us in a circle, transfixed.

I was so happy that I was dancing on air. Literally: when I looked down, I saw that my feet were hovering a few inches above the ground, my magical shoes enveloped in a red mist, holding me aloft. No one noticed. They were too distracted by how happy they were.

The Lion was sitting on his haunches, ready to take me up in the next dance. He extended a huge paw, cutting in, and I was about to reach out for it when something bumped against my shoulder, hard. Cold, fizzy liquid splashed against my back, and then I heard the sound of glass crashing against the ballroom floor.

When I turned around, I saw Aunt Em standing there with a guilty look on her face, a shattered crystal goblet lying in a puddle of purple liquid on the floor.

I came back down to earth.

"Oh, Dorothy, I'm sorry," Aunt Em said. "I wasn't paying attention to where I was going, and I just bumped right into—"

I put a hand up to interrupt her. "Stop," I said. "You were thoughtless. You were careless. I was dancing, and you weren't even watching. Everyone *else* was watching me." I reached back and felt the dampness of my gown. "You could have ruined my dress."

"I'm sure . . . ," Aunt Em began. Her lips began to quiver. Tears came to her eyes.

I'd always hated seeing Aunt Em cry, and now I hated it even more. It was like she was doing it to spite me. Like she was trying to make me feel guilty on a day when I should have felt nothing but happiness.

"Clean it up," I said.

She looked at me in surprised horror, her tears still streaming down her cheeks. "Well—I'm sure Miss Ozma can ask someone else . . ."

"No," I said. "I want *you* to clean it up. Immediately."

Uncle Henry was at her side now. "Now see here, Dorothy," he said, taking my aunt's arm. "This has gone too far." For a moment, it seemed that he was going to be angry, but then he saw the look in my eyes and the expression on his face turned quickly to one of fright. He went silent.

"Clean. It. Up," I instructed Aunt Em again. When she made no move to do as she was told, I took the choice out of her hands. Things had changed, and the two of them needed to learn that. I was their niece, and they had raised me, but we were in Oz now. Here in Oz, I wasn't just another prairie girl. I commanded respect.

My shoes were urging me on. I could hear them whispering in my ear in a voice that was almost Glinda's but not quite. It was low and urgent and sweet. It was the voice of Oz; the voice of magic. It was the voice of my mother.

Do it, it was saying. *Teach them a lesson or they'll never learn.*

Show her who you are. Show them that this is where you belong. Show them that you are the one with power here.

My whole body was burning; not just my feet. Every bit of me was singing with the power the shoes spoke of, and the music from the orchestra faded into just a distant hum as the song of my true self took its place. This was what I had been born for. Everything that had happened before had been preparing me for this moment, preparing me for my destiny. For who I really was.

I tugged at the strings that controlled my aunt, and she bent to the floor, onto her hands and knees, and began to wipe up the mess she'd created with a wet rag that had materialized for her.

"I'm so sorry, Dorothy," she said. "You are so wise and beautiful. I'm lucky to know you. To be able to have kept you safe all these years. Please, I beg your forgiveness."

"And now the dress," I said, and Aunt Em stood, and began to dab at my back with the rag. I could have cleaned it myself, with just a thought, but I didn't want to.

"It's such an honor," Aunt Em was saying. "To be able to serve you like this."

Then Ozma was standing in front of me. I hadn't seen her approach.

She looked different than I'd ever seen her. This was so much more than the Ozma who I'd seen in the maze, the day I'd met her. It was like she had been hiding part of herself from me. She no longer looked like the girl I knew. She no longer looked like a girl at all.

Her skin was fiery and glowing like the sun; her green eyes

were huge and iridescent. Her hair haloed her face in oily-black tendrils that coiled and twisted like snakes.

The wings she'd showed me in the garden that day had revealed themselves again, but they were bigger now, twice as big as her body, and they sizzled with magical energy.

She looked like a fairy, and not even a fairy princess. She looked like a queen.

"*Dorothy*," she said. Her voice reverberated throughout the ballroom. "It's time for you to leave."

"No," I started to say. But the words wouldn't come out.

I knocked my heels together, trying desperately to use my magic against her. It didn't work. Nothing happened at all. My feet felt cold. Too cold. Like the magic had been drained from them.

And then, with everyone in the ballroom staring, I felt myself turning and walking away. I had lost it. I had lost my magic, lost everything I had worked so hard for. I couldn't fight back— Ozma was controlling me.

"Wait!" the Scarecrow called. I found I couldn't answer him.

Before I knew what had happened, I was back in my bedroom, where I settled into a black and dreamless sleep.

EIGHTEEN

I woke up to find Aunt Em sitting on the edge of my bed. She'd opened the windows, and the light was streaming through, casting her in a silhouette. The breeze hit my face. It smelled like grass and dirt and rain. It smelled like home.

For a second, I thought we were back in Kansas, and that it had all been a dream. I always hated it when stories ended that way.

"Dorothy," Aunt Em said. I rubbed my eyes, still disoriented, and tried to think back to last night. It was foggy in my memory. There had been some kind of party, and I'd been dancing with the Lion and—

Oh.

I pulled the pillow over my face and groaned, trying to block it all out. If only I could go back to sleep, maybe everything would be okay.

"Dorothy," Aunt Em said again. She pulled the pillow away.

I grabbed for it, but she held it at arm's length. "It's nearly afternoon."

"I need to sleep," I said. "I think I ate something I shouldn't have last night. I don't feel so good."

She pushed a lock of hair behind my ear and looked down at me. I expected her to be mad, but there was something tender in her expression. "I know, dear," she said. "You know, you're not in trouble."

I sat up slowly and slumped against the silk-upholstered headboard. "I'm not?" I asked cautiously.

"Of course not. We all know that you didn't mean to do any of that."

"You do?"

"Yes, dear. Your uncle and I have had a long talk about it with Ozma, and we all agree that you're not to blame. It's those shoes. They've been doing something to you. Something terrible."

"It's not—"

"We just think it's time for all of us to go home. We've stayed here too long already."

"No!" I jumped out of bed and threw on the brocade robe that was draped over the armchair by the window. "Don't you see?" I asked angrily. "It's *her*. Ozma. She's making you think that there's something wrong with me, when really it's just that she's afraid I'm more powerful than she is, and now she wants to get rid of me, just like she got rid of Glinda. Well, the princess can't always have her way. I'm not going anywhere."

When I turned around, Ozma was standing in the doorway.

In the late morning light, wearing a simple white shift, she looked more like a little girl than ever.

"You're right," she said sadly. "About one thing, at least. I *was* afraid of Glinda. She's used to getting her way around here, you know. She was trying to manipulate me. I had to send her away. Oz has seen too many cruel rulers already. If Glinda had gotten what she wanted, I would have been another. I couldn't let that happen."

"Spare me," I said. "I don't believe anything you say. You've been tricking me all this time. Trying to make me think you're this kind, innocent, little girl, when really you're just like the witches—you just want Oz for yourself."

Ozma shook her head sadly. "Don't you see? When she couldn't control me, she thought she might be able to control *you*. So she sent you those shoes, and brought you here to do her work for her. And it's working."

"You're lying! Glinda sent me the shoes because she knew I was the only one who could save her. Which is exactly what I'm going to do."

I didn't know why I was even bothering talking to her. This could all be solved with a simple knock of my heels.

All I had to do was wipe Ozma's mind clean. I'd done it once before, and I could do it again.

I tried to summon a spell, but where my magic had once been, all I found was a deep, aching emptiness. A hunger. I had gotten so used to having it—even if I couldn't always use it, it was always *there*. Comforting me, protecting me. Feeding me.

Now it wasn't.

I looked down in a panic. My shoes were still on my feet. They were as red and shiny and beautiful as ever. But where they had once felt alive—like a part of my body, as important as my arms or legs—they now just felt heavy and separate. Just two ordinary shoes with extra-high heels.

Ozma gave a half shrug and looked away when she saw the distraught expression on my face. "I'm sorry," she said. "I can't take the shoes away from you. Whatever spell binds them to you is already complete, and magic like that is irreversible, even for me. But I can block your access to the power they possess. And I have. I didn't want to—I thought maybe you would be able to handle it, that maybe you were strong enough to resist the corruption. You *are* Dorothy, after all. If anyone could fight off Glinda's manipulations, it's you. But the Sorceress is powerful and ruthless. She didn't outlast the other witches by playing fair, you know."

"No one could have resisted," Aunt Em said. She had risen from my bed and walked over to me, placing a hand on the small of my back. I suppose it was meant to be comforting, but I slapped it away. "It's too tempting," she said. "It's not your fault, Dorothy. You'll see, someday. This is for your own good. It's time to go back to Kansas."

"No!" I screamed, whirling around in a rage, looking for something—anything—that I could use against the princess. But it was too late. Ozma waved her scepter and my palace bed-chambers faded to white.

* * *

When the world re-formed, I found myself standing in the middle of an endless field of waving green grass. I felt dizzy and
nauseated, and I struggled to stay on my feet. Was this Kansas?
Had it been that easy to undo it all?

No. We were still in Oz—the Emerald City was still visible in the distance, and Ozma was still standing in front of me.
Aunt Em was here, too, stumbling around a bit from the tran-
sition, and Uncle Henry was a few paces away, holding Toto
in his arms. As soon as my little terrier saw me, he wriggled
out of my uncle's grip and raced over to where I was struggling to stay on my feet. Toto circled my ankles, sniffing my
shoes in confused concern. He could see that something was
missing.

"I sure feel terrible," Uncle Henry was saying. "You won't
believe me, but I know how much you wanted to be here. I hope
you can understand, someday."

"Sending you home isn't simple," said Ozma. "I really didn't
know how to do it for a while—so little is known about the walls
that separate your world from ours. I needed to find something
that already knows the way."

I didn't know what she was talking about, and I didn't care.
All I wanted was to find a way to stop her.

"When you arrive home in Kansas, none of you will remember any of this. I think it's better that way. It will just seem like a
pleasant, faraway dream. Something that happened to someone
else in a story."

"No!" I screamed one more time, lunging for her. She might have cut me off from my magic, but I still had two hands, and I would use them to strangle her if that's what I needed to do to stay here.

But before I could reach her, she raised her scepter, and I hit a wall. I punched and clawed at it, but my fists bounced uselessly against the invisible barrier.

"I'll always be grateful to you, Dorothy," Ozma said, ignoring my screams. "You saved Oz. And I'll always think of you as a friend."

With that, Ozma threw her head back and lifted her scepter to the sky. Her wings materialized, and she rose up into the air as a column of blinding light shot down from the clouds and surged through her. She began to shine so brightly that she was barely even visible anymore—she was just a vague, burning ball of radiance.

Even in my fury, I couldn't help being impressed. I had met witches and sorceresses and wizards, but I had never met anyone who could turn themselves into a star.

Uncle Henry put his arm around Aunt Em. Even Toto sat back on his hind legs and stared up in amazement.

As Ozma cast her spell, wind whipped through the treetops. Dark clouds swirled overhead. It looked like a storm was coming. The light changed; the sky around us was now a sick, pale, greenish shade.

In that moment, I felt something happening to me. My feet began to tingle, and then the rest of my body was tingling, too, until it was almost vibrating with power.

No one noticed what was happening.

Ozma must have been too consumed with her own spell to realize that whatever barriers she'd placed on my shoes were falling away. She must not have been able to manage both spells at once.

My magic was coming back.

In the distance, I saw it approaching. The old house—the shack that had brought me to Oz—was flying across the sky, spinning like a top as it drew nearer, getting bigger and closer by the second. That was what Ozma had meant by *something that already knows the way*. She was going to put us all back in that awful, ramshackle old house and she was going to make it take us back to Kansas.

I wouldn't stand for it. My shoes gripped my feet so hard it hurt.

It all happened so fast. Important things always seem to, don't they?

The house was careening through the sky, traveling faster than I thought possible, and then it was right over our heads and it began to hover in place as it made its descent.

My hair was whipping past my face; my whole body was twitching with fear and rage and power. More power than I'd ever felt before. More of *anything* than I'd ever felt before.

I didn't know how long it would last. I only had one shot.

And I didn't really even think about what I was doing. I just knew I had to do something. So I reached out in fury and desperation. I summoned every ounce of magic I could find, and I grabbed it. That's really what it felt like. It felt like I was reaching out with giant hands and pulling the house from Ozma's magical clutches. It was easy.

I just plucked it up and I threw it at her—sent the house hurtling for the princess like I was tossing a handful of chicken feed onto the ground for Miss Millicent.

Ozma saw it coming a second too late. Just before it was about to hit her, the column of light that held her suspended dissipated, and her body returned to her. She screamed, her black hair swirling around her as her wings flapped furiously. Acting on instinct, she flung her arms out in front of her to protect herself. A glowing green shield materialized in front of her.

Like I say, it happened fast. Too fast for me to react.

The house crashed into Ozma's force field. But it didn't shatter. Instead, the farmhouse ricocheted off of it with a thunderous crash and went sailing gracefully through the air, straight toward where my aunt and uncle were standing, frozen in place.

"*Dorothy!*" Aunt Em screamed, seeing it coming toward her.

"*Do som—*" Uncle Henry shouted.

Toto let out a howl, and I put my hand up, summoning another spell to stop it, but even as I did I knew I was a second too slow.

When the dust settled, the house had come crashing to the earth, still in one piece, and all that was visible of my poor aunt Em were her two feet sticking out from under our old front porch.

NINETEEN

Silence.

Terrible, awful, horrible silence.

It was only broken by the sound of my voice cracking. "Aunt Em!" I screamed. "Uncle Henry!"

There was no response. I knew there wouldn't be.

I fell to the ground in front of the house, sobs racking my body.

What have I done? She was dead. Uncle Henry was dead. Tears rolled down my face. My throat closed up. It hurt so much. They were my only family. They had loved me, despite everything.

I choked on my tears. Why had I ever brought them here? I should have left them in Kansas, where they would have been safe. And happy. They hadn't asked to come. All they'd wanted was to go home and I wouldn't let them.

No. It wasn't my fault. It was hers. *She* had done this to them.

I shook with rage as I saw Ozma, back on the ground, crawling to her feet from where she'd made her own crash-landing.

The clouds thickened, growing darker above me. My shoes hugged my feet like a vise, glowing like they were made of red lightning. Ozma stared up at me in shock.

"*You* did this," I shrieked. "*You* killed them!"

I walked toward her, the rage burning me alive. It felt *good* to hate her this much. Natural.

Small forks of lightning flickered off the shoes as they throbbed with a magical pulse. But the heels weren't alive. *I was.* The pulse was my heartbeat. Their magic was part of me now.

A scream ripped out of me as another magical surge punched through my body. I felt like I was about to explode into flames as I walked steadily toward Ozma, screaming louder and with more anguish than the Screaming Trees in the Forest of Fear.

She staggered backward as I rushed at her. Her face contorted in fear. "No, Dorothy! Please! Don't let it control you! Don't give in to it!"

"Too late for that, *Princess*," I screamed. As I said it, I felt all of Oz screaming along with me.

"Please, calm down. You've no idea what you're doing. You can still save yourself. Think about this."

With a roar louder than the Lion's I unleashed every last bit of magic that had been building unstoppably inside me since I got to Oz.

It was wondrous.

It surged through my body, flowing like a thousand rivers

cascading violently and crashing on the shore.

It drained from the land and the sky, up through me and right at her.

She screamed as I hit her with pure energy, streams of purple and green and red lightning shocking and sparking as it struck the ground around us over and over and over again.

She didn't fight back. Maybe she couldn't—maybe she'd used up everything she had summoning my house. Or maybe she didn't want to. Maybe she was too scared. I didn't know and I didn't care. I just wanted her dead. I wanted it to hurt.

But she didn't die. When I'd used up everything I thought I had, I was sure that I'd see her lying on the ground in a mangled, bloody heap. But Ozma rose to her feet. Easily, steadily, as if it was nothing.

She was more powerful than I'd realized. She had changed. I hadn't hurt her a bit. I might have even made her stronger.

Ozma's entire body turned the color of midnight and shadows. It looked alive—like there was black smoke churning just beneath her skin. Her eyes were hollow, golden caverns; her scepter was a lightning bolt that stretched into the thick clouds overhead.

"You have no idea what I am," she screamed with a hundred voices. "I am the blood of Lurline and the daughter of the Ancient Flower. I am the first and the last and the in-between. I am *Oz*."

She slammed her scepter into the earth, and a swarm of black moths came bursting forth out of it. They flew for me, knocking me backward, clinging to my skin, trying to suck the life out of me.

But the shoes protected me. Without me even trying, they wrapped me with red light, and the moths burned away as if I was a candle whose flame they'd been drawn to in the dark.

I regained my composure. Ozma had taken everything away from me. Everything I cared about or would ever care about. She had taken away Glinda, and my aunt and uncle, and my magic. She had tried to take away my kingdom.

"I am *Dorothy*," I screamed back at her.

I closed my eyes and knocked my heels three times, begging the Land of Oz to fill me with darkness and power and all the enchantments it possessed.

It did.

It all came bursting out of me. This time, it was more than magic. It wasn't just the shoes at work. It was me. It was the reason I had been brought here in the first place. It was the reason I had been brought back again.

It was that *wanting* I'd known my whole life. All that hope that there was something better out there, something that could be mine and mine alone.

Ozma was no match for it. She'd never felt anything like it, I don't think. She had all this, and she didn't even care about it.

But I cared. I wanted. I wanted *more*. My desire was a tornado that twisted out of my body and danced toward the princess, catching her up in its funnel, lifting her into the air as easily as if she was a feather. She screamed and struggled against it, but there was nothing she could do.

It was no use. She was powerless against me. She may have been the One True Princess, the delicate peach blossom and the blood of whatever-her-name-was, but I was the girl who rode the cyclone, the girl who had slayed the witches. I had been brought here against all odds—not once, but *twice*. I wouldn't be denied.

Within the cone of the maelstrom, I watched calmly as Ozma's dark form began to tear itself apart in a gruesome explosion of black and gold. It was like she was unraveling. Like she was *melting*.

And then she was gone.

For the third time, Oz had chosen *me*.

The sky had returned to normal. Everything was quiet. The storm I had summoned faded away into the distance. It was like none of it happened, except that my head was throbbing and all of my limbs were aching in exhaustion.

And the old farmhouse was still standing there, invincible and mostly undisturbed, with my poor aunt's feet still sticking out from underneath it. I looked away. I couldn't bear the sight of it.

Then my eyes caught sight of *her*.

Ozma was lying on the ground, her crown knocked from her head and her scepter ten feet away. Her dress was streaked with blood and dirt and her face was bruised and swollen. But she was breathing.

She sat up and looked around. I took a step forward, ready

to keep fighting. Ready to do whatever it took. Then I saw that she was smiling. It wasn't a normal smile either. It was dazed and vacant and her eyes were empty, like old, tarnished marbles. She looked at me and cocked her head.

"Who are *you*?" she asked stupidly.

I lowered my arms. "Ozma?"

She giggled an idiotic giggle.

I pointed at her and tried to call up more magic. Just a little bit more, enough to snuff her out once and for all. But all that shot forth from my fingers were a few useless red sparks that faded away as quickly as they had come. I had used it all up, for now, I figured. It would take some time to recharge.

Ozma didn't seem to understand that I wasn't exactly her friend. She clapped her hands. "Oh that's *lovely*!" she cried. "Do it again."

Before I could try anything, a high-pitched yipping noise filled my ears.

"Toto?" I spun around.

In all the commotion, I had forgotten about my dog, and when I searched for him, I saw Glinda standing there, right next to the farmhouse.

Her pink dress looked like it was made from the sunset itself; her eyes were kind and gentle. She bent down to pet my Toto, who was bouncing up and down happily at her feet, and when she stood up, she caught sight of me and beamed, picking up the skirt of her dress and racing forward through the grass to greet me.

"Dorothy!" she called, her voice strong and sweet and joyful. "My beautiful, powerful, *angry* Dorothy. I knew I could count on you, and I was right. Just look how right I was!"

She gestured toward Ozma, who had her arms outstretched and was whirling around, making herself dizzy as she laughed and tripped over herself, oblivious to everything that was going on.

"What did I *do* to her?" I asked.

"Oh, you did what you had to," Glinda said with a shrug. "You couldn't kill her. I don't think it's possible to kill her, at least not without destroying Oz. But still, *ding dong*, as they say!"

Glinda threw her head back and let out a long, melodious chortle.

I was a little confused. "What do you mean?" I asked.

"Think of it this way," Glinda said, when she'd stopped laughing. "You've taken Ozma's power and you've given it back to the land. Back to Oz, where it belongs. She was trying to hoard it all for herself, you know—that's been her goal all along. That's why she hated me, and why she wanted your shoes so badly. She just wanted to hoard the magic, like fairies always do."

"I thought the fairies *gave* Oz its magic."

"Oh, she told you that old taradiddle, now did she? I'm sure you didn't believe her. These fairies are *greedy* little creatures. She just couldn't *stand* to see anyone else with even a drop of magic to speak of. You did what you had to. You did what was right. And Oz will thank you for it, someday. For now, you'll have to settle for *my* thanks. You saved me, Dorothy. You can't think of how horrible it was for me to be locked away like that."

"How did I . . ."

"Once you took care of Ozma, the prison she's been holding me in ceased to exist. Poof! Just like that. Of course I came to find you right away. I've been so worried about you all this time. It's a miracle I was able to get you those shoes at all. But you know—even all chained up, even in the darkest of dungeons—this old girl had a few tricks up her sleeve." She wiggled an eyebrow at me and laughed again, but this time she stretched out her arms as she did it and gestured for me.

"Oh, come here, you foolish, dear thing." As soon as she said it, I fell effortlessly into her embrace and suddenly found myself sobbing as she pulled me tight against her bosom.

"My aunt," I managed to say through my tears. "My uncle . . ."

Glinda held me close. She kissed my head and squeezed me even tighter. Aunt Em had hugged me before, and of course I knew that she had loved me, but there had always been a certain distance between us. She had never wanted children, and even though she had tried her best with me, I always knew I wasn't quite part of her plan.

Now, as Glinda kissed me and hugged me and stroked my hair, I wondered if I finally knew what it was like to have a mother.

"Darling," she said kindly. "I'm so sorry about what's happened to them. But it just couldn't be helped. And, you know what?"

"What?" I asked as she let me go and I stepped back. She took my arms, held them at my sides, and looked lovingly into my eyes.

"You'll have a *new* family now. A family who loves you more than you can imagine."

"Who?" I asked.

"Why, *me* of course, you silly goose! And the Scarecrow, and the Lion, and the Tin Woodman, and, oh, just about everyone in Oz, I imagine. You're to be their new princess, you know, and you're sure to be the most beloved girl in the land, before long. If you're not already!"

"I'm to be *princess?*" I asked.

"Who else would be?" Glinda asked. "Her?" She pointed to Ozma, who was kneeling in the grass sniffing curiously at a patch of buttercups. "Well, they'll still *call* her princess, I guess. All that fairy magic makes it unavoidable. La-di-dah! But as you can see, she won't be good for much from now on. When we get back to the palace, I'll see to it that she issues a decree making you Deputy Princess and Protector of the Crown. Won't be too difficult. We'll set her up with some dolls and toys and let her run wild in her own quarters while you sit on the throne and do all the important princessing work. With my help and guidance, of course. They'll forget all about her soon enough; the people of Oz have short memories, bless their hearts. And they absolutely *adore* a new monarch. Oh, the coronation we'll throw for you!"

I looked over at Ozma, and Glinda, and then over at the farmhouse. I wasn't sure about any of this. Aunt Em's feet were pointing away from each other at odd angles. She was wearing the same ordinary leather boots she'd worn on the farm—for all the fancy new shoes she'd been offered here, she'd refused to give them up.

Glinda saw the doubt in my eyes. She frowned sympathetically. "You poor thing. You always *were* such a sentimental sparrow."

She waved her hand at the house. "Poof!" she said, and as soon as the word escaped her lips, my old home—along with my aunt and uncle—disappeared in a shower of pink bubbles, like there had never been anything there at all.

I felt a weight lifting from my shoulders. I felt my sobs easing.

"There, doesn't that feel better?"

"It does," I said. As soon as the reminders were gone, everything that had happened in the past couple of weeks felt very far away.

"It doesn't *matter* where you came from," Glinda said. "I came from someplace, too, you know. Someplace not that different from Kansas. I'll tell you the story someday, if you can *possibly* stand the boredom!"

"I'd like that," I said softly.

Glinda smiled back at me. "Good. *Very good.* Now, why don't we leave all this useless sadness behind and go back to the palace? We need to pick you out a nice crown." She put her arm around me. "Doesn't that sound like a good idea?"

It did. It really did.

Glinda turned to Ozma. "You, too, darling," she said, and

the princess scampered toward us, almost tripping over her own feet. "You two can be like wonderful sisters!"

Ozma nodded eagerly and took my hand.

Glinda winked knowingly. "Well, maybe more like distant cousins," she said to me in a stage whisper. She put her arm around my shoulder, and we began the walk back to the Emerald City.

"Now," Glinda said, "you must tell me *all* about your adventures. I was able to watch some of them while you were having them, but I have to say it all came in a bit garbled. Like listening to a radio with a broken antenna."

I looked back over my shoulder. The house was gone. My aunt and uncle were gone. Ozma was flapping her arms as she skipped aimlessly through the fields.

She wouldn't be much company. But Toto was racing behind us. And I had Glinda and all my friends in the palace. I had my kingdom.

My shoes sent a happy wave of magic shooting up through my body, and, on impulse, I grabbed a fistful of it and tossed it into the blue sky, where it burst into a pink and gold firework.

"That's my girl!" Glinda exclaimed proudly. "Oh, I can't wait to show you what you can really do with it. You were *born* to be a sorceress, you know."

It was too good to be true. It was almost like Kansas was just a dream and I was waking up to a wonderful new morning where everything was bright and sunny and full of life.

They say you can't go home again. Well, I'm proof that's not true. Home isn't just where you're born—it's where you belong. I found my home and I let it go. But I came back. Now I was home for good, and I would never, *ever* make the mistake of leaving again. The past was gone forever. There was no place like here.

THE WITCH MUST

BURN

ONE

Things have been pretty weird lately in Oz. I mean, if you're not from around here, things are always a little weird in Oz. There're the flying monkeys, sure, and the Road of Yellow Brick, which isn't exactly the most reliable freeway in the world (it moves around). We have magic—more about that later—and animated soldiers that used to be toys, and a city made out of emeralds, and trees that talk. We have an enchanted palace—that's where I work as a servant—and we have a Wizard with extra-special powers. We *had* a Wizard, anyway, until he disappeared. We have cornfields that grow pre-roasted corn on the cob and talking animals and a Cowardly Lion who's actually not so cowardly and is becoming a little bit scary. (He talks, too.) But for us, all of that is no big deal. We're used to it. The really weird thing about Oz these days?

Her name is Dorothy. And she's my boss.

Technically, Ozma is my boss. She's the rightful ruler of Oz, and when she was running the show, things were great for us here in the Emerald City. I don't know anything about where I'm from—I was left on the doorstep of the Emerald Palace as a tiny baby. Ozma and I grew up together there. I knew she'd one day be the ruler of Oz, too, but she never acted like someone who was about to be a queen. She was just my friend, and the palace servants became my family. I've never known anything else.

Then Dorothy showed up—the first time—and everything changed. She killed the Wicked Witch of the East and with the help of the Tin Woodman, the Scarecrow, and the Cowardly Lion, the Wicked Witch of the West. She saved Oz. Then she vanished back to the Other Place—the world she came from, where magic doesn't exist. Ozma took her rightful place on the throne, and things were basically perfect. Although I still didn't know anything about my real family, I'd lived in the palace for my whole life and Ozma and the servants were the only family I needed. I loved my work in the palace, as strange as that may sound—it gave me a real sense of pride to do a good job keeping everything running. Nobody plans a banquet like I do. I can remember the names of every single dignitary of Oz—*and* their children, pets, favorite foods, preferred seating arrangements, wives, husbands, ex-wives, ex-husbands, and what room in the palace they most like to stay in when they visit. My detail-oriented nature is what makes me so good at my job, and it's why Ozma ultimately promoted me to be the youngest head maid in the history of Oz. I wasn't going to be a famous queen or a powerful sorceress, and I was fine with that. I was good at something that I loved, and I'd get to spend my life doing it.

And then Dorothy came *back*, and that's when things got weird. She was different—she wasn't the sweet, innocent girl we all adored who had saved Oz. Dorothy moved into the palace, and this time she was here to stay. And then, after a palace ball one night, suddenly Ozma wasn't herself anymore; overnight she went from our vivacious, caring, generous queen to a vacant ghost of herself wandering the halls of the palace like the world's creepiest talking doll. Sometimes she didn't even recognize us. At first, Dorothy pretended she was helping out, ruling on Ozma's behalf. She kept Ozma close by her side.

But then Dorothy dropped the pretense pretty quickly, and none of us knew how to stop her, or even if we could. Suddenly, our peaceful palace was full of soldiers. They looked like the Tin Woodman, but there was something about them that didn't feel right. The Scarecrow left his own corncob mansion out in the hills of Oz and moved into the palace, where he shut himself up in his suite of rooms and began to work on something mysterious that Dorothy referred to as his "experiments." The Scarecrow had always seemed so harmless before, just kind of dopey and pleasant despite his brain upgrade, but the maids who took him his meals came back from his rooms with stories about sinister equipment and cages covered in blankets, behind which they could hear rustling and faint, soft moans, like something crying out in pain. We'd see lights coming from his rooms at all hours, and hear crashing and banging in the middle of the night. Pretty soon I had to bribe my staff with extra time off in order to get them to so much as clean the hallway outside his room. And the stories of what they saw *inside* sent chills up my spine.

Dorothy acted as though nothing was wrong—as though whatever was happening was totally normal. If any of us asked her about it, she'd fly off the handle in one of her infamous tantrums. So we left it alone.

I also quickly realized that Dorothy doesn't like me, but I am careful to keep myself useful. I want to figure out what's going on in the palace, and with Ozma, and I can't do that if Dorothy kicks me out. And I think even she realized that dismissing me out of hand would clue the rest of the servants in to the fact that something was *really* wrong. Ozma would never condone such a thing, and for all intents and purposes, Ozma is still the ruler of Oz. I make sure for the time being to keep everything the way Dorothy likes it. I make sure her rows and rows of dresses are hung neatly, organized by color, occasion, and material (and yes, of course, season). Her bacon is extra crispy, the floors are extra scrubbed. I know exactly what it takes to keep the palace running like clockwork, and Dorothy knows I know, and so for now we're in kind of a standoff. She hates me, but she can't get rid of me, and I intend to keep it that way.

She is the only one who's allowed to use magic in the palace. She says there's too much of a risk of disaster otherwise. But I think the real reason is that she doesn't want anyone to have more power than she does.

I'm not sure how much longer I can stand it here. Every once in a while, I'll get a chance to pause for a moment at a window, looking out over the glittering green towers of Oz and day-dreaming about what life used to be like when Ozma was in charge and Oz was the way it should be. When Dorothy was a national hero, not a national menace. When—

"*Jellia!*" Dorothy's voice tore through the air, a piercing shriek that made me flinch. I'd been scrubbing the palace floors since sunrise. Dorothy had been on a tear since she staggered out of bed long after the palace was up and bustling, and I'd had the bad luck to be standing next to her when she decided the floors were filthy, despite the fact that we'd cleaned them the day before. I sat up from my brush and bucket as the relentless *tap-tap-tap* of her heels came storming into the room, and just barely scrambled to my feet and executed a clumsy curtsy.

"What are you *doing?*" she snarled. "Why are you *filthy?*" She'd used magic that morning to dress herself—there was no mistaking the way she was stuffed into her corseted and impossibly short dress, or the glittering haze that surrounded her as she moved. Her hair was curled into tight, childish ringlets that were a strange contrast to her glossy red mouth and heavily rouged cheeks. As always, her magical red heels glowed like the fires of Hell. If you got close to those shoes, it was almost as though you could hear them talking to you in a low, seductive whisper.

"You look terrible," Dorothy said. *So do you*, I thought.

"You asked me to scrub the floors this morning." I kept my eyes downcast.

"I most certainly absolutely did no such thing, *Jellia*." She always said my name like it was the worst insult she could think of. It drove me nuts. I dared a look up at her through my lashes, trying to judge her mood. If she'd truly forgotten, I'd only make her angrier by contradicting her. If she was trying to torment me, she'd only leave me alone once she saw me squirm like a worm on a hook. She was looking out the window with a scowl, her attention already elsewhere, which meant I wasn't on her hit list for the day. Yet.

I rolled my eyes and swallowed my pride. "I must have misheard, Your Majesty," I mumbled.

"Get yourself cleaned up at once," she snapped. "I'm throwing a banquet and it has to be perfect. And I want all my dresses laid out—and the ballroom prepared—and I want all the Munchkins *out* of sight. *Every* last one of them, especially that filthy little blue one. Is that clear?"

"Of course, Your Majesty. Someone is visiting the palace?"

"Glinda is returning tomorrow," she said coolly.

Even I, practiced as I was becoming in keeping my emotions out of my expressions, couldn't hide my shock. Glinda was one of the most powerful witches in Oz—possibly *the* most powerful witch in Oz. Rumor had it that she was somehow responsible for Dorothy's return, although no one knew exactly what she'd done.

Then Glinda had vanished shortly after Dorothy had moved into the palace. I know I wasn't the only one who'd breathed a sigh of relief.

"Glinda is coming *here*?" I blurted. Dorothy narrowed her eyes, studying my face, and I cursed my big mouth. If she was back in the Emerald City now, I was pretty sure it wasn't to deck us all out in ball gowns and tiaras.

"Surely you're thrilled," she said, and I recognized the danger in her voice.

"Oh, of course." I scrambled to cover my slipup. "I'm just— it's just a surprise to have such a, um"—I was hit with a burst of inspiration—"such an *exalted* guest. It will be an honor to receive her."

An expression of disgust crossed her face. "And change your dress," she said. "You look like you crawled out of a sewer." She laughed out loud at her own joke, pivoting on one glittering heel and stalking out of the room. Her ridiculously short dress swished back and forth with each stride. I sighed and scowled down at my mop bucket. Something was up, and I had the sinking feeling whatever was about to happen wasn't going to be good.

TWO

The morning of Glinda's arrival, the palace was a hive of activity. Servants ran back and forth, putting up decorations and frantically cleaning. Delicious smells from the kitchen filled the halls. I inspected every maid I passed, making sure everyone's uniform was spotless and perfectly fitted. When I heard the clatter of carriages from the courtyard that signaled Glinda's arrival, my heart skipped a beat. If everything wasn't perfect, I'd be the one to pay for it.

Dorothy and Glinda shut themselves up in Dorothy's chambers as soon as Glinda entered the palace. I spent the rest of the afternoon making sure that everything in the banquet hall was ready for Glinda's big welcoming dinner. The long table was heaped with white flowers that released a gentle aroma of jasmine into the air. The crystal chandeliers glittered. The tablecloth was a snowy, spotless white, richly embroidered with silver thread. Every place was set just so. Even Dorothy, I thought, couldn't find fault with anything here.

But that night, as we served dinner to Dorothy, Glinda, and her entourage, everything in the palace felt off. The air snapped with tension, and all the servants were nervous. I looked around and noticed Ozma wasn't present. Dorothy sulked at her end of the table, her habitual fake smile replaced with a sullen scowl. Glinda sat next to her, and the two of them talked quietly on their own. I moved back and forth between the kitchen and the banquet hall, trying to catch snippets of their secretive conversation.

"How are the Scarecrow's experiments coming, Dorothy? Are we on schedule to begin mining?"

"He's doing his best," Dorothy mumbled. "But we're all worried about you-know-who. If you had better control over your sister—"

"My sister is unimportant," Glinda snapped, cutting her off sharply.

"But he's a danger to all of us," Dorothy said petulantly. "Who knows why he's returned? Or what his plan is?"

"My spies tell me that he hasn't returned; he never left Oz at all. He may be throwing his lot in with the Wicked . . ." Glinda's voice was cool and calculating. I couldn't quite catch the end of her sentence, and it wouldn't do to show I was listening. *The wicked what?* I wondered. "And we don't yet know for a fact that he means to depose you," Glinda said, her voice low. "His power—"

She cut herself off, looking at me. I lowered my eyes. "Go

get more wine, won't you, Jellia?" she said sweetly. "And you mustn't pay attention to Dorothy and me. We're just indulging in silly gossip!" She tittered gaily; it was like watching an eagle try to sound like a mouse.

"Yes, Your Eminence," I said, curtsying quickly and turning to obey her request. *The Wizard*, I thought, my mind spinning as I went back to the kitchen. They were talking about the Wizard—they had to be. And Glinda was helping Dorothy—which meant that she must know about Dorothy's slow takeover of the palace. Did Glinda know what was wrong with Ozma? Could the Wizard really have returned to Oz? And if he had, what did that mean for us? Had he returned to overthrow Ozma and take back the throne? Or did he realize that Dorothy was out of control? Was he trying to regain control of Oz—or protect it? And what *exactly* was the Scarecrow working on?

Astrid, one of the youngest servants, tripped on her way from the kitchen to the dining hall, bringing my thoughts back to the moment. I was right behind her and watched in dismay as she dropped the platter of roast beef she was carrying and burst into tears. "I'm—I'm—I'm sorry," she sobbed, falling to her knees and trying to pick up the shattered pieces; she only succeeded in soaking her dress in the messy remains of the roast. I looked around quickly. Thankfully, we were alone in the corridor and no one had seen her blunder.

"It's all right," I said gently, hauling her to her feet. "I'll make sure a Munchkin cleans this mess up." I eyed her dress. Magic in the castle was strictly forbidden among the help, but I'd risked it before when trouble brewed. Besides, Dorothy was already tipsy, so I didn't think she'd notice, and being shorthanded at the banquet could end in disaster.

"Here," I said, tugging at her dress and concentrating. I could feel the warm buzz in my hands, and Astrid gasped as the stains disappeared.

"Th-thank you, Jellia," she whispered. She seemed shocked— almost as if she'd never seen a staff member do magic before. I'd always assumed everyone else here used it when they were in a fix.

"You can't go back into the hall with that face. Smile." I dabbed the remaining tears out of her eyes with the corner of my apron and looked at her sternly as her mouth quivered. "I mean *really* smile, Astrid. Go back to the kitchen and don't carry anything to Dorothy until you look like you mean it." It would be handy, I thought, if there were some spell that could keep all of us permanently smiling; Dorothy was only too happy to dole out punishment at random to anyone who didn't look like they were having the absolute best time of their lives in her company. That was a hard level of happiness to fake.

"Yes, Jellia," she whispered, and fled.

But that wasn't the end of her mishaps for the evening. A few minutes later, as I topped off Dorothy's wineglass yet again, a rigid grin fixed across my own features, Astrid came back into the banquet hall with a fresh platter of roast beef. Instead of a smile, her face bore an expression of terror. I caught her eye and tried to signal her to turn around, but it was too late. Dorothy could spot suffering from across a room like a cat on the prowl for errant mice. "Annabel," she crooned, her voice dripping with lethal sweetness. "Come over here with that." Astrid's eyes went wide in fear. At Dorothy's feet, Toto growled from his jeweled velvet pillow. Not for the first time, I thought that I'd have sacrificed a body part if it meant I could throw that wretched dog out a window. A very high window. Astrid rounded the banquet table with her platter and came to stand on Dorothy's other side.

"Your Majesty," she said, her voice shaking. Technically, Ozma was the only person in the palace we should have addressed as "Your Majesty," since technically she was still the queen. But Dorothy was only too happy not to correct us. *Soon we won't even notice she's taken over everything*, I thought. The expression on Dorothy's face was different than I'd ever seen it—instead of her usual scowl of adolescent petulance, she looked positively malevolent. A chill ran down my spine. Something was very, very wrong. *I have to get Astrid out of here*, I thought frantically, taking a step forward. But it was too late.

"Annie," Dorothy crooned. "I've been *waiting* for the roast *all evening*. Jellia told me it's *extra* special tonight. Was there a *problem* in the kitchen, Astrid?"

"A p-problem, Your Majesty?"

"Something that might cause such a significant delay with the service," Dorothy said, her voice dripping honeyed menace. I closed my eyes and took a deep breath. Whatever happened next was not going to be good. "It must have been something simply *disastrous*, to keep a guest as honored as Glinda waiting."

Astrid's mouth trembled, her smile widening desperately and then faltering altogether. From the other end of the table, Glinda laughed. "Now, Dorothy," she said. "There's no need to be upset. I'm perfectly content."

"This is my palace!" Dorothy shrieked, all the syrupy sweetness gone from her voice. Her eyes blazed as she reached out and grabbed Astrid's arm, sending the platter clattering to the floor and the roast flying for the second time. Dorothy's glossy red talons dug into Astrid's flesh, and tears filled Astrid's eyes as a trickle of blood ran down her arm. "You know what we *do* in my palace with servants who cannot perform their tasks properly?" She released Astrid's blood-streaked arm and leaned back in her chair.

Glinda put one pale hand on Dorothy's arm. "Not yet, Dorothy," Glinda said, so low I almost missed it. "The time is not yet." I stared at Dorothy, my mouth half open in horror. She'd been cruel before, entitled and prone to outbursts. But I'd never seen her do anything like this.

"No, Your Majesty!" Astrid cried, sinking to her knees and sobbing. "Please, Your Majesty, I'm sorry—I'm so sorry—it will never happen again—miss, please, don't hurt me—"

"That's enough," I said sharply. Dorothy looked up at me, her eyes narrowed with surprise. "I made a mistake with the order of the dishes. There's no need to punish Astrid." I added a hasty and belated, "Your Majesty."

"Is that so," Dorothy said. Her sudden calm was even more terrifying than her rage of moments ago. "Really, Jellia, you disappoint me."

"The servants are my responsibility," I said.

"Are you disagreeing with how I choose to discipline them?"

I took another deep breath. If I could distract Dorothy and calm her down, we might all get out of this banquet unscathed. "Of course not, Your Majesty," I said. "As always, your wisdom is boundless. But I should have known that—that"—I racked my brain and hit on an idea—"I should have known that Astrid was too young to wait on such an important guest. The pressure was too much for her. She's just nervous, Your Eminence— please, there's no need to punish her." I curtsied in Glinda's direction for good measure, and caught an evil little smile flicker across her face and vanish again.

"Your head maid is a feisty little thing, isn't she?" Glinda said, turning from Dorothy to me. "Come here." Surprised, I looked at Dorothy, whose expression was uncertain. Astrid, forgotten, began to creep away from the table on her hands and knees.

"Obey Glinda, Jellia," Dorothy snapped. I curtsied again and walked over to where Glinda was seated. She'd barely touched her food; her plate was still full. From a distance, she was beautiful; up close, she was even more so. Her soft strawberry-blond curls framed her heart-shaped, ageless face. Her eyes were a bright, cornflower blue. She was wearing a pale pink ball gown sewn together out of what looked like tiny scales of leather; the effect was almost like armor, but still managed to be pretty. She stretched out one delicate, immaculately manicured hand and gripped my chin, turning my face back and forth as she studied me like a bug under a magnifying glass. Her blue eyes bored into me and I felt as though I were falling into a bottomless pool, sinking deeper and deeper below the surface as I helplessly watched the sunlight recede above me and the darkness intensify all around me. *You're supposed to be the* Good *Witch*, I thought faintly. But the look in Glinda's eyes was cold, hard, appraising.

"You can't just have my maid," Dorothy said indignantly. Her voice broke the spell. I inhaled sharply, as though I'd just been underwater. "She's *mine*." What was she talking about?

"Just for the summer," Glinda said, her eyes not leaving my face. "You can have her back just as soon as I'm done with her, Dorothy. You wouldn't begrudge me this one favor, would you? After everything I've done for you?" Her voice was so syrupy I swore I could see the words oozing out of her mouth and flowing across the table toward Dorothy like a pink, sugary tide. Dorothy blinked, her mouth falling open a little, as the thick, shimmering liquid slid up the front of her dress and into her open mouth. Dorothy licked her lips, which glistened as though they'd been dipped in sugar. I blinked. I wasn't imagining it.

"Just for the summer," she whispered. But Glinda wasn't looking at her; she was still staring at me.

You see it, don't you, little girl? You can see *the magic, not just feel it.* I heard her voice inside my mind, but her lips weren't moving. Her fingers tightened on my chin and I went rigid with terror. I had never been so frightened in my life. *You don't even know what you are, do you? You haven't the faintest idea,* she crooned inside my skull. *I can make much use of you, child. Much use indeed.* She let me go and I staggered backward, nearly falling to the floor.

Around us, the guests who'd fallen silent during Dorothy's tantrum began to chat nervously again, and the buzz of conversation filled the banquet hall. The servants, moving hesitantly at first and then with more confidence, refilled glasses and cleared plates, brought out trays piled with colorful desserts. The room returned to normal for everyone but me.

"Just for the summer," Glinda said pleasantly. "I think it will be such a wonderful time. Don't you, Jellia?"

My heart hammering in my chest, my limbs finally released from her terrible power, I answered in the only way I could. I turned and fled the room.

THREE

Packing for the journey to Glinda's was simple. I told myself that Glinda was telling the truth, no matter how much she'd scared me the night before: this would just be for the summer. There was no need to clean out my room in the Emerald Palace. Just a few dresses and pairs of shoes. Glinda would probably have her own servants' uniforms, but I added my work dress just in case. I looked over my tidy little room and neatly arranged possessions, wondering if I'd ever see them again, and quickly squashed that thought. Of course I'd be back. Dorothy would insist on it, and Dorothy was in charge now. I had made myself indispensable to her. I tried not to think about how easily Glinda had overruled Dorothy the night before, or just how powerless Dorothy had been when confronted with Glinda's magic. Or to wonder what Glinda wanted me for.

I snapped my fingers, and an image of all the other servants wavered into life before me, transparent and iridescent as a soap bubble. I could summon up their images whenever I wanted, I told myself. I could probably even send them messages, though I'd never tried to use my magic over long distances before. This summer I would learn how much I was capable of doing.

The hardest part was saying good-bye. Astrid had already burst into my room first thing that morning, her face wet with tears. "Jellia!" she wailed, flinging her arms around me and almost knocking me over onto my bed. "You can't go! It's all my f-f-fault," she sobbed into my shoulder. "Who will look after us when you're gone? Who will protect us?"

"It's just for the summer," I said firmly, gently moving her head off my shoulder before she blew snot all over me. "You'll have to be strong, Astrid. You can't always rely on other people to fight your battles for you. This summer will be your chance to grow up." *She's just a kid*, I thought, patting her back awkwardly. *How can she stand up to Dorothy? What will they do without me?* Technically, *I* was just a kid, but I'd always had a good head on my shoulders and a lot of responsibility. I felt about a million years older than Astrid, even though we were nearly the same age. And though I tried not to let her see it, inside I was almost as upset as she was. Glinda was seriously scary—and I had no idea what lay in store for me.

Despite our hasty departure, word had spread fast around the palace, and all the servants were assembled in the courtyard to see me off. I took a deep breath, determined not to cry. I looked around for Ozma but wasn't totally surprised by her absence. I couldn't remember the last time I'd seen her walking around in the palace, and it made me worry even more about Dorothy's plans.

Glinda hovered a few feet away—literally, her glittery heels floating a few inches off the cobblestones. She had dressed for the journey as if she were headed to a ball. Her pale pink dress was embroidered with glittering gold thread and the bodice was studded with clear gemstones that caught the sunlight and refracted it into a blinding dazzle. Her hair was piled on top of her head and secured with more gems. A small squad of the Tin Woodman's soldiers stood at attention behind her mechanical carriage, their metallic bodies gleaming in the bright courtyard as the automaton horses—wired together out of tin and wood and gems—stamped their feet mechanically, their tinny neighing breaking the still air. Glinda beamed benevolently while the other servants came forward one by one to say good-bye. It wasn't like Dorothy to allow the servants a moment's respite, but Glinda's departure seemed to have put her in a good mood. She stood a few feet away from the witch, decked out in a tiny-waisted leather dress pieced together out of blue and white squares. As always, her red shoes emitted a rosy halo of light.

Astrid was still sobbing like the sweet little idiot she was; I had to resist the urge to pat her on the head like a dog. Hannah, the maid who was closest to me in age—and the closest thing I had to a best friend—came up to hug me. The Munchkin cooks surrounded me, flinging their arms around my knees and crying "Jellia! Jellia! Don't go!" in unison. I was touched, even if they made walking a little awkward.

"It's just for a few months," I reassured them, hugging them one by one. "I promise. You'll barely notice I was gone. Take good care of Dorothy—don't forget about the bacon—"

"—and color-code her dresses," Hannah finished. "We know, J. It'll be okay." Astrid wailed aloud, and Hannah rolled her eyes. I laughed. She always knew how to cheer me up.

"*Jellia*," Glinda cooed, "we *really* must be going. You'll see all your little friends again before you even know it! I need your help at *my* palace now."

I gave everyone one last wave before I climbed reluctantly into Glinda's carriage. To my surprise, I saw the Scarecrow stumble out of the palace, carrying an enormous satchel. Behind him stretched a line of the Tin Woodman's soldiers, carrying various pieces of mechanical equipment and machine parts. Another carriage drew up behind Glinda's, and the soldiers busied themselves loading it with their burdens while the Scarecrow supervised.

"He's always late," Glinda said, and sighed. Gone was the terrifying witch of the night before; in the afternoon sunlight, she looked radiant and gentle, although her voice had a peevish tone that belied her sweet expression. Finally, the second carriage was loaded to the Scarecrow's satisfaction, and he gave Glinda a jaunty wave.

"Everything will work as we discussed?" she called in a honey-eyed voice. He nodded jerkily, his black button eyes flashing in the sun.

"If the girl has enough magic to power the device," he said.

The Scarecrow only spoke rarely, and his dry, straw-like voice always sent chills through me. What girl was he talking about? Did he mean *me*? What magic could I possibly have?

"Oh, I'm confident of that," Glinda said gaily. "I believe in the power of positive thinking, don't you? If everything's ready, I think it's time we were going." She rapped sharply on the roof of the carriage, and the driver snapped to life with a whirr of clockwork. "Good-bye, Dorothy!" Glinda sang merrily. "Good-bye, Emerald City! Say good-bye, Jellia! We've got such adventures ahead of us!"

I did not like the sound of that at all. I waved out the window as the servants shrank behind us in the distance, and I didn't turn back to face the road until they were nothing more than tiny dots against the glittering green of the Emerald Palace. Whatever happened next, I was on my own now.

FOUR

I had only been outside the Emerald City a handful of times in my life, and despite my anxiety about what lay ahead of me, I couldn't help a surge of excitement as the carriage passed through the immense gates of the city and onto the Road of Yellow Brick. Next to me, Glinda lay back against her seat with her eyes closed, looking for all the world like a pretty young girl taking a nap. If I'd hoped she would give me some clue as to what she wanted with me, I clearly wasn't going to get it. I used the brief respite from her razor-sharp attention to look out the carriage window at the countryside. Once we were out of the gates, the radiant green aura of the city dissipated. Hills gave way to rolling farmland; cornstalks bobbed in the wind, and neatly tended orchards stretched toward the horizon in even rows. The trees didn't talk anymore—that had been one of Dorothy's first decrees, she said they gave her a headache—but their silence didn't affect the views. We'd been traveling for an hour or so when Glinda opened her eyes next to me and sat up, rapping on the roof of the carriage with her knuckles. We drew to a halt, and she stepped out of the carriage. I stayed where I was, confused, until I heard her call sweetly, "Jellia! What on earth are you waiting for? Surely you're not shirking your duties already?" I got out hastily.

We'd stopped next to a broad meadow of periwinkle grass, bordered on one edge by a thick, lush forest. The second carriage had followed us, and I only now saw that a large contingent of the Tin Woodman's soldiers had ridden along in the carriage. Glinda was directing them to unload the Scarecrow's machinery from the other carriage—a bewildering array of pipes and wires and instruments. The unloading took some time, and I could sense Glinda's impatience, although her face remained unnaturally serene. When the soldiers had finished they stood expectantly, staring at her.

"Now put it together," she said. This time there was no mistaking the irritation in her voice, and the soldiers got busy at once, assembling the pieces in the middle of the field. Glinda didn't seem to expect me to do anything, so I stood awkwardly at her side as she surveyed the construction.

The soldiers were moving with sharp, jerky motions, like sped-up windup toys, and soon a structure began to take shape. It was a giant contraption that looked almost like a complicated windmill with a long, flat piece that stretched out from the main body of the structure and balanced on another, smaller structure, like a seesaw. *What on earth?* I wondered.

"It's a drill, of course," Glinda said, as if she could read my mind.

"A drill, Your Eminence?"

"For magic," she said. I looked up at her. The rubies in her crown dazzled in the afternoon sun. "It's simply everywhere in Oz, as you know, going to waste. It's high time we put all those natural resources to work, don't you think?"

"You're drilling magic out of the ground?" I stared at her in surprise and she raised one eyebrow. "Your Eminence," I added quickly.

"Of course. Now that we have the technology to extract it, there's no reason not to. Think of how much that power will improve the lives of your fellow citizens!" I wasn't fooled by her sugary rhetoric; I was pretty sure that the only citizens whose lives would be improved by Glinda's crazy plan were Glinda herself, and Dorothy.

"But Your Eminence, doesn't Oz depend on that magic to survive?"

She waved a hand dismissively. "Jellia, I thought I saw something special in you in the palace, but now you sound positively old-fashioned. There's plenty of magic to go around. Oz won't feel a thing."

I shut my mouth. The months ahead would be hard enough without starting out on Glinda's bad side. We watched as the soldiers finished tightening the last nuts and bolts on Glinda's drilling machine, and then she pushed me forward. "Now, Jellia, it's time to do your duty for your country."

"Me?" I blurted in surprise as two soldiers grabbed me by the arms and dragged me toward the machine. "But—"

"I need magic to power the drill," Glinda cooed. She floated delicately after us, her heels sparkling silver several inches off the ground. "You certainly don't expect me to use *mine*, do you?" Now that we were closer to the machine, I could see a leather harness and silver helmet attached to one end of the giant see-saw. I struggled desperately, but the soldiers strapped me in and jammed the helmet down on my head. What was happening? Glinda looked me over with an assessing gaze, and then nodded.

"Begin," Glinda said, and one of the soldiers flipped a switch on the seesaw's platform. I screamed as a blinding wave of pain surged through me. It felt as though I was being electrocuted. Over my own cries I could hear the machine give out a huge, creaking groan, and the platform I was strapped to shifted as the machine began to move. The pain was unbearable and unending; my nostrils filled with the scent of burning, and I realized in horror that it was the smell of my own flesh. Nothing I had been through in my life had prepared me for pain like this.

"I'm very disappointed in you, Jellia," I heard Glinda say, and then everything went black.

I woke up on my back in the long, sweet-smelling grass. Every part of my body ached, and when I tried to open my eyes my vision was so blurry I shut them again. My head pounded with a dull, throbbing pain.

"Awake, lazybones?" Glinda's voice came from a few feet

away, but I couldn't bring myself to look at her. "I'm afraid you've failed me rather badly this afternoon, and it will take quite a lot of effort on your part to make it up to me. I've had to revamp the entire mechanism, and all that wasted time is your fault."

"What happened?" I croaked, my voice barely above a whisper.

"You should have had enough magic to power the device yourself. But you simply weren't up to the job, Jellia, and now I'll have to find a way to run it manually. How inconvenient for me." She sniffed delicately. "I suppose I need to think of something for you to do all summer at my palace. You're not nearly as valuable to me as I thought you would be."

Every muscle in my body cried out in protest as I struggled to sit upright, cradling my pounding head in my hands. "Now stand up and make yourself useful," Glinda said, her voice sharper. I heard her snap her fingers, and I yelped aloud as my body was jerked into a standing position. I was afraid I'd fall over, but her spell held me there. "Open your eyes," she said, and my body obeyed her. Slowly, my vision returned. We were still in the field, and the sun was still high in the sky—but that didn't mean anything. Dorothy controlled the passage of time in Oz, and she liked long afternoons with lots of sunshine. Something was moving next to Glinda's terrible machine. I squinted, and saw that the soldiers had corralled a handful of terrified Munchkins. While a few soldiers guarded the Munchkins, another was busy taking apart the harness and helmet they'd strapped me into. When they finished, they began lifting the Munchkins up to the platform part of the seesaw.

"Munchkin labor," Glinda sniffed, her honeyed voice underscored with disgust. "Unreliable, ineffective—and impossible to leave unsupervised. I'll have to station some of my soldiers here, and even return myself to make sure the job is getting done properly. All of this could have been avoided, Jellia, if your magic was sufficient to power the machine." She studied her device thoughtfully, and then looked back at me. "Perhaps with some refinements you'll be able to help me again." One of the soldiers barked an order, and the miserable-looking Munchkins began jumping up and down in place. With a terrific, earsplitting groan, the machine began to turn. Glinda sighed and turned away. "Onward to my palace, I suppose," she said.

Magic. Glinda was mining magic, pulling it out of the soil as if she was just digging a well. It was everywhere—it was in the land itself.

I struggled to stay awake in Glinda's carriage, but my body had other ideas, and I passed out again as soon as it moved forward. I had no idea how much time had passed when Glinda shook me impatiently and I snapped back to consciousness. My muscles still ached, but the rest had done me a little good; the headache had subsided, and my vision was much clearer. "Look sharp, you lazy girl," she said. "We're almost to the palace, and I won't have you setting a bad example."

I'd heard about the Summer Palace, Glinda's famous home, but I'd never seen it with my own eyes. It was nearly a full day's journey from the Emerald City, and Glinda's domain wasn't exactly a hot vacation destination. Outside the carriage, the countryside was remote and desolate. Lonely-looking blue hills, barren and rocky, surrounded us, and the trees were twisted and thorny. Here and there, huge craters dotted the landscape, and I wondered if she'd already tried out her magic-mining experiments closer to home. We were approaching a huge, sparkling pink gate, made out of some stone that refracted the setting sun's light and sent it in dazzling sparks across the desolate, rocky ground. Beyond the gate, candy-cotton-pink towers stabbed upward to dizzying heights. As soon as Glinda's entourage was within the castle walls, the gate swung shut. Like it or not, I was home.

Glinda's palace was as pink on the inside as it was on the outside. The walls were coated with a textured pink paint that looked as though someone had smeared sugar over everything. Chandeliers, crusted with pale pink gems, hung from the high ceilings. Pink-framed mirrors reflected the pink light, and everywhere hung pink-hued portraits of Glinda in an endless series of pink ball gowns. Waist-high pink vases held huge bouquets of pink flowers, which released little puffs of sickly-sweet perfumed pink smoke into the air at regular intervals. I tried not to gag as a waft of scent hit me, leaving a faint pink smear like a slug's trail on my uniform. Glinda, who didn't seem to walk if she could help it, floated ahead of me, gesturing me to follow her down the pink-floored main hall of the palace. "I have the perfect place for you, Jellia," she singsonged as I trotted after her, wincing at my still-sore muscles. "We'll start you in the kitchen."

"I'm trained as a lady's maid, Your Eminence," I panted as I hurried after her.

"Too good to start out at the bottom, are we?" she cooed.

"It's not that, Your Eminence, it's just that I thought—" She whipped around in midair, her ball gown swirling, and stared down at me.

"In my palace, you don't think, Jellia," she said. "Is that clear?"

"Yes, Your Eminence," I said.

She smiled. Despite her pretty face, the expression made her look like a shark. "That's more like it, Jellia. And don't think I won't be keeping an eye on you. Is that clear?"

"Yes, Your Eminence." In a puff of pink glitter, she vanished. I stood blinking in the hallway, uncertain what to do next, when a tall, lean boy about my age with thick dark hair rounded a corner and stopped in front of me. He was one of the best-looking people I'd ever seen; I was very happy to see that he wasn't pink.

"You're the new girl," he said, his curt demeanor at odds with his charming looks.

"Yes," I said, and curtsied for good measure. He snorted.

"Save it for Glinda," he said. "I'm here to help you stay alive."

FIVE

I was taken aback by his bluntness, but after what I'd been through on my way to the palace, I was grateful that someone was finally being level with me. "I'm Nox," he said, stalking away from me. I realized I was supposed to follow, and hurried after him. "I oversee the kitchen, where you'll be stationed for the time being until Glinda . . ." He paused, and a look of pity crossed his face for a second before he returned to stern indifference. "Until Glinda promotes you."

"Promotes?" I asked as we walked. The maze of pink corridors was hopelessly disorienting; I couldn't imagine ever being able to get my bearings.

"She has a habit of it," he said, his tone discouraging further questions.

"What happens to people she promotes?" I persisted.

"To be honest? I'm not sure you want to know."

"Oh," I said, and was quiet for a moment. "I'm only here for the summer. I work in the palace in the Emerald City, normally."

"I know," he said.

"You seem to know a lot about me."

"Your reputation precedes you."

"What's *that* supposed to mean?"

He didn't slow down. "Glinda's not the only one who's kept an eye on you. It's my job to know what happens in the palace."

"I thought you just said you worked in the kitchen."

"Among other things." With this cryptic answer, he pushed open a pink-paneled door at the end of yet another pink hallway, and I followed him into what was obviously the palace kitchen. A bank of ovens took up most of one wall; next to them, pink pots bubbled on a huge pink stove. But the rest of the room was mercifully ordinary; the long counter that stretched the length of the kitchen was just plain old wood, the floors were gray stone, and the walls were painted a clean white. "Glinda doesn't come in here," Nox said, as if to explain the color scheme. Three Munchkin cooks bustled back and forth in front of the stove, and a bedraggled girl who looked about ten was washing dishes in the kitchen's huge sink. Nox didn't introduce me, and none of them looked up as we came into the room. "Glinda only eats pink food—mostly cake, which is why there are so many ovens," Nox said. "She likes strawberry ice cream, too. If she wants something that isn't ordinarily pink, we have to enchant it. Just hope you don't get stuck on cleanup after bubble gum fondue night."

"Bubble gum fondue?" He was kidding, right? But his

expression was serious, and based on his demeanor so far, it didn't seem like he kidded anyone about much of anything.

"Listen," he said, "I don't know how they do things in the Emerald City, but if you want to survive here you'd better not let Glinda overhear you say anything she might find unflattering. And she has ears everywhere in the palace." He looked meaningfully at the cooks.

"Right," I said. "Thanks."

He took a tiny pink bird covered with pink rhinestones out of his pocket and fastened it to my apron with a little pink clip. "Don't ever take this off, even when you go to sleep. She'll know, believe me. This is how she summons you when she needs you. It'll direct you to wherever she is in the palace." As if on cue, the bird let out an earsplitting blast of noise, and I jumped about a foot in the air. Nox didn't even flinch. "Jellia!" Glinda's voice, tinny and compressed, shrieked across the kitchen. "Bring me a strawberry sundae!"

Nox crossed the kitchen to a tall freezer, which he opened to reveal a row of strawberry sundaes, already prepared. "When she wants something, she wants it right away. We make her favorite dishes ahead of time so she doesn't have to wait." He took a pink platter and a pink vase down from a shelf, filled the vase with pink roses from another cooler, set a sundae and the flowers on the platter, and handed the platter to me. "Good luck," Nox said. "I'll see you back here when you're done."

I'd hoped I would get some time to rest after my ordeal in the field, but clearly that wasn't going to be the case. I did a mental self-assessment; I was still sore, but I'd manage. The bird pin barked directions at me as I hurried back through the palace corridors and up spiraling flights of pink stairs. Finally, I found myself at a set of pink double doors. I knocked lightly, and the doors swung open.

SIX

Glinda's personal chambers looked as though a pink marshmallow had gotten into a losing fight with a cotton candy machine. The walls were a lighter version of the ever-present shade of the palace, and the floors were carpeted with thick patterned rugs piled on top of each other, in some places inches thick. Heavy pink velvet drapes hung on either side of the big picture windows, which let in a view of the surrounding countryside through rose-tinted glass. A huge, pink-canopied bed dominated one corner of the room, where Glinda lounged against a raft of immense, ruffled pink pillows. She had let her hair down and her soft curls framed her heart-shaped face. She looked almost vulnerable, and surprisingly young—despite what she had put me through, I found myself wondering what she was really like when she wasn't busy being a manipulative, magic-stealing monster. She had to be pretty desperate for friends, if Dorothy was the closest thing she had to someone to hang out with.

"That took you long enough, Jellia," she said sweetly. "You may bring the tray over here."

"Yes, Your Eminence," I said, trying not to trip on the carpets as I crossed the room.

"How are you finding the palace, Jellia?" she asked as she took the tray from me and settled it on her lap. Was she serious? I looked at her out of the corner of my eye. Her face was serene. She *was* serious.

"It's as lovely as you are, Your Eminence," I said cautiously.

She smiled. "You *are* very clever, aren't you, Jellia? Tell me honestly—were you happy working for Dorothy?"

I kept my eyes on the floor. We were definitely on thin ice. What did she want from me?

"I'm always happy," I said, and she actually laughed.

"Look at me, Jellia." Cautiously, I looked up. She was still laughing, holding her bowl of ice cream so carelessly that it was in danger of spilling over onto her dress. "Jellia, I know you're not stupid. And I *know* you're not happy. Dorothy is . . ." She paused. "Dorothy can be quite difficult," she said, although I didn't think that was what she had meant to say originally. "But you have run her palace very well, and remained very modest—admirable qualities, in someone with your power."

Was this about her machine? Or the magic she was mining? I had plenty of practice keeping my expression blank after all the time I'd worked for Dorothy, but something told me Glinda was going to be a lot harder to fool. "Perhaps you can be of more use to me than I thought," she mused. She looked down at her ice

cream and a sudden frown marred her perfect features. "But this
ice cream has melted, Jellia, because you took so long to bring
it to me."

"But Your Eminence, we've been talking—"

Her frown deepened. "Now, Jellia, I don't want to hear your
excuses. I want you to do better next time. Is that clear?"

"Yes, Your Eminence. It won't happen again," I said. Next
time I would have to use a spell on her sundae to keep it cold.
No one had said anything about a ban on using magic in *Glinda's*
palace.

Glinda studied me and sighed deeply—a sigh that seemed
to come all the way from where her puffy, feathered, pink
high-heeled slippers dangled from her perfectly manicured pink-
glitter-coated toes. "Tell me, Jellia. Do you *enjoy* your job?"

I blinked. "Enjoy, Your Eminence?"

"I mean, do you take real *satisfaction* in your work? At the
end of the day, do you feel pride in what you've accomplished?
Is it meaningful for you to be here?"

I had no idea how to respond to this. "I'm sorry, Your Eminence, I don't mean to be disrespectful—it's just that it's my first
day, and I—"

"Because the thing is, Jellia, I get the sense from you that
you just don't *care*," Glinda interrupted, her fructose-sweet voice
tinted with genuine sadness. "It's as though you're just going
through the motions—you're clearly very smart, and very effi-
cient, but I need you to understand that we're all at the palace
because we want to be here. Because our work is meaningful to

us. I give my heart every day to magic, Jellia"—at this, Glinda laid her beautifully manicured hands over the bony area of her sternum that I imagined housed this, also doubtless pink, organ—"I show up for my work with joy, Jellia, because there simply isn't anything I'd rather do than be Glinda the Good Witch. But you—I think you'd almost rather be anywhere else. Mistakes like this"—she indicated the bowl of melted ice cream with a gentle, regal nod of her golden head—"tell me that you think you're too *good* to be here with us. Don't get me wrong, you're very competent. But I need to feel that you *care*, Jellia. I need to see *caring* from you. Can you do that for me?"

"I—I think so, Your Eminence," I said, utterly confused.

"I'm sure things were different when you worked for Dorothy," Glinda said, her voice losing none of its gentle sweetness. "But here, we don't make mistakes." In her hands, the sundae bowl began to glow red-hot, and the ice cream melted into a steaming swirl. Without changing her expression, Glinda threw the bowl directly at me.

I flung up my arms without thinking, as if to protect myself—and felt a strange buzzing surge through me. The air around me shimmered, and to my astonishment, the bowl shattered in mid-flight, as though it had hit an invisible brick wall. With a series of little pops, the fragments vanished before they even hit the floor. A few blobs of pink ice cream hung forlornly in the air before they, too, disappeared with a faint, sticky noise. I stared in disbelief, but Glinda was smiling.

"I thought so," she said. "Oh, I had a feeling about you, Jellia, and I'm simply never wrong when I have a feeling."

I was too startled to keep up my perfect servant act. "What—happened?"

"All in good time," Glinda said, and this time the gentleness in her voice seemed almost real. "I moved too quickly with you this afternoon. But there's much, much more to you than meets the eye, and together we're going to find out just how much you can help me."

"I don't understand," I said.

"Leave the understanding to me," she said briskly. "You're dismissed, Jellia. We'll have plenty of time to perfect your—education." She waved a hand in my direction and turned back to the window.

Nox took one look at me when I finally found my way back to the kitchen and told me I was done working for the day. His demeanor was as gruff as ever, but I thought I saw sympathy in his eyes. "What happened up there?"

"I—to be honest, I'm not sure," I said, and told him everything—Glinda's sudden niceness, the ice cream, the thing I'd done to somehow make it disappear. When I got to that part, his eyebrows went up.

"You mean, you did magic?"

"But it wasn't something I did on purpose," I said. Before Dorothy and her rules, everyone in Oz had used magic all the time in the palace for little things, like polishing the silver, or making the flowers in the garden grow a particularly vibrant shade. Ozma had magic, of course—Ozma was a fairy, with all the powers of Oz at her disposal. And Dorothy had power, too: the power to control the weather, set the seasons to her liking, bewitch the Scarecrow's weird experiments into more than just lifeless ideas strung together out of wood and wire—though none of us really knew where Dorothy's power came from, or if she'd had it in the Other Place. But what I'd done in Glinda's room was something different from the common household magic all the servants shared. It was far more powerful—and seemingly out of my control.

"You've never done anything like that before?"

"I don't think so," I said, and then stopped. I *had* done something like this once before when I was a little girl. I'd been playing with some hand-me-down dolls that the other servants had given me. I was lonely—I was the only child in the palace, and one day I'd decided I wanted some real live friends, so I made my dolls come alive. I still don't know how I knew the magic to make that happen, but I do remember when Ozma walked in on me and my animated friends. She'd instantly made them go back to being just stuffed dolls, and she'd made me swear to never do that again—and to never let anyone else know that I could do something like that. I always wanted to make her happy, so I'd never again tried to summon that kind of magic—I didn't want to upset Ozma.

I'd always kept the extent of my magic a secret from everyone else in the palace. Adding a little extra shine to the silverware was no stretch for most Ozians, but ever since that day, I knew that my own powers were different—and stronger—from everyone else in the palace. Except Dorothy. And Ozma.

"You're different, aren't you," Nox said, interrupting my reverie. I didn't confirm his suspicions—he seemed to know without me saying anything. "That must be why we—" He cut himself off.

"Why what? And who's *we?*"

"I promise I'll tell you everything when it's time," he said. "But for now you'll have to trust me."

"Right," I said. "Clear as mud." I sighed, annoyed, but whatever he knew, he wasn't going to tell me anything else now.

"You've had a long day," he said. "Why don't you get some rest, and you can get a fresh start tomorrow." He lowered his voice again. "Whatever she says to you—whatever she lets you see—don't trust her. Understood? She can act vulnerable, but it's just an act."

Nox summoned another Munchkin to show me to my room in the servants' quarters. It was tiny, like my room at Dorothy's, but it had none of the comforts of my room at home, where I'd spent my entire life. It was bleak and bare bones, with just a narrow bed, a low dresser, and a single small window that overlooked the palace gardens. The room was a stark reminder of how different my new life was, but at least here, I could be alone. *Just the summer*, I told myself again. *I just have to make it through the summer.* I collapsed on the bed, too exhausted to even change out of my dress, and fell immediately into sleep.

SEVEN

The next day the little bejeweled bird woke me up with a horrific shriek right in my ear. I sat bolt upright, my heart galloping in my chest, and it took me several minutes to remember where I was and what had happened to me. I looked down in dismay at my wrinkled, dirty dress. The bird fell silent after its initial blast, and I realized it was just some kind of alarm, not a call from Glinda. I splashed cold water on my face, brushed my hair, and muttered a quick spell over my dress; the previous day's grime melted away, and the wrinkles dropped from the fabric. I didn't exactly feel my usual chipper self, but the night's rest had loosened up some of my aching muscles and done away with my headache at least. I put my hair up in a demure twist, pinched my cheeks to add a bit of color, and ran down to the kitchen.

Nox was already there, going over a complicated-looking chart spread out on the big counter. "You're late," he said tersely without looking up as I entered the kitchen.

"I'm sorry," I said. "I didn't wake up until the alarm."

"It's not an alarm," he said. "It's the signal that means you should be at your post already. Don't let it happen again."

"I won't."

Finally, he looked up, and his expression softened a little. "I'm just working out the schedule for the rest of the day," he said in a low voice, gesturing to the chart. "I'll try to keep you out of Glinda's way today. After yesterday, I imagine you could use a break. I can't do much if she summons you directly, but at least this way you won't be right in front of her. I'll try to keep her occupied. Hopefully she won't come after you until the afternoon." In a more ordinary tone—one the cooks could easily overhear—Nox explained the workings of the palace to me. "This chart is posted in the kitchen with the day's schedule. Sometimes we have various guests and dignitaries who are served meals in the dining hall, but right now Glinda is here alone. If she doesn't have guests, she usually eats in her chambers. Servants eat in the kitchen after the main meal is served. I'm sure we're a much smaller staff than you're used to in the Emerald City; we all do a bit of everything. You'll meet the rest of the maids today at dinner. But in the meantime . . ." He trailed off and studied me thoughtfully. His dark hair fell into his eyes, and he had that kind of mournful, beseeching look about him that would have suggested poetic depth to a girl with a slightly less pragmatic disposition than mine. I imagined he probably did pretty well among the ladies of the palace, although Glinda couldn't have had much interest in his considerable charms if she kept him relegated to the kitchen. Then again, it was hard to imagine the words *Glinda* and *romance* in the same sentence. I couldn't exactly picture her swooning over photos of heart-throbs, or waiting anxiously at fancy restaurants for her dinner date to show up. I wondered suddenly if Glinda's interest in the Wizard was more than academic—after all, they were more or less equals. But it seemed more likely that she was trying to rope him into her crazy magic-mining plan somehow.

Nox was looking at me with one eyebrow raised, and I real-ized I'd been staring at him. "Sure," I said, trying to remember what we were talking about. Meeting the maids—schedul-ing—dinner. "Dinner! Do I need to do anything to set up? At Dorothy's my job was pretty . . ." I waved my hand around. "I mean, I was responsible for basically everything. Although Dorothy didn't care what color her food was. I might need some help with the pink thing."

But he shook his head. "That's really what I'm here for," he said.

I couldn't help the note of petulance that crept into my voice. "Then why am *I* here? Really?"

He paused and looked over his shoulder. Right. The cooks. Eyes and ears for Glinda everywhere. Or else he was using them as an excuse not to tell me what he knew, what he meant by "we" yesterday. "Glinda wants to know how she can use you," he said softly.

I saw out of the corner of my eye one of the cooks half turn in order to hear us better.

"It's just that I want to be certain I do the best possible job for Glinda," I said loudly, in a sugary voice. "It's so important to me that I serve Her Eminence well." One corner of Nox's mouth twitched, and I realized belatedly he was hiding a smile. *Score one for me*, I thought. I'd made the Stone Man himself crack a grin. He reached forward, as if to touch my hand where it rested on the table, and then seemed to change his mind and picked up his pen again.

"I'll send you out to the gardens for the morning," he said. "You don't need to worry about tending them or anything like that. Most of the landscaping is done by magic, and there are a few Munchkin gardeners who take care of the rest. But here in the kitchen, we use herbs and vegetables from the main garden, so you should make yourself familiar with it."

"What should I do if Glinda calls me while I'm outside? She was"—I paused, making sure my voice was under control— "unhappy with me for my tardiness last night."

"Punctuality is very important to Glinda," Nox said drily. "But you should be safe for the morning, at least. Take this basket with you. Here's what we'll need for the day," he said, handing me a basket from a shelf overhead and a neatly printed list of various vegetables, fruits, and herbs. "I imagine it will take you a few hours to find everything," he added. That wasn't even close to true, I thought, looking over the short list he'd handed me. He was basically giving me the morning off to wander around outside. If I didn't know better, I would have hugged him. "Yes sir," I said, and he smiled.

"Nox," he said. "Please. There's no need for formality in the kitchen." And he smiled at me again—a real smile this time, winning and full of charm. I couldn't help myself; I smiled back.

EIGHT

Dorothy's palace in the Emerald City had gardens far grander than Glinda's, though never in a million years would I have been dumb enough to point that out. Even so, Glinda's gardens were nothing to sneeze at. A little heavy on the pink flowers for my taste, of course—rows and rows of sweet-smelling singing roses in a dozen variations of the shade; towering pink lilac trees, which released visible puffs of perfumed smoke at intervals; an orchard full of pink-barked trees, each of which bore a different pink fruit: peaches, apples, hot-pink pomegranates (points for creativity, I guess, even if not for realism). There were even tiny pink flowers that covered the winding paths through the decorative portion of the gardens like a carpet, and when you stepped on them, they shot out little jets of pink glitter. By the time I got back to the kitchen I was going to look like a disco ball.

It took me a while to find the vegetable garden, which was more or less hidden behind a low, pink brick wall, and which bore little resemblance to the rest of the landscaping. The plants here had a distinctly practical feel: unlike the rest of the gardens, which were beautiful but obviously designed to cater to Glinda's unnatural passion for pink, these more humble rows of vegetables and herbs were comforting in their hominess.

I'd been so young when my parents died that I had no memory of them. All I knew was what Ozma had told me: that I'd been born in a small village in the Oz countryside, to people who were too humble to leave me anything other than my name. Ozma had taken me in because I had no other family and nowhere else to go.

Wandering the rows of the vegetable garden, I wondered if my own parents had grown food like this; if maybe they'd sat down every night to a dinner of crisp green lettuce and ruby-red tomatoes pulled from the earth just moments earlier. I rarely thought about my parents—what good did it do me to wonder?—but for a moment in Glinda's garden I stopped to consider what my life might have been like if they hadn't died. Maybe I'd be out in the countryside somewhere, lying in a field napping underneath the warm sun, or reading a book. Maybe my life would be my own, not Dorothy's. But thinking like that was useless, and bound to get me nowhere. There was no point in crying about it. My life was what it was. There was no way I'd ever get away from Glinda, or Dorothy, or whatever they had in store for Oz.

I was lucky to even *have* a job; since Dorothy came back, there were rumors of Munchkins going hungry for the first time in Oz's history. The winged monkeys were little more than zombies these days, only too eager to obey whatever the Tin Woodman ordered them to do—even if it meant harassing innocent citizens. Some of the servants at the palace talked about friends and relatives who were out of work—something that had never happened before in our history. It was like Dorothy had brought some terrible disease with her from the Other Place, one you couldn't see.

I shook my head, trying to rid myself of such dark thoughts. There was nothing I could do to solve Oz's problems from Glinda's garden. And it was such a relief to be outside, alone, with the sun on my shoulders and the trilling of birdsong in my ears. As Dorothy's head maid, I'd had little time to myself in the Emerald City, and I'd imagined that Glinda would be watching me like a hawk out here. But Nox had given me the gift of a morning out from under her scrutiny, and I was determined not to let a second of it go to waste.

When I had filled my basket to Nox's specifications I went out of the vegetable garden back into the flower garden. Despite the overwhelming influence of Glinda's dubious taste, it was still a beautiful place on a sunny morning. I sat with my back against one of the fruit trees and closed my eyes. It wouldn't do to fall asleep out here, but surely no one would notice if I took a moment to rest before I went back inside to face whatever Glinda had in store for me next.

Suddenly, the sinister, dulcet tones of Glinda's voice cut through the serene air, and I froze in terror. "Of course, we're so delighted to see you," she trilled.

How had she found me out here? Had Nox sent her after me? Why hadn't she just used the bird pin megaphone? I flung myself up against the nearest tree, my heart pounding, as she continued.

"We have so much to discuss, my *dear* friend. . . ." I craned my neck around the tree, desperately hoping she couldn't see. She obviously wasn't talking to me, and I didn't recognize the little man at her side. But in an instant, I knew exactly who he was.

The Wizard, I thought.

NINE

Glinda strolled casually through her pink pom-pom of a garden, the Wizard by her side. He was dressed snappily in a brocade suit with a top hat, and he carried a silver-tipped cane that he swung as he walked. Though they were a ways away, and thankfully the tree hid me from their view, I could hear most of what she was saying. ". . . and of course I'm certain Dorothy and I would be only too happy to work with you to clarify a vision of Oz's future, if only we knew something more about your intentions. I know things ended on a . . . *difficult* note during your last visit to the palace, but there's no reason to continue what I know was simply a terrible misunderstanding. Dorothy is just torn up about it. As, of course, am I."

Glinda's voice was so sweet it was practically dripping syrup, but even from where I was sitting I could hear the steely resolve underneath her words. The Wizard made a noncommittal noise and Glinda tried again. "I mean, you haven't even told us how long you plan to *be* in Oz!" she cooed, adding a giggle for effect that sounded more sinister than flirtatious.

What on earth was the Wizard doing here—and what could he possibly want with Glinda and Dorothy? I quickly refocused my attention as his words carried across the garden.

"I'm sure we'll have plenty to discuss," he was saying. "But as you know, the well-being of Oz is of utmost importance to me. It remains to be seen whether Dorothy is the leader we need in this difficult time."

"Certainly she's young," Glinda interrupted smoothly, "but she was clever enough to defeat you, Wizard, with all due respect. And please, you can't imagine she's to be the true leader of Oz. That role has always fallen to those with real power. She's simply a heroine of the people. They cherish her. They're only too happy to obey her every command. But make no mistake, my dear friend, those commands come from me."

The Wizard laughed. "Dorothy's arrival was . . . foreseen, Glinda. But do not make the mistake of underestimating her. I know you think you control her, but she most certainly has plans of her own—and she's far more dangerous than you can imagine. And what's this I hear of your magic mining? You know Oz doesn't have the infrastructure to support that kind of a power draw. In fact—"

They were moving away from me and though I strained so hard to hear the rest of what he was saying I nearly fell over, his words were unintelligible. I sat back against my tree, my mind racing. I hadn't heard enough to tell me much, but it seemed more than possible that my initial assumption about the Wizard was wrong.

He hadn't seemed pleased with Glinda at all—and her own wheedling, ingratiating tone suggested she was well aware of the fact. Were they working together, or was she trying to convince him to side with her? What did it mean if he'd been in Oz all along? Were they double-crossing Dorothy—or was he double-crossing Dorothy *and* Glinda? And it seemed pretty clear that Glinda really was trying to steal Oz's magic. Whatever was going on, it was definitely something big. And maybe I didn't want to know the answer. It was far easier to be a servant girl, oblivious to the political machinations of the real powers of Oz. What could I do to stop them?

And then I had a sudden, terrible image of Ozma, wandering with unseeing eyes through the halls of Dorothy's palace, and my heart sank all the way into my scuffed boots. Who was I kidding? Of course I cared. If there was anything I could do to help Ozma, to turn her back into the vibrant, powerful, generous ruler she'd once been . . . Well, there wasn't much I wouldn't give to have the palace back the way it should be. And when you got right down to it, that meant no Dorothy. And no so-called Good Witch either.

I'd been in the garden for a long time, and even though Nox had cut me a break this morning, I didn't want to push my luck. I picked up my basket, looked around one last time to make sure Glinda and the Wizard were out of sight, and hurried back to the kitchen.

Nox was there, more or less where I'd left him, although now instead of going over the schedule he was overseeing the decoration of four enormous pink cakes that the Munchkins must have baked that morning. Each cake had been frosted in a slightly different shade of pastel pink, and a young Munchkin baker was painstakingly creating elaborate portraits of Glinda on each one—a radiantly beautiful Glinda holding a bouquet of enormous pink roses; Glinda, looking benevolent, distributing pink cupcakes to beaming Munchkin children; Glinda with a festive background of fireworks and a cheering crowd; Glinda reclining on her immense pink bed, looking sultry.

The portraits were so detailed they looked as though she was about to spring to life. I gave an involuntary shiver. Nox looked up as I came into the kitchen and set my basket on the counter, careful not to jostle the surface and upset the Munchkin's work.

"That last one seems a little scandalous," I said without thinking. Nox raised an eyebrow at me and the Munchkin looked startled. "Nice pictures, though," I added to the Munchkin. It wasn't his fault Glinda was a power-hungry despot trying to suck Oz dry of all its magic. He was just trying to do his job and stay alive.

"Remember what I told you yesterday?" Nox asked in a warning tone.

"Yeah," I said. "I'm just feeling a little revolutionary, I guess." The Munchkin dropped his container of frosting and stared at me in fear, and Nox's eyes widened. He rounded the table and grabbed my arm.

"That's enough," he hissed in my ear. I shook him off angrily.

"No, you know what's enough?" I snarled at him. "This charade is enough. Glinda is destroying Oz, and you know it. We can't let her get away with this! She's the one who's making Dorothy into a monster, and she's the one who's stealing our ma—" Nox clapped a hand over my mouth and wrapped his other arm around me.

"I said that's *enough*," he snapped. The Munchkin was staring at us, his mouth open. "Get back to work," Nox told him. "I'll deal with this. Understood?" The Munchkin nodded, turning back to his cake. Nox dragged me outside into the hallway.

"Listen to me, and listen carefully," he said in a low voice. "Talking like that will get you killed, do you understand? I know you don't understand why—I know I haven't been able to tell you everything. But you can't die. We need you."

"So that's why you've taken an interest in my welfare?" I was suddenly furious. "I can't die because you *need* me? For some mysterious cause? I don't even know what the cause *is*, Nox! I just know Glinda has some kind of crazy, sinister plan for me, and I have magic I don't understand, and what if Glinda tries to put me back into that terrible machine, and—"

"Look," he said so quietly I had to strain to hear him. "I know. Believe me, I know. I'm on your side, Jellia. But you can't draw attention to yourself like that. You're risking your life. You need to be strategic." He looked as if he was struggling with a decision, and then he sighed. "There are other forces at work here you don't know about. Just—you're not the only one in Oz who feels this way, Jellia. Be patient."

"Don't tell me to be patient," I retorted, and then I thought about what he'd just said. "Wait, do you mean the Wizard?"

His gaze sharpened and he pulled me in again. "What do you know about the Wizard?"

"He's here. I saw him. In the garden with Glinda." He looked around, his eyes wide, as if checking to see if the Wizard were standing behind us, but the hallway was empty.

"Tell me everything," he said. "But not here. It's not safe. Meet me—" He stopped, thinking. "Meet me in the garden. At sunset."

"Why should I trust you? Why do you even want to know?"

He laughed. "You shouldn't trust me. You shouldn't trust anyone in this palace. But I give you my word that I'm on your side. You'll have to decide for yourself if that's enough. I can tell you more tonight."

The tiny bird clipped to my dress let loose with a piercing shriek and we jumped apart. "Jellia!" Glinda cooed, her voice so loud I wanted to clap my hands over my ears. "I need you at once, Jellia!" I stared at Nox, my heart beating hard.

"You'd better go," he said, his face worried.

"Do you think she—"

"I don't know. You have to be careful, Jellia. Promise me you'll be careful."

"I'll try."

"Do better than that." The concern in his voice was genuine, I was sure of it.

"No promises," I said, and then Glinda's magic yanked me away from the hallway. The last I saw of him was his handsome features twisted into a mask of worry.

TEN

Glinda was in her chambers, in a terrible temper—I could only guess because of the way things had gone that morning with the Wizard. She'd torn through her closet in a fit of pique, and the floor of her room was strewn with ball gowns and high-heeled shoes and gem-studded necklaces. "Pick that up," she said as soon as I materialized in her room, dizzy and nauseous from the spell she'd used to transport me through the palace. She sat on her bed huffily and watched as I obediently collected the dresses off the floor and hung them carefully in her huge closet.

She was wearing a revealing gown that plunged deeply, showing a considerable amount of cleavage, and her soft strawberry-blond hair hung loose around her shoulders. Her pretty features had a childish set to them, and she looked more like a sulky teenager than a terrifying witch.

I wondered what it was like being Glinda. She had outlasted all of Oz's other witches, and from what she'd told the Wizard in the garden, she was the real power behind Oz. When I was growing up in Oz, she'd always had a reputation for being the Good Witch, but I had a more than sneaking suspicion that she was responsible for whatever had transformed Ozma from our regal, powerful, beloved princess to the vacant shell she was now. But in a strange way, as much as I hated Glinda, I also felt sorry for her. There was something deep in those blue eyes that looked almost like loneliness.

"You know," she said conversationally, "we'll be having another guest soon, Jellia." My back was to her; I could feel her eyes boring into me as I gathered up her scattered jewelry.

"Is that so, Your Eminence," I said politely.

"An old friend of yours, I believe. The Scarecrow."

"The Scarecrow is coming here?" I couldn't keep the surprise out of my voice, and I could tell Glinda was pleased to have caught me off guard.

"Of course, Jellia. Who do you think invented the magic-mining machine?" I flinched involuntarily, remembering the nightmare of my journey to her palace. She examined her nails, a tiny frown marring her perfect features. "I really don't think magic makes for the best manicures," she mused. "Why don't you try, Jellia?"

"As you wish, Your Eminence," I said. She summoned a tray of nail polish out of the air with a snap of her fingers and leaned back against her pillows.

"You pick," she said. "I don't care anymore." There was something in her voice that was so genuine and vulnerable that

I looked up at her in surprise. I examined the bottles of polish—all pink, of course—and selected a vibrant coral. She held out one delicate hand and closed her eyes, and I went to work. The repetitive motion of brushing on the polish was almost soothing, and Glinda's silence was a relief. My mind wandered, taking me back to the Emerald City, to the days when Ozma ruled Oz and my life had been much less complicated—and filled with much more joy. Ozma had taken me once to the Rainbow Falls, and I remembered now the feel of the spray on my face as we stood on a rocky promontory overlooking the majestic, vibrant colors of the falls. The air had been cool and gentle, the breeze scented with Ozma's heady perfume of bergamot and sandalwood; the cobalt and crimson and deepest emerald of the falls glowing vividly underneath a clear blue sky.

"My goodness, Jellia," Glinda murmured, her words snapping me back to myself. "What a talent you have." I looked down at her nails and saw that somehow, without realizing it, I'd painted a perfectly detailed series of tiny pictures on each nail: Ozma looking out over the Rainbow Falls, the Lion bounding across a field, his heavy golden mane so perfectly rendered that I could almost see it moving as he leapt; the periwinkle field where Glinda had set up her terrible machine . . . Each image was impossibly lifelike. My hands tingled. Glinda was regarding me with an expression I couldn't quite read: triumph, but something else, too, something sadder. "You have real power, Jellia," she said quietly. "You have the very magic of Oz itself moving through you. Did you really never know?"

"I don't—I don't understand," I said, dazed. What had I just done?

"You will," Glinda said. "When the time is right, Jellia, you will." Her tone was gentle, but her words sent a chill all the way through me. I couldn't meet her eyes.

"You've done very well, Jellia," she said. "You may go back to the kitchen for now. But I think perhaps it's time for you to take on more . . . responsibility. The Scarecrow and I have much to discuss." I couldn't control my shudder, and Glinda chuckled, all trace of her vulnerability gone. "Sleep well tonight, Jellia," she murmured.

ELEVEN

That evening, I could barely finish my dinner. My stomach was knotted in fear, and my head was a jumble of conflicting thoughts. Finally, the meal was mercifully over. When I was sure no one was paying attention, I slipped out a side door into the gardens. There was Nox under the same tree I'd hid behind to eavesdrop on the Wizard and Glinda that morning. His back was to me as he scanned the garden, on the lookout for anyone who might see us.

He heard my footsteps and turned as I approached the tree. "We have to be quick," he said in a low voice. "If we're both gone for too long at the same time, someone will put two and two together. It's not safe for us to be seen together like this."

"Why would Glinda suspect you of anything? What exactly is going on here? Who are you?"

He raised an eyebrow. "What do you mean?"

"You know who I am. You seem to know more about my

magic than I do. You know more than you should about what Glinda's doing. You haven't told me the truth about anything since the moment I came here. And if Glinda has some plan for me, and you know what it is—"

He cut me off. "Jellia, I know how difficult this must be for you. And believe me, I'm not trying to lie to you—it's just that the less you know about some things, the better. For your own safety."

"What do you mean, 'about some things'?" I asked, my fear and confusion turning to anger. "Nox, what are you *talking* about?"

He took a deep breath. "I'm talking about defeating Glinda," he said quietly. "About sending Dorothy back to the Other Place. About restoring Oz to what it once was—and what it should be."

Defeat Glinda. Get rid of Dorothy. I couldn't believe he'd said it out loud. We weren't just meeting to swap secrets—Nox was openly talking treason. But if Nox was serious, he couldn't be acting on his own.

"Nox, what are you planning? And how does it involve me?"

He shook his head. "I'm sorry, Jellia. There's so much I can't tell you—not yet. Glinda brought you here because she knows your magic is special. And she wants to keep an eye on you because she knows we'll reach out to you—and she can use you to find us."

"Who's 'we'?" I asked. "What aren't you telling me?"

"You'll find out when it's time," he said. "But not now. I'm sorry. I know it's a lot to ask of you, but it's for your own safety."

I shook my head. "A lot to ask doesn't begin to cover it." But for some reason, I was willing to give him a chance. And if he truly knew of a way to bring the real Ozma back, I would do whatever it took to help him.

I thought again of being at the falls with Ozma. Of what my life had been like when she ruled Oz. Of how everything had been different—and better. "Promise me you'll tell me everything," I said. "Not now—fine. I understand that. But soon."

"I promise," he said instantly. "When the time is right, you'll know. Now tell me everything you saw this morning in the garden. If the Wizard is back—if he's allied with Glinda—we have to know."

"I'm not sure, but I don't think they're working together," I said. I quickly told him everything I'd overheard of Glinda and the Wizard's conversation. Nox's frown deepened as I talked, and when I was done he let out his breath in a deep sigh.

"I wish I knew what it all meant," he mused. "But it sounds like the Wizard is refusing to forge an alliance with Glinda. At least for now. And that's good news, I think."

"What do you know about the Wizard?"

"Nobody knows anything about the Wizard, except that he's from the Other Place. Dorothy's world."

"And he can send Dorothy back?"

"I don't know for sure. If Glinda brought her here, she might be the only one with the power to return her. But if he isn't helping Glinda, he might be willing to help us—and that could make all the difference." He paused, thinking. "Just keep doing what you're doing," he said finally. "Glinda wants you close to her for now, and I don't think she'll do anything to hurt you until she knows more about your magic."

That wasn't exactly comforting. "And then what?"

"For now, you'll have to wait. Listen, we have to go back inside. They'll miss us soon. Wait a few minutes before you follow me." And with that, he turned around and walked off through the twilit garden.

I sighed and watched him go, my head spinning. Revolutionary conspiracies, bargains with wizards, all these secrets—it was going to be hard to find my way through all of this to the truth. But Nox was right—I didn't have much of a choice. If he was willing to tell me that he was part of some secret group planning to send Dorothy back to the Other Place, that meant he was putting his life in my hands. I had no other option but to return the favor.

TWELVE

A few days after Glinda brought up his visit, the Scarecrow arrived. He constructed a makeshift laboratory on the palace grounds and shut himself away as soon as it was completed. Glinda spent long afternoons holed up with him there, and sinister sounds of clanking and hissing emitted from the hastily constructed shack at all hours.

The Scarecrow never slept. He didn't need to. The servants took turns bringing him his meals at his lab. One of the girls didn't come back until the next morning—that night, we heard terrible screams from the Scarecrow's laboratory, and at breakfast the servant girl was dead-eyed and silent. Nox sent her to her room to rest, but when he asked her what had happened in the laboratory, she just shook her head and refused to talk. I knew Nox was as curious as I was, but there was nothing we could do without putting ourselves at risk, and so we went about our duties and kept our eyes open.

My days at Glinda's palace stretched into weeks, and slowly I relaxed. Nox was right: Glinda kept me close. After the day when I'd painted her nails, she declared that I was "indispensable." She demoted her previous personal maid, and now every morning she summoned me to her pink chambers and demanded I help her with her hair and makeup, lace her into her tight corsets, and offer her advice on which of her endless dresses to wear. Her obsession with fashion and her looks was even bigger than Dorothy's, but she didn't need my help. She had more innate fashion sense than Dorothy and she always picked out the perfect ensemble on her first attempt. After just a few days of composing obsequious compliments and picking up after her as she discarded clothes on her bedroom floor, I was exhausted—but I couldn't let her see it, and so I made my face into a mask of good cheer. Sometimes I'd see flashes of the other, secret Glinda—the lonely witch who'd let me paint her nails—but they were few and far between; and she kept the powerful witch who'd strapped me into her terrifying machine well hidden, too. I had to remind myself not to be lulled into a false sense of security. I met Nox again in the garden a few more times, but I had nothing to report. Other than the Scarecrow's secret project, there was nothing out of the ordinary happening in the palace.

If Glinda was somehow pulling Dorothy's strings, she was careful not to let me see it. She spent her afternoons in the garden, or holding court in her elaborate throne room, where she lounged on an immense, overstuffed pink chaise longue and nibbled pink bonbons off a pink tray. Messengers flitted back and forth between her palace and the Emerald City, reporting on the daily doings of the metropolis—Dorothy's elaborate banquets and balls, her increasing number of new decrees, another statue erected in her honor. Once, as yet another messenger delivered yet another flowery speech on Dorothy's magnificence, I saw the muscles of Glinda's jaw tighten, and I wondered if she regretted her choice of a puppet. For a moment, I almost felt sorry for her. Glinda and I had at least one thing in common: we both thought Dorothy was insufferable.

And then, one morning one of the Tin Woodman's soldiers arrived at the palace carrying an elaborate scroll, which he unfurled dramatically and read from in a deep, mechanical voice. "By order of Her Majesty, the Regally Benevolent and Eternally Beautiful Dorothy, Rightful Ruler of Oz and Mistress of the Deadly Desert—"

"The introduction is unnecessary," Glinda interrupted smoothly.

The soldier sputtered and cleared his throat with a noise like a teakettle whistling. "Dorothy demands that her maid be returned to her," he said in a more subdued tone.

Glinda raised one elegant eyebrow. "Dorothy *demands*?"

The soldier shifted his weight from one metal foot to the other, clanking nervously. "That's what it says here, Your Eminence," he said.

Glinda's nostrils flared and she lifted one delicate hand from her couch. For a moment, I thought she might blow the soldier to smithereens. But then her expression cleared, and she smiled.

"Of course," she said. "It's been so wonderful to have Jellia here that I'd simply gotten used to her. She's been tremendously helpful." The soldier and I exchanged glances, both of us unsure if we were expected to respond to this. "I don't know what I'll do without her," Glinda continued, "but you may tell Dorothy I'll send her home tomorrow."

My heart leapt in my chest, and then sank again. I'd done it— I'd survived, and it was finally time to go back. But what about Nox and his secret plans to restore order to Oz? What could I do from the Emerald City, if he was here? And what did I have waiting for me with Dorothy when I got back?

Word of my pending departure traveled quickly through the palace, and that night he pulled me aside after dinner. I expected him to give me instructions, or some kind of message, but all he said was, "Stay safe. I'm worried she has something else up her sleeve."

"Wonderful," I muttered. "That's comforting."

"I'm looking out for you," he insisted. "Don't do anything foolish. But don't worry."

I nodded, but all I could do was worry.

THIRTEEN

The morning of my departure Glinda summoned me to her room as usual. She was already dressed in a low-cut pink dress that was fairly simple—for her, anyway. Her eyes had a dangerous glitter to them, and my heart sank. After all these weeks of relative calm, the real Glinda was back.

She wasn't alone—the Scarecrow was there with her. His gangly frame was stuffed into his habitual too-small suit, and the clothes combined with his painted-on face, button eyes, and the bits of straw sticking out from under his hat should have made him look charming and harmless. But there was nothing harmless about the Scarecrow.

"As you know, our dear friend has been helping me with a project that's very close to my heart," Glinda cooed. "And before I return you to Dorothy, he'd like to see all his hard work come to fruition. I hope you're aware of what a tremendous honor it is for you to be asked to help him."

"Me?" I asked uncertainly, and Glinda laughed.

"My dear Jellia!" she burbled merrily. "You don't think I've forgotten about how eager you were to do your duty for Oz, do you? We've been working nonstop all week to perfect the machine I designed that will siphon Oz's leftover magic to where it's needed most."

My eyes widened in terror and I took an involuntary step backward. "I thought the machine didn't work, Your Eminence," I whispered. Her brow furrowed with displeasure.

"Jellia, that skeptical attitude is simply hateful, and I won't tolerate it. Of course my machine works. It simply needed some—adjustments." She smiled at the Scarecrow. "Now, are you ready?"

Before I could open my mouth to answer, everything went blurry, and I felt as though I was being pulled through a tub of molasses while trying to cross a stormy sea in a rowboat. When the world solidified around me again, Glinda, the Scarecrow, and I had been transported to a meadow of pale yellow grass, dotted here and there with bright red flowers that grew more thickly at the meadow's center. The air had the faint, ozoney crackle of magic. A handful of Munchkins were busy setting up what I recognized with a sinking heart as a simpler and more compact version of the mechanical apparatus she'd used on me on the journey to her palace.

"You know what they say, Jellia," Glinda said, smiling at my stricken expression. "If at first you don't succeed—try, try again." She seized my arm and dragged me, struggling, toward the machine, the Scarecrow following after us. "You should be very honored, Jellia," Glinda added. "Even though he's terribly busy, the Scarecrow agreed to come out and help me make a few adjustments to my magic drill. Isn't that generous of him? He knows how important the well-being of Oz is, and how much this magic will help keep Oz the wonderful place it is."

As Glinda dragged me closer the Scarecrow turned to look at us, his awful button eyes glinting as he examined me like I was one of his science experiments. "This is the fairy?" he grated.

"Only part," Glinda said, "but she'll have to do." My mind reeled. Part fairy? Me? But that was impossible.

"It may not be enough. I've already told you, Munchkin labor—"

"Is inefficient," Glinda interrupted sharply.

"Perhaps. But it may be the only way to operate the machine."

"I didn't bring you all the way out here to give me excuses," Glinda said brightly. "There's no excuse for this negativity when it comes to serving Oz."

The Scarecrow shrugged. "I made the adjustments you specified, but I haven't had enough time to experiment. Another few weeks in my laboratory, and I might have something for you. But I can't guarantee this machine will work."

"We don't have another few weeks. Dorothy wants the girl back now," Glinda said, shoving me forward into the Scarecrow's arms. "And we wouldn't want to disobey the illustrious ruler of Oz, would we? Start the machine."

His fingers closed around my arms, and I shuddered with

revulsion. It was almost impossible to believe this monster was the same lovable buffoon who'd once—briefly—governed Oz before Ozma took her rightful place on the throne. His fingers dug into my flesh as he strapped me to a smaller, more compact version of the platform Glinda had harnessed me to before and fastened a metal collar around my neck. Metal pieces curved upward from the collar and ended in rods that he inserted in my eardrums. I couldn't move my head without impaling myself, and so I gave up struggling and held myself as still as possible. His eerie, dead eyes didn't even register me as he worked. He tightened the straps that crossed my chest and stepped away from me. "It's ready," he said to Glinda, and she smiled.

"Let's begin, Jellia," she said sweetly. "Try not to let me down this time, my dear."

I braced myself but there was no preparing for the agony that followed. Excruciating waves tore through me, each one worse than the last; the metal pieces in my ears were like red-hot pokers driving into my brain. Glinda and the Scarecrow watched dispassionately as I sobbed in despair.

"She's too weak," I heard the Scarecrow say as my vision began to go dark. "I told you, it's not going to work."

"Then both of you are terrible disappointments," Glinda said coldly. "But I'm done wasting my time here. If she survives, the Munchkins can take her back to Dorothy. I have no more use for her."

The pain overwhelmed me, and then I didn't feel anything at all.

FOURTEEN

When I opened my eyes again the darkness around me was so thick there was no difference from when I'd had them closed. I was lying on my back on something hard. When I shifted cautiously, the pain shooting through my body was so awful that I gasped aloud.

"Ah, she's awake," said a gentle voice nearby, and the darkness was suffused with a cool white glow that gradually brightened until I could make out what surrounded me.

I was lying next to a clear pool in the middle of a huge cavern whose ceiling was lost somewhere in the darkness overhead. The cavern's purplish stone floor was polished smooth, as though by generations of feet, and its walls glowed with a gentle, phosphorescent light that eased the darkness around me and illuminated the person who had spoken.

I turned my head with difficulty to study her. She was the oldest person I'd ever seen; her body was round and shapeless beneath her sack-like white dress, and her face was so seamed with lines and wrinkles that it was hard to make out her features. Her hair stuck up in a silvery halo that wafted gently in the cool air like an undersea plant. "Don't try to move," she said. "You've been through quite a lot, my dear." The wrinkles around her mouth wriggled and shifted, and I realized she was smiling at me.

"What—who are you? Where am I?" I croaked, wincing as a whole new set of aches flared up in my body. In the cave's light, I could see what a mess I was. My dress was torn and bloody where the Scarecrow's harness had dug into my skin. My bare arms and legs were purpled with bruises and streaked with more blood. And every part of me hurt, from my scalp to the tips of my toes.

"You can call me Gert. Grandma Gert, if you like. But who I am and where you are can wait until you've healed. You're dying, Jellia."

"Dying?" I struggled to sit up and cried out as my broken body refused.

"Lie still." Gert's voice was gentle but firm. "What you've been through would have killed anyone without your power. Glinda's machine—"

"You know about my power?" I wheezed.

"I said lie still, Jellia." She scooped me up in her soft arms, so lightly that I barely felt the movement. It didn't seem possible that someone so soft could be so strong. She waded into the pool with me still in her arms. "This may hurt a little, my dear."

The clean, clear water of the pool rose around us. It was as warm as bathwater, but it felt thicker than ordinary water—almost like oil. Gert lowered me fully into the water and I felt it move against my skin insistently, almost as if it wanted something from me. I became more and more aware of the pain in my body—the pool was pulling it from me, bit by bit. I cried out in anguish and my open mouth filled with water; I swallowed involuntarily and felt a mouthful of the strange liquid move through my body as if it had a will of its own, worming its way through my veins.

I looked down at myself and saw that a thick, dark substance was seeping out of my pores, forming a black cloud around me that slowly dissipated in the pool. The pain in my body was slowly replaced with a warm, drowsy sense of bliss. Dimly, I felt Gert lift me up again and set me down gently at the pool's edge. The bruises and blood were gone; my skin glowed, and my ruined dress had been replaced by a thick, soft white robe. Instead of feeling broken and exhausted, I felt refreshed.

"What was that?"

Gert was looking at me with an expression that was hard to read. It almost looked like pity. Though she'd just gone into the pool with me, her clothes were dry. "Magic," she said.

"I figured that much out."

She smiled. "It's good to see you back to normal, Jellia. I must admit I was worried about you. We were aware you might encounter danger at Glinda's, but we weren't prepared for things to move so quickly. Come," she said, offering me her hand and pulling me to my feet. "It's time for some explanations." But instead of continuing to talk, she took off at a brisk pace. I had no choice but to follow her as she led me away from the healing pool and down a bewildering series of tunnels, all lit by the same glowing phosphorescence that seeped out of the walls.

Sometimes the tunnels opened up into more caverns, each one of them full of marvels: a shimmering, underground meadow, radiating silver light and dotted here and there with towering wildflowers that rose into the darkness; another pool, this one so big I couldn't make out its far side, where bright golden fish jumped and fell back into the water with a splash; a series of mysterious, enormous machines, which sent a shard of terror stabbing through me until I realized they were putting together elaborate clocks that slid past on a conveyor belt.

We were moving too fast for me to catch more than the briefest glimpse of each cavern before Gert dragged me along to the next tunnel. Finally, she stopped at a low wooden door, rapped sharply, and pushed it open without waiting for a response. I followed her into a smallish room, furnished with a huge black table and rough wooden chairs that took up most of the space. Three people sat at the table: a cloaked figure, a mean-looking old woman I didn't recognize, and Nox, whose expression was distinctly worried.

"What are *you* doing here?" I asked him.

"He saved your life," the cloaked figure said, and lowered her hood. I flung my hands up and took a step backward. Her perfect face, her heart-shaped mouth, her strawberry-blond curls—Nox hadn't saved me, he'd betrayed me. Because the woman in front of me was Glinda.

Without realizing it, I'd backed up to Gert, who held me firmly in her fleshy arms. "It's all right, Jellia," she said, her soft tone doing nothing to slow my pounding heart. "It's not her. I'd like you to meet Glamora—Glinda's twin sister."

I blinked and stared at the woman seated at the table. What Gert was saying made a kind of sense. This woman had Glinda's face, but where Glinda's eyes were like cold, hard chips of ice, hers were kindly. The set of her mouth was friendly, not cruel.

"Have a seat, Jellia," Gert said, steering me to a chair. "We have much to discuss. And I imagine you're hungry." With that, she sat down next to me and snapped her fingers, her eyes twinkling. I was used to magic, but I was still taken aback by the feast that appeared on the table almost instantaneously—big platters piled high with fruit and cheese, fragrant loaves of steaming bread accompanied by creamy butter and honey, a huge tureen of some kind of soup that smelled like heaven. Gert handed me a plate and a gleaming silver fork that she plucked out of the air, and I helped myself.

If this was going to be my last meal, I might as well make it a good one. Nox, Glamora, and Gert filled their plates, too—but the fourth person sat at the far end of the table, glaring at the food as if she expected it to bite her. I eyeballed her surreptitiously as I ate.

She looked more like a troll than a witch. Like Gert, she was short and squat, but where Gert came across as nurturing, there was nothing generous about this woman. Her nose was the most extraordinary feature in her wrinkled face: huge and bulbous, with a wart at its very tip. She was dressed in purple rags that hung haphazardly from her stout body and a battered, pointed black hat rested on her greasy, stringy black hair at an alarming angle. "Why don't you paint a picture, it'll last longer," she growled at me. Embarrassed at being caught staring, I quickly looked away, mumbling an apology. Next to me, Gert chuckled.

"Don't you mind our Mombi," she said. "She has a terrible attitude problem."

"Remind me of my attitude problem the next time I save your skin," Mombi snapped. "Are you done stuffing your faces? We don't have all day. It's time to get down to business."

For the first time, it occurred to me to wonder what Glinda would think about my disappearance. How long had I been in the cave? What would happen when—if—I returned to her palace? And how had I gotten here in the first place?

"One at a time, dear," Gert said, and I realized that she was answering me even though I hadn't spoken aloud. "Bad habit," she added, reading my thoughts again. "But it saves time. I won't look in on anything that's none of my business, don't worry."

"Fine," I said, trying not to show her how unnerved I was by her magic mind reading. "How did I get here?"

"I can answer that," Nox said. "I followed you when Glinda summoned you. I knew if she'd brought the Scarecrow to the palace, she was up to something really bad. We"—he indicated the others seated at the table—"didn't realize she'd move again so quickly. I could protect you inside the palace, but by the time I got to you, it was almost too late. She and the Scarecrow had left you for dead. I thought there was still a chance we could save you, so I brought you here." I thought of the Scarecrow's machine and shivered, covering my eyes with my hands. I felt Gert put an arm around my shoulders.

"I'm sorry we couldn't prevent you from experiencing so much pain," she said. "We had no idea she would try again so soon after she brought you to the palace. Glinda and Dorothy have been looking for a way to tap into Oz's magic since Dorothy took over the Emerald City. Glinda's machine will be slowed down now by the fact that she'll have to use Munchkin labor. But that won't stop her for long. Oz is in danger, and we're the only people who can keep the country safe."

"Who's 'we'?" I asked. Mombi drew herself up to her full height.

"The Revolutionary Order of the Wicked," she said proudly. "The only thing standing between Oz and its destruction." If the only thing standing between Oz and its destruction was this ragtag bunch, I thought, then Oz was in even bigger trouble than I'd thought—but I kept my mouth shut. Gert was probably reading my mind anyway. "We're witches, too," Mombi continued. "But for years, we've kept to ourselves, letting our more attention-hungry sisters steal the spotlight. When Glinda brought Dorothy back to Oz, we knew it was time to come together to find a way to stop her."

"You said you knew about me already," I said to Nox. "Back

at Glinda's palace. What does that mean? Does it have something to do with your—Order?"

"We have eyes everywhere, including in the Emerald City," he said. "We've known about you for a long time. You're part fairy, Jellia. It's why Glinda thought she could use you to tap into Oz's magic."

"But how could I be part fairy?" I asked.

"It's not common," Gert countered, "but it's certainly possible. Why do you think your magic is so powerful? You've always been different, and you know that."

I struggled to process what Gert was saying. I did have stronger magic than most—I knew that. But how could this be? How had I never known?

"Did Ozma know?" I said finally.

"I'm sure she did," Nox said. "Anyone with enough magic can recognize your power, Jellia."

"Why didn't she ever tell me?"

"Ozma has always had her own reasons for doing what she does," Glamora said. "The fairies aren't like the other citizens of Oz. They literally *are* Oz; their magic is Oz's magic. If she didn't tell you, it was because she felt it was for the good of Oz. But everything is different now. You have to learn the extent of your powers if you want to help send Dorothy back to the Other Place and heal Ozma."

"You're not any better than Glinda," I said, hurt surging up in my chest. "You only helped me out because you think I can do something for you."

"Not because you can do something for us," Mombi said curtly. "Because you can do something for Oz."

"I know this is difficult, dear," Gert said, her gentle voice countering Mombi's gruffness. "But these are desperate times. We've protected you because you're special, it's true. But you have the power to help us heal Oz—to bring Ozma back and restore the rightful order. You can't choose who you are. But you can choose what you'll become."

"But I don't even know how to use my magic," I said. "I never even knew what I was. How can I help you?"

"Nox is our eyes and ears in Glinda's palace," Gert replied. "And you can do that work for us in the Emerald City. No one is as close to Dorothy as you are."

"And Glinda hasn't told her about your magic," Glamora added. "As far as she knows, you're just as ordinary as anyone else in Oz—if anyone in Oz can be said to be truly ordinary."

"If Glinda recognized me as part fairy, why hasn't Dorothy? She has magic, too," I pointed out.

"Dorothy doesn't have magic of her own," Gert said. "All her power comes from those infernal shoes of Glinda's. Dorothy is learning how to use that power for her own ends, but for now Glinda can still control her."

I sat for a moment, digesting what they'd told me. "You're asking me to risk my life when I don't even know what you're trying to do," I said finally.

"That part is simple," Mombi said. "The witch is going to burn." Everyone else at the table fell silent. Mombi slapped her hands on the table and heaved herself to her feet, trundling around the table to where I sat. "Listen, little girl," she said, grabbing my chin and forcing me to meet her eyes. "You don't think much of us now, and I can't blame you. I know more about your life than you think. I know what you've seen and I know how much Dorothy and Glinda have hurt you. Not just you— your friends. I know you remember what it was like to live in a free Oz. We might not look like much, but we can do it. We can make Oz free again."

Her tone was gruff, but underneath her harsh words there was something almost sympathetic.

As if she could sense me softening, Mombi continued. "We're asking you to risk your life, sure. You know that. You're not stupid. But your life is already at risk, every day you work for Dorothy. Glinda's already figured out she can't use you in her machine. You're no more use to her. Do you really want to be Dorothy's head maid for the rest of your life? This is your chance, Jellia. It's your chance at something better. We're not going to pretend it's not risky. But Oz deserves better—and you have the power to help."

Her grip on my jaw was firm, but when I met her eyes again they were full of compassion. "I know," she said, so quietly I didn't think the others at the table could hear her. "I know how much you want the real Ozma back. In that, if nothing else, we're together."

I jerked away from her grip, and she let me. She took a few steps backward, put her hands on her broad hips, and stared at me. They were all watching me now.

"I need some time," I said.

"We can give you a few minutes, but that's all," Gert said. "We can bewitch the Munchkins who were tasked with taking you back to Dorothy so that they won't realize you were gone, but the longer you're here, the harder it will be."

"Fine," I said. Without another word, Gert led me back to the cavern with the healing pool and left me there.

FIFTEEN

I sat staring into the pool as the soft slap of Gert's bare feet on stone faded away. A pale pink mist had formed over the water, which was now an opaque, rich blue and smelled of honeysuckle. I had no idea how long I'd been sitting there when something in the air changed and I realized Nox was sitting beside me. He'd come up behind me and sat down so silently I hadn't even noticed.

"I'm sorry," he said in a low voice, looking at the water.

"Why did you join them?"

He was silent for a long time. "It might not seem like it," he said at last, "but you've been protected in the Emerald City from the truth of how evil Dorothy is. Glinda has been trying to tap into Oz's magic for a long time, and Dorothy is helping her. It's not just that machine—Glinda's been digging mines deep under Oz, looking for ways to pull magic out of the earth. The Tin Woodman's soldiers have been kidnapping people and using them as slave labor."

I thought of the rumors that had swirled around Dorothy's palace ever since Ozma had changed. The stories of Munchkins going hungry, of the winged monkeys turning evil. They hadn't just been stories, then. "That still doesn't explain how you got here," I said.

"The Tin Woodman's soldiers burned my hometown to the ground when I was just a boy," he said quietly, not looking at me. "They tried to take all of the adults, but everyone fought back. No one was left alive—except me. Mombi rescued me and brought me here. She raised me to be a fighter. I owe the Order my life." He looked up at me. "But it's more than that. More than just gratitude. I believe in the possibility of a better Oz, Jellia. I *have* to. I won't let Glinda and Dorothy keep destroying our country. And if I can avenge my parents' deaths—well, so much the better."

I searched for the right words. "I'm sorry," I said simply, though it hardly seemed like enough. "I didn't realize."

He shrugged. "You didn't know. But now you have to decide, Jellia. Will you help us?"

"I've already made up my mind," I said, and his face fell. But as soon as the words were out of my mouth, Gert materialized next to me in a little puff of purple smoke.

"I knew we could count on you, Jellia," she said, her voice full of pride. She wrapped me up in a big, soft hug, and after a moment I returned the gesture. I could see Nox's confused expression over her shoulder.

"You're not the only one who wants to see the real Oz restored," I said to him, and his face was transformed by a real, full smile.

Gert released me from her embrace and I found that I missed her comforting warmth as soon as she did. I hadn't had much mothering in my life. "Down to business," she said briskly. "I'm sorry to be curt, my dear, but we haven't much time. We must return you to the meadow where Glinda left you, and Nox has to get back to Glinda's before she notices his absence." She paused, smiling at me. "Welcome to the future of Oz, Jellia. We're proud to count you among us." When she put it like that, I couldn't help but be a little proud of myself, too.

After that, there wasn't much else to do. Mombi, Gert, and Glamora assembled in the pool cavern to see me off. Glamora waved her hands, and my soft white robe was replaced with the tattered, bloody dress I'd been wearing when Nox brought me to the cavern. Glamora waved her hands again, and bruises sprang up painlessly across my skin. I poked one cautiously; it didn't hurt at all, but it sure looked convincingly gory. "Just a glamour," she said. "They'll fade eventually, like real bruises." I looked down at my ruined dress. I was really going to do this. I was really going to spy on Dorothy—and put my life on the line for the future of Oz. What was I thinking? Why had I agreed to this?

"Because you know Oz needs you, dear," Gert said. I faced her and opened my mouth, ready to tell her I knew no such thing. But the words didn't come. Instead, I thought of the tiny girl who washed dishes all day long in Glinda's kitchen. I thought of Nox's murdered parents. I thought of poor Astrid—how was she faring, back in the Emerald City without me to look after her? I thought of Glinda's Munchkin cooks, so afraid of Glinda's power they were willing to spy on the people who they should have been united with. I thought of Ozma, and how things used to be. I cared about them, all of them. I cared about their chance for a better life. For freedom. I cared because they deserved it. I took a deep breath and adjusted my dress so that it looked even more askew.

"Let's get this over with," I said. Gert smiled.

"You're very brave, dear," she said. "Very, very brave."

Hopefully, I wasn't about to be very, very dead.

Gert took my hand and put it in Nox's. His grip was cool and reassuring. Gert took his free hand and Mombi took mine. The last thing I saw before the cavern disappeared was Glamora's face, a haunting mirror image of Glinda's, her big blue eyes looking deep into mine.

We rematerialized in the meadow where Glinda had left me, next to the Scarecrow's machine. It was night, just before dawn; overhead, the constellations of Oz gleamed like gems in the lightening sky. A handful of astounded Munchkins huddled around the machine, gaping at our unexpected arrival. Gert marched over to them briskly; I could see the air shimmering with magic around her upraised hands.

"Listen, Jellia," Nox said, and stopped, searching for the right words. "Good luck," he said finally. "Be careful."

"You too," I said. He nodded again and then, to my surprise, he gave me a brief, fierce hug. Without another word, he turned his back on us and loped off into the darkness.

Gert walked back toward us with the Munchkins trailing after her, blinking and dazed. "It's time," she said. "Be strong, Jellia. We have faith in you. We chose you because we knew you could do what we asked of you. Not many people are that brave."

"Or that stupid," I said.

Mombi grinned and patted me on the back. "Don't get killed, kiddo."

Gert turned to the Munchkins. "You remember nothing," she said gently, and they nodded as one with their mouths open. She smiled at me. "Good-bye, dear. And good luck." The witches' outlines wavered, and I watched as they shimmered and then disappeared with a pop, like a bubble bursting. That was it: I was on my own.

The Munchkins were looking around them as though they'd just woken up from a dream. One of them caught sight of me and stood up a little straighter. "You're alive," he said slowly. "We're to take you back to Dorothy, if you're alive. To the Emerald City."

I took a deep breath. "What are we waiting for then?" I said. "It's time to go home."

THE WIZARD

RETURNS

ONE

Sometimes you just have to cut your losses, the Wizard thought as the rolling green fields of Oz dropped away below his balloon. It had been a decent run: parties in the palace, everyone scampering to and fro at his command, all the banquets. One merged into the other now in his memory: the smeary blur of china platters and singing toast, pastries bursting into flames, wine pouring in waves down the sparkling white tablecloths without leaving a stain and hurling itself into goblets. But in the end none of it had ever been enough. There had been too many late nights in the dark of his vast chambers, staring down the bleak interminable chasm of the future; day after day, never changing, all the sycophants and toadies, the yammering masses, the damn monkeys—he shuddered, and closed his eyes against the memory. Never another monkey. The best thing he'd ever done in his entire tenure in Oz was sell them out to the Wicked Witch.

He closed his eyes. Who was he fooling? He didn't want to go back to the Other Place. It was a hard step in the wrong direction, going from Wizard of Oz to the tired sidewalk con artist he'd been before he came here. The dusty streets of Omaha, that tired blue sky. The circus he had traveled with—its dispirited, jaundiced elephant; the aging aerialists in their shabby old costumes; the strongman, who could only manage barbells made of tin painted to look like iron. He might have detested Oz, but it had been a vast improvement over his old life. Its people, fools that they were, had thought he was a magician capable of anything. They had rushed to do his bidding. He'd been a king—and now he was nothing.

And he had the girl to thank for it.

That awful girl in her awful checkered dress and her whining, high-pitched voice. He had been quite content to rule the childlike citizenry of Oz until she came along with her little dog and revealed him for what he truly was: only a man like any other, though perhaps a little less kind and a little more clever than most. He'd left her standing in the courtyard of *his* palace, her mouth a round, astonished *O* as his balloon rose into the sky. He'd promised her a way home, but he'd never been one to keep his promises.

Now he leaned his head against the ropes of the hot air balloon, rough hemp scratchy against his ear, and looked carelessly out at the horizon. The Emerald City still sparkled on the horizon like a cheap necklace in the distance; far below, a golden plain gave way to a vast red field of poppies. But what caught his gaze were the storm clouds massing in heavy gray drifts. Even at this distance he could see their unnatural—though *everything* in this disgusting country was unnatural—sheen. Their staticky haze of magic, real magic, sparking across the roiling surface of the storm.

The clouds moved closer at a surreal pace, swelling like ink spreading through water, rolling across the sky until the clear summery blue was swallowed up in darkness. The cool breeze that had carried the balloon at a brisk clip away from the Emerald City picked up, gusts howling past his ears and jerking the balloon wildly until the basket swung madly below it like a yo-yo on a string and he was thrown against the ropes. A menacing rumble of thunder was followed by an earsplitting crack of white-purple lightning so close to the basket that he could feel his hair standing on end. The wind whipped at his clothes. In its fury he thought he could almost make out a taunting chorus of voices—but what words they snarled, or in what language they spoke, he could not have said.

Holding fast to one of the ropes, he struggled grimly to lower the burner, thinking he might try and safely land the balloon. Lightning snapped furiously and the wind swirled around in a terrifying vortex with the balloon at its heart, spinning him faster and faster like a top—but when he looked up from the burner he saw that the clouds that had streaked across the sky were gathered directly overhead. Past their edges, the sky was as clear and calm as it had been only moments earlier. Whatever this storm was, it wasn't ordinary.

Perhaps this unexpected development was the chance he was

hoping for: Oz wasn't ready to let him go. Someone had sent the storm to keep him here.

Resigned, he settled back into the heaving basket, concentrating firmly on not being sick over its edge, and waited for the inevitable. It was only a matter of time before the balloon went down. With a grim sense of satisfaction, he watched as one particularly spectacular streak of lightning tore through the silk of his balloon, leaving a smoking rent that only widened as the wind pulled at it. With a slow, majestic shudder the balloon held for a moment, caught in an updraft, and then it began to plummet toward the sea of poppies below. As quickly as it had come upon him, the storm blew itself out like a birthday candle: the wind died, the lightning popped and vanished, and the clouds dissipated into faint gray wisps that dawdled off toward the horizon. One last gust cupped the balloon, buffering its fall to earth. "Please," he said aloud, in the event he was being watched by whatever entity had sent the storm. "Just no more monkeys. It's all I ask." He could have sworn the gust snorted.

With a bone-jarring thud, the balloon hit the ground and bounced into the air once—sending poppies flying—before thumping down again. The Wizard was flung from the basket and went head over heels into the poppy field, tumbling through a rich red cloud of petals and at last coming to rest in a drift of seed heads and silvery-green leaves. He lay there for a moment, stunned, and then took stock of all his limbs. Nothing seemed to be broken, or even bruised. Whatever magical force had brought down the balloon had apparently had no intention of harming him. He sat up, and found that the heady smell of the poppies had induced a wonderful languor; his limbs seemed deliciously heavy. The golden sunlight poured over him like butter and his eyelids began to drift closed. He sank back into the poppies as if into the most decadent and luxurious of feather beds.

"I really should have tried this sooner," he murmured, and then darkness took him.

TWO

"Wake up," said an insistent voice in his ear. "It's time." He had no interest in doing so. He'd been having the most lovely dream, floating in a warm honey-scented bath while colorful balloons sailed by overhead and a beautiful talking lion sang lullabies in a voice that rivaled the great blues singers of his homeland. But the voice would not let him sink back into glorious oblivion. "I mean it," it said, more firmly this time. "Wake *up*."

He opened his eyes and found himself staring into a pair of uncanny emerald ones. *Emerald*. There was something about the color that he couldn't quite put his finger on. His own eyes refused to focus properly, and he only wanted to go back to sleep, but the person in front of him was now tugging fiercely at his shoulder. "We have to get you out of here," Emerald Eyes said. "You're high as a kite."

"Balloon," he mumbled, allowing himself to be dragged along as the young man hoisted one arm over his shoulder and towed him through—where was he? His vision was improving a little; there was more color all around him, red and green, and overhead a lot of blue. A sky, he remembered. The thing overhead was a sky. He protested feebly as he was pulled away from the last of the huge red flowers, and dumped, unceremoniously, onto a grassy hillock. Emerald Eyes smacked him briskly on the cheeks, but when this did nothing to wake him up, heaved a sigh of disgust and let him go. "Nighty night," he murmured, and drifted off into sleep again.

The next time he woke up, it was early in the morning, and the pleasant fuzziness had faded to a dull buzz. He was in a cornflower-blue field, under a bright blue sky. He sat up and looked around. A patch of fat pink flowers next to him was singing a cheerful high-pitched ditty. Two huge yellow-and-black butterflies fluttered lazily through the air, arguing halfheartedly about who was better-looking. Emerald Eyes was stretched out with his back against a nearby tree, watching him. "Good," he said. "You're awake. The poppies should be wearing off now that you're out of the field. Do you know where you are?" Emerald Eyes cocked his head. "Do you know *who* you are?"

He considered the questions. There was the dream about the lion—but before that, everything was a hazy blur. He had a vague sense that flowers did not ordinarily sing and butterflies were not meant to talk, but that was it. "Not really," he admitted.

Emerald Eyes looked at him for a long time. "You're the Wizard," he said finally. "Not that you were ever very good at being one. But we can't call you that on the journey we're about to take. You really don't remember, do you?"

Wizard? He didn't know anything about being a wizard. Something stirred in his memory. A card table—he'd sat at a card table and done sleight-of-hand tricks, and passed a battered top hat. A shabby one-room apartment that smelled of cabbages. His face in the mirror, sallow and pale, with dark circles under the eyes. A young face, but hardened and cynical. A brown suit with fraying cuffs, worn shiny at the elbows, and underneath it a stained white shirt with a collar that had long since lost its crispness. He shook his head violently, and the images dissipated into wisps of smoke. "I played tricks," he said uncertainly.

Emerald Eyes laughed, and there was something in the sound that was almost bitter. Or cruel. "That you certainly did," he said. "For the time being, let's call you . . ." He trailed off, thinking, and then smiled. "Let's call you Hex," he said with a grin. "And you can call me Pete, though you used to know me as something else."

"I did?" the Wizard asked. No. He wasn't a wizard. This strange boy had just told him as much. Hex. His name was Hex now. He studied Pete closely, and something flickered at the back of his mind. A baby? A monkey? But then the flicker died down, and whatever he'd been about to remember was gone.

"You did," Pete said, "but that was a long time ago. Do you have any idea how long you've been down for the count in that poppy field? Twenty-five years, my friend, give or take a few. You should be an old man by now. But as you know—or used to know anyway—time doesn't move the same way in Oz that it does in your world. And time *definitely* doesn't move the same way in the poppy field." Pete sighed. "Kind of jealous, actually. A quarter-century blissed-out nap sounds pretty good right about now. You wouldn't believe how much work it took to get out of the palace—the only reason I could get away at all was because Dorothy is so wrapped up in whatever she's up to with Glinda. Anyway, I've been sent to help you get home."

"Sent? By who?" Hex thought more about what Pete had just said. The name *Dorothy* had set off a tiny alarm in his brain, though he wasn't sure why. "Where is home, if it isn't here?"

"The Other Place," Pete said impatiently. "You were trying to get there when your balloon crashed. That's where you're from, and that's where you belong. But you can't cross the boundary between here and there until your memory returns. The fairies are the only people in Oz who can help you, which is why I'm taking you to them. But they won't help you without getting something in exchange—and they'll test you to make sure you're worthy of their assistance."

"Test?" Hex asked nervously. "What kind of test?"

"The Three-Part Test," Pete said. "Wisdom, Courage, and Love. It's part of your journey. I can guide you to the fairy kingdom, but you'll have to pass the test on your own to prove your selflessness. The fairies won't help you unless they believe it's for the good of Oz."

Test? Other Place? Fairies? What Pete was saying didn't make any sense at all. And why did Pete care if he stayed here or went to what was supposedly his home? If he thought about it for too long his head hurt. "Why now?" he asked suddenly. "Why didn't you just leave me to sleep?"

Pete pulled Hex to his feet, ignoring his protests. "It's time to start walking," he said. "No one will be looking for you, or expect to see you out here wandering around, but we can't take any chances."

"Why does it matter if anyone recognizes me?"

Before Hex even realized what was happening, Pete had taken hold of his face in both hands, staring deep into his eyes with his own uncanny green ones. "Hold still," Pete said. "This might hurt." He pushed his palms into Hex's cheeks with a terrible cracking sound. The sudden flare of pain was overwhelming, and Hex uttered a muffled yell. He could *feel* the bones of his skull shifting as Pete's hands—almost unbearably hot now—continued to push at his cheeks and jaw. His skin was burning; his scalp felt as though it might peel away from his skull in flayed pieces, his teeth as though they were crumbling in his jaw. Tears sprang to his eyes, and a flash of contempt crossed Pete's face before he finally took his hands away. Hex sank to his knees, gasping for breath, and touched his face, afraid of what he'd find there. His skin was cool and ordinary to the touch. The agony lessened to a dull throb.

"I could have just glamoured you," Pete said, "but this will last longer. I'd show you in a mirror, but I don't have one—and anyway, you don't remember what you looked like before. But trust me, no one in Oz is going to recognize you now." Hex rubbed his jaw, wincing at the remembered pain. "You'll need new clothes, too," Pete added, tossing him a pair of pants and a shirt that he'd somehow summoned out of thin air and then pointedly turning his back. After a moment, Hex changed into the new clothes. They fit him perfectly. He carefully folded the clothes he'd been wearing and cleared his throat. Pete turned around again, and Hex handed Pete his old suit. Pete snapped his fingers, and the clothes disappeared.

"Thanks," he said, and laughed. Pete looked at him in surprise.

"You're welcome," he said. "Let's get going."

Pete was already walking away from him, striding briskly through the tall, pale blue grass. Hex scrambled after him, his mind burning with questions. Why, after twenty-five years, had Pete woken him up now? Why did it matter if anyone recognized him? Who *was* Pete, and why did he call Hex a wizard? Who were the fairies, and why was Pete taking him to them? Hex stared at Pete's back and sighed. It didn't take a wizard to know his questions weren't going to be answered anytime soon.

THREE

They walked through the pale blue fields for a long time, stopping briefly to eat some bread and cheese that Pete summoned out of thin air. ("*That's* magic," Pete said. "Not like the flashy tricks you used to do.") Their shadows lengthened on the grass; by now it was late in the afternoon. Pete occasionally squinted up at the sun as if gauging their direction, but when Hex asked him about it he only laughed. "This is Oz," he said. "The directions change all the time. I'm following the feel of the Old Magic— that's what's telling me where to go."

"Old Magic?" Pete didn't answer at first, and Hex thought he was ignoring the question, but after a moment, he shrugged.

"You really don't remember anything, do you? The Old Magic is the lifeblood of Oz. The power that runs through this place and keeps it alive. It's like a huge web that connects everything together. The people, the landscape, the animals, the palace—Old Magic flows through everything. Only the most powerful witches in Oz can tap into it. And the fairies, of course, because technically it's their magic—but I don't think even they truly understand how it works."

"The fairies who will be testing me?" Hex asked.

"The fairies are the original citizens of Oz," Pete replied, apparently content to continue his history lesson. "They were the ones who first crossed the Deadly Desert, long before Oz existed, and used their blood to give Oz its magic and bring life to the desert. They created Oz out of the wasteland. Because of that, the fairies are the rightful rulers of Oz. There have been other guardians of the throne over the years, of course." Pete shot Hex an inscrutable look. "But none of those rulers are legitimate unless they've been authorized by the fairies. Anyway, if anyone can help you get home, it's the fairies." He put a strange stress on the word *legitimate*, and Hex wondered what he was getting at. Fairies? Old Magic? It all sounded like a bad penny dreadful. He frowned. Penny dreadful. An image of a cheap, flimsy booklet, its cover printed in lurid colors, a fanged vampire leering over a cringing blond girl in a low-cut dress. Something he'd once owned? He felt as though he were surrounded by a translucent but impermeable wall—he could almost see through to the other side, where his old self awaited him in his real life, memories intact. But every time he tried to reach out he crashed into a barrier as solid as glass.

He had stopped walking, trying to remember, and Pete was watching him with an unreadable expression that seemed almost sympathetic, in contrast to his previous hostility. "It must be strange," Pete said. "Not knowing who you are."

Hex struggled to keep hold of the memory, but it dissolved again into the blurry recesses of his mind. He felt almost queasy, and realized belatedly that the strange sensation was shame. "I wasn't a very good person, was I?" he asked quietly.

Pete looked surprised. "No," he said after a moment. "Not really."

"Maybe it's better I don't remember," Hex said. "Maybe I should just start over."

Pete's expression grew hard again. "Do you really think that's how it works? You forget about all the bad things you did, and they just go away? The people you hurt still remember. They have to—" Abruptly, Pete stopped, as if he'd thought better of what he had been about to say. "Get moving," he said gruffly. "We have a long way to go."

The blue field gave way to rolling hills of flowers that moved like waves even though there was no wind, stretching all the way to the horizon on either side. In front of them loomed an immense black forest, with trees so tall that even at a distance Hex had to tilt his head all the way back to see where their inky tips speared the blue sky. As they drew closer, he saw that the trees grew so closely together they almost resembled a wall. The forest had an unmistakable air of menace—and they were unmistakably headed directly for it. "You want us to go in there?" Hex asked, trying to keep his voice casual, and though Pete's back was to him he could hear the sneer in Pete's response.

"Don't like it? Too bad." After that, Hex resolved not to ask any more questions. His situation was bad enough without giving Pete any more opportunities to make him feel like a fool.

Suddenly, an earsplitting howl echoed across the sea of flowers, and Hex saw half a dozen jagged black shapes bounding toward them through the blossoms at a terrifying speed—wolves, he thought, but like no wolves he had ever seen. They were twice as big, and from their brindled backs sprouted huge, leathery black bat wings that flapped madly as the animals raced toward them. Every so often one of the wolves would give its wings a tremendous pump, propelling itself several feet into the air and hurtling even more quickly toward them. "Wolves! *Run*," Pete yelled, and took off for the forest. Hex didn't need to be told twice. His throat closed up in terror as he ran after Pete. But the wolves were gaining on them; they would never make the forest in time. Pete risked a glance backward and stumbled. Hex, unable to stop his momentum, thumped into him, sending them both tumbling to the ground. Pete cursed aloud, and then the first of the wolves was upon them. Pete threw up his arms. A crackling curtain of purple energy sprang up behind them. The wolf skidded to a halt, but too late: it crashed into Pete's magical wall and yelped frantically as its fur caught fire. Pete scrambled to his feet, dragging Hex up with him. The other wolves had stopped, eyeing the wall of magic warily, but one of them was already trying to push through, and Hex saw in horror that rather than burning its snout, the wall was beginning to give. "That's not going to hold them," Pete gasped. "Come on."

Hex was pretty sure he had never run so hard in his life—of

course, he couldn't remember, but it didn't seem likely. Behind him, he heard a triumphant yip, and knew one of the wolves must have broken through Pete's spell. He put his head down and pumped his legs harder. "Almost there," Pete said at his side. Dimly, Hex realized that Pete had slowed down to match his pace. And then the wall of trees reared up before them, and Hex nearly crashed into one of the enormous trunks before Pete grabbed his arm and pushed him at a narrow opening between two trees. Up close, the forest was more like a fortress. The huge trees loomed over them, sinister and forbidding, like an army of conjoined soldiers forming a hermetically sealed barricade. Hex struggled to squeeze through the trees. The wolves had reached them; Pete held them off with crackling sparks of magic, but they were so close Hex could smell their awful, meaty breath and see the serrated edges of their huge fangs as they snarled. One leapt through the magical barrier, yowling but undeterred as its fur caught fire, and Hex hurled a rock at the wolf with all his might, hitting it squarely on the nose. It jumped back, growling. *"Go!"* Pete yelled, giving him one final shove, and with that Hex popped through the wall of trees and tumbled to the ground on the far side. Pete heaved himself through the opening after him, landing on top of him as the trunks snapped together like a door slamming. First one, then several more disappointed howls rose up on the other side of the wall. Hex lay where he had fallen, gasping for breath. They had done it. They were safe.

Something sharp jabbed him in the neck and he looked up. A monkey loomed over him, dressed incongruously in a velvet jacket and neatly tailored velvet pants. A small, red velvet fez with an ostentatious black tassel sat at a rakish angle on its head, and a pair of pince-nez was perched on the end of its nose. The sight was so ridiculous that Hex would have laughed. Except the monkey was holding a very serious-looking spear, and the business end of the spear was shoved up against Hex's throat. Hex turned his head just enough to look for Pete; maybe he had some idea what was going on. But Pete had vanished as if into thin air, leaving him alone with a crazed overdressed monkey on the verge of impaling him.

"Who the hell," the monkey said, "are you?"

FOUR

"I'm just a traveler," Hex whispered, barely able to get the words out past the pressure of the monkey's spear. It seemed like a bad time to explain that he had no more idea than the monkey did who he was or what he was doing here.

"What, like a tourist?" The monkey snorted. "Are you kidding? Nobody comes here without a reason. What do you think this is, the Riviera? Look around you, human." If Hex had tried to look around, the monkey's spear would have decapitated him, but now did not seem the best time to point out this small fact.

"I came with a—" He faltered. A what? Pete was hardly his friend. "A guide," he wheezed.

"Don't you think I would have noticed two of you?"

"I don't know where he is. He was just with me, I swear it. I lost my memories in the poppy fields, and he—"

"Oh, *great*," the monkey groaned. "A delusional hallucinating junkie. *Just* what we need. As if Oz isn't going to hell in a handbasket already. Do you even know how busy I am right now? I've got fourteen reports to finish by the end of the week, and my boss is on a rampage, I have all this data on the rival factions and no one will listen to me when I point out their strategic flaws because they say my methods are too newfangled, as if we're supposed to just swing around in trees hooting for the rest of our—" The monkey sighed deeply in frustration. "Anyway, what am I supposed to do with you?"

"You could move that spear," Hex whispered. The monkey scowled down at him, but it lessened the pressure of the spear a little and gestured roughly for him to sit up.

"Thank you," Hex said in a normal voice, gingerly rubbing his throat.

"Don't thank me just yet," the monkey said curtly. "Dealing with you is way over my pay grade. I think it's time for your first audience with the queen, human. Get up."

The monkey kept the spear trained on him as he cautiously got to his feet, surreptitiously looking around for Pete. There was no doubt about it: the mysterious boy had vanished. He was totally on his own—and he had no idea why he was even here or what he was supposed to do next. "Thanks a lot," he muttered under his breath, but the monkey heard him.

"Are you *sassing* me?" it snapped. "I've always thought humans were stupid, but you seem to be an extra-special case of idiot. Can't you see I'm a fierce warrior?" The monkey waved its spear threateningly. Hex considered responding to this, and then decided his safety was worth more than his dignity—for now anyway. "Come on. I don't have all day. If you hold me back I'll make *you* finish my statistics reports—and believe me, anyone as dumb as you won't make it through the *first* of my equations. Customized them all myself. You wouldn't be able to make head nor tail of them." The monkey poked him firmly, and Hex obediently began to walk. On this side of the wooded wall, the forest looked a little more like an ordinary jungle. Heavy green vines dangled from the treetop canopy far overhead. Brightly colored birds flitted past in a whoosh of jasmine-scented air. The ground was covered with thick, broad-leaved plants that gleamed wetly in the dim green light that filtered through the branches. It was a beautiful place, actually, although his first choice of companion would definitely not have been a talking monkey with an itchy trigger finger.

After they had been walking a little while—the monkey's spear at his back the whole time—they came to an immense rock face. At its base, a monkey-high crack fissured the rock. Hex could see light on the other side. "In you go," the monkey said. "Better duck. You don't want to lose your head until Queen Lulu decides it's time." It cackled hysterically. Hex, gritting his teeth, stooped low enough to clear the top of the natural doorway. The monkey followed him nimbly. Hex caught sight of the scene around him and stopped short, his jaw dropping in awe.

The monkey village looked like some little kid's dream. Hundreds of feet up, the huge trees were filled with wooden houses that seemed to grow directly out of the trunks. The houses were connected by an intricate system of hanging walkways that swayed gently in the breeze. And there were monkeys every-where: monkeys swinging from vines, monkeys leaning out the windows of their little houses, monkeys hurrying along the walkways, monkeys lounging on park-like platforms where bright flowers grew in carefully tended patches. Even from the forest floor Hex could see they were all dressed, like his captor, in well-fitted but incongruous clothes. He made out monkeys in suits, monkeys in dresses, monkeys in uniforms—even one lone monkey in a wedding dress and veil, looking for all the world like a monkey cupcake. His captor did not allow him much time to look around, shoving him roughly forward. "No funny business on the stairs," the monkey snapped, pushing him to a perilous-looking staircase that wound its way up from the ground, looping dozens of times around the trunk of one of the trees until it reached the dizzying heights of the forest canopy. "You're my first prisoner, and I'm not going to lose you! *Finally*, the queen will have to pay attention to me. I've captured a human! You'll probably be executed! Everyone will take me seriously!"

The staircase didn't even have a railing; each of its steps had been cleverly wedged into the living wood of the tree itself. Hex swallowed past the lump in his throat, wondering if his former self had been as afraid of heights as his present self was. He took a deep breath and started up the stairs.

The climb was a nightmare. As he made his way up the stair-case, the insistent breeze tugged at his limbs and threw him off balance. Behind him, the monkey, obviously enjoying his palpable fear, alternated between laughing at him and poking him in the back with the spear, more than once almost causing him to lose his footing. With no railing, he could only cling desperately to the rough bark of the tree as he made his way up.

At last, after what felt like a century, the staircase joined up with one of the hanging walkways. Hex collapsed on the slats, not even caring anymore if the monkey stabbed him in the back. The narrow, dangling walkway, swaying alarmingly under his weight, was hardly the safest place, but after the staircase it seemed as good as solid ground.

"Well, well, well," the monkey said behind him, a note of grudging admiration in its voice. "You're made out of sterner stuff than you look. I didn't think you'd make it. We always end up having to carry humans the last part of the way. Trial by fire, they say. Pain in the ass, I tell you, and if you ask me it's an outdated system, but nobody asks me anything around here. I have so many ideas about streamlining efficiency and data management—you should see the spreadsheet I designed last week—but they don't even care. 'Not the monkey way,' they tell me. As if we should be stuck living in this backward—"

Hex interrupted the monkey's beleaguered monologue. "The stairs are a *trial*? You mean the monkeys don't use them?"

The monkey shot him an amused glance. "Are you kidding? We use the elevator. Look, I'm sure the queen is going to execute you—probably even with torture. Since you won't live to see tonight, we might as well introduce ourselves. I'm Iris." Hex gaped stupidly at the monkey.

"Iris? But that's a girl's name."

The monkey gave him another look, this time one of disdain. "Because I *am* a girl, you moron. You think only men can crunch numbers and be honored members of the queen's guard?" Iris brandished the spear at him.

"No!" Hex yelped hastily. "No. Of course not. Forgive me." Apparently mollified, Iris looked at him expectantly. "Oh, right," he said. "I'm Hex. Sorry." Iris offered him a paw and he shook it gravely.

"Pleased to meet you, Hex," she said. "And now it's time for me to escort you to your doom."

FIVE

To reach the monkey queen's palace, Hex had to climb yet another flight of stairs. This one, however, wasn't half as bad as the first; there was even a handrail. His fear of heights had settled into a kind of numb dread in his belly. Soon enough he'd be swinging around on vines like the monkeys themselves, he thought drily. Iris's attitude had improved considerably since their formal introduction. She was whistling cheerfully behind him, and, though he had no doubt she'd be delighted to stick him again if he made any attempt to flee, she had laid off poking him with the spear.

The queen's palace was a hut, a little larger and grander than the others Hex had seen but otherwise unremarkable. It sat in the center of a broad platform of planks that had been built above the treetops. From the platform, Hex could see for miles in every direction. There was the wall of trees, and just beyond it the heaving sea of flowers where the wolves had attacked; there was the blue plain he had crossed with Pete, and in the distance he could see the crimson splatter of the poppy field. He thought wistfully of how wonderful it would be to be back there again, nodding off under a huge red flower without a care in the world, but there wasn't much point in longing for something that clearly wasn't going to happen anytime soon. He wondered again what had happened to Pete. Had he been captured by the monkeys, too? But Iris's disbelief had seemed genuine when she'd found him just after the wolf attack, and surely he would have seen if someone else had abducted Pete after they'd escaped from the wolves. No, Pete had abandoned him. Did this have something to do with the mysterious test he was supposed to take? Either way, he was on his own, and there was nothing he could do about it.

Iris cleared her throat loudly, and Hex realized he'd been staring off into space like an idiot. "Sorry," he mumbled, slouching toward the door at Iris's prompting. The hut was windowless, its smooth round walls interrupted only by a single door—monkey height, like everything else in the village.

"Go on," Iris said impatiently, and he stooped and entered.

The inside of the hut belied its humble exterior. Its smooth, round walls were painted an eye-searing yellow; here and there, the yellow was augmented by even brighter murals depicting the queen floating regally over her subjects, outfitted for battle, and surrounded by bunches of bananas that looked—well, as though they had been finger-painted by a monkey. An elaborate chandelier hung from the low ceiling, looking rather out of place. It had no doubt once been very fine, but was now bedecked with dried banana peels in various stages of decay.

Queen Lulu herself was lounging against a raft of brightly colored pillows with a surprising amount of dignity for a ridiculously dressed monkey. She wore a vibrant, ruffled pink dress, leopard-print stockings, and rhinestone-studded sandals, and her eyes were hidden behind enormous sunglasses. In one hand she held a jeweled scepter; in the other, a half-eaten banana, which she was busily gnawing. She swallowed the last bites as Hex approached the throne and chucked the peel up at the chandelier, where it added to the collection.

He had never met a royal monkey before, but it seemed prudent to err on the side of caution. He executed a sweeping bow, so low his forehead nearly brushed his shins, and the queen grunted with approval through a mouthful of banana. "This one has manners, at least," she said. Her voice was rough and heavily accented—and strangely familiar. Staring at her, he thought he'd surely seen her before—and then a flash of memory leapt to the surface of his mind. *A stooped, haggard old woman in a black hat—he was giving her a shapeless old felt hat that he knew was terribly important despite its appearance. "This seals our bargain," the old woman hissed. "Giving me control of the monkeys? You're even crueler than I am, human, and that's saying something. They must raise you differently in the Other Place."* And then the memory was gone as quickly as it had come, but looking at the queen, he was flooded with a sudden sense of sick, terrible shame. The hat had had some kind of power over the monkeys, and it had been his.

Why had he given it away? What had his past self done?

The queen was looking at him quizzically, and it was evident that whatever he had done, she had no memory of it—or, more likely, she didn't recognize him thanks to Pete's transformation spell. He patted his cheeks cautiously. The soreness was gone, but their shape was still unfamiliar. The queen was still staring at him, and he realized he was behaving like a lunatic.

"Er, Your Royal, um, Highness," he stammered. "May your, uh, bananas be plentiful and the branches that hold your houses aloft remain strong."

The queen raised an eyebrow. "Well, you're an odd duck, but you're charming enough," she said. "Where'd you find this one, Iris?"

"I caught him trying to invade!" Iris piped up excitedly. "At the Wolf Gate! I think he might be a barbarian! He tried to tell me some nonsense story about a guide, but he's clearly a spy."

"A barbarian or a spy?" Queen Lulu asked drily, bemused by Iris's enthusiasm. "How perfectly terrifying."

"He could be both!"

"I'm neither!" Hex protested. "I'm only trying to—" What *was* he even trying to do? Without Pete, he was at a loss.

"I think we should execute him!" Iris was bouncing up and down on her heels in excitement. "For treachery! I mean treason!"

The queen reclined even further and waved a paw. Another monkey—this one dressed in a black velvet suit with a dapper red ascot—sauntered out of the shadows, bringing her a fresh banana, which she peeled languidly. He shot Iris an unmistakably evil look, which Iris returned haughtily. "Iris, calm yourself," the queen said. "We haven't executed a human in— well, we haven't executed anyone ever."

"Think how fun it would be!" Iris squealed in glee. "May I be the executioner, Your Majesty?"

"Be silent, you little fool," snapped the monkey in black. Iris drew back, an expression of genuine hurt flashing across her face.

"Quentin, there's no need to be cruel to the young and enthusiastic," the queen said. "But I *am* rather curious as to how a lone traveler managed to cross the Sea of Blossoms and penetrate the Wolf Gate with no weapons." She pushed up her sunglasses, revealing intelligent brown eyes, and studied him carefully. "And no supplies."

Hex was somewhat curious himself as to how he'd managed all those things, but he wasn't about to tell her that. For all her monkey sass, the queen was obviously no dummy, and he had a feeling she'd know right away if he lied. Plus, he had no idea what he should even lie about. "I lost my memory in the poppy fields," he said. "I'd been there for a long time—a really long time. I was rescued by a boy who told me he could help me find out who I was. He guided me here, but disappeared just after the wolves attacked. Then Iris found me and—well, here I am."

The queen was staring at him incredulously. "Do you actually expect me to believe that?"

"A spy!" Iris shouted in excitement. "A traitor! Death to

enemies of the queendom!"

"I know how it sounds," Hex admitted. "But you have to believe me. I swear—"

He was interrupted by a tremendous clamor from the forest floor below. He wondered in terror if the wolves had broken through the wall. But these sounds were unquestionably monkeyish—shrieks, cackles, and almost-human-but-not-quite howls. There was a tremendous explosion and a cloud of foulsmelling smoke drifted past the queen's hut. She leapt to her feet. "Those cursed rebels and their wretched demands! Iris," she snapped, "take our prisoner to one of the guest huts at the edge of the forest. He'll be safe enough there until we've quashed this little squabble and I can decide what to do with him."

"But—" Iris protested.

"*Now*, Iris," the queen said. "I have work to do!"

Grumbling, Iris grabbed Hex by the shoulder—none too gently—and shoved him out the door and down the stairs. The queen bounded after them, seized a vine hanging from a nearby tree, and swung off toward the sounds of battle. Her departure was punctuated by another explosion, this one even more impressive than the first.

SIX

Still grumbling, Iris led Hex away from the chaos over a wobbly series of interconnected walkways. The sun had set, and the monkeys' city was lit by hundreds of glowing yellow balls that floated in the air. "Sunfruit," Iris said, in answer to his unasked question. "You can eat it if no one remembers to bring you dinner, but then you won't have a light."

Hex soon lost any sense of direction. If he wanted to find his way out of here again, he wouldn't be able to do it without the monkeys' help. Finally, Iris stopped at a low hut, more roughly built than others they'd passed but still as neatly constructed as a ship. He followed her inside to a little room lit by another, smaller sunfruit. The room was sparsely furnished with just a hammock and a single table and chair, but everything was tidy and clean. Iris rang a little bell shaped like a banana, and in a few moments another monkey dressed in a butler's outfit brought in a tray of . . . bananas. Hex almost groaned out loud. At the very corner of the tray was a small, steaming bowl. "Oatmeal for you, sir," the butler said politely as Iris helped herself to several bunches of banana.

"Oatmeal?" Hex wondered aloud as the butler bowed and left them. "For dinner?"

"Humans *love* oatmeal," Iris said authoritatively.

Hex decided not to argue. "What's going on out there?" he asked, sinking down onto the hammock to eat his oatmeal—which was burnt. Iris hovered awkwardly for a moment, still chewing, and then frowned and settled into the chair.

"The monkeys are split," she said heavily, swallowing the last of her banana. "Before Dorothy"—there was that name again—"came back to Oz, all the monkeys had wings." She flapped her arms, as if to demonstrate. "We flew all over Oz as we pleased when Ozma ruled. But then Dorothy took over and Ozma went—well, wherever she is. Our wings have always been vulnerable to magic—we've been enslaved by one ruler after another, including that cursed Wizard."

Wizard? Hex thought. *Was that me? Was that what I remembered in the queen's palace?* He shifted uncomfortably, but Iris didn't notice. "This time," she continued, "some of us decided losing our wings was worth our freedom. You're in the Queendom of the Wingless Ones—the last free monkeys in Oz." Iris puffed her chest proudly, and then her expression sank again. "But some of the monkeys don't *want* to be free anymore. They think it's better to side with Dorothy"—Iris spat the name out as if it were a curse—"and that Dorothy's creepy sidekick the

Scarecrow can make us new wings. They say Dorothy is on our side and wouldn't make us her slaves again—as if! Even back when she first came to Oz all she did was make us fly her around like we were some kind of taxi service. But now that she's returned, she's downright *evil*." Iris sighed. "The rebels have been causing all kinds of trouble in the queendom—sabotage, arson, waylaying supplies. Some of the poorest monkeys are going hungry. I *know* that human-loving—no offense—traitor Quentin is behind the rebels, and I can prove it, too—I've been tracking the queen's accounts with a data management system I developed, and by comparing royal expenditures I can prove that Quentin is siphoning food and supplies from all our imports," she said excitedly. "Only he's the chancellor, and I'm just a lowly guard. I can't say anything against him the queen will believe."

"Not even with all your data?" Hex asked.

She sighed again. "No one else understands double-entry accounting. Unless you know what the data means, it's all just a bunch of meaningless numbers. And—well, the queen is very wise, of course, but she doesn't think my work is serious," Iris said quietly. "No one does. They all think I'm just young and—and silly. I'm the only one of the monkeys who's even *interested* in numbers, and I can't make them see how important data management is."

But you are *young and silly*, Hex thought. *I wouldn't take you seriously either, if I were the queen*. Iris seemed to have a good heart, but she couldn't possibly think her endless spreadsheets would have any impact on the queen's decisions. She wasn't even a particularly effective guard. Was *he* meant to stop Quentin? If so, how? "I don't have any other proof," Iris was saying, "and Quentin knows that I can't do anything to stop him because no one will listen to me." Her brown eyes filled with tears. "The monkeys are going to destroy themselves, and I can't do a thing to stop it," she sobbed. She was so distraught that Hex forgot a few moments ago she had been clamoring for his execution. He patted her awkwardly on the back, and she wept heavily into his shoulder.

"I just c-c-care so m-m-uch!" she wailed, her runny nose dripping onto his shirt. "I want the monkeys to b-b-be happy! The only way to end the unrest is to prove he's at the heart of it. And I c-c-can't do anything!"

"There, there," Hex murmured, continuing to pat her gently as she erupted into damp, hiccuping sobs. "Why don't we go to the queen in the morning, and you can convince her you're right? I'm sure you can figure something out. You're very clever." But his mind was racing. Pete had said he was being tested—was that why he'd been brought here? And if it was, what was he supposed to do? Convince the monkeys to side with Dorothy? It was hard to take the monkeys seriously, but that Quentin had still seemed like a nasty piece of work. Iris snuffled and blew her nose on her sleeve.

"*I* should be Lulu's adviser, not Quentin!" Iris hiccuped furiously. "He's a traitor and a f-f-fraud! Do you really think I can convince the queen?" Her lower lip quivered and she looked dangerously close to bursting into tears again. Hex hastily handed her a banana.

"Of course," he said firmly, though he had no idea. "You've

already convinced me—and I'm a total stranger." This made no sense at all, but seemed to reassure Iris.

"You're right," she said more confidently. "First thing in the morning. I'll tell her! I'll—"

Suddenly, another loud explosion went off in the distance. Hex and Iris hurried outside, peering over the balcony of the guest hut. Below them, a small, seething group of monkeys battled each other furiously on the forest floor, their fight lit by more sunfruit. Monkeys in velvet suits that matched Iris's—presumably the queen's guard—carried prisoners, tightly wrapped in banana leaves, away from the battlefield, while more suited monkeys whacked the upstarts with bananas. "It all started with peaceful protests, but now we're on the verge of all-out civil war," Iris said, her eyes filling with tears again. "And it's all Quentin's fault! If he wasn't spreading lies, they'd realize siding with Dorothy means death—or worse." She sighed heavily. "It's been a long day, and I can't do anything until the morning. You might as well get some rest."

Iris sat at the table again, apparently taking her guard duty seriously enough to watch over Hex as he slept. He tried to get comfortable on the swaying hammock, at last falling into a fitful sleep. A strange, sonorous noise woke him later in the night, and he sat up in confusion. Iris had fallen asleep on the table, her shoulders hunched in defeat, and the room echoed with her snores. Hex sighed and lay back in the hammock again, waiting for dawn.

SEVEN

The next morning, after a breakfast of (to Hex's dismay) more oatmeal, Iris marched him briskly back to Lulu's hut. Her velvet suit was rumpled, but otherwise she was back to being the cocky, confident monkey who had marched him up the endless stairs.

Iris burst through the palace door, shouting, "Your Majesty! Your Majesty!" Queen Lulu, startled, turned from where she had been giving terse instructions to a small group of nervous-looking monkeys dressed in battered armor and carrying monkey-sized swords. Behind the queen, Quentin leaned against the wall, his dark eyes glittering as he watched the scene. *He looks like a monkey who just found himself a banana tree*, Hex thought. Iris stopped short. "Your Majesty," she whispered, "what are you doing? Monkeys have never used weapons on monkeys before now."

"We're past that point," Queen Lulu said tiredly. "Iris, I have to put a stop to this before our people destroy each other."

Lulu and Iris stared at each other as if they were frozen in time, while Quentin sneered. Hex's thoughts raced. Quentin wanted the monkeys to side with Dorothy, and everybody hated Dorothy—including Pete. Defeating Quentin's plot *had* to be his test. Iris was too naive and foolish to convince the queen—clearly, that was why he had been sent here. Pete had said he wasn't a real wizard, but that didn't mean he couldn't pretend to be one. He swiftly palmed one of the floating sunfruits and hurled it at the ceiling so quickly the monkeys only saw the bright shower of light that fell around him as the fruit splattered. "ENOUGH!" he boomed, and the monkeys stopped short and gaped at him. "I have come to you to demonstrate my powers and end the conflict that tears apart your nation!" Even his speech had changed, he thought, awed at himself. His back was straighter, his arms upraised as if he were sweeping an invisible cape behind him. His voice filled the little room. He pointed at Quentin. "You cannot hide from the might of my powers, ape!" he shouted. "I see all! I know the trick you have played upon your people and the deceit you have sown! The heart of this conflict lies at your feet, foul thief!" He turned to Queen Lulu, who was staring at him with her mouth hanging open. "Ask him what has been happening to your supplies, mighty queen! Ask him where he has hidden what he has stolen from you! Ask him why he is working in concert with"—*oh bother*, he thought, *what was her name again?*—"er, Dorothy's minions!"

Lulu pushed up her sunglasses, seeming a little less impressed. "These are serious accusations against one of my most trusted advisers," she said. "Do you have any proof?"

"He doesn't," Iris said, practically jumping up and down in her eagerness. "But I—"

Hex interrupted her. "I have seen the traitor at work!" he boomed in the most authoritative voice he could muster. "Last night, while you slept"—he hesitated for the barest moment, and then hit on the perfect lie—"I sent my astral body through the Queendom of the Wingless Ones, and saw the traitor Quentin meeting with the rebels!" This story seemed suddenly preposterous, even as he said it, but the trick with the sunfruit had apparently impressed the queen more than he'd realized. She raised one eyebrow, seeming almost convinced.

"That's nonsense!" Iris exclaimed. "But he's right, and I can—"

But the queen cut her off, turning to Quentin, who was edging toward the door. "Is this true?" she asked, her voice low and angry. "Have you betrayed my trust?"

"I can explain, Your Majesty," the chancellor said smoothly. "It's all a misunderstanding." He shot Hex a nervous glance. "The sorcerer is exaggerating—I was merely storing away some of our supplies for safekeeping—" Hex's accusation had been a shot in the dark, but it had hit home, he saw. Quentin *had* snuck out of the palace to meet with the rebels, and his slick demeanor faltered as the queen gave him a withering stare.

"You're *lying*," she snarled. "I can see it in your eyes, you thief! Under my very nose, you've torn apart our people! For this, you'll rot underground, never to swing from a vine in this city again—but first, you'll give back what you've stolen and end this strife!"

She gestured at her monkey soldiers, and they seized Quentin and dragged him outside. She turned to Hex. "I don't know what gift of fate brought you here, sorcerer," she said, "but I owe you my queendom."

"But I——" Iris began. Lulu ignored her and waved one hand imperiously. A soldier hastily brought her a banana. "Humans have never sat at the side of monkeys in all the history of our people," Lulu said, chewing thoughtfully, "but these are new times for all of us. If you choose to remain among us, you may have Quentin's old job. Which is a *real* honor, I'll have you know."

Of course, it was Iris who'd actually exposed the traitor. He could tell Lulu, but Iris was just a young hothead with no sense for politics. She wasn't suited for Quentin's position; really, he was doing her a favor, saving her from future embarrassment when she couldn't handle the responsibility. And if defeating Quentin had been his test, surely this was his reward. He could always award Iris an extra banana allowance once he was officially made chancellor—he wasn't *heartless*. Hex bowed politely. "Your Majesty, I'm honored. I'll certainly consider your offer." She nodded and tossed the banana peel over her shoulder; a guard hurried forward to catch it.

"Now," she said, "I must attend to my people." With that, she swept out the door, a scatter of rhinestones sparkling in her wake and the guard trailing behind her.

Next to Hex, Iris was almost speechless with fury. "You—you

human!" she gasped. "You're no *sorcerer*! You're just a stupid cheat who stole the credit for *my* work, and now Lulu thinks *you're* the one who exposed the rebellion!"

"Iris, there was nothing I could do," he lied in his most conciliatory tone. "The queen saw what she wanted to see. I would never have undermined you on purpose. Besides, you never said you wanted Quentin's *job*—just that you wanted him defeated. Really, I've only helped you get what you want."

"You don't even have the decency to tell me the truth," Iris said furiously. "You humans are all alike. You'll sell out anyone if you think it'll get you ahead." She gestured toward the door. "If you're so all powerful, you can find your own damn way to the guest chambers." She stalked out the door, but not before he caught a glimpse of her face and realized she was crying.

Hex watched her small back recede down the walkway, her shoulders shaking. Why couldn't she see how reasonable he was being? He was cleverer than Iris—didn't he deserve the queen's praise? A strange, unfamiliar sensation tugged at his heart— was it *guilt*? If he had done the right thing, why didn't he feel better about it?

"Nice one, Hex," said a sardonic voice behind him in the formerly empty room. He whirled in surprise. Pete lounged against a wall, one leg crossed over the other, chewing on a blade of grass and eyeing him with distaste. "I guess you can take away the memories, but you can't take away the man. Somehow I'm not surprised."

"I didn't mean to hurt Iris," Hex said. "I didn't think—"

"You never thought about anything except yourself," Pete said bitterly. "I thought the whole amnesia thing might give you a chance to start over, be a better man. Use wisdom and judgment for once, instead of deceit. Looks like I thought wrong, huh?"

"No!" Hex cried. He remembered the terrible flood of shame he'd felt the moment he'd first seen Queen Lulu. "I did something else to the monkeys, didn't I? Something worse?"

Pete snorted. "Yeah, you could say that," he said coldly. "You betrayed them, Hex. You gave power over them to the Wicked Witch of the West. You knew she would enslave them, and you didn't care."

"Why would I do that?" Hex whispered.

Pete shrugged. "You tell me, Hex. Convenient you forgot about that part, huh?"

"What else did I do that I don't remember?" Hex asked, his heart sinking. "What kind of person was I?"

"I already told you," Pete said. "A crappy one." He stared at Hex for a long time, his expression unreadable. For the second time, Hex wondered if maybe it wasn't better to leave his memories behind forever. "That was the test of your Wisdom, Wizard," Pete said. "You didn't do very well."

"How was that a test?" Hex protested.

"If you cared about Oz instead of yourself, you'd have used your wits to help Iris restore peace to the monkeys—not sell Iris out and make yourself look like the hero. Wisdom should be used for the good of all, not just one. It didn't occur to you to work together with Iris to find a way to defeat Quentin? To tell the queen that Iris was the one who deserved the credit?"

"But she's just a monkey!" Hex sputtered. "How was I supposed to know that was the test?"

"Here's a hint for the next stage," Pete snapped. "In the future, try thinking about someone other than yourself." Pete grabbed Hex by the wrist, and the air around them began to glow with the now-familiar purple crackle of Pete's magic.

"But now I'll never get to be chancellor," Hex said sadly, and then the hut around them vanished in a shimmer of purple light.

EIGHT

Hex felt as though he was being pulled through the air in a thousand different directions. He opened his mouth to shout in terror and a surge of purple magic poured down his throat. His entire body glowed with the same purple light. Was Pete so fed up with him that he had finally decided to just kill him? But before Hex could worry that he was experiencing his last moments on earth—or wherever he was—the purple light faded and he fell to the ground as if dropped there by a giant, none-too-careful hand.

"Sorry," Pete said from somewhere behind him, although he didn't sound sorry at all. "Teleportation can be a little rough if you're not used to it. Or if, in your case, you don't remember that you're used to it."

Hex ignored him, determined not to let Pete get the best of him—again. Instead, he stood up and looked around. They were in another forest, but this one looked significantly different from the monkeys' jungle home. Where that forest had seemed tropical, this one was cool and still. No brightly colored birds flitted from branch to branch. No sparkling waterfalls cascaded down soft, grassy hillocks between trees. This place was severe, almost stark; the air was much cooler, and as a sharp breeze brushed past the back of Hex's neck, he shivered. There was something about the dim, silent wood that was downright disturbing. He felt as though invisible eyes were peering at him from the shadows between the trees, assessing him as a potential lunch option.

Pete seemed unperturbed by the forest's haunted feel. He was dressed in the same clothes he'd been wearing when he'd pulled Hex from the poppy field, though he'd added a coat to stave off the forest's chill.

"What the hell happened to you?" Hex asked, fury battling out fear in his chest and ultimately winning.

"What do you mean?" Pete asked breezily.

"After the wolves—you just left me there! I was practically attacked by those dreadful monkeys, and nearly taken prisoner—it was only my ability to think on my feet that kept me safe!"

Pete stared at him. "You're already changing the story to suit yourself," he said coolly. "Amazing. 'Think on your feet'? Is that what you call what you did back there?"

Hex faltered. "Well, I—I mean, it's true the little monkey was the one who helped me expose the chancellor as a charlatan and restore peace to the queendom, but I'm the one who was able to get through to the queen when no one else could. Doesn't that count for something?" He resolutely avoided thinking about the hurt on Iris's face when he'd claimed sole credit for exposing Quentin. He didn't have time to worry about that now—he had to find out what the next test would be, and fast, before Pete disappeared again. "You yourself basically said I was a con man," he added. "Maybe I'm just remembering who I am. You're the one who won't tell me anything except that I'm from somewhere that isn't here and that it's my job to help you save a place I don't remember anything about. Why should I even want to do anything you ask of me?"

Pete sighed, and his harsh expression softened. "Look, I don't like this any more than you do. But Oz has always had a complicated relationship with the Other Place. It took someone from there—Dorothy—to set Oz's decline in motion. And we think it will take someone else from there to repair what she's done to our country. Right now, you're our only hope—assuming you remember who you are in time to stop her. And I know you don't remember, but I promise, Oz is worth saving."

"*Our?*" Hex asked.

Pete looked at him for a long time, mixed emotions playing on his usually impassive face. Finally, as if making a decision, he nodded. "I'm . . . helping the fairies, let's just say. We're fighting to make Oz the place it once was, before you—" He cut himself off. "Before everything changed."

"Before I what?" Hex asked. "Why can't you just tell me?"

Pete shook his head. "That's not how it works. You have to

remember—truly remember—who you are."

Hex looked at the ground, where tiny golden flowers with smiling faces beamed up at him. One of them appeared to be humming some kind of catchy jingle under its breath. "Did I— did I care about Oz?" he asked hesitantly. "Can you at least tell me that much?"

"You cared about yourself," Pete said. "As for Oz—only you can know that, once your memory has returned."

"Did it *seem* like I cared about Oz, when you knew me— before?"

"I've already told you all I can," Pete said curtly, and the stony-faced, inscrutable boy was back again. "You can ask me all the questions you want, but that's not going to get you any real answers. Those you have to find on your own."

"You're leaving me again, aren't you?" Hex said.

Pete smiled, though the grin didn't quite reach his brilliant emerald eyes. "You catch on quick."

"I still don't even know what I'm being tested for."

"The future of Oz," Pete said. "No pressure. Like I said, so far, your score is pretty low."

Hex thought of what he'd done to poor Iris and winced. If he'd known that his time with the monkeys had been a trial of some kind, would he have done anything differently? Iris's hurt, heartbroken face flashed before him again, and he closed his eyes against the memory. "What happens if I fail?" Hex asked.

Pete shrugged. "We'll throw you back in the poppy field, I

guess. If you fail you're of no use to anyone, let alone Oz. We don't need cowards and cheats on our side. Dorothy has plenty of those if you want to throw your lot in with her."

That name again. *Dorothy.* It rang the faintest of bells in his subconscious. Blue and white checks . . . something silver and glittering. *Shoes*, he thought suddenly. *There had been shoes.*

"I liked the poppy field," Hex admitted. "That doesn't seem much like punishment."

"In that case," Pete said calmly, "I guess we should just kill you." It was impossible to tell if he was joking.

"Are you a fairy?" Hex asked quickly, hoping to change the subject. But Pete looked troubled.

"I've already told you more than I should," he said. "The fairies sent me, and that's all you need to know."

"But how will I know when I'm being tested?"

Pete smiled like a cat with a cornered mouse. "Oh, believe me," he said. "You'll know."

"How will I know where to go?" Hex asked, but Pete had already vanished in another flash of purple electricity.

Hex looked down at his battered shoes—the only thing, he realized, that he had that was left over from his life before, whatever that life had been. Just beyond his toes, he noticed for the first time a sandy path that led off into the dark woods. He was sure—well, almost sure—that the path hadn't been there a moment ago. He looked up again; all around him, brambles and bracken had closed in. Their thick, waxy leaves waved eerily even though there was no wind, and huge, glossy black thorns sprouted from the branches, oozing a viscous slime that looked distinctly poisonous.

He had no other option but to follow the path through the thick underbrush. The only way out, it seemed, was forward.

NINE

Hex followed the path through the trees for what could have been hours or days. In the dark, endless forest, he lost all sense of direction and even the time of day. Anytime he so much as thought of stepping off the sandy path or heading in a different direction, the leaves around him rustled menacingly, and the branches clacked their thorns together as if to say, "Don't even bother."

Finally, when he felt as though he couldn't possibly walk any farther, he stumbled into a broad clearing whose ground was covered with the same dry, sandy earth as the path. He sank gratefully to the ground. Pete hadn't said anything about not stopping for the night—if it was even night. Nothing about the dim woods had changed in any way to indicate whether it was daytime or nighttime, or whether the sun was proceeding across the sky at all. The sinister, diffuse light seemed almost to come from the trees themselves.

Hex was also beginning to wonder what exactly he was supposed to eat or drink, when he spotted a brown knapsack at the far side of the clearing that he could have sworn wasn't there a second ago. Too hungry and thirsty to be cautious, he got to his feet to investigate. Inside the pack was a rough woolen blanket. Underneath it, there were a few pouches containing some stale bread and hard cheese. He realized the last actual meal he'd eaten had been his oatmeal breakfast with Iris, however long ago that had been, and his stomach grumbled loudly. He had a feeling that if there was anything alive in the woods around him, it would be a lot more likely to make a dinner out of him than to bring him a menu. He washed down the bread and cheeses with water from a bottle he found in the pack. The water, at least, was sweet-tasting and clear, and after another long drink he felt refreshed and clearheaded.

Below the water bottle, he found the clothes he'd been wearing when Pete pulled him out of the poppy field. He took them out and carefully unfolded them, fingering the soft material as though it could tell him who he was: a jacket, vest, spats, a pair of pants, a dapper collared shirt, and a top hat. But as much as he racked his brains, nothing came. If Pete was right, he hadn't yet passed the test that would unlock his past and show him how to help Oz—assuming he wanted to. But what if he uncovered his memories and discovered he couldn't stand this country of talking monkeys and flying wolves? What if Pete was right, and his true self was a terrible, selfish person? Wouldn't it be better to stay as he was, in this state of oblivion? The cheerless forest did nothing to distract him from these depressing thoughts.

His body was aching, and he was ready for a rest. He unrolled the blanket, stretched out on the ground, and was asleep almost as soon as his head hit the earth. But his dreams were awful: the monkeys battled each other savagely with their miniature swords, hacking at one another until the ground ran red with their blood, screaming in rage and pain—and then he jerked awake and realized the screams were real, and they were coming from somewhere ahead of him in the forest. His heart pounded in his chest. The screams were alarmingly near, and somehow familiar. Someone was in desperate trouble.

"Pete!" Hex shouted. "Help! Pete!" His voice barely carried past the clearing, and there was no response. The screams wavered for a second, and then continued even more awfully. He saw that there were now two paths leading out of the clearing—one toward the source of the noise, and the other away. He groaned aloud. Was this a test, or a trap? Either way, not very subtle.

Abruptly, the screams cut off with an awful gurgling sound. He stood poised in the clearing, listening intently. Perhaps it was too late. Whatever was happening out there, it was over. There was nothing he could do. Far better to protect his own skin; after all, he could hardly recover his memories if he was dead. And then, through the trees, he heard a faint, pleading—and familiar—wail. "Somebody please help me!" The voice sobbed. There was no mistaking it for anyone but Iris.

He stood a second longer, wavering with indecision. He was

a bad person. Pete had told him as much. And bad people put themselves first—and came out ahead. No one could possibly fault him for wanting to protect himself. It wasn't his problem. He thought of the pain and reproach in Iris's face as he'd betrayed her in front of the queen, and sighed. So far, he'd done nothing but prove Pete right: that he was nothing more than a con man and a coward.

But the feeling of persistent shame kept nagging at him, and he suddenly found himself wanting to do better. Even if it meant putting himself in danger. Even if he was risking his life for a cranky, spear-happy monkey with a persecution complex. He might not go down in the annals of history for trying to rescue Iris from whatever terrible thing was happening to her, but a more noble quest had yet to present itself. Maybe he had been a terrible person in the past, but being a terrible person in the present wasn't turning out to be very much fun. He took a deep breath, wishing Pete had thought to pack him a weapon of some kind, and took off running on the path that led to Iris.

He didn't have to go far before he found her. She was in another clearing like the one he'd left, so covered in blood she was almost unrecognizable. She cowered in a heap at the far edge of the clearing; opposite her, a huge, awful lion, spattered with her blood, lounged against a tree picking his teeth with one giant claw. The lion's mane was filthy and matted, and his huge muscles bulged grotesquely. Iris was sobbing, which at least meant she was still alive. The lion looked up as Hex entered the clearing. He grinned savagely, exposing his terrible, jagged fangs.

"Two for the price of one," he growled. "It's my lucky day: dinner buffet special."

"Leave her alone!" Hex said faintly, and the lion laughed.

"I don't think so, little man," he said, sneering. "I'm hungry. And when the Lion is hungry, the Lion gets his meal . . . or else." The Lion? Something about the horrible animal sparked at Hex's memory as fear flooded through him. The Lion's voice had a terrible power; across the clearing, Iris whimpered, even though the Lion hadn't been speaking to her. Hex's chest flooded with a sick, nameless dread. It was as if the Lion was fear itself, formed into the body of a terrible, powerful creature. "That's right," the Lion sneered, gloating. "Now you understand why I rule the forests of Oz. No one can withstand their fear of me. And now, little man, I'll feed on your terror—and then I'll feed on *you*."

The Lion rose to his feet, lashing his long, sinuous tail like a whip as he advanced toward Hex. His tail. Something about his tail. And then a whole memory came back to Hex, sudden as a tidal wave: a different Lion, a real one, cowering before him, begging for the gift of courage. *"Only you can help me," it cried, its golden fur gleaming in the warm Oz sun. "Please, Wizard! If only I had the courage of a real lion, I could stop being ashamed of myself—I could be free."* So Hex *had* been a wizard, then—but what kind? Had he somehow created this awful monster out of an ordinary beast? Would he have done something like that? Once, long ago, the Lion had wanted to be braver—but this perversion wasn't just a creature filled with ordinary courage. Pete had said Oz was changing, its very magic twisted. Was the Lion a part of that? Was this transformation somehow Hex's fault—or was he a victim of it, too?

He'd deliberated too long, and the Lion had crossed the clearing and was standing in front of him, leering at him. Up close, the Lion's breath smelled like a slaughterhouse crossed with a sewer.

"Don't they teach you to brush your teeth in this crazy country?" Hex said, and suddenly he found that his fear had fallen away from him. He *remembered*: not everything, and not enough, but he knew this terrifying creature had once been something else. Something desperate and even more cowardly than he was. Something ordinary and cowering and meek. And without fear, the Lion had no power over him.

The Lion halted in mid-pounce, rearing back so quickly that he almost fell over backward. "You fool," he snarled, a menacing growl so deep it almost seemed to come from the very earth itself. "Do you really think you can challenge me and win?"

Hex wasn't swayed. "Be strong," he called to Iris. "I'll be there to help you as soon as I can."

"Oh-ho!" the Lion chortled, leaping away from Hex and toward Iris. "Have I found your weakness, human? It's all well and good for you to think I can't hurt you, but your monkey friend here is a different story." The Lion stood over Iris, one enormous paw upraised, as though he meant to disembowel her.

"Leave her alone," Hex hissed, and the Lion laughed, bringing his paw down with all his might—and stopping just short of a killing blow, cuffing Iris roughly on the side of the head.

"No," the Lion said, "I don't think I will. But the longer she suffers, the more I get to enjoy watching you squirm. I don't know who you are, but I don't like you." He nipped lightly at Iris's arm, tearing away a piece of flesh. Iris howled in pain and fear.

Hex suddenly found that he was furious. Furious with Pete, for telling him nothing and leaving him here to battle this awful creature; furious with Iris, for getting herself into such an awful predicament and—worse—making him *care* about her; and above all else, furious with this disgusting, brutal lion, sneering and tormenting someone so small and helpless. Anger flooded through Hex's body, and with it something else—a force that seemed to come from the very earth itself. Something strange and powerful rushed through his body, but instead of feeling swept away he realized he was in total control. "ENOUGH," Hex said, and he could *see* his voice traveling across the clearing in a roiling wave of dark energy that surged toward the Lion and knocked him to his knees. The Lion roared in anger, springing to his feet again, but Hex held up one hand and pushed against the wall of power, and the Lion flew away from Iris and crashed into a tree.

"I made you what you are, animal," Hex said, and his voice was as strong and fierce as a thunderstorm. "To me, you are still nothing but a coward. Begone from this place." He raised his hand again and the Lion rose into the air; with a flick of his fingers, he summoned more power and sent the Lion cartwheeling through space, head over tail, before slamming him into the ground again. The Lion moaned feebly, his own eyes wide with fear. "Now you know how it feels," Hex said. "Think twice, before you inflict pain on the innocent. And get out of here, before I regret sparing you." The Lion grabbed his greasy, lashing tail, staring at it in bewilderment, before he shot Hex a look of pure hatred and bounded away through the trees. All the power rushed out of Hex in a flood and he stumbled, almost falling to his knees. Iris was struggling to prop herself up on her elbows. "No!" he said, scrambling over to her. "You must rest. You're badly wounded." Up close, he saw just how much blood she had lost, and his heart sank. Her uniform was so soaked he couldn't even tell its original color. Her eyes were glazed, and her breathing was fast and shallow.

"That was a dirty trick you pulled back there in the palace," she wheezed, staring up at him. "But I think you just saved my life. Does that mean I have to thank you?"

"No," he told her. He stripped off his jacket and shirt, tore the shirt into strips, and did his best to bandage the worst of Iris's wounds. If it had been magic that he had somehow summoned back there battling the Lion, it was gone now. But without it, he didn't know if he could save the plucky little monkey he'd risked his life for.

"That hurts," she said crossly as he tied off a bandage too tightly.

"Complain to the Lion," he said, trying to keep the fear out of his voice. There was no mistaking it: Iris was close to death.

And, he realized, he desperately wanted to save her. The feeling was so alien he didn't know what to make of it. Another fit of coughing racked her broken body, and he hushed her gently, cradling her in his arms. She closed her eyes. "Too bad you went to all that trouble," she coughed. "I was following you, you know. To stab you in the back."

"Iris, hush," he said. "Save your strength. You wouldn't really have stabbed me anyway."

"Probably not," she conceded, and then her head rolled back and she lost consciousness. Hex lowered her to the ground, frantically feeling for a pulse. There it was, at the side of her throat—faint, and growing fainter. "Iris," he pleaded. "It's my fault you're even here. Please don't die." He felt an unfamiliar wetness coursing down his cheeks. Was he bleeding? But his hands came away wet with something clear.

"Tears," a voice said behind him, and he whirled around. Pete was looking over his shoulder, staring at Iris with an expression of intense concern.

"Tears? You leave me like this—leave her like this—and that's all you can say?"

"You're crying," Pete said curtly. "Now get out of my way if you want her to live."

Hex moved aside, and Pete knelt over Iris's body, holding his hands just above her chest. As they hovered over her, they began to glow. This time, Hex could see tendrils of magic rising out of the earth, forming a web that wrapped Iris's body over and over again until she was an Iris-shaped purple light. Pete's face was tense with concentration, his eyes closed, his lips moving silently as the magic intensified. His arms began to tremble and his forehead grew slick with a sheen of sweat, and Hex worried that he might faint. Finally, with a gasp, Pete slumped backward and opened his eyes. Iris was still out, but her breathing had evened, and the worst of her wounds had stopped bleeding.

"She'll be all right," Pete whispered. "But the Lion did more than just harm her body. His power is to feed on others' fear—on their very essence. She has to rest for a while, and so do I."

Hex covered Iris with the blanket from his pack; mysteriously, two more had appeared beneath it, along with a loaf of bread that looked decidedly fresher than what he'd eaten earlier. He spread out the blankets while Pete did his best to start a fire. It took him several tries, but finally he coaxed a feeble magical blaze out of the air.

"Will the Lion come back?" Hex asked, tearing the loaf of bread in half. He handed the bigger half to Pete, who took it without commenting on Hex's sudden generosity.

"Not tonight," Pete said. "We're safe for a little while at least." He settled back onto his blanket, chewing on his hunk of bread, and after a moment Hex did the same. While Iris snored softly, Pete and Hex stared into the fire, neither of them ready for sleep.

"You knew," Hex said, and Pete started.

"Knew what?"

"You knew the Lion had Iris. You knew he would kill her, if I didn't stop him somehow." Pete was silent. "She'd be dead," Hex repeated. "If I hadn't found a way to save her—if I hadn't been brave enough to face down the Lion—you would have left her there to die."

"She didn't die," Pete said.

"But she would have."

"None of us know what would have been," Pete said quietly. "We only know what is."

"How is leaving her there to die any different from what I did in the palace?" Hex asked angrily. "We're not so different, you and me. You tell me I only think of myself, and maybe that's true—maybe it's always *been* true. But you were willing to sacrifice Iris for some stupid test, to see if I'm eligible for some quest you want me for—"

"Saving Oz is not 'some quest,'" Pete said. "And the circumstances of the test choose themselves. I didn't know Iris would be in danger."

"If you had known the test would put her in danger, would you have consented to it?"

Pete raised one hand in a helpless gesture. With a loud snort, Iris turned over and settled herself again. "I don't choose the magic," Pete said. "The magic chooses us. Oz chooses us. We can only do what it asks of us, and do our best to keep it safe. Sometimes that involves sacrifice, yes."

"But not *your* sacrifice," Hex said.

"I've sacrificed more than you will ever know," Pete said sharply. "You don't know the first thing about sacrifice, Wizard."

Hex was silent, watching the flames flicker silently from blue to pink to green and back to blue again. Though they burned for hours, they didn't seem to require fuel. Just one more thing in this crazy country that didn't make any sense.

"I felt something strange," Hex said quietly. "Back there, when I was trying to save Iris. I think it might have been something I've never felt before at all. Not even before, when I knew who I was."

Pete was silent for a long time. "Selflessness," he said finally. "That feeling's called selflessness."

Selflessness. Hex turned the word over in his mind. He'd cared about Iris's well-being more than he'd cared about his own—maybe it was only for a few minutes, but it had opened something up inside him that felt different and new. He couldn't undo the person he had been before, whoever that was, and whatever he'd done to make Pete feel such contempt for him. But he didn't have to be tethered to that idea of himself either. The Wizard. The words still meant nothing, though they'd obviously meant something to Iris.

"When I was the Wizard," he said. "You said I didn't have real magic, just a bunch of flashy tricks. But when I fought the Lion . . ." He trailed off, not sure how to ask.

"That was magic," Pete said. "The Old Magic of Oz. When you saved Iris, you tapped into it for the first time."

"Can I do it again?" he asked. Pete sighed. "I know, I know," Hex said hastily. "There's so much you can't tell me. Of course. But what I did back there—that was new?"

"Oz is changing fast," Pete said. "And we're all changing

with it. Everything is going to be different now for all of us." He looked at the dancing flames. "Get some rest," he said. There was something new in his voice, something different. If Hex didn't know better, he would have said it was respect. "You still have one more test to pass. And this one's going to be the worst of them all."

TEN

Hex expected Pete to leave him again in the morning, but to his surprise, Pete made the three of them a tasty breakfast of porridge and scrambled eggs—where he'd gotten the eggs, Hex didn't ask—and showed no signs of departing after he had magicked away the breakfast dishes. The rest seemed to have done wonders for both him and Iris; Pete's terrible pallor of the night before was gone, and though he moved stiffly, he had clearly regained most of his strength. Iris had a noticeable limp and difficulty moving one arm, but she babbled at them a mile a minute. The Lion had damaged her body, but he'd certainly done no permanent harm to her spirits.

Pete was mostly silent, and Hex couldn't help but wonder what his sullen mood meant. Iris chattered on at them both about a new formula she had developed to track banana consumption by age, happily oblivious, and Hex was grateful for her cheer. She hadn't forgiven him exactly for what he had done in Lulu's palace, but since he had saved her life, she seemed somewhat appeased, and she'd apparently forgotten all about her plan to murder Hex in his sleep. (He seriously doubted she had ever been capable of such an act, anyway, as much as she wanted them to believe she was a ferocious warrior.) She'd given them a detailed rundown of the current political situation among the Wingless Ones: with Quentin's treachery exposed, Lulu had been able to restore order among the rebel factions. The chancellor had been storing away most of the supplies he'd stolen, and Lulu was busy redistributing them among the poorest of the monkeys. Anyone else would have managed to report this news in a few sentences, but Iris was only too happy to go off on long digressions about statistical analysis, equations for determining equitable distribution of goods, and cost-benefit analyses. While Queen Lulu still credited the mysterious sorcerer with exposing the chancellor's wrongdoing, Iris said, shooting Hex a menacing look, Iris herself had been promoted out of the guards to a management position as soon as he'd left, and couldn't be happier about it.

"Now that everything's settled with the Lion," she said finally, "I should be getting back to the Wingless Ones. Lulu's a great ruler, of course, but she doesn't have a head for numbers. I'm badly needed back at the palace." She puffed her chest importantly, and then winced.

"You shouldn't travel alone," Pete said. "You're still hurt, and vulnerable."

"I can take care of myself!" Iris said, immediately furious.

"The Lion may return at any time," Pete said, and she deflated.

"I suppose you're right," she said, and her bravado fell away. "I thought I was going to die back there," she said softly.

"The Lion is far less likely to attack again if the three of us are together," Pete said. "Especially now that he knows Hex is a match for him. And I think we got rid of the wolves for now. We'll escort you back to the Sea of Blossoms. You should be safe enough the rest of the way to the queendom."

Hex looked at Pete in surprise, but didn't ask any questions. Was this part of his third test? And why was Pete sticking around? But Pete was as infuriatingly inscrutable as ever as they rolled up their blankets and prepared to leave. Pete suggested they fashion crutches for Iris, but she scoffed at the idea. Her indignation was so comical that even Pete cracked a smile.

At some point while they rested, the other path—the coward's path, Hex thought—had disappeared, leaving them only one way out of the clearing. The trees were just as ominous, the weird perpetual twilight just as creepy, but Iris's happy chatter lightened Hex's mood, and it seemed as though they had only been walking for a few hours when the thorny underbrush thinned out and the trees began to grow farther and farther apart. Soon, real sunlight filtered down through the forest canopy, and at last they emerged, blinking, into a sunny meadow dotted here and there with huge, lush fruit trees that grew in tidy rows. A broad blue stream ran through the meadow, burbling merrily. The whole place was such a welcome contrast to the forest that

Hex felt his heart lift immediately.

"Beautiful, isn't it?" Pete said. Hex nodded, and Iris sighed in pleasure.

"I should get out of the queendom more often," she said happily. "There's nothing like a good vacation to make you appreciate home, right?" Hex almost laughed out loud. Iris was the only person—well, monkey—he could imagine who would describe being attacked by a monstrous Lion while plotting a murder as a "vacation." He wondered again about his own home. Had he wanted to go back? Or had he been happy here?

"We should keep moving," Pete said. "The Lion isn't stopped by pretty scenery. Neither are the Tin Woodman's soldiers."

"Soldiers?" Hex asked in surprise.

Pete nodded. "Not everyone in Oz can access the kind of magic you did in the clearing. The Lion is doubtless on his way to warn Dorothy and Glinda, if he hasn't already. And once they learn that someone with that kind of power is just wandering around Oz—well, it won't be long before they're hot on our trail."

"Dorothy," Iris said, and spat on the ground. Hex was shocked.

"Who *is* this Dorothy?" he asked.

"She used to be the best thing that had happened to Oz," Iris said, "but then she turned out to be the worst." Hex waited for Pete to cut her off, but to his surprise, Pete let her continue, her voice growing even more passionate as they walked. "For a long time, a terrible usurper ruled Oz," she explained. "He came from the Other Place in a beautiful balloon that floated in the sky. This was a long time ago, of course—the citizens of Oz were much more trusting then. He deceived everyone in Oz and made them believe he was a good and kind Wizard, when he was nothing of the sort! He didn't even have magic—just a bunch of fancy tricks. He made the people of Oz build him the Emerald City, and then he shut himself up in the palace so no one would realize he was a fraud. He stole the throne from the fairies, the rightful rulers. We tried to stop him, but he was too powerful."

"That's not exactly true," Pete said drily. "The citizens of Oz have never done much to stop anything from happening."

"The monkeys did!" Iris said hotly. "We saw through him from the very first! We knew he was trouble! We called him the Traitor! We never bowed down to him!"

"You didn't try to stop him until it was too late," Pete said. "Until he sold you into slavery. And all of this happened before you were even born, Iris."

"Are you going to let me finish or not?" Iris snapped, and Hex was surprised to see tears in her eyes. Pete relented, waving at her to go ahead. "That was when Dorothy first showed up," Iris continued. "She came from the Other Place."

If Dorothy was from the Other Place, and *he* was from the Other Place—did that mean they were related somehow? Had he known her? Something stirred at the back of his mind. He was so close, he thought, to putting it all together. So close to remembering who he was. But understanding was still on the far side of that shimmering wall—close enough to touch, but separated from him by a barrier he couldn't yet cross.

"Dorothy defeated the Traitor, and sent him back to the Other Place, and no one has heard from him since. Good riddance, if you ask me. She went back, too, and Ozma took the throne"—Iris gave a respectful little curtsy, as if this Ozma could somehow see her—"and everything was as it should be. But then Dorothy came back. Nobody knows how or why she got here, but this time everything was different. *She* was different. It was as if something—or someone—had brought her back to destroy Oz. At first, no one realized anything was wrong. She stayed in the palace with Ozma, and they had all sorts of banquets, and everyone who was anyone was invited—*I* didn't want to go, of course," Iris said quickly, "even if I'd had an invitation, I would have turned it down, I don't care a thing about parties." The wistful look in her eye belied her words. "But then Ozma changed somehow, and suddenly it was Dorothy this, Dorothy that. The Tin Woodman's armies marching around and laying waste to villages. It's like Oz has been wounded; the whole land is bleeding magic, and unless someone puts a stop to Dorothy, we're all doomed."

Iris's tone had grown more and more somber as she spoke, and even the weather echoed her mood: a huge thunderstorm was piling up in the distance, moving toward them rapidly, and the temperature was dropping. They were almost across the meadow; at the horizon, Hex could make out something bright and undulating that must have been the Sea of Blossoms. They were close then. Pete looked up at the sky. There was something unnatural about how quickly the storm was moving. Something almost—magical. "You wanted to know what the third test was," Pete said, looking at him. "It's coming for you now."

Hex stared up at the sky. The thunderclouds, directly overhead now, swirled and coalesced, taking the shape of giant men who battled each other fiercely. As each blow landed, thunder cracked and boomed and jagged spears of lightning shot down toward the earth. Iris shrieked as a white-purple streak of lightning struck the ground just a few feet from where they stood. Hex recognized nothing about the meadow, and yet everything about this scene was familiar: the heaving purple clouds, the thunder, the color and sound of the lightning—*he was in a basket, a basket floating in the air, while all around him a thunderstorm just like this one raged; he was fleeing something, or going somewhere. He was leaving Oz. It was so close*—he grasped desperately for the tangled threads of memory, but they slipped away again, just out of reach. An earsplitting rumble of thunder followed another terrific crack of lightning that struck the earth in front of them so fiercely it split the ground open. Purple and gray smoke poured from the fissure, forming itself into a stairway that led down into the darkness.

As quickly as it had come upon them, the thunderstorm dissipated into a few scattered clouds that veiled the bright sun and cast long shadows across the now-chilly meadow. Hex shivered and wrapped his arms around himself. Iris gaped at the staircase, her expression so comical that Hex would have laughed if he himself had not been filled with fear at the sight of it.

"This is as far as we go," Pete said calmly, as if nothing out of the ordinary had happened. "I'll see Iris safely to the edge of the Sea of Blossoms, and then I must return to the palace. I've already been away far too long. Dorothy will be suspicious."

"What about me?" Hex said, his voice more plaintive than he would have liked.

"*I* wouldn't go down there if you paid me," Iris said vehemently.

"You're not the one who has to," Pete said to her. He pointed to Hex's pack. "Change into the clothes you brought with you before you go," he said. "You won't need anything else."

Hex swallowed. "What if I refuse?"

Pete raised an eyebrow. "If you refuse? Do you really want to wander around forever like the village idiot, never knowing who you are and where you came from?"

"Maybe I do. Maybe I'm happy this way."

Pete shrugged. "In that case, you're no help to us. I'll take away your protection—and your disguise. There are a lot of people in Oz who won't be too happy to see you as you are— and you won't even know why, or who to protect yourself from."

"You'd leave me to die?"

"We do what's necessary for the greater good of Oz," Pete said dismissively. "Nothing comes without sacrifice."

Iris was looking back and forth between the two of them, her eyes wide. "I think you should probably do what he says," she said to Hex. "He sounds kind of serious." She limped forward and stuck out a paw. After a minute, Hex realized she meant for him to shake it, and obliged. "You started out kind of a rat," she said. "But then you made up for it. You're not so bad, human. Thanks for saving my life."

"You're welcome," he said, bemused. "Good luck with your—"

"Double-entry accounting is not a matter of *luck*," she said. "It is an operation of *skill*." She limped off toward the Sea of Blossoms, not looking back to see if Pete was following.

"Good luck," Pete said. "Iris is right, you know. You are doing a pretty good job lately, for a human." His tone had the same begrudging respect he'd had back in the clearing, after Hex had fought the Lion to save Iris.

"Can't you at least warn me what the last test will be?" Hex asked.

Pete laughed. "You should know better by now than to even ask. But when it comes time for you to make a choice, remember: you're the Wizard. Once you ruled Oz, and now Oz is a part of you. Think about that, before you accept any gifts that are offered you."

With that cryptic remark, Pete turned to follow Iris. "Good-bye!" Hex called after him, but he didn't turn around or acknowledge Hex's farewell. "And thanks for nothing," Hex muttered under his breath. He dug his old suit out of the pack Pete had left him, feeling a little silly, and changed behind a tree—as if there was anyone around for miles who could see him. He adjusted his top hat on his head and straightened his jacket. The clothes might make the man, but they didn't tell him anything new about who he was. With that, he laid the pack tidily under the nearest tree, took a deep breath, and started down the stairs.

ELEVEN

Although the lightning had opened up the earth just moments ago, the staircase into the earth seemed ancient. The steps were as worn as if generations of feet had passed over them. Torches burned along the walls at intervals just regular enough to light the way, but their flame was cold and blue, not the cheery orange of real fire, or even the flickering multihued warmth of Pete's magical campfire. The air was chilly, and Hex pulled his jacket close.

The staircase ended at last at a long, dim corridor that stretched before him into more darkness. He looked around him for some kind of light, but the torches were firmly fastened to the walls. Did *he* have the magic to make a lantern? Even as he thought it, the air around him sparked and crackled, crystallizing into a kerosene lantern with a metal handle and a cheerful golden flame. He plucked it out of midair: it was solid and unmistakably real. What else could he conjure up? A five-course dinner? A trip home? A fur coat to stave off the chill? But no matter how he concentrated, nothing else happened. Magic, apparently, was fickle. No surprise there. He held the lantern aloft, advancing cautiously down the corridor. After a few minutes, the hallway abruptly ended in a rough wall. He stared in disbelief at the wall. He rapped it with his knuckles: solid stone. Was he supposed to cast a spell? Say a magic word? He racked his brains for any kind of clue Pete had given him, anything that would indicate what he was supposed to do next, but came up with nothing. He was at a literal dead end.

Well, he thought, no one could say he hadn't tried. He'd done his best to meet the test, and nothing had happened. There was no reason for him to stick around in this big, empty hall. Pete would have to understand. Maybe Pete wouldn't even know—he could find a nice village somewhere, settle down. Perhaps he'd try being a farmer, or a grocer. What did people do for work in Oz? Maybe he didn't even need to work, if he was such a powerful magician. He could get a nice set of robes and a wand, maybe teach himself to fly. He could visit Iris and the monkeys, impress them with his powers. Perhaps Queen Lulu would award him some kind of honorary decree. He'd be esteemed above all other humans, loved—and maybe feared, just a little—by all.

Buoyed by this cheerful thought, he turned around to leave. As he took the first step, there was a powerful *whoosh* and hundreds of torches flared to life all around him, nearly blinding him. He threw one arm over his eyes and yelped in surprise.

"At last," said a cool, dry, sardonic voice behind him. "We

have the immeasurable honor, brethren, of meeting the Wonderful Wizard of Oz."

Hex turned around very, very slowly, blinking until his eyes adjusted to the light's dazzle. The rough stone hallway was gone: he was standing in an immense, palatial room lit by huge crystal chandeliers; the light was not so extraordinarily bright after all, but had just seemed so in contrast to the dim hallway. The room was luxuriously appointed; the walls were draped in black velvet, and the floor was covered with rich, tapestried carpets piled three or four deep. And it was full of people. They stared at him curiously from where they reclined against carelessly stacked overstuffed velvet pillows or slouched in ornately carved armchairs that rested next to enameled tables bearing platters of glossy, dark fruits he didn't recognize. They were all alarmingly beautiful, but eerily identical, with bone-pale skin and hair a shade whiter. They were dressed alike in black clothes that blended into the walls so that their cruel, fox-like faces seemed to float, disembodied, in the darkness. The nearest of them shifted in his chair and there was something inhuman about the way he moved, almost as if he was double-jointed. At the center of the room there was a flat black pool, perfectly round and still, whose waters reflected nothing but instead seemed to absorb the light like a black hole.

There was no mistaking the speaker, who lounged regally in a throne-like chair that was bigger and more elaborate than all the other furniture in the room. Carved out of some dense, shiny black stone, it was studded with blood-colored rubies that

gleamed dully in the soft light of the chandeliers. Its occupant
was even paler than the other people in the room, with long,
sleek white hair that spilled down his shoulders and over the rich
black robes he wore. One long, leather-clad leg was slung over
the throne's armrest, and he kicked idly with one booted foot
against its side. A long black cigarette burned between the first
and second knuckles of his fingers; he flicked ash disdainfully
on the carpet before taking a long, decadent drag. His expression was one of utter, all-consuming boredom, but his black eyes
glittered dangerously.

Hex coughed, trying not to stare around him. "You seem to
know who I am," he said cautiously, "but I'm afraid you have me
at a disadvantage."

The man threw his head back and laughed. "It speaks, brethren!" he chortled, and all around him the other people in the
room tittered. Hex flushed an embarrassed red. "Oh, come now,
Wizard, don't be so easily flustered," the man said, still laughing.
"There was a time when all of us here were under your estimable
thumb, was there not? We were simply *terrified* of your *incredible* powers." At this, everyone around him only laughed harder.
Hex scowled and balled his hands into fists, determined not to let
these strange people get the best of him.

"Ah, my dear Wizard, I apologize," the man said, still chuck-
ling. "Come forward, and let me greet you properly. Welcome to
the Kingdom of the Fairies."

As he skirted the pool, Hex saw that the fairy's black cloak
was actually a pair of tightly folded wings—and, his glance

darting around the room, he saw that the other occupants of the
room all sported wings as well. Some of the fairies yawned and
stretched as he passed, unfurling their wings—black, but lacy
and delicate as a butterfly's—and waving them gently. Others
stared at him openly, craning their heads to get a better look at
him. At last he was standing before the throne, unsure of whether
or not he should kneel.

"Do not humble yourself before me, Wizard," the fairy said.
It sounded a lot like the fairy was making fun of him. "We are
practically—well, I wouldn't say *equals*, but my people are the
rightful rulers of Oz, and you, once upon a time, usurped the
throne—so we have a certain degree of experience in common,
do we not?" The mockery in his voice was now unmistakable.
Hex felt stupid and small. Pete had said he hadn't been much of
a wizard, but he'd just been dragged through all kinds of trials,
and the last thing he needed was some stupid creep in a weird
getup making him feel small.

"You know I don't remember anything," he said angrily. "I'm
here because Pete said you could help me if I passed your stupid
test. Is that true, or should I just leave?"

The fairy laughed, and this time his laughter seemed genuine
rather than malicious. Hex almost rolled his eyes in frustration.
What was the deal with these people? Were they just toying
with him? Did they even mean to help him at all? He'd had no
reason to trust Pete to begin with, and now he was beginning to
wonder if Pete had had some ulterior motive all along.

"I can give you back your memories, Wizard," the fairy said.

"But a choice lies in front of you; a crossroads of a kind. You must choose your path before we can give you back what you have lost."

"A choice?" *So this is it*, Hex thought. *This is the final test.* The monkeys had tested his Wisdom—and he had failed. The Lion had tested his Courage—and he had passed. What was left? What happened if he failed? Would they really kill him, like Pete said?

"What do you think is left, Wizard?" the fairy king said. "Wisdom, Courage—what other virtue before you remains but Love?" He said the word *love* with a tone of such contempt that Hex nearly flinched. "Do you accept my challenge? Am I so much more frightening than the Lion that you cannot trust the test I lay before you?"

That was not exactly reassuring. Hex raised an eyebrow. "What happens if I fail?"

The fairy sat up in his chair, and looked at Hex with a gaze that pinned him like an insect. "Then you are of no more use to us," he said, "and people who are of no use to the fairies do not last long in Oz."

"I thought Ozma was supposed to be good!" Hex protested.

"Ozma," the king snorted, and a titter ran through the assembled crowd. "Ozma has her uses, but she is the least of all of us. Wizard, I grow impatient. Will you begin the test, or keep yapping all day?"

Hex stared at the fairy king, who blew a set of lazy smoke rings at the ceiling. "Take off your clothes," the king said flatly, "and enter the pool. And then, Wizard, we will see what stuff you are made of."

"Here?" Hex asked, bewildered.

"Where else?" It all seemed like some elaborate practical joke. Hex would take off his clothes, and they'd all laugh at him, and that would be the end of it; he'd be humiliated, they'd have had their fun. Suddenly, he found that he didn't care. He was tired of cryptic pronouncements, inexplicable quests, mysterious allusions to a past he knew nothing about. If this was his chance to find out who he was and end it, he was willing to take it. And if not? If they killed him? So be it. It couldn't be worse than the Lion, whatever they did. At least, it didn't *seem* like it could be worse than the Lion. He stripped off his jacket and trousers and undergarments; the fairy king raised one eyebrow, but said nothing, and Hex sensed that he was almost impressed. *He didn't think I could do it.* He stood before the fairies with his back straight, naked as the day he was born. "I accept your test," he said, and then he walked to the pool and jumped in.

The water was as thick and viscous as oil, and he sank like a stone, realizing belatedly that he had not thought to ask how deep the pool was—and it seemed that the person he had once been had no idea how to swim. Without thinking, he opened his mouth to shout in terror, and the black liquid poured down his throat and entered his body, turning his limbs heavy and his thoughts slow and strange. He was drifting through darkness— he found, to his surprise, that he could breathe, although the air was heavy and close and scented with something unfamiliar but not unpleasant. Faintly sweet, like a delicate wildflower.

"Welcome, Wizard," said a gentle voice. It came from every-where and nowhere, surrounding him like the water itself; it was kind, but underneath the kindness was steel.

"Who are you?" he asked, and found that he could speak as easily as he could breathe—where was he? What kind of pool was this?

"You are in a place between places," the voice said. "A place between times. Between what has come before, and what is yet to pass. The pool of the fairies is a very old and very powerful thing. It is here that you must make your final choice. But first, I have something to show you."

"Who are you?" he asked again, and the voice laughed.

"I am Ozma," it said, "and Lurline before her, and all the fairy queens who have ruled this country. I am made out of the magic of Oz itself. I *am* Oz, Wizard. Now pay attention." The darkness around him swirled into an image of what he knew must be Oz, but not the Oz he had traveled through: this vision was a terrible one. Dark factories scarred the once-verdant landscape, belch-ing black smoke into the toxic air. Munchkins in chains toiled miserably in the fields, drawing magic out of the earth with ter-rible machines as a glittering pink witch floated over them, her mouth drawn into a horrible grin. The Lion tore through a vil-lage, leaving a pile of corpses in his wake, his mouth and hands red with blood as he laughed mercilessly. The clanking armies of the Tin Woodman marched endlessly across the barren plains where flowers had once bloomed, crops had once grown. Iris, her wrists bound, wept piteously as a soldier dragged her behind him toward the Emerald Palace.

And then Hex saw himself and knew somehow that he was in the Other Place. He was in a huge room—a study or a library—filled with rich, expensive furniture. Bookcases stuffed with leather-bound books and curios lined one wall, and framed posters featuring his picture plastered another. His side table was crowded with flowers and cards; baskets of fan mail were piled beneath them. He was reading a book about magic, seated at an impressive oak desk covered in ornate carvings, while a butler brought him a glass of whiskey in a crystal highball glass on a little silver tray, bowing deeply.

"You can leave Oz," the voice said. "You can return to the Other Place. This is the life that awaits you there—the life of a conjurer, a stage magician of great renown. You will be wealthy beyond your wildest dreams; you will perform for presidents and kings. Your magic will not be real, not the magic of Oz, but it will not matter—because audiences around the world will believe it is. You will live a long, illustrious life, and die a very old and very respected man."

"But Oz . . . ," he said.

"But Oz will become what you have seen. There will be no stopping the tide of Dorothy's dark magic. Oz will fall."

"And if I stay?"

"There are no certain things," the voice said. "There is no way to see the end of this story until we are upon it. You have magic here, real magic. You have been transformed. If Oz is to

have a chance, it will be because you stay. But there are no guar-
antees."

"I could give up everything and still fail?"

"You could."

"The fairies mocked you."

"Our line is . . . different from our kindred," said the voice,
and now it seemed impossibly sad. "The burdens of ruling Oz
alone have changed us. Lurline's descendants are true to Oz,
but the other fairies have become corrupt and weak. They see
only themselves. If you choose Oz, Wizard, you must be wary
of them."

He drifted through the dark water, confused and lost. "What
about Pete?"

He could almost hear the voice smile. "What do you think of
Pete?"

"I think he's a jerk."

Now the voice was definitely laughing. "Do not be so quick
to judge, Wizard. Pete has his own burdens to carry, and his own
secrets. All will be revealed to you in time—if you choose the
people of Oz. If you do not . . ."

"If I don't, the fairies will kill me."

"The fairies are malicious, but not evil. Whatever they told
you, they will not kill you. You will be returned safely to your own
time, your own home. All of this will be behind you." The voice
grew sad again. "You will forget your time here, even as Oz ceases
to exist. But you must know what you were, before you can choose
what you will become. I give you your memories, Wizard."

The terrible vision of Oz, of Iris with her bound and bleeding wrists, vanished. And suddenly, his memory—the memory of who he had been, what he had done, his days in the palace and in the Other Place, the entire long, tangled ribbon of his life, spilled back into his head like wine pouring from a jar, until he was dizzy with it. The petty tricks he had played on the people as soon as he had arrived in Oz, the deceit—forcing them to build him the Emerald City, betraying the monkeys, avoiding the witches like the plague lest he be exposed as the fraud he so essentially was. His entire time in Oz had been marked with his craven cowardice and chicanery. He had made the worst possible choice at every turn. No wonder the monkeys had cursed him; no wonder Pete had treated him with such contempt. He was filled with an overwhelming shame. How could he face the people of Oz after what he had done? How could he possibly stay here? The only answer was to go somewhere no one knew him and start over.

It hardly seemed like a choice at all. "I choose—" He opened his mouth to ask her to send him back, send him home at last—but something stopped him at the last minute. What would happen to him if he returned to the Other Place? If he left behind what it was he had found here—the possibility that he was something far more than an ordinary man? He had felt the power of Oz's magic running through him like a drug in his veins. To abandon that forever, once he had tasted it—what would that do to him? All the money and fame in the world could never come close to that elation, that exhilarating moment in the clearing when he had felt the full power of Oz coursing through him, when almost anything had seemed possible. What if that power was the chance to redeem himself? What if it would make him a better man than he had been? If he left now, if he went back to the Other Place, he would live with the regret of his loss for all the rest of his years. He would lose the chance of undoing the terrible things he had done, and never be able to forgive himself for it. And more than anything else, even if he went back to riches and fame, he would never use magic—real magic—again. Never know what it was like to summon the power of Oz. Never find out what he was truly capable of, now that he could tap into Oz's magic. And he knew, deep down, that regret would undo him, like a cancer in his heart.

"I choose Oz," he said. All around him, he could hear the fairies crying out—in joy, in exhilaration, in triumph, he could not say. "I am the Wizard!" he cried aloud, and then all at once he had the sensation of flying through the air at a tremendous speed until he landed with a sudden, ungainly thump on the carpet at the fairy king's feet, stark naked and dripping wet.

The fairy king sneered down at him. "So you have chosen us after all, Wizard," he said, and beckoned to one of the fairies behind him. "Bring our Wizard a towel," he added, laughing mockingly. "If you are truly to be the savior of Oz, Wizard, you might want to start by putting on some clothes."

TWELVE

The fairies bustled about, wrapping him up in soft robes, rubbing dry his hair until he batted their hands away with irritation. They tried to dress him, but he turned his back to them and put his clothes on with as much dignity as he could muster. He was acutely conscious of the king's amused gaze. A fairy brought him a mirror and a comb, and as he tidied his hair as best he could he saw that the face in the mirror was his own, his real face; Pete's disguise had melted painlessly away. Another fairy offered him a glass of something hot and steaming. The surface of the liquid appeared to be glowing from within. "What *is* that?" he asked, eyeing it dubiously.

"Sunfruit Schnapps!" the fairy said cheerfully. The Wizard took a cautious sip and the fiery liquid slipped down his throat, setting him to coughing furiously. But soon a warm glow filled his stomach, and he found he didn't mind the burn nearly as much after another few sips. The fairies tittered as he chugged down the rest of the liquor and waved his cup around, which magically refilled itself.

"You have made your choice," the fairy king said, and the excited buzz of the fairies fell silent at once.

"I have," the Wizard said.

The fairy king smiled, a smile that did not reach his eyes. "We do not give, Wizard, without asking something in return. We have given you back yourself; we have offered you the power of Oz itself. And now, we will ask of you a tiny favor before you devote yourself to the glory of Oz." Again, it was almost as though the fairy was making fun of him, the Wizard thought, his mind racing. Pete had been infuriating, but the Wizard had never doubted how much he cared about Oz. The fairies seemed different, though. The voice in the pool had said they were corrupt and weak. Was it possible they were trying to trick him? Was Pete working for them—or being used by them?

The Wizard narrowed his eyes. "Describe this . . . favor."

"Long ago, you gave three gifts to three children of Oz—all of whom asked you for something they lacked. This much, I assume, you remember now?"

"The Cowardly Lion," the Wizard said slowly. "The Scarecrow, the Tin Woodman—but that was nothing. Those gifts weren't even real. I had no power then."

"Indeed, you thought nothing of answering their pleas, knowing that the magic they believed you had was nothing but an illusion. But what if I told you the illusion itself was a lie?"

"I don't understand," the Wizard said helplessly. "I was

never—I never had magic, before now. I don't even know what happened back there with the Lion. It's out of my control."

"The journey from the Other Place transforms your kind in ways we do not yet understand," the fairy king said. "In the crossing, you become something more—and perhaps something less—than what you once were. Like Dorothy, you had no magic in your world; like Dorothy, Oz has altered you. You have had the power of Oz at your disposal all this time, Wizard. When you created the three gifts—the Lion's courage, the Tin Woodman's heart, the Scarecrow's brain—you thought you were only offering them a kind of panacea. But there was real magic, Old Magic, in those gifts—and when those from the Other Place make that discovery it often leads them down a path of perversion and abuse.

"Make no mistake, Wizard, the magic of Oz is our magic, the magic of the fairies—and we want those gifts *back*. The corruption of the Lion, the Scarecrow, and the Tin Woodman is on your shoulders. You must bring back to us what was not yours to give."

"You want the gifts back?" the Wizard asked, his mind whirling. "But why?"

The king rose from his throne, fierce and imperious. "The doings of my people are no business of yours, Wizard. The magic of Oz is ours to keep safe, ours to protect. You have let loose something that must be stopped, and it is up to you to make amends. The pool offered you a choice, and you chose Oz. Do not challenge Oz's rightful rulers."

"Look," the Wizard said crossly, "I went through kind of a lot to get here. Pete said you could help me, and now you're asking me to go off on some crazy quest. Is he one of you?"

The fairies stirred restlessly, and the fairy king looked almost shifty. "Is that what he told you?"

"He didn't tell me anything," the Wizard said. "Except that you had the key to my memories, and that I'd be tested—a test I just passed. I'm not helping you until you tell me who Pete is and why you sent him to me in the first place."

The fairy king considered the question, his eyes half lidded, before he answered. "Pete is one of us, in a way," he said finally. "We have been waiting a long time, Wizard, to see if you might be able to help Oz with your . . ." The king paused delicately, and someone behind him snickered—"*powers*."

"What do you mean, you *waited*? You knew I was in that field? For twenty-five years?" The king didn't answer. And then the worst thought of all occurred to him. "Someone sent that storm to keep me in Oz—someone with real magic. That was *you*, wasn't it?" The fairy was silent, but his expression gave him away. The Wizard felt fury rise in his chest. The fairies had been using him all along, and for longer than he'd even imagined. They'd left him in that field until they thought he might be useful—and they would have continued to leave him there forever if he wasn't. And if the king lied about that, no doubt he was lying about the gifts—lying about protecting Oz. He wanted the gifts for himself—but to what end? Did the fairies want to restore Ozma to the throne, when the pool itself had told him they were corrupt? Was the fairy king imagining *himself* on the throne in the Emerald Palace? The Wizard schooled his features, keeping his expression neutral. He couldn't let the fairy king guess that he knew there was more to the fairies' demand than simply the well-being of Oz. And suddenly he was angry again, angry like he hadn't been since he'd faced the Lion. The voice in the pool had made him believe he could be good again— but this lying pack of fairies was only out for themselves. Why should he be selfless, when no one else in Oz was? What did he care about their petty power plays? Who was to say that Ozma was any better? *Maybe everyone who rules Oz is destined to put themselves first*, he thought bitterly. *Maybe it's not me. Maybe it's this place—and now I'm stuck here.* Ozma had tricked him in the pool—tricked him into believing in the possibility of his own goodness. But what felt good about being good? He squashed down the thought of Iris—after all, even she had been trying in her own way to stab him in the back. No, the only thing that felt good was power. He'd had power once. And now he wanted it back.

"We felt you had more to do in Oz," the fairy king said smoothly, interrupting his thoughts. "Bringing your balloon down was not the most graceful way to keep you here, and for that I apologize." The king coughed, and the Wizard noted how difficult it was for him to so much as admit to the slightest wrong-doing—even if he was only doing it to sweet-talk the Wizard into doing his bidding. "I hope you can forgive us. Sometimes when the good of Oz is concerned we—ah"—the fairy king looked as though he was about to bring up a hair ball—"we can, er, make mistakes. Not that that happens *often*, of course," he added hastily.

The Wizard drew himself up to his full height—which was, admittedly, not very tall. "I accept your apology," he lied, "and I accept your task. I will not fail. Do not forget that I *did* rule Oz, and well."

"*Well* is not precisely the word I would have used," the fairy king said, laughing, "but I have no doubt you will do your earnest best on our behalf. I offer you a token—and a reminder—of our . . . esteem." The fairy king bent forward and scooped up a palmful of water from the black pool. He took his palm away, and the globe of water floated there; with both hands, he pinched and shaped it, drawing it out into an ebony cane. When it was finished, he presented it to the Wizard with a flourish. "Do not forget us," he said lightly. "We will be watching you, Wizard. Of that, you can be certain."

"I have no doubt," the Wizard said coolly. "But I have no need of your gifts."

"I insist," the king said coldly, holding it out. The Wizard hesitated, and then accepted the cane. He tapped it experimentally against the ground; it was as solid as an ordinary cane, though the wood was shot through with an obsidian slickness that echoed the water of the pool. As he looked at it, an eye opened in the dark wood and winked at him before disappearing again. So this was how they would watch him. He would have to be very careful, indeed. He had no doubt that if he found a way to get rid of the cane they would punish him for it some-how. Now was not the time to defy them. No, he'd wait until the moment was right.

"Then we are agreed," the fairy king said, and the Wizard smiled, matching the king's oily grin with one of his own.

"But of course." A flicker of uncertainty crossed the fairy's face before vanishing again, and the Wizard smiled to himself in triumph. *Not so sure of yourself now, are you?* he thought.

"Then let us celebrate," the fairy king said, "and afterward, we shall return you to the world above to begin your most noble quest." He clapped his hands, and a parade of extraordi-nary creatures—lithe, beautiful girls with the bodies of human women and the heads of deer, a fat little troll in an ermine coat far too big for him, a frog the size of a man dressed in a tuxedo with tails—capered into the throne room, bearing platters of steaming dishes and a host of folding tables. Wine poured itself from floating bottles into heavy goblets of silver and gold that settled themselves onto trays, to be whisked about by mournful-looking specters as insubstantial as mist—as the Wizard saw when a fairy walked right through one of them, snatching up a wineglass as the ghostly waiter dissolved and then re-formed. The king himself served the Wizard a heaping portion of roast venison on a white china plate and drew up a folding table and a comfortable little chair before returning to his throne with a plate of his own. And though the room was full of merriment—fairies chatting, gossiping, exclaiming over this delicacy and that—they all ignored the Wizard as completely as if he were invisible, so that a miserable sense of loneliness punctuated the feast and turned the taste of the meat to ashes in his mouth.

"I had better be going," he said aloud. No one paid him any attention as he pushed away the table and got up. Without his even reaching for it, the cane found its way to his hand. A dull, shabby corridor that bore a resemblance to the one that had led him to this awful room opened up in the wall before him. And as he stumbled down it, the Sunfruit Schnapps churned in his belly, and he wondered if he was going to be sick. As he left, the fairies' laughter echoed behind him, high-pitched and cruel, and it rang down the hallway after him for a long time.

THIRTEEN

The climb up the stairs from the fairies' kingdom was not as long as he remembered it, and he soon emerged, blinking, into the sunlit meadow where Pete and Iris had left him. Pete was sitting with his back against a tree, eating an apple.

"So you made your choice," Pete said. "And you remember now what you are."

"So I did. And yes, I do."

They were both quiet, looking at each other.

"The fairies can be—"

"Awful?"

"I was going to say complicated," Pete said, smiling a little, "but yes, that, too. But you have to understand, the good of Oz is what they care about most. No matter how they seem to the . . . unprepared visitor."

"Is it," the Wizard said. Pete looked at him, surprised, and for the first time since the Wizard had met him he looked uncertain.

"Of course," Pete said. "That's all any of us want. What's best for Oz."

"Of course," the Wizard echoed.

"That's why you chose this," Pete said. "That's why you chose to stay. To fight for what Oz once was—and will be again. We won't fail. We'll defeat Dorothy, and restore the balance."

"That's all I want," the Wizard said smoothly, and Pete's face collapsed into relief.

"Good," he said. "I'm sorry I—underestimated you." Pete took a deep breath. "Listen—I owe you an apology. All along, I expected the worst from you."

"I can't really blame you," the Wizard said gently. "I did things that were unforgivable. I can hardly expect you to simply forget the past."

"I can't forget the past," Pete said nobly. "But I did forget something just as important. I forgot that people can change. Even people who have done terrible things."

"I've learned so much from you," the Wizard said easily. Pete smiled, and the Wizard almost laughed. So easy to fool them; so easy to play the part of penitent revolutionary, vowing to do right by his adopted home. What would they say, Pete and the fairies, if they could see what he really wanted?

Oz had been his once, and it could be again. Not just his in name, as it had been before, but his wholly—now that he knew he had real power, now that he could access the Old Magic of Oz. He had liked the throne, liked it very much. He didn't know why the fairies wanted the three gifts so badly, but the answer had to be their power. If he had the Old Magic, the gifts, the throne—nothing would be able to stop him. Not Dorothy, not Glinda, not a bunch of goths in black bathrobes, chain-smoking cloves underground and longing for the good old days. And Dorothy—oh yes, he remembered her. Dorothy owed him. And he was going to make her pay.

Pete took a step forward, and the long grass parted to reveal the most familiar highway in Oz: the Road of Yellow Brick. Waiting, as it always was, to take travelers to the Emerald City, no matter where their journey began. The Wizard smiled to himself. Like Dorothy had once said, there was no place like home. He found he was very much looking forward to his return.

"Are you ready?" Pete asked, taking the first step onto the golden road.

"Oh yes," the Wizard said, tapping his cane lightly against the yellow bricks. "I am very ready indeed."

Follow Amy Gumm's mission to take down Dorothy in:

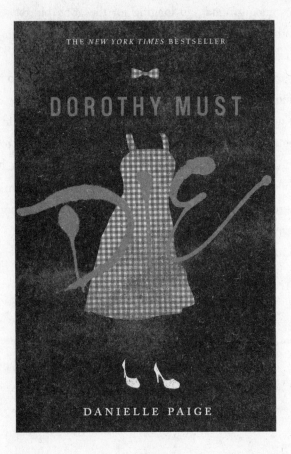

ONE

I first discovered I was trash three days before my ninth birthday—one year after my father lost his job and moved to Secaucus to live with a woman named Crystal and four years before my mother had the car accident, started taking pills, and began exclusively wearing bedroom slippers instead of normal shoes.

I was informed of my trashiness on the playground by Madison Pendleton, a girl in a pink Target sweat suit who thought she was all that because her house had one and a half bathrooms.

"Salvation Amy's trailer trash," she told the other girls on the monkey bars while I was dangling upside down by my knees and minding my own business, my pigtails scraping the sand. "That means she doesn't have any money and all her clothes are dirty. You shouldn't go to her birthday party or you'll be dirty, too."

When my birthday party rolled around that weekend, it turned out everyone had listened to Madison. My mom and I were sitting at the picnic table in the Dusty Acres Mobile Community

Recreation Area wearing our sad little party hats, our sheet cake gathering dust. It was just the two of us, same as always. After an hour of hoping someone would finally show up, Mom sighed, poured me another big cup of Sprite, and gave me a hug.

She told me that, whatever anyone at school said, a trailer was where I lived, not who I was. She told me that it was the best home in the world because it could go anywhere.

Even as a little kid, I was smart enough to point out that our house was on blocks, not wheels. Its mobility was severely over-sold. Mom didn't have much of a comeback for that.

It took her until around Christmas of that year when we were watching *The Wizard of Oz* on the big flat-screen television—the only physical thing that was a leftover from our old life with Dad—to come up with a better answer for me. "See?" she said, pointing at the screen. "You don't need wheels on your house to get somewhere better. All you need is something to give you that extra push."

I don't think she believed it even then, but at least in those days she still cared enough to lie. And even though I never believed in a place like Oz, I did believe in her.

That was a long time ago. A lot had changed since then. My mom was hardly the same person at all anymore. Then again, neither was I.

I didn't bother trying to make Madison like me anymore, and I wasn't going to cry over cake. I wasn't going to cry, period. These days, my mom was too lost in her own little world to bother cheering me up. I was on my own, and crying wasn't worth the effort.

Tears or no tears, though, Madison Pendleton still found ways of making my life miserable. The day of the tornado—although I didn't know the tornado was coming yet—she was slouching against her locker after fifth period, rubbing her enormous pregnant belly and whispering with her best friend, Amber Boudreaux.

I'd figured out a long time ago that it was best to just ignore her when I could, but Madison was the type of person it was pretty impossible to ignore even under normal circumstances. Now that she was eight and a half months pregnant it was really impossible.

Today, Madison was wearing a tiny T-shirt that barely covered her midriff. It read Who's Your Mommy across her boobs in pink cursive glitter. I did my best not to stare as I slunk by her on my way to Spanish, but somehow I felt my eyes gliding upward, past her belly to her chest and then to her face. Sometimes you just can't help it.

She was already staring at me. Our gazes met for a tiny instant. I froze.

Madison glared. "What are you looking at, Trailer Trash?"

"Oh, I'm sorry. Was I staring? I was just wondering if *you* were the Teen Mom I saw on the cover of *Star* this week."

It wasn't like I tried to go after Madison, but sometimes my sarcasm took on a life of its own. The words just came out.

Madison gave me a blank look. She snorted.

"I didn't know you could afford a copy of *Star*." She turned to Amber Boudreaux and stopped rubbing her stomach just long enough to give it a tender pat. "Salvation Amy's jealous. She's had a crush on Dustin forever. She wishes this were her baby."

I didn't have a crush on Dustin, I definitely didn't want a baby, and I absolutely did not want Dustin's baby. But that didn't stop my cheeks from going red.

Amber popped her gum and smirked an evil smirk. "You know, I saw her talking to Dustin in third period," she said. "She was being all flirty." Amber puckered her lips and pushed her chest forward. "Oh, Dustin, I'll help you with your algebra."

I knew I was blushing, but I wasn't sure if it was from embarrassment or anger. It was true that I'd let Dustin copy my math homework earlier that day. But as cute as Dustin was, I wasn't stupid enough to think I'd ever have a shot with him. I was Salvation Amy, the flat-chested trailer-trash girl whose clothes were always a little too big and a lot too thrift store. Who hadn't had a real friend since third grade.

I wasn't the type of girl Dustin would go for, with or without the existence of Madison Pendleton. He had been "borrowing" my algebra almost every day for the entire year. But Dustin would never look at me like that. Even at forty-pounds pregnant, Madison sparkled like the words on her oversize chest. There was glitter embedded in her eye shadow, in her lip gloss, in her nail polish, hanging from her ears in shoulder-grazing hoops, dangling from her wrists in blingy bracelets. If the lights went out in the hallway, she could light it up like a human disco ball.

Like human bling. Meanwhile, the only color I had to offer was in my hair, which I'd dyed pink just a few days ago.

I was all sharp edges and angles—words that came out too fast and at the wrong times. And I slouched. If Dustin was into shiny things like Madison, he would never be interested in me.

I don't know if I was exactly interested in Dustin, either, but we did have one thing in common: we both wanted out of Flat Hill, Kansas.

For a while, it had almost looked like Dustin was going to make it, too. All you need is a little push sometimes. Sometimes it's a tornado; sometimes it's the kind of right arm that gets you a football scholarship. He had been set to go. Until eight and a half months ago, that is.

I didn't know what was worse: to have your shot and screw it up, or to never have had a shot in the first place.

"I wasn't . . . ," I protested. Before I could finish, Madison was all up in my face.

"Listen, Dumb Gumm," she said. I felt a drop of her spit hit my cheek and resisted the urge to wipe it away. I didn't want to give her the satisfaction. "Dustin's mine. We're getting married as soon as the baby comes and I can fit into my aunt Robin's wedding dress. So you'd better stay away from him—not that he'd ever be interested in someone like you anyway."

By this point, everyone in the hallway had stopped looking into their lockers, and they were looking at us instead. Madison was used to eyes on her—but this was new to me.

"Listen," I mumbled back at her, wanting this to be over. "It was just homework." I felt my temper rising. I'd just been trying to help him. Not because I had a crush on him. Just because he deserved a break.

"She thinks Dustin needs her help," Amber chimed in. "Taffy told me she heard Amy offered to *tutor* him after school. Just a little one-on-one academic counseling." She cackled loudly. She said "tutor" like I'd done a lap dance for Dustin in front of the whole fourth period.

I hadn't offered anyway. He had asked. Not that it mattered. Madison was already steaming.

"Oh, she did, did she? Well why don't I give this bitch a little tutoring of my own?"

I turned to walk away, but Madison grabbed me by the wrist and jerked me back around to face her. She was so close to me that her nose was almost touching mine. Her breath smelled like Sour Patch Kids and kiwi-strawberry lip gloss.

"Who the hell do you think you are, trying to steal my boy-friend? Not to mention my baby's dad?"

"He asked me," I said quietly so that only Madison could hear.

"What?"

I knew I should shut up. But it wasn't fair. All I'd tried to do was something good.

"I didn't talk to him. He asked me for help," I said, louder this time.

"And what could he find so interesting about you?" she snapped back, as if Dustin and I belonged to entirely different species.

It was a good question. The kind that gets you where it hurts. But an answer popped into my head, right on time, not two seconds after Madison wobbled away down the hall. I knew it was mean, but it flew out of my mouth before I had a chance to even think about it.

"Maybe he just wanted to talk to someone his own size."

Madison's mouth opened and closed without anything coming out. I took a step back, ready to walk away with my tiny victory. And then she rolled onto her heels, wound up, and—before I could duck—punched me square in the jaw. I felt my head throbbing as I stumbled back and landed on my butt.

It was my turn to be surprised, looking up at her in dazed, fuzzy-headed confusion. Had that just happened? Madison had always been a complete bitch, but—aside from the occasional shoulder check in the girls' locker room—she wasn't usually the violent type. Until now.

Maybe it was the pregnancy hormones.

"Take it back," she demanded as I began to get to my feet.

Out of the corner of my eye, I saw Amber a second too late. Always one to take a cue from her best friend, she yanked me by the hair and pushed me back down to the ground.

The chant of "Fight! Fight! Fight!" boomed in my ears. I checked for blood, relieved to find my skull intact. Madison stepped forward and towered over me, ready for the next round. Behind her, I could see that a huge crowd had gathered around us.

"Take it back. I'm not fat," Madison insisted. But her lip

quivered a tiny bit at the f-word. "I may be pregnant, but I'm still a size two."

"Kick her!" Amber hissed.

I scooted away from her rhinestone-studded sandal and stood up just as the assistant principal, Mr. Strachan, appeared, flanked by a pair of security guards. The crowd began to disperse, grumbling that the show was over.

Madison quickly dropped her punching arm and went back to rubbing her belly and cooing. She scrunched her face up into a pained grimace, like she was fighting back tears. I rolled my eyes. I wondered if she would actually manage to produce tears.

Mr. Strachan looked from me to Madison and back again through his wire rims.

"Mr. Strachan," Madison said shakily. "She just came at me! At us!" She patted her belly protectively, making it clear that she was speaking for two these days.

He folded his arms across his chest and lowered his glare to where I still crouched. Madison had him at "us." "Really, Amy? Fighting with a pregnant girl? You've always had a hard time keeping your mouth shut when it's good for you, but this is low, even for you."

"She threw the first punch!" I yelled. It didn't matter. Mr. Strachan was already pulling me to my feet to haul me off to the principal's office.

"I thought you could be the bigger person at a time like this. I guess I overestimated you. As usual."

As I walked away, I looked over my shoulder. Madison lifted

her hand from her belly to give me a smug little wave. Like she knew I wouldn't be coming back.

When I'd left for school that morning, Mom had been sitting on the couch for three days straight. In those three days, my mother had taken zero showers, had said almost nothing, and—as far as I knew—had consumed only half a carton of cigarettes and a few handfuls of Bugles. Oh, and whatever pills she was on. I'm not even sure when she got up to pee. She'd just been sitting there watching TV.

It used to be that I always tried to figure out what was wrong with her when she got like this. Was it the weather? Was she thinking about my father? Was it just the pills? Or was there something else that had turned her into a human slug?

By now, though, I was used to it enough to know that it wasn't any of that. She just got like this sometimes. It was her version of waking up on the wrong side of the bed, and when it happened, you just had to let her ride it out. Whenever it happened, I wondered if this time she'd be *stuck* like this.

So when I pushed the door to our trailer open an hour after my meeting with the principal, carrying all the books from my locker in a black Hefty bag—I'd been suspended for the rest of the week—I was surprised to see that the couch was empty except for one of those blankets with the sleeves that Mom had ordered off TV with money we didn't have.

In the bathroom, I could hear her rustling around: the faucet running, the clatter of drugstore makeup on a tiny counter. I guess she'd ridden it out again after all. Not that that was always a good thing.

"Mom?" I asked.

"Shit!" she yelped, followed by the sound of something falling into the sink. She didn't come out of the bathroom, and she didn't ask what I was doing home so early.

I dropped my backpack and my Hefty bag on the floor, slid off my sneakers, and looked over at the screen. Al Roker was pointing to my hometown on one of those big fake maps. He was frowning.

I didn't think I'd ever seen America's Weatherman frown before. Wasn't he supposed to be reassuring? Wasn't it, like, his job to make us feel like everything, including the weather, would be better soon? If not tomorrow then at some point during the extended ten-day forecast?

"Hey," Mom said. "Did you hear? There's a tornado coming!"

I wasn't too worried about it. They were always predicting disaster around here, but although nearby towns had been hit a few times, Dusty Acres had always been spared. It was like we had cliché to shield us—Tornado Sweeps Through Trailer Park, Leaves Only an Overturned Barbecue. That's something that happens in a movie, not in real life.

My mom emerged from the bathroom, fussing with her hair. I was glad to see her vertical again, freshly scrubbed with her face all done up, but I had to wince at the length of her skirt. It was shorter than anything I owned. It was shorter than anything Madison Pendleton owned. That could only mean one thing.

"Where are you going?" I asked, even though I knew the answer. "For three days, you're one step away from a coma and now you're heading to the bar?"

It was no surprise. In my mother's world, there were only two pieces of scenery: the couch and the bar. If she wasn't on one, she was in the other.

She let out an accusatory sigh. "Don't start. I thought you'd be happy that I'm back on my feet again. Would you rather I just lie on the couch? Well, you might be content to mope around the house all day, but *some* of us have a life." She fluffed up her already teased hair and began looking for her purse.

There were so many things wrong with everything she'd just said that I couldn't even begin to process all the ways it was infuriating. Instead, I decided to try the sensible argument. "You're the one who just told me there's a tornado on the way. It's dangerous. You could get hit by a tree or something. Won't Tawny understand?"

"It's a *tornado* party, Miss Smarty-Pants," Mom said, as if that explained things. Her bloodshot eyes lit up as she spotted her purse lying on the floor next to the refrigerator and slung it over her shoulder.

I knew there was no point arguing when she got this way. "You need to sign this," I demanded, holding out the slip of paper Strachan had given me. It was to show that she understood what I'd supposedly done today, and what the consequences were.

"I got suspended," I told her.

It took her a few seconds to react, but when she did, her face registered not surprise or anger, but pure annoyance. "Suspended? What did you do?" Mom pushed past me again to get to her keys. Like I was just a thing that was in the way of something she wanted.

If we lived in a regular house, with one and a half bathrooms, I wondered, would she still hate me this much? Was resentment something that grew better in small spaces, like those flowers that Mom used to force to bloom inside in little vases?

"I got in a fight," I said evenly. Mom kept staring. "With a pregnant girl."

At that, Mom let out a long, whistling sigh and looked up at the ceiling.

"That's just great," Mom said, her voice dripping with something other than motherly concern.

I could have explained it to her. I could have told her exactly what happened; that it wasn't my fault. That I hadn't even hit anyone.

But the thing is, at that moment, I kind of liked having her think I'd done something wrong. If I was the kind of girl who got in fights with pregnant girls, it meant it was on her. And her stellar lack of parenting skills.

"Who was it?" Mom demanded, her plastic purse slamming into the counter.

"Madison Pendleton."

She narrowed her eyes but not at me. She was remembering

Madison. "Of course. That little pink bitch who ruined your birthday party."

Mom paused and bit her lip. "You don't see it, do you? She's already getting hers. You don't need to help it along."

"What are you talking about? I'm the one who was suspended."

Mom flung her hand out and gripped the air, mimicking a pregnant belly. "I give her a year. Two tops before she's got a trailer of her own around the corner. That boy she's with won't stay. And she'll be left with a little bundle of karma."

I shook my head. "She's walking around like she's God's gift. Like she and Dustin are still going to be prom king and queen."

"Ha!" Mom hooted. "Now. But the second that kid comes, her life is over." There was a pause I could drive a truck through.

For a split second, I thought of how things used to be. My *before* Mom. The one who'd dried my tears and challenged me to a cake-eating contest at that fateful birthday party. "More cake for us," she'd said. That was when I was nine. After Dad left, but before the accident and the pills. It was the last time she'd even bothered remembering my birthday.

I didn't know what to do when she acted like this. When we were almost having a normal conversation. When she almost seemed like she cared. When I almost saw some glimmer of who she used to be. I knew better but I leaned into the kitchenette counter anyway.

"One second, you have everything, your whole life ahead of you," she said, fluffing her hair in the reflection from the stove.

"And then, boom. They just suck it all out of you like little vampires till there's nothing left of you."

It was clear she wasn't talking about Madison anymore. She was talking about me. I was her little vampire.

Anger pricked in my chest. Leave it to my mother to turn any situation into another excuse to feel sorry for herself. To blame me.

"Thanks, Mom," I said. "You're right. I'm the one who ruined your life. Not you. Not Dad. The fact that I've been taking care of you every day since I was thirteen—that was just my evil scheme to ruin everything for you."

"Don't be so sensitive, Amy," she huffed. "It's not all about you."

"All about me? How could it be, when it's always about you?"

Mom glared at me, and then there was a honk from outside. "I don't have to stand here and listen to this. Tawny's waiting." She stormed to the door.

"You're just going to leave me in the middle of a tornado?"

It wasn't that I cared about the weather. I wasn't expecting it to be a big deal. But I wanted her to care; I wanted her to be running around gathering up batteries for flashlights and making sure we had enough water to last through the week. I wanted her to take care of me. Because that's what mothers do.

Just because I'd learned how to take care of myself didn't mean I didn't still feel panic setting in every time she left me like this—all alone, with no clue when she'd be back, or if she'd ever be back at all. Even without a tornado on the way, it was always an open question.

"It's better out there than in here," she snapped.

Before I could think of a good enough retort, she was gone.

I opened the door as she slid into the front seat of Tawny's Camaro; I watched as Mom adjusted the mirror to look at herself and saw her catch a glimpse of me instead, just before the car vroomed away.

Before I could have the satisfaction of slamming the door myself, the wind did it for me. So maybe this tornado was coming after all.

I thought of Dustin and his wasted scholarship, and about my father, who'd left me behind just to get out of here. I thought of what this place did to people. Tornado or no tornado, I wasn't Dorothy, and a stupid little storm wasn't going to change anything for me.

I walked to my dresser, pushed up flush against the kitchen stove, and opened the top drawer, feeling around for the red-and-white gym sock that was fat with cash—the stash of money I'd been saving for an emergency for years: $347. Once the storm cleared, that could get me bus tickets. That could get me a lot farther than Topeka, which was the farthest I had ever gone. I could let my mother fend for herself. She didn't want me. School didn't want me. What was I waiting for?

My hand hit the back of the drawer. All I found were socks.

I pulled the drawer out and rifled through it. Nothing.

The money was gone. Everything I'd spent my life saving up for. Gone.

It was no mystery who'd taken it. It was less of a mystery what she'd spent it on. With no cash, no car, and no one to wave a magic wand, I was stuck where I was.

It didn't matter anyway. Leaving was just a fantasy.

In the living room, Al Roker was back on TV. His frown was gone, sort of, but even though his face was now plastered with a giant grin, his jaw was quivering and he looked like he might start crying at any second. He kept chattering away, going on and on about isotopes and pressure systems and hiding in the basement.

Too bad they don't have basements in trailer parks, I thought.

And then I thought: Bring it on. There's no place like anywhere but here.

TWO

I had to admit it looked a little scary outside: the darkening sky stretched out over the empty, flat plain—a muddy, pinkish brown I'd never seen before—and the air seemed eerily still.

Usually on a day like today, even with bad weather, the old guy next door would be out in the yard, blasting old-fashioned country songs—the kind about losing your car, losing your wife, losing your dog—from his ancient boom box while the gang of older kids I never talked to would be drinking neon-colored sodas from little plastic jugs as they sprawled out on the rusty green lawn furniture and old, ratty sofa that made up their outdoor living room. But today, they were all gone. There was no movement at all. No kids. No music. No nothing. The only color for miles was in the yellowed tops of the dried-out patches of grass that dotted the dirt.

The highway at the edge of the trailer park, where cars normally whizzed by at ninety miles an hour, was suddenly empty.

Mom and Tawny had been the last car out.

As the light shifted, I caught a glimpse of myself in the reflection in the window and I saw my face, framed by my new pink hair. I'd dyed it myself and the change was still a shock to me. I don't even know why I'd done it. Maybe I just wanted some color in my stupid, boring gray life. Maybe I just wanted to be a little bit more like Madison Pendleton.

No. I didn't want to be anything like her. Did I?

I was still studying my face when I heard squeaking and rustling, and turned around to see my mom's beloved pet rat, Star, going crazy in her cage on top of the microwave. Star has got to be the world's laziest rat—I don't think I've seen her use her wheel a single time in the last two years. But now she was racing frantically, screaming her gross little rat screams and throwing herself against the sides of her home like she was going to die if she didn't get out.

This was new.

"Guess she abandoned both of us, huh?" I tried to ignore the twinge of triumph I felt at this. I'd always had the sneaking suspicion that Mom loved Star more than me. Now she couldn't be bothered with either of us.

The rat stared right at me, paused, and then opened her mouth to reply with a piercing squeal.

"Shut up, Star," I said.

I thought she'd stop after a second, but the squeal just kept coming.

Star didn't stop.

"Fine," I said when I couldn't take it anymore. "You wanna come out? Fine." I unlatched the top of her cage and reached in to free her, but as I wrapped my hand around her body, she thanked me by sinking her tiny teeth into my wrist.

"Ow!" I yelped, dropping her to the floor. "What's wrong with you?" Star didn't answer—she just scurried off under the couch. Hopefully, never to be seen again. Who even keeps a rat as a pet?

Suddenly the door of the trailer swung open.

"Mom!" I called, running to the open door. For a split second, I thought maybe she'd come back for me. Or, if not for me, then at least for Star.

But it had just been the wind. For the first time, it occurred to me that the impending tornado might not be a joke.

When I was twelve, when it all first started, I didn't get it at first. I thought Mom was actually changing for the better. She let me skip school so we could have a pajama day. She took me to the carnival in the middle of the school day. She jumped on the bed. She let us eat pizza for breakfast. But pretty soon she wasn't making breakfast at all, she was forgetting to take me to school, and she wasn't even getting out of her pajamas. Before long, I was the one making breakfast. And lunch. And dinner.

The mom I'd once known was gone. She was never coming back. Still—whoever she was now—I didn't want her out there on her own. I couldn't trust Tawny to take care of her in a disaster. More than that, I didn't want to be alone. So I picked up my phone and punched in her name. No service. I hung up.

I went to the door, still open and creaking back and forth on its hinges, and took a step outside to scan the horizon, hoping I'd see the red Camaro zooming back down the highway. A change of heart.

As soon as I put my foot on the first stair outside the trailer, I heard a whooshing noise as a plastic lawn chair flew through the air toward me. I hit the ground just in time to avoid getting beaned in the face.

Then, for a moment, everything was still. The lawn chair was resting on its side a few feet away in the dirt like it had been there all along. It began to drizzle. I thought I even heard a bird chirping.

But as I hesitantly got to my feet, the wind started back up. Dust swirled and stung my eyes. The drizzle turned into a sheet of rain.

The sky just overhead was almost black and the horizon was a washed-out, cloudy white, and I saw it, just like in the movies: a thin, dark funnel was jittering across the landscape and getting bigger. Closer. A low humming sound, like an approaching train, thrummed in my ears and in my chest. The lawn chair shot up into the air again. This time, it didn't come back down.

Slowly, I stepped backward into the trailer and yanked the door closed, feeling panic rising in my chest. I turned the deadbolt and then, for good measure, pulled the chain tight, knowing none of it would do any good.

I pressed my back to the wall, trying to keep calm.

The whole trailer shook as something crashed against it.

I had been so stupid to think this might be a joke. Everyone else was gone—how hadn't I seen this coming?

It was too late now. Too late to get out of town—even if I'd had the money to do it. I had no car to get to a shelter. Mom hadn't even thought to ask Tawny to drop me off somewhere. I was trapped here, and whichever way you sliced it, it was my mother's fault.

I couldn't even lie down in the bathtub. We didn't have a bathtub any more than we had a basement.

Al Roker's voice on the TV had been replaced by the buzz of static. I was alone.

"Star?" I squeaked. My voice barely made it out of my chest. "Star?"

It was the first time in my life that I'd been desperate for the company of my mother's rat. I didn't have anyone else.

As I sank onto the couch, I couldn't tell if I was shaking, or if it was the trailer itself. Or both.

My mom's stupid Snuggie was rancid with the stench of her Newports, but I pulled it over my face anyway, closing my eyes and imagining that she was here with me.

A minute later, when something snapped on the right side of the trailer, everything pitched to the side. I gripped the cushions hard to keep from falling off the couch. Then, there was another snap, and a lurch, and I knew that we'd come loose from our foundation.

My stomach dropped and kept dropping. I felt my body getting heavier, my back plastered to the cushions now, and suddenly—with a mix of horror and wonder—I knew that I was airborne.

The trailer was flying. I could feel it.

Dreading what I would see, I peered out from under the blanket and toward the window, squinting my eyes open just a crack to discover my suspicion had been right: Pink light danced through swirling clouds. A rusted-out car door floated by as if it were weightless.

I had never been on a plane. I had never been higher than the observatory, the tallest building in Flat Hill. And here I was now flying for the first time in a rusty old double-wide.

The trailer bounced and swayed and creaked and surfed, and then I felt something wet on my face. Then a squeak.

It was Star. She had made it onto the couch and was licking me tenderly. As her soft squeaks filled my ear, I let out a breath of something like relief just to have her here with me. It wasn't much, but it was something.

Mom was probably on her third drink by now, or maybe huddled with Tawny in the basement of the bar, a stack of kegs to keep them happy for as long as necessary. I wondered what she would do when she got back—when she saw that the trailer was gone, and me along with it. Like we were never here. Would her life be better without me in it?

Well, I had wanted to be gone. I'd wanted it for as long as I'd known there was anywhere to go. I wanted other places, other people. Another me. I wanted to leave everything and everyone behind.

But not like this.

I scratched my index finger against Star's furry spine and waited for the falling part. For the crash. I braced myself against the cushions, knowing that my tin-can house wasn't going to protect me when we hit the earth. But the crash didn't come.

Up and up and up we went. More white-pink light, more pink clouds, and every kind of junk you could imagine all swirling around in the surreal air blender: an unbothered-looking Guernsey cow. An ancient, beat-up Trans Am. An old neon service-station sign. A tricycle.

It was like I was on the world's most insane amusement park ride. I've never liked roller coasters. Going up would be fun if you didn't have to think about what always came next.

THREE

When I came to, the first thing I saw was the spongy gray floor of the trailer above me. Star was scampering around my achy body like it was a racetrack, trying frantically to wake me. It took me a second to realize that I was lying on the ceiling.

Light streaked through the dirty windows—normal, bright, white light again, not the blushy pink I'd seen during the tornado or the watercolor brown just before it.

I was alive. And someone was talking to me.

"Grab my hand," he was saying. "Step lightly." I turned my head and looked up to see a torso leaning in through the open door, half-in, half-out, and an arm reaching for me. It was a he, silhouetted by light pouring in from behind. I couldn't make out his face.

"Who are you?" I asked.

"Just take my hand. Try not to make any sudden movements."

From my side, Star squeaked and scrambled into the pocket of my hoodie.

I rose slowly to my feet and dusted myself off. Nothing seemed to be broken. But everything hurt like I was a rag doll that'd been thrown around in a giant tin can. When I took a step, the double-wide lurched beneath me. I rolled back on my heels, trying to get my balance, and it rocked with even more menace. I stopped.

"Just two steps and you're home. Hurry," he said. The distance between his hand and me seemed farther than two steps. I wanted to move again. But I didn't.

"It's okay," he said. "Don't panic. Just move."

I took another step, careful not to upset the equilibrium, and then another. I put my hand in his.

As my skin touched his, I saw his face, and I felt electricity shooting through my body. His eyes were the first thing I noticed: They were emerald green with flecks of something I couldn't even describe to myself, and they seemed to be glowing, almost floating in front of his face. There was something about them that seemed almost alien.

Was he a rescue worker? And if so, how far from home was I, exactly?

"Am I dead?" I asked. It certainly seemed possible. Likely, even. It was hard to believe that I had survived any crash.

"Of course not. If you were dead, would we be having this conversation?"

With that, he gave my arm a sharp, strong yank and pulled me through the tipped doorway. We fell backward, tumbling onto the ground outside.

I scrambled quickly to my feet and turned around to see that

I was standing on the edge of a deep ravine. My poor little trailer was barely holding on, teetering on the precipice.

The chasm was more like a canyon: it was as wide as a river and stretched on for as far as I could see in either direction. The bottom was all blackness.

"What the . . . ?" I whispered.

My trailer heaved, and then, with a final, aching creak, it lurched backward, letting go.

"No!" I screamed, but it was too late. The home that had once been mine was spinning down and down and down into the hole.

I kept expecting to see it crash and shatter into a million pieces, but it just kept on falling as I stood there watching it disappear into the abyss.

It was gone without even a sound. I had almost gone with it.

Everything I owned was in there. Every piece of ugly clothing. Every bad memory.

I was free of all of it.

"I'm sorry about your house," my rescuer said. His voice was soft, but it startled me anyway. I jumped and looked up to find that he was standing at my side. "It's a miracle you made it out. A few inches to the left and you'd have gone straight into the pit. Lucky, I guess." The way he said it made it sound like he thought it had been something more than luck.

"Did the tornado do that?" I asked. I stared back into the pit, wondering how far down it went. Wondering what was down there. "I didn't know tornadoes made giant holes in the ground."

"Ha. No." He laughed, but he didn't seem to think it was all that funny. "The pit's been here for a long time now." He didn't elaborate.

I turned to face him, and when I saw him standing there in the pale, blue-gray sunlight, my breath caught somewhere beneath my ribs. The boy was probably my age, and about my height, too. He was slim and sinewy and compact, with a face framed by dark, shaggy hair that managed to be both strong and delicate at the same time.

His skin was paler than pale, like he'd never left home without sunscreen or like he'd never left home period. He was part rock star, part something else. I couldn't put my finger on what the something else was, but I knew that it was somehow important.

And those eyes. They were glittering even brighter than before, and there was something about them that made me uneasy. It was like he had whole worlds behind his eyes.

He was beautiful. He was too beautiful. It was the kind of beautiful that can almost seem ugly; the kind of beautiful you don't want to touch, because you know it might burn. I wasn't used to talking to people who looked like him. I wasn't used to being *near* people who looked like him.

But he had saved my life.

THERE'S A NEW GIRL FROM KANSAS IN OZ . . . AND SHE HAS A MISSION.

THE *NEW YORK TIMES* BESTSELLER

DOROTHY MUST DIE

DANIELLE PAIGE

See where Amy Gumm's story began.

HARPER
An Imprint of HarperCollins*Publishers*

www.epicreads.com

GOOD IS WICKED.
WICKED IS GOOD.

In the sequel to *Dorothy Must Die*, only one thing is certain:
the wicked will rise again.

An Imprint of HarperCollinsPublishers

www.epicreads.com

KEEP UP WITH ALL THINGS WICKED IN THESE *DOROTHY MUST DIE* PREQUEL NOVELLAS!

A PREQUEL NOVELLA TO
DOROTHY MUST DIE

NO PLACE LIKE

OZ

DANIELLE PAIGE

A PREQUEL NOVELLA TO THE *NEW YORK TIMES* BESTSELLER
DOROTHY MUST DIE

THE WITCH MUST

BURN

DANIELLE PAIGE

Available only as ebooks.

HARPER
An Imprint of HarperCollinsPublishers

www.epicreads.com

ENDGAME IS REAL.
ENDGAME HAS STARTED.

ENDGAME IS REAL. ENDGAME IS NOW.

ENDGAME
THE CALLING
—
JAMES FREY
AND
NILS JOHNSON-SHELTON

Twelve ancient cultures were chosen millennia ago to represent humanity in
Endgame, a global game that will decide the fate of humankind. Endgame has
always been a possibility, but never a reality . . . until now. Twelve meteorites
have just struck Earth, each meteorite containing a message for a Player
who has been trained for this moment. At stake for the Players: saving their
bloodline as well as the fate of the world. And only one can win.

HARPER
An Imprint of HarperCollinsPublishers

WWW.THISISENDGAME.COM

JOIN THE
Epic Reads
COMMUNITY

THE ULTIMATE YA DESTINATION

◀ DISCOVER ▶
your next favorite read

◀ FIND ▶
new authors to love

◀ WIN ▶
free books

◀ SHARE ▶
infographics, playlists, quizzes, and more

◀ WATCH ▶
the latest videos

◀ TUNE IN ▶
to Tea Time with Team Epic Reads

Find us at **www.epicreads.com**
and **@epicreads**